M000101248

Four Women

Four Women

Nikesha Elise Williams

NEW Reads Publications

Copyright © 2017 by Nikesha Elise Williams

Library of Congress Cataloging-In-Publication Data

Williams, Nikesha Elise.
    Four Women/Nikesha Elise Williams

PUBLISHER'S NOTE
This book is a work of fiction. Names, characters, places, and incidents
either are the product of the author's imagination or are used
fictitiously, and any resemblance to actual persons, living or dead,
business establishments, events, or locales is entirely coincidental.

Without limiting the rights under copyright reserved above, no part of
this publication may be reproduced, stored in or introduced into a
retrieval system, or transmitted in any form, or by any means
(electronic, mechanical, photocopying, recording or otherwise), without
the prior written permission of both the copyright owner and the
above publisher of this book.

The scanning, uploading, and distribution of this book via the Internet
or via any other means without the permission of the author is illegal
and punishable by law. Please purchase only authorized electronic
editions, and do not participate in or encourage electronic piracy of
copyrighted materials. Your support of the author's rights is
appreciated.

To the mothers and fathers of the movement… may your pain never be in vain.

Part 1

". . . weeping may last for the night but joy comes in the morning."
— Psalm 30:5

1.

Thursday, March 13, 2014

She lays on her back. Eyes trained to the ceiling. Mouth closed, covered, but she can still breathe through her nose. Tears fall from her eyes. They make a flat splash on her white cotton sheets. She cries silently to herself, but remains still, eyes still trained on the ceiling. There she sees a spider. It crawls along the jagged, seven-inch crack toward the fan. She concentrates on it's eight-legged dance as it creeps along the ceiling, preparing a web of life and insect lies. The cracked, spackled ceiling has slight water stains. The spider creeps closer to the ceiling fan's spinning blades. It's eight legs walk in time with the fan's high whine and whir. Red, green, and blue wires hang visible from where the fan was once sturdily mounted. Now those mangled and twisted wires barely hold the weight of the fan in its place. The fan whirs and whines as the blades beat the air around and around. She studies the ceiling fan and wishes . . . She wishes it would fall on his fucking head.

He's here. Again. On top of her. Again. Pounding at her insides with his dick. Again. His pounding rhythm is in time with the fan. The headboard punches a deeper hole into the wall. Her head bangs a deeper dent into the headboard.

She wishes he would stop. He doesn't. She knows that when he is like this he doesn't care. She knows that when he is like this he's having fun. He is sadistic pleasure personified, prostrate over her body as she lays there and takes it. Her eyes never move from their trained stare at the ceiling.

It is in this state where she reflects the most.

The vaginal tearing.

The chlamydia.

The gonorrhea she had twice.

I think he wants me to have something forever. So I'll always be reminded I belong to him.

I wish I had herpes.

"Bitch, I'm talking to you."

"What?" She blinks rapidly.

Spittle from his latest verbal assault lands at the corner of her mouth. It rolls down her face, to her chin and lands on her chest, mixing with his wet drips of perspiration. She tries to turn her head to wipe the spit from her face onto the edge of her pillow, but she c move. She can't even turn slightly to get a glimpse of the mid-March sunset falling behind the tall trees surrounding her apartment complex. It's not much of a view by Jacksonville's beach standards, but it's something for her to see other than his fucking face dripping with spit and sweat.

"See that's exactly why I do this shit. You're always ignoring me, you Stupid Bitch."

He backhands her across her face. His large hands contact her skin from cheek to cheek, but her head doesn't turn from the blow. There is not enough force to make her head reverberate against the crush of pillows supporting her neck, and plow another hole into the headboard. He's getting tired.

They've been fucking for the last twenty minutes. A stamina she would appreciate if he were not like this. If he were different. *If* he were different. It is this *if* that fuels her fantasy where she matches him thrust for thrust. It is inside this *if* where she grinds her hips into his, meets him with a smile on her lower lips and allows herself to quiver and quake until he wrenches every last drop of anxious passion from her body. *If* he were different she would allow him to see how uninhibited she could be behind closed doors. But he's not. He's him. So she lays there, motionless, her back straight, legs rigid. They only open as far as he pushes them; her private resistance to his presence.

"Bitch, you're still not talking. I asked you a mother-fucking question. Who the fuck does this pussy belong to?"

"You." Her response is weak. But it's a response. He pumps away with his eyes clenched together and the crows feet corners touch, making one thick, long wrinkle.

He pumps.

She lays there refusing to match his thrusts or grind her hips, or make it wet for him. She doesn't give him any leverage to reach her G-spot. Frigid and straight, her body does not lower into the bed so his friction rubs against her clitoris, creating a sensation for phantasmic ecstasy. She lays there taking pleasure in denying him pleasure. Proud of her self-training not to come, she is satisfied watching him struggle for release. It is her own version of an orgasm. But he is adamant. Deliberate.

He pumps.

Like a jack rabbit. Hard, long and fast. His strokes are meant to fuck her into submission, but submission is not derived from sex. It is not gained from fucking for fucks sake. Submission comes from love and is done willingly. Not by force. She lays there and waits for him to finish, wishing the fan would fall on his fucking head.

He pumps.

Slowly she turns her head from his face just enough so it appears she is still focused on him. Scanning her bedroom, her eyes jump until they settle on his reflection in the dresser mirror. His body is prone and pumping away against her. She averts her eyes, not wanting to see his body on hers, their complexions entwined; his in hyper-sexual discipline, hers in protest. Past the glass image her eyes find the unadorned white walls. The space is clean and clear; uncluttered of images meant to evoke emotion or elicit subconscious responses to unanswered questions only asked as the mind drifts off to dreamland. She looks around her room. The vaulted ceiling leads to the dangling ceiling fan. Nightstands are placed on either side of her bed, which slouches on its bent metal frame. It is one of many furniture casualties in her room. The dented headboard made of wooden carrying crates was her very first DIY project. It didn't turn out just right, but it wasn't completely wrong.

The sagging weight of the broken bed is the center of the near emptiness in the room. The pounding sound of the headboard into the wall forces her to scrunch her head on her neck to keep it from punching completely through the crates and into the hole in the wall.

He pumps.

She stares, focusing on the rooms only oddity: a woven white rocking chair. His first gift to her from their encounter that started it all. The gift arrived at her doorstep even though she had only given him her last name. The note written in an inky, cursive script was camouflaged as an extension of their bantering puffery, but was really his first stake of possession. The strokes of ink curled around the s's of her name. Soleil St. James. The strokes of his pen then were as deliberate as his painful pumps are now. She stares at the chair, focusing on the pattern of the painted wood. Her mind teleports her body to the chair. She sits relaxed, calm, and unafraid.

From the broken bed to the empty chair, Soleil is now an observer to her torrid affair. She watches the body lay straight, neck scrunched, not moving, barely breathing. Only seeing parts of a scene she does not want to behold. A leg. An arm. Fingertips.

He pumps.

Soleil's mind game breaks. She is no longer a spirit outside her body in her rocking chair. She is in her bed, beneath him instead of across from him, not in the chair. She is no longer an observer, but an unwilling participant.

He pumps.

In two minutes she knows he will finish. Soleil counts backwards. 120. 119. 118. He's speeding up. 117. Straining. 116. She squeezes her pubococcygeus muscles to encourage his pace. 115. Hold. Squeeze. One. Two. Three. Hold. Squeeze. One. Two. Three. Four. Hold. Squeeze. One. Two. Three. Four. Five.

He grips her hips with his hands and tries to raise them to meet his, but Soleil wills her weight into her ass and allows gravity to keep her down. Her private resistance wins again as he struggles to his finale. Grasping to hold on to their connection, his hands mold like baseball mitts against her skin; gripping, leather rough and battle hard.

He comes violently, slamming into her one last time. She feels his seed as it rushes through her walls; hot, thick, and fast. He collapses on top of her breathless.

"Oh, shit," he mutters in her ear. "Damn, Gorgeous. That shit was good."

His breath is humid, putrid and rank, just like the rest of him. His heart beats through his chest into her own. Shaved chest hairs prick her sweat-wet skin. He snores lightly. The grotesque growling sound bounces against the drums of her ears. His bald head resting against her cheek leaves a trail of drool down her face, past her chin, onto her neck, and then over the mounds of her breasts where it sticks and dries between the folds of her fatty tissue. She is as trapped as his spit, once again unable to turn her head. Soleil lays flat on her back. It is the only movement she can manage with his head obstructing her view of anything that could ever be beautiful.

If he were different she knows she would enjoy this; feeling the weight of a man after a battle of the sexes. But his weight is not one she enjoys. Stuck, trapped beneath his slack body, Soleil tries again to turn her head toward the wide windows of her bedroom. Desperate to see the North Florida sunset through her sheer curtains, the moment when the sky turns colors and the moon begins to rise remains elusive. Soleil can't turn her head more than a few inches. She is paralyzed by his weight, resigned to wait another round staring at the ceiling.

The beating blades of the fan hum out their own song. She listens past their high whine and whir, drowns out the snoring beside her, to find the sounds of the apartment. Her ears pick up the volume of the television. The white noise of the news she left for his unprovoked assault. The voice of a woman comes in clear. *Good evening,*

I'm Dawn Anthony. You're watching Dawn in the Evening. Soleil listens to the anchor she intended to take notes of, as she lays paralyzed beneath his body. She listens to the woman who will read to her class tomorrow, while staring at the ceiling the fan dangling over their heads.

Your time now is 8:30. Right now on Dawn in the Evening, the anchor woman says as Soleil wriggles her body from beneath him. He is still sleeping. She slides out the other side of the bed and tiptoes around the bent metal frame. He doesn't stir. Soleil walks the few steps to her en suite slowly; careful not to let her insides touch as she goes. She smells him with each step. Damp with his sweat, her pores are full of his Southern Comfort and Swisher Sweet residue.

Inside the bathroom she closes and locks both doors. Soleil takes her hand mirror from beneath the vanity and looks at her reflection magnified side up. A trickle of blood is dried on her forehead. The rest of her tanned, crema fresca complexion is hidden beneath his handprint. A five-fingered pink rouge on her right cheek. In the morning it will be blue, but she is thankful her nose isn't bleeding and her eyes aren't blacked. She knows ice on her face will handle the swelling, and the passing of the night will help heal her body if a bath doesn't make what's left of her better.

Hot water fills the shallow, ceramic tub at full stream. The scalding water surrounds her body. Bubbles, courtesy of dishwashing liquid foam and fizz around her. She lays like a child in the womb; her hair floating deep beneath the water's surface. Soleil sees the light brown ringlets succumb to the sloshing water as she lets her head loll around on her neck. With her knees hugged tightly into her chest, and her nose peeking just enough above the water to take in air, she closes her eyes in the tub and waits. She waits in the water, knowing she will not come out until she hears Cole Haan loafered feet pad across her carpet, down the hallway, and on to the other side of her door.

This is their routine. Small talk. Yelling. Arguing. Beating. Fucking. Fucking. Beating. Beating and fucking. Snoring. Bathing.

SLAM

She waits until she knows he is gone. Until she thinks she can hear the rev of his German engineered car starting up. The familiar streaks of burning rubber leaving the parking space in front of her building. She listens for his car, not knowing that there is more than one engine purring; that there is more than one set of wheels speeding out of her parking lot. Soleil listens until the sounds from outside are no more, not knowing the extended sound of streaking tires belongs to

12

another foreign car, following closely behind him. She listens until outside is silent, and only the murmur from her TV remains inside. Soleil lays in the tub and waits as the woman sitting in the car beside his did in the parking lot. They both know he is gone for now. They both know he will be back tomorrow, but only one of them wishes the other won't be there.

2.

Across the darkened city, away from the ever expanding urban sprawl, in a nondescript building on the edge of Jacksonville's burgeoning downtown, Dawn Anthony sits poised in front of the camera of the cold studio.

"Five. Four. Three. Two. One. Cue Dawn."

Welcome back to 'Dawn in the Evening.'

In tonight's 'Sound Off' . . . Back to the budget . . . and more specifically the city's pension problem.

City council needs to find a solution to fix the police and fire pension fund . . .

By raising taxes,

The retirement age,

Increasing contributions, something.

It also wouldn't hurt to cut unnecessary spending on projects that will never begin, let alone get completed.

The budget and the final pension plan should protect the people it affects.

Without accounting for all of these issues, the certainty of our city's credit rating, and meeting our obligations will remain as certain an unknown, as the future of Detroit.

Thank you for joining us for this edition of 'Dawn in the Evening.'

As always we'd like to thank our special guests . . .

Economist Bryan Michael White and local author and activist, Shelby Lincoln.

Thank you to you both . . .

And to you at home.

I'm Dawn Anthony, and we hope to see you right here tomorrow night for 'Dawn in the Evening.'

"Clear, Dawn," John, the floor director, yells in a burly voice.

"John, I'm leaving my mic on the desk," Dawn says, the anchor and managing editor of *Dawn in the Evening.*

"Dawn, keep the mic. We need to shoot three promos for tomorrow night before you head out," John says.

"Are we doing them here in the studio or in the newsroom?"

"Ask Kelly." John wrangles the robotic cameras together.

"Is Kelly still on headset?"

"No, Dawn, I'm behind you," Kelly, the producer, says as she approaches Dawn at the anchor desk.

"Did you write the promos for tomorrow?"

"Yes. They should be behind your 'Sound Off' script."

Dawn rifles through her pink paper scripts until she finds the three pages she's looking for. She puts on her black square rimmed glasses to read through the copy, pen in hand. At 35, she is the only woman in the Jacksonville, Florida market to anchor an hour long news magazine show five nights a week. Covering local, national and international politics, policies, and crises, the show steals viewers from the primetime lineup on the broadcast networks, and rivals the cable networks for ratings in the 8 o'clock hour.

"One script in and I already see a problem," Dawn says, marking through her scripts.

"Yes, Dawn." Kelly responds.

"I know the budget and pension thing is big, but I really don't want to promo that. We talk about it almost every day. It's news. It's a given. Is there something sexier we can lead with?"

"We've got the pension and the budget, the Marine that just returned home from working in Australia and found his wife cleaned him out and that their marriage wasn't even real, and then the update on Governor Rick Scott's push to drug test welfare recipients."

"Kelly, I like the Marine story for the emotion and the governor drug-testing thing for the outrage factor; though at this point it's just inside baseball. We don't have anything else we know we're going to talk about tomorrow, besides the budget and pension?"

"Um, no. The news hasn't happened yet."

"You don't say. Then I guess we'll just shoot two promos."

"But you have to do three," Boyce Butler, WABN's news director, says as he steps into the brightly lit set.

"Boyce, I understand that, but as my producer has informed me, the news hasn't happened yet, and I'm not teasing this budget bullshit one more night."

It was known around the 9 News Now newsroom that Boyce and Dawn hated each other. They tried to respect one another to keep peace, but friendly they were not. Dawn made a decision and Boyce vetoed it, pulling rank as the news director. Boyce made a decision and Dawn threatened to break her contract and take *Dawn in the Evening*, which she owned the creative and editorial rights over, to rival station WNNB.

This rift over a promo was going to explode and the *Dawn in the Evening* crew knew to steer clear. Pale, burly John, and Kelly, who sported a near orange spray tan and *I Love Lucy* red hair, backed slowly across the set. They slipped silently into the weather office at the back of the studio. Through the office's frosted window, they watch as brown-eyed, licorice-skinned Dawn looked into the ruddy, freckled face of Boyce.

He feigns nicety, "Dawn, you can't just decide you're not going to shoot three promos because you don't like the content."

"Yes, I can. It's my show, my name, my promo." She says, brushing her medium length jet black hair from her face.

"Your show, my station, my rules."

"You're right, your rules. So here's what we're going to do. I'm going to shoot two of the three promos for *my show*. Then we'll have Tarren Tyler shoot the last promo for her story on the Marine that's airing in *my show*. That work for you, Mr. Butler?" Dawn smiles but it doesn't touch her eyes.

"Yes, Dawn. I can always count on you to take care of your responsibilities."

"Great. Kelly! Let's get these things shot so I can go."

"Uh, sure," Kelly stutters stumbling out of the weather office.

And Three. Two. One.
Duped down under . . .
I'm Dawn Anthony . . .
Tomorrow night on 'Dawn in the Evening . . .'
The story of one of our hometown heroes taken for the ride of his life, by a woman who only pretended to be his wife.
Tarren Tyler reports, how she cleaned out his accounts without him ever noticing the money was missing.
That's tomorrow night on 'Dawn in the Evening.'

"And we're clear," John says.

"Thanks, John. Kelly, I'll see you tomorrow. No post meeting tonight. Email me any notes you have, and tell Jennifer to cancel my appearance at the SENT conference. I can't make it."

"But you're already late," Kelly and Jennifer, an associate producer, say together as they follow their mile-a-minute anchor out of the side door of the news studio and down the hall toward the back exit. Another anchor passes by the trio; the longtime face of the station, Julia Gillé. A woman who'd anchored the 5, 6, and 11 p.m.

shows for as long as Kelly and Jennifer had been alive. Botox, running, and hair color saved her career when natural beauty and youth had run out. The viewers adored her because they knew no one else.

To Julia, Dawn was an enemy poised to take her chair. To Dawn, Julia was a missed opportunity for a mentor on how to survive in a business where Barbie beauty was rewarded over journalistic integrity. In an age where a pretty face is the only quality capable of capturing leftover attention after viewer scourings of Facebook, Instagram and Twitter were maxed out, being a woman of a certain age still on air meant something.

"Goodnight, Julia," Dawn says as the two pass each other. "Have a good 11."

Julia gives a small wave and wide smile to Dawn's goodbye. Her lips turn up, her mouth opens slightly, and her teeth barely touch. It is her anchor smile. The one that greets viewers as they make dinner, do laundry, and tuck their children in bed at night. The smile that assures them they are safe in their homes despite headlines highlighting the opposite.

"No thanks to you," Julia mutters.

Dawn stops her speed walk to the door to watch Julia's slow stroll down the hall. She stares at Julia's brunette and blonde highlighted head until she disappears around a corner into the newsroom.

"Are you sure you want me to cancel your SENT appearance tonight?" Jennifer asks standing beside Dawn.

"Yes. I never agreed to go in the first place." Dawn snaps. "I received an invitation. I never RSVP'd. Then I see a commercial blasting my name as a panelist for an event whose organizers never called to ask if I would attend, let alone participate as a public figure and use my likeness to garner them more attention."

"Okay, I'll call and cancel."

"Don't worry about it. I'll call Johnnie and tell her I'm not coming myself." Dawn resumes her march toward the door.

"Okay. What does SENT stand for anyway?"

"Single, Ethnic and Not Taken," Dawn and Kelly say in unison.

"Seriously?"

"Seriously," Kelly answers.

"And that's the other reason I'm not going," Dawn says playfully. "I no longer fit the criteria of the ideal SENT woman."

"Ooh, Dawn. Does that mean you have a date tonight?" Kelly asks.

"Don't sound so surprised. I do indeed, my producer extraordinaire. So girls it's been fun but I've got to be going. Email me anything and I'll get back to you before show time."

Dawn whips out her cell phone and leaves her producers standing in the doorway behind her.

"That early, huh?" Kelly snickers.

Dawn smiles, not hearing Kelly's final comment. She dials Johnnie's phone number while crossing the parking lot.

"Hello," A tired voice answers.

"Hey, Johnnie, what are you doing?"

"I'm about to go in the grocery store. Why?"

"Well, then I guess you're not going tonight either."

"Going to what?"

"To SENT."

"Shit, that's tonight?"

"How are you one of the people supposed to be giving a testimonial about the wonders of being a SENT woman, and you're not even going to be there?"

"Then I guess I won't be giving a testimonial then."

"Obviously."

"You're supposed to be speaking tonight, too. Are you going?"

"No, ma'am. I don't know why they put my name all over the flyer, the Facebook and Instagram page. I told you and Margo Westcott, SENT was not for me."

"I don't know why not. You're still single; and I've been married 16 years, Dawn. Sounds like one of us is losing at love, and it sure as hell ain't me."

"For your information, Johnnie, I'm going on a date tonight."

"Really?"

"Yes. Really. Why is everyone I tell so surprised I'm going on a date?"

"Because you don't date."

"I mingle."

"Yeah, right. When?"

"When I need the itch scratched."

"Ho."

"Now why I gotta be a ho? Don't act like you didn't have your years of hoeism either, Johnnie."

"I did and I still do. You gotta be a ho for your husband."

"So I've been told."

"What you won't do, some other woman will."

"I see. Well, I'm going to let you get back to grocery shopping, and hoeing for your man and I'll talk to you later."

"Call me in the morning and tell me about your date."

"I have to read to a class in the morning, but I'll call you after."

"Okay, I'm supposed to be off tomorrow, but if I get called in, we can catch up at the luncheon on Saturday."

"Sounds good. I'm so excited to present you with your award."

"Thanks, Babes. Love you."

"Love you too, Johnnie. Talk to you later."

3.

Johnnie hangs up the phone and pushes it into the thigh pocket of her scrubs. Before getting out of her car, she reaches for her water bottle in the side pouch of her book bag in the passenger seat. Johnnie brings the bottle to her lips, pulls the black cap open with her teeth, and drains the contents inside. She smacks her lips and releases an "ah" as she tosses the bottle back into the seat, gets out of her car, and makes her way inside her own personal hell.

For Dr. Jonelle "Johnnie" Edwards, the grocery store after 5 p.m. on a Thursday is the second worst place to be in the world on a Thursday after 5 p.m. The first worst place being the Shands emergency center operating room. The former name of the hospital before the University of Florida decided to assert all of its monetary authority with the eponymous UF Health. That's the worst place to be in the world on any day.

Johnnie found herself able to leave early, if you call stopping at 36 hours instead of going for the full 48, leaving early. The week had been one shooting victim after another. Some victims were women and children; most of them were men. If they made it to the operating room the majority of them lived.

Johnnie praised God for her quick, nimble fingers. But sometimes victims died. A regrettable feeling she let worm its way inside her heart until she was standing in the grocery store after 5 p.m. on a Thursday, looking for something quick and effective to erase the memory of the face who died on her table two hours ago. Johnnie plans to drink away her failure today, and again after her victim's funeral. A ritual she began when she lost her first patient two years after her residency.

Maneuvering the grocery side of one of the world's largest discount retailers, Johnnie finds herself facing the back racks of cheap wine and no spirits. She desperately searches for a 12 dollar bottle of anything hoping the higher price will mean better quality, but the shelves filled with nine dollar bottle after nine dollar bottle force her to settle on Beringer's White Zinfandel deciding, *you don't have to be fancy to be drunk*.

Wine bottle in hand, Johnnie pushes her way to the front of the store where she stands in the long line for people with 20 items or less; reminded once again why she hates the grocery store on a Thursday after 5 p.m. 18 cash registers man the front of the store. Only six are open, not including the chaos of the self-checkout square.

Johnnie waits, tapping her feet. Crossing and re-crossing her arms. She sighs loudly, clears her throat, and stares down the cashier, daring her to say anything other than "May I help you?"

The line crawls until finally, Johnnie is able to set the wine bottle down on the conveyor belt. She brings her hands to her temples and massages her head, regretting not picking up the bottle of aspirin from the pharmacy when she had the chance. Stretching her neck to each side, muscles and tendons crack. Forcing herself to relax, Johnnie scans the racks of magazines. Paper tabloids that make no bones about what they are, stand next to glossy tabloids putting on airs as respectable publications. They are all the same — telling the same story from cover to cover. One fat pop star; one skinny celebutante. A picture of a post-pregnancy, wedding-planning Kim Kardashian on every cover, even if she isn't the cover story. None of the pictures are new. Stock photos plaster the covers of the tabloids; all of them old and outdated. The only thing separating one from another are their headlines; each one more sensational than the last.

Johnnie roves across the magazines stacked high on the display shelves, until her eyes fall to the candy crates where children can easily reach and beg their tired parents for a sugar high.

"Will this be all for you today, ma'am?" The cashier asks dryly.

"No," Johnnie says. "Add these too."

She places four cans of Altoids on the sliding conveyor belt thinking, *I need to restock anyway.*

"Mama, what'd you buy at the grocery store?" Five-year-old Danielle asks as Johnnie enters the front door.

"Baby, let Mama get in the house before you bombard her with questions." Johnnie smiles at her daughter who she hasn't seen in two days.

"Mama, what does bombard mean?" Danielle asks.

"It means don't ask Mama too many questions before she puts her groceries down and can take off her shoes," Johnnie answers. "Where's your Daddy?"

"Mama, don't bombard me with so many questions."

"Girl, where's your Dad?"

"He went to get pizza, Mama," Danielle stutters.

"And he left you here by yourself?"

"No. I'm here," Johnnie's 14-year-old son Tyler calls out, coming down the stairs from the second floor.

"Tyler, how long ago did your father leave to get the pizza?"

Johnnie kicks her shoes into the front hall closet and walks from the foyer to the kitchen, not waiting for Tyler to answer. He and Danielle dutifully follow behind. They find their mother in the middle of her after-work routine. The double-bagged bottle of Beringer's is gently placed on the quartz island. Beside the bottle are her backpack and purse with the cans of peppermints rattling around inside.

"Tyler and Danielle."

"Yes ma'am."

"Did you do your homework?"

"Yes ma'am."

"Go get it so I can check it over."

Tyler and Danielle dart out of the kitchen giving Johnnie a glimpse of what she created. Tyler looks just like his father with the same dark chocolate complexion and wiry frame. Danielle has his chestnut brown eyes and full lips, but managed to maintain Johnnie's honey complexion. They bound up the stairs to gather their school work. Meanwhile, Johnnie pulls her white sports water bottle from the side pouch of her book bag. She unsheathes the wine bottle and uses the corkscrew on her key chain to open the top. Uncapping the opaque water bottle, she pours the rose-colored liquid inside, not spilling a drop on the island.

With the contents of the wine safely stored, Johnnie takes the bags and wine bottle through the kitchen's side door into the garage, where Nathan is pulling in. She stops in front of the large green garbage can, bags and bottle behind her back, watching her husband park the Toyota SUV. He closes the garage door from the button inside the midnight blue 4Runner. Johnnie stays frozen in front of the garbage can.

"Hey, Baby what are you doing out here?" Nathan asks grabbing the pizzas out of the backseat of the SUV.

"I heard the car pulling up outside. I was in the kitchen," Johnnie lies as she quietly places the bags and bottle on top of the overloaded garbage heap while Nathan's back is turned.

"Where are the kids?" Nathan asks closing the door with a smile.

"They're getting their homework. I was about to check it."

"Do that later. I've got pizza."

Johnnie gives her husband a lopsided shrug of her shoulders as he leans in to give her a half hug and quick peck on the lips. She inhales his scent. The cologne doesn't register. Nathan breaks the embrace and heads through the open door into the kitchen. Johnnie follows, closing the door behind her.

Tyler and Danielle sit on barstools at the island. Nathan moves Johnnie's water bottle and purse to make room for the pizzas. The peppermint cans rattle inside.

"Kids, take your homework upstairs, I'll check it later." Johnnie stares at her purse.

"What do you guys want to drink?" Nathan asks Tyler and Danielle as they scramble back up the stairs.

"Juice," Danielle yells behind her.

"That'll work," Tyler says nonchalantly.

"And for you, My Dear?" Nathan asks Johnnie.

Johnnie swipes the white bottle from the island with one hand. She gives a half smile as she pops open the black top with her teeth.

"I'll just drink my water, Babe."

"Suit yourself."

Johnnie hops up on the counter top next to the stove, and lets her head rest against the oak-colored cabinets. She watches Nathan dish out pizza onto four plates. Sipping her wine, Johnnie feels the last two days spent between body after body dissipate from around her. She stifles her moan as she savors the fruity liquid thinking *this is heaven*.

4.

Friday, March 14, 2014

"Class, we have a very special guest this morning," Soleil says to get the attention of the 25 kindergarteners in her class.

Murmurs of "who is it," buzz between the children as they struggle to sit still and learn more about the surprise they'd been promised all week.

"Dawn Anthony, from channel nine is here this morning, and she's going to read you a story."

"Who is that?" A ruddy faced boy with spiky hair shouts aloud in the class.

"She's my Mommy's friend." Danielle defends to the boy behind her. "She works at the news."

"You're right, Danielle. Dawn Anthony hosts her own show every night on Channel 9, but today instead of telling you the news, she's going to read you a book."

"Is she here yet?" The loud mouth boy pipes up again.

"Jeremiah, she's standing right outside the door, but if you want her to come inside, I'm going to need you to mind your manners."

"Yes ma'am." Jeremiah slouches and hides his head behind Danielle.

Soleil walks to the door and opens it wide for Dawn Anthony, who had been talking on her phone.

"They're ready for you now, Ms. Anthony."

"Call me Dawn," Dawn says with a wide, smile that shows off her teeth. "Sorry for the delay; had to make sure everything was on track for tonight's show. My producers were called in early for some breaking news."

"No worries. They're just happy to have someone else read to them today instead of me; especially Danielle Edwards. She seems to know you already."

"I didn't know this was her school," Dawn whispers. "Her mom and I are friends."

"So she's said."

"Everyone," Soleil says addressing the class. "This is Dawn Anthony. She's going to read to us today from *The Very Hungry Caterpillar.*"

"Hi, Ms. Dawn," Danielle says bouncing out of her seat to wave.

Dawn mouths "Hi" to Danielle as she sits in a small, yellow chair at an empty desk in front of the room.

"You can sit on the stool." Soleil suggests.

"This is fine. I like being on their level. That way we're all the same."

"Good morning, everybody!" Dawn says brightly, smiling at the class. "Are you guys ready to read?"

"Yeeeeeeeessssssssss!" The children drag out in a chorus of small voices.

Soleil hands Dawn the beloved children's book and then sits behind her at her desk.

"In the light of the moon a little egg lay on a leaf," Dawn reads in a sing-song voice that booms across the room.

Soleil closes her eyes and listens to Dawn read through the book with as many theatrics as she can lend to the only character. She listens to the narration she's told to every class since she began teaching. While Dawn's cadence is different, Soleil is reminded of the voice that began speaking to her from the television the night before. The voice that said "welcome" and "good evening" as she lay trapped beneath him. Soleil is back in her bed where she laid naked and hot, stuck beneath his pounding sweat, his humid breath, and cigarette-stained teeth.

Quickly digested Southern Comfort and mouth bacteria assaults her olfactory glands. Soleil shakes her head and coughs, muffling the sound in her hands. His hands. His large, gnarled knuckles, and well-manicured nails dig into her skin. Soleil touches the side of her body where his hands dug in, where he tried to lift her, and she willed her body to refuse. His smell and touch consume her as she coughs her muffled cry.

"He built a small house, called a cocoon, around himself," Dawn reads to the class.

She coughs.

"He stayed inside for more than two weeks."

She coughs.

"Then he nibbled a hole in the cocoon,"

Soleil coughs as she stands up from her desk, strides across the room, and steps out of her door. Dawn's voice becomes as drowned out as it was the night before — white noise in the background of her present tense. A sound distanced from her reality. The warm morning air carries whatever is cooking in the nearby lunchroom into Soleil's lungs. She breathes in her present. Her class. Her guest. Awareness of her abrupt departure returns. She steps back inside.

"What do you want to be when you grow up?" Dawn asks another student as Soleil steps back in the classroom.

She gives her a grateful smile.

Dawn nods, continuing her interview of the students.

"Everyone, why don't we thank Ms. Dawn for that wonderful story today."

Dawn stands from the tiny chair as a cacophonous sound of student voices say their own version of thank you.

"Are you okay?" Dawn whispers to Soleil.

"I'm fine. Allergies. They're the worst this time of year, and being in these portables doesn't help."

"Everyone," Soleil commands, "take out your notebooks for art. Before we go to lunch I want you to draw a picture from the story Ms. Dawn read. We'll use them for our spring-time collage at the back of the classroom. If you have any questions Miss Lisa will help you." Soleil nods toward her teacher's assistant sitting at the back of the classroom.

Soleil and Dawn walk outside as the classroom leaps alive with the commotion of small children.

"Thank you for coming in and reading to them. We all really appreciate it."

"Anytime," Dawn says; her phone back in hand, eyes focused on the screen. "I would love to do it again. Gives me a chance to see Dani. Lord knows her mother and I rarely catch up."

"Dr. Edwards is a rare site around here too, but she calls at least twice a week to check-in" Soleil reveals. "Mr. Edwards, though, is very hands-on. Sometimes too hands-on," Soleil murmurs.

"It works for them." Dawn taps the glass screen of her phone. "I've got to head to work, but seriously, I will come back and read to them anytime."

"Thank you. I'll hold you to that."

"Please do." Dawn hands Soleil her card.

Soleil accepts the thick, embossed card stock. She watches Dawn make her way beneath the shade of the portico-lined sidewalks through the maze of portables, until she disappears around a corner.

"Miss St. James, Miss St. James, Miss St. James," Danielle squeals, running up to the front of the class as Soleil returns inside.

"Yes, Danielle."

"Will you look at my picture I made for you. It's a butterfly, on a rose, in the grass, by the beach, with the waves and the sky and the clouds and a sun and a bird." Danielle says, looking at Soleil with an innocent sparkle in her chestnut-colored eyes.

"Danielle, your picture is very beautiful. Is this the butterfly at the end of the story?"

"Yes. He's on a new adventure at the beach, see."

"I see. Write your name on it and I will hang it on the blackboard when everyone else finishes their pictures."

Danielle runs to her desk. Ponytails flop on either side of her head, red barrettes bounce on her small, gold hoop earrings. Soleil stares at her, as she grabs the large black pencil and carefully writes her name, remembering when she, too, used to be a sparkle of innocence.

Danielle runs back to Soleil, her drawing flapping in the momentum wind she creates behind her. Her gapped-tooth grin stretches from ear to ear. Soleil smiles lovingly despite the incessant throbbing of the bruises on her battered body.

"Soleil St. James, I see you're wearing purple blush again. I think I know what that means."

"Troy, can you not yell my business across the teachers' lounge."

Troy Mackie, the fifth grade teacher whose classroom is just above Soleil's, strides over to where she sits in the small, stuffy lounge.

The two met at the Shady Grove Elementary school teacher orientation eight years ago and have been teaching together ever since. He teaches the older, smart aleck kids who think they're grown. She prefers the babies she can mold into everything she was supposed to be.

Sparkling. Innocence.

"Soleil, how many shades of purple blush did you have to mix today to get the right color of Barker's hand?" Troy asks sitting beside her.

He wears a purple shirt and navy blue, pin-striped pants. No tie, no vest, no jacket. The top button to his shirt undone, the sleeves rolled to the elbow. Troy's only flamboyant vanity is his hair; gelled and spiked to perfection. The epitome of patience, his ice-blue eyes bore into the bruised side of her face, waiting for an answer.

Soleil averts her gaze and mumbles, "Not today, Troy."

Troy never liked Barker. The feeling was mutual. Barker tolerated him because he wasn't a threat. He took one look at Troy's pasty white skin, five foot five inch frame, blonde hair, frosted tips, and flamboyant style of dress, and dismissed him without a second look. Troy, on the other hand took one look at Barker and told her he was a piece of trade who could be found on his knees on the wrong side of Philip's Highway, every night.

"Soleil, answer my question."

"What was your question, Troy?"

"Obviously, your late-night ass kickings are getting to your hearing. I said how many shades of purple did you have to mix to get the right color of Barker's hand."

"Eight. Damn. I'm not in the mood today, Troy. Leave me alone."

"No. I won't leave you alone. You need to tell that overgrown, steroid-injecting son of a bitch to leave you alone. I respected your wishes by not calling the police on his ass when you first told me that wannabe, featherweight champion was beating on you. But that was three months ago and it has only gotten worse."

"Troy, why don't we go for a walk, the kids are at recess."

"Soleil, there is no need to take this outside. Everyone knows something is wrong with you because your makeup gets darker and more purple by the day. They may not know what's going down but they know something ain't right."

"Well, can we go outside for my sanity at least." She begs.

"Your sanity? If you were halfway sane you would slice that faggot motherfucker until his intestines fell out and untangled like a tape worm."

Troy's last statement is punctuated by three invisible exclamation points. His gay-bashing candor says with strength, the words Soleil has never given her mouth the opportunity to form. She does not defend her defenselessness, acquiescing instead to Barker's brutal wiles.

"Thank you, Troy, for your most colorful suggestion."

"You're welcome. I told you that faggot wouldn't be good for anything except swallowing my kids."

"Aren't you offending yourself by calling Barker a faggot."

"No, baby, I told you, it takes a real man to be gay."

5.

Six months ago, before Troy's threats to do Barker bodily harm increased in violence, Soleil sat alone on a Sunday afternoon in a rocking chair outside Cracker Barrel near Regency shopping center. She had just left church and stopped in for a quick breakfast by herself. Before going home, she decided to sit in one of the rocking chairs, lining the outside patio of the restaurant. It was an urge she felt every time she ate at the restaurant. That day she gave in to the temptation.

Barker came strolling down the breezeway in front of the rocking chairs with two or three friends. She felt him before she saw him. His eyes blazoned her seated body from the messy bun crowning the top of her head, to the cajun shrimp polish peeping from the toes of her shoes. She ignored the heat from his eyes, never looking up to meet his stare. Instead she focused on the sleek black car circling the building. She counted the loops the car made until it finally parked in a spot behind the man who kept staring at her. The man who stared at her past the point of appreciation; past the threshold of rudeness. Staring in patient anticipation, refusing to be ignored, as if she owed him an explanation for minding her own business, he never said a word. His friends had long ditched him for the cool inside of the restaurant. But he stood there, in the September North Florida heat, lips never moving yet demanding words from a woman who didn't know what he was waiting on.

"May I help you?" she asked raising one eyebrow.

He responded with arrogance, "Don't mind me, Gorgeous, but it seems as if you've already helped yourself."

Soleil didn't smile. Ego, while attractive to some, is an anaphrodisiac to others. But there he stood, ego personified. Crisp navy suit, no tie, white shirt with the collar starched stiff, soft leather shoes without creases from wear and tear, and a large, bold-faced watch that twinkled in the sun light. He looked like a politician; bald, no facial hair whatsoever, resilient smile, and tired eyes. The type who worked long hours but never wanted anyone to know. His smile, white teeth against ebony skin, gave nothing away. Only his eyes, the crows-feet corners, showed the truth in his demeanor.

Soleil turned her gaze, from the black car where no one had yet to emerge, to stare at him through her lashes, openly and rudely, for the same length of time that he gawked at her. He reveled in her stubborn curiosity, opening his arms as as if to say "take it all in" as she looked on from her seated perch in the rocking chair.

She inhaled distinct dislike and exhaled the familiar tingles of desire that tickled at the zenith of her thighs. Looking at him with half of her face hidden from his gaze, she felt urges from her ovaries that made women wonder questions of what if, what about, and could we be, before declaring to their innerselves, *I bet he makes pretty babies.*

"So," he said after an inordinate amount of time passed.

"So," she said back.

"Did you help yourself?"

He asked the question in a way that made Soleil know he was talking about more than just the rocking chair. His question answered her thoughts, engaged her desire, dissipated her dislike, and increased the intensity of the feeling swirling on her womanhood that caused her to scoot to the edge of her chair and rock steadily with her legs tightly crossed. They both knew by the tells of her femininity that she was no longer relaxed, but Soleil smiled just the same, giving him just half of her face, refusing to give him the satisfaction of engagement in his metaphoric banter, even if her body already belied the truth.

Determined by her own refusal to acknowledge his question, she stood from the rocking chair. At her full height he arrested another of her senses with his scent. Light, intoxicating notes of money, power, and prestige permeated the air around him. She knew whatever he was wearing — cologne, soap, deodorant, or the combination of the three, was custom-made specifically for his biology. His aura of smell drifted in a halo around him and wafted its way to where she stood. The air around her was thick with him. Propelled by the forces of nature and thoughts of nurturing, Soleil lifted her entire head and turned, giving him her full portrait instead of just her profile.

He stared, taking in more than what he was given the right to do before. His eyes gazed at the angles in her face that comprised what he had been allowed to behold. Her focus drifted, from his face, to the car behind him where a woman with two sleek dutch braids had finally emerged. She looked at the woman leaning against her car with her arms stuffed in her front pocket. The woman seemed to stare right back at her. Soleil shifted her focus from her to a single element on his face. The corners of his eyes where exhaustion was evident. The tight lines of crows feet marked his otherwise flawless skin. Lines that made her wonder what secrets he was hiding that manifested on his face. The moment was ephemeral. It passed with the same quickly-fading magic of a good dream. Her prescient wonder erased as she stood a stone's throw away in his commanding presence, trying and failing to be unbothered by his affects.

Abruptly, Soleil turned away from his paralyzing stupor, kicking the edge of the chair she'd been sitting in. It rocked with all the anxiety she felt in her body. She had given him her face, taken in his own, and was now running from whatever she forgot she saw. Down the covered patio she walked, taking the same direction as he and his long-forgotten friends. She mumbled a contrived explanation only meant for his ears, "I need to get going."

"I hope I didn't keep you from your chair, Ms. . . . " he said fishing for her name.

Soleil stopped. Dead in her tracks she stopped, turned, and obliged the beautiful man, who failed to hide all of himself in plain sight.

"Miss St. James," she said, looking past his face at the black car where the woman once stood behind them. The car's brake lights flashed as the woman backed out of the parking spot.

"Do you have a first name, Miss St. James?"

Soleil waited for the car to pull out of the spot and leave the restaurant, but it didn't. It paused when she had paused to speak to him once more. She refocused her eyes, squinting to see the corners of his, then relaxing to look at all of him. Admiration crept over her countenance for his smile, tired eyes, and crows feet juxtaposed against his clean shaven skin. She saw his own sentient self-awareness that presented the face he wanted her to see. It was almost *all* she could see, her teacher's intuition that correctly judged the character of children and their parents, was only running in the background of her brain. The intuition that would have normally made her question aloud the peculiarity of the circling car and the mystery woman driver, took a seat to the pressing needs of her female self that made her answer as arrogantly as he was egoistic, "You look like a resourceful man. If you really want to know my name you'll figure it out."

"I am smart. And I am resourceful," he said complimenting himself. "And maybe, just maybe, if you're lucky, I'll figure you out."

"One, I never said you were smart. Two, don't act like you're doing me any favors," Soleil said, letting what she thought would be her last words to the beautiful stranger resonate before she rushed off to her car. She didn't see that as she walked away the black car behind them finished pulling out of the parking spot and disappeared away from the restaurant.

On the ride home Soleil was overcome with laughter at his ridiculous sense of self-importance, but the impropriety of his initial gaze nagged at her. It found her alone in her shower that night, after their first introduction, with the warm water of the adjustable head spraying a steady stream of pleasure. She put on an operatic show for an imagined audience of one, choosing to remember her desire more than her dislike, and the curve of his lips in his smile, more than the lines of crows feet at his eyes that manifested what she did not yet know, and what he would never tell.

Working the shower head as an extension of her hand she forgot the black car and the mystery woman, choosing only to remember the baritone of his voice that was regionally indistinguishable. His dictating cadence, stored for her dreams, guided the rhythm of her hand in the shower. With her eyes closed, and pleasure ever building, the remembered scent of him that wrapped around her like a warm hug that afternoon, mounted her hand-held shower head and exploded around her body. Her fragmented memories kept her dazed with desire, warmed by passionate ambition to conquer the hidden part of the preeminent man, and wet with lust for the next three days.

Three days later, Soleil came home from school and found the same Cracker Barrel rocking chair she'd sat in that past Sunday, leaned up against her apartment door. A pink bow and a small yellow card with a pretty printed script were attached to the seat. It said:

Hope you help yourself, Miss Soleil St. James.
From a smart and resourceful Barker Gordon.

It was arrogant, but sweet. Egotistical and promising. Soleil took her new chair into her apartment shaking her head "no" while saying a silent "yes" to questions unasked. She sat the chair in the corner of her bedroom, beside the large window where she would be able to catch the sun while rocking to sleep or lucidly day dreaming.

It is in the chair she first discovered with a quick search on her laptop that Barker was a judge; a navy veteran, who ran and successfully won several terms as state attorney, turned Governor-appointed judge. His resume was as impressive as his stature. Soleil read through bio after bio on the beautiful stranger she could now call Barker. Just as she figured, while staring at him in the rocking chair at the restaurant, he was a politician; resourceful and apparently smart. Soleil read about the man who's life seemingly began in the military, was highlighted by high-profile prosecutions in murders where self-defense proved indefensible, and who's career remained unpunctuated because it was far from over. At the end of her search, Soleil knew the man she met was on the short list for an appointment to the Florida Supreme Court. She knew if he wanted anything else from her, he'd call or show up.

Then, three days after their first encounter, the thought of his unannounced, uninvited arrival at her doorstep, or on her phone did not scare her. She did not know to be afraid. She did not know that beyond the facade of his ego she would find a very real man who fed his self-aggrandizing, messianic complex on her fear. Three days after their first meeting it did not occur to her to recall the fleeting feeling she had when she first looked at his face. She did not know she needed her anamnesis to remind her that she saw something more than just crows feet in the corners of his eyes. The memory of the mystery woman who stood outside of her car as she traded short sentences with Barker was long forgotten. As was the lesson that internal turbulence causes external manifestations of any emotion. She did not know to heed her clairvoyant response of initial dislike when he stared at her, so that when he did call, when he did show up, she would know to be a sentinel for herself instead of unguarded, and openly inviting all because she had the urge to just sit and relax in that damn rocking chair.

The rocking chair still sits in the corner of Soleil's bedroom, beside the large window, where her often beaten and bruised, black and blue body catches the sun. The bow that arrived with the chair has since been discarded. The card attached to the bow remains tucked into the deepest corner of the top drawer of her nightstand; easily accessible.

Sometimes after he leaves; after one of their rage-filled, fucking-filled, beating-filled nights, Soleil reads, and re-reads, the card, trying to discern between the two lines of text what he really meant. What he was really trying to say. What unspoken warning he refused to impart.

Hope you help yourself.

Soleil helped herself to all of him. To his attentiveness, his jealousy, his anger, his penchant for no kissing and rough sex, his tempestuous fits of rage that stunned her silent the first time his hand ran across her face. Her fleeting feeling of his hidden self became the foreground of their fortuitous affair that she called a relationship for convenience, and others' need for clarity. Soleil helped herself to him.

He helped himself to beating her ass, and as she lay prostrate beneath him night after night, never cowering, never crying, she held on to the desire she felt when she looked at him and he smiled. The feeling she felt when he spoke to her and his voice bounced around her body. The drunken daze that arrested her being when she smelled the heady concoction of what she would later learn to be body oils mixed specifically for his chemistry. Soleil continuously helped herself to him, holding on to the nascent sincerity and humor of when they first met to keep her calm through his chaos.

6.

Chaotic is the only way to describe the scene Dawn walks into when she steps inside the 9 News Now newsroom after reading to the kindergarten class at Shady Grove Elementary. Morning anchors Marcus Jordan and Kirsten Little are still on the air an hour after their noon show ended. Her producer Kelly, is in the control room, taking the lead on breaking news coverage with Jennifer at her side, while Boyce barks orders standing behind them. The scene, while not unusual for Dawn, is still jarring after a morning spent with children who care less about the news.

Dawn tips into her office amidst the ordered craziness and begins working on the show. A show that is supposed to be focused on the city's military community and the struggles they face in and out of the service. That coverage anchored by the story about the Marine, who lost everything to a scam artist who opted for the long con over the quick fix, is bumped to the second half hour, co-opted by the breaking news.

Sex, lies, and deception.
Tonight on 'Dawn in the Evening,' meet Corporal Jon Jacobson.
"I just couldn't believe she would do this to me."
Standing guard at an embassy in the outback.
Working to give his family a better life.
When all of a sudden . . .
"Everything was just gone, vanished, like it never even happened."
A runaway wife, empty bank accounts, and 200-thousand dollars in debt.
How he says it happened to him.
"I should have never turned my back. I just should have never turned my back."
The mirror deception that left Corporal Jon Jacobson duped down under.

"I like it," Dawn says. She removes her glasses and leans back in her thick leather office chair stifling a yawn.

"Any changes you want to make?" Donald, the lead editor in the promotions department, asks. "I still have the sequence open in Avid."

"No. I think it looks good as it is. What time is this running?"

"It's 10 to 6 now so in about 25 minutes in the break before the quarter. And then twice more. Once during network and again during the 7 o'clock hour."

"Sounds like a plan. Send it up to master control now so they have it and don't start freaking out."

"Will do. Talk to you later."

Dawn takes off her phone headset. Bringing her fingers to her face she slowly massages her temples. The breaking news she saw unfold through her email while reading at the school, exploded when she walked into the newsroom.

It began with a police shooting on the outskirts of the city, during a funeral for a local gang member. Extra police presence had been requested for the service, just in case rival gang members showed up. They did. Shots were fired as the casket was being lowered into the ground at the cemetery. One gang member hit an officer. Three officers returned fire. In the end four people were hit with the officers' return fire. Three gang members had flesh wounds; the mother of the opposing gang member who was being buried was killed when she threw herself in front of the fire fight.

This was now her lead story, but she would not promote it. She would not give it any special attention. A decision she was sure Boyce would want to fight about once he saw the first two promos at 6:15 and 6:45. That gave Dawn less than an hour before she had to defend her editorial decision.

She looks around her office. Her golden-yellow walls are adorned with plaques giving accolades for excellence in journalism. Her degree from Northwestern's Medill School of Journalism hangs on the wall directly behind her. Below that is a bookcase with very few books. The latest edition of the AP Style Guide and Strunk and White *The Elements of Style*. Next to those stands a combination dictionary and thesaurus. On the shelf below the books sit her five Emmys collected throughout her peripatetic career.

Her desk, a dark red-wood laminate, looks nice but is cheap. The two chairs for visitors in front of her desk are cloth. The nicest thing in her office is her own chair. The one she bought out of her own paycheck. In it she could sit for hours in the high-backed soft Italian leather working until her show was as near to perfect as possible.

There are no pictures on Dawn's desk. Only a framed yellow Post-it Note that reads in a faded, red scrawl, "I'm not your enemy."

She received the note before coming to 9 News Now, at one of her previous stations where she was the young reporter and fill in anchor. The note was sticking to the middle of her computer screen when she arrived at work. She didn't know who sent it and therefore, couldn't ask whether it was a joke or if she was being chastised for her attitude; what she preferred to refer to as her unwavering ambition. After all these years the note, left quite possibly with malicious intent, had become a badge of honor. She smiles at it fondly as if it were a joke left between old friends. Only she isn't sure if her life and career are the punch line.

Dawn closes the media file open on her computer where she watched the promo for "Duped Down Under," and opens the show rundown to look it over. She reaches for her phone headset, places it on her head, and presses speed dial number one.

"9 News Now, this is Kelly."

"Kelly, Dawn. Grab Jennifer and come to my office so we can talk about this show."

"Be right there."

"Where the hell is the promo on the funeral shooting," Boyce yells aloud in the newsroom.

Quiet falls over the room as producers, anchors, editors, assistants, and the five people sitting at the assignment desk stare at their boss. No one says anything. They just wait for Boyce to explain what he's raging about.

Kelly, Jennifer, and Dawn stay seated in her office.

"Dawn," he rages again.

She doesn't move. She doesn't raise her voice in the hushed newsroom.

"In my office," she calls.

Boyce crosses from the center of the newsroom to the office on the back wall nearest the studio in seconds. He reaches the door, red-faced, and breathing hard. Kelly and Jennifer don't move. They stay seated in the straight-backed cloth chairs facing Dawn. She keeps her face trained to the computer screen; typing furiously through the scripts, making notes when needed on the steno-pad beside her computer mouse and phone. She keeps busy to appear indifferent, insouciant and united with her producers. They simmer in her self-confidence; their aplomb unshaken and undeterred.

"Dawn."

"Yes, Boyce."

"Where the hell is the promo on this afternoon's shooting?"

"I didn't have Donald do one."

"Why the hell not?"

"Because it has no news value. People get shot every day. There's a police shooting once a month. I'll lead with it because it's big, but don't count on a promo."

"Jennifer, Kelly, would you excuse us," Boyce says, altering his tone toward the two producers.

"You two, don't you move." Dawn commands.

Boyce looks at Dawn, mouth agape. The redness in his face creeps into the bare scalp of his half-bald head.

"They've been here since 11 this morning working on the breaking news in addition to tonight's show. Called in an hour early at your request. If you want to make any changes you do it with the three of us."

"Fine by me. Kelly, why didn't you write a promo for Donald on the shooting when it happened?"

"Because as a general rule on *Dawn in the Evening*, we don't do shootings unless it's something out of the ordinary," Kelly answers.

"And you don't consider a shooting at a funeral where the decedent's mother is killed by police, out of the ordinary? Is that not compelling?"

Kelly and Dawn don't respond. Jennifer sits quietly next to Kelly in the chair closest to the corner of the office. She is an observer to the showdown; an unwilling participant. She fidgets with her black skirt. Pulling the hem below her brown knees. She plays with her fingers, scratching the chipped red polish off of her nails. She alternates her movements from the hem of her skirt to her fingernails. She adds smoothing the collar of her leopard blouse to her ministrations as every eye in the office watches.

"Jennifer, do you have something to add?" Dawn asks with her anchor smile stapled to the corners of her mouth.

"No." Jennifer begins. "I just don't see the big deal about not promoting the shooting. We've been covering it all afternoon. At 8 o'clock it's old *and* repetitive. I agree on leading with it. A gang shootout at the funeral for a rival gang member. Four people injured, including a cop, and one person killed, the mother of the gang member who's funeral got shot up. It's a great story, a lot of moving parts. But it's not new."

Jennifer looks up from her fingers to see Dawn's ice smile melt into one of muted pride. Kelly remains nonplussed. Boyce stares them all down.

He begins slowly. "Dawn, your show is not just about what *you* want. It's about what *our* viewers want."

"I think I know what *our* viewers want. Have you seen my ratings? They're up 50 percent over last year and we're winning every demo including men 25 to 54."

"You may be right, but this story still needs more attention than you're giving it."

"I'm giving it plenty of attention. Owen Major will report live from the cemetery with exclusive sound from the dead gang member's aunt, the mother's sister. Our gang analyst at the FBI is coming into the studio to discuss the different gangs and what causes these turf wars to flare up. And we've pulled the latest gun violence numbers and police shootings for the year to let *our* viewers know just how safe they are. The only attention this story isn't getting is a 15-second promo to run during national news or one of those stupid-ass judge shows."

"Dawn, I don't care if you spent your entire hour on this story and nothing else, if you don't promo the story to sell it so people see it, then it doesn't matter how good your team coverage is off the top. People need to know it's coming first. You can't just assume they're going to tune in because it's you."

"They've been tuning in for me."

"They also tuned in when Tarren Tyler filled in for you when you were on vacation last month. Do you want to see if they tune in for her while you're suspended indefinitely for insubordination?"

"Try it and I'll sue this station for everything it's worth. Don't threaten me with legal action, Boyce. You won't win. Trust me. Furthermore, it's 7:30, we go on air in half an hour and I need to finish briefing *my* staff on the final rundown."

"Dawn, don't overplay your hand. *Trust me* when I say that when I'm through, you won't even be able to get this show cleared for YouTube."

Dawn stares at Boyce. Defiant. Brown eyes to green.

Boyce huffs, "This isn't finished."

"It never is." Dawn replies cooly. "Kelly, you and Jennifer gather the crew in the studio. I'll be there soon to go over the changes. Make sure both directors are there."

Kelly and Jennifer rise out of their seats and leave Dawn's office. They squeeze past Boyce, uncomfortably brushing against his bulbous stomach as they exit.

"Boyce, is there something else I may help you with?" Dawn asks, returning her attention to the show rundown on her computer.

"Yes. I got a call today from Margo Westcott. She says you didn't show up for the panel discussion last night. Said Jennifer called an hour and a half after the program started to cancel."

"That isn't a question, Boyce."

"Dawn, don't play coy with me. Why didn't you attend?"

"I wasn't aware I was required to."

"Required. No. Good station business, yes."

"Having cocktails, and discussing why I do or don't have a man in my life at 8 p.m. on a Thursday evening is hardly what I call, 'good station business.' Besides, I had other plans."

"What other plans, Dawn?"

"That's for me to know, and you to never find out. Now if you'll excuse me I have a show to do."

Dawn stands from her chair and heads out of her office toward the studio. A buzz vibrates inside her white suit jacket. She takes her phone out of her pocket and smiles.

A text message from Victor Russell:

Have a good show beautiful.
I'll be watching.

Dawn smiles to herself, not minding the text. *A little too familiar, but compliments will get you everywhere.*

7.

"*We're following breaking news tonight on Dawn in the Evening*," says the pretty dark-skinned anchor on channel nine. Ebony reaches for the remote sitting between her and James on the couch and turns up the volume.

Dawn in the Evening is on. Dawn Anthony departs from her usual political fare to talk about a murder. Ebony puts the remote down and leans forward on the sofa, closer to the TV news. A gang member's funeral shot up by rival gang members. The mother of the dead gang member killed by police. She studies the faces on the screen. The rolling montage of images shows first a picture of the man whose funeral was interrupted. A dated photo, probably from high school, was used for his obituary. Then mugshots of the three suspects. The trio who fired on the funeral, injured an officer, and are now responsible for the return fire that injured them and killed a grieving mother. Blood splatter stains their hardened faces, subsumed with anger in the last pictures they'll probably ever take. Ebony studies them and one word comes to mind. Freedom.

"What are the charges against them?" Ebony asks.

"They'll get attempted murder on a law enforcement officer for sure, firing a deadly missile, and possibly first degree murder in the death of the mother, and maybe an accessory after the fact, and possession of a weapon by convicted felons," James answers. He picks up the remote and turns the volume back down.

"Is that what you were working on at the office all day?"

"Pretty much. With the shooting so early this morning, they made their first appearances at the jail this afternoon. Their arraignment is next week, and then the pre-trial process starts sometime next month in front of Judge Gordon."

"So I've heard," Ebony mutters as she stares at the young men's faces. None of them are older than 21, and none of them will ever be free again. Yet something in them believed they would achieve some level of freedom if they shot up the funeral; even if it was just having one less corner-boy beef. They marked the loss of life with their own blood, searching for freedom and ending up condemned. Doomed to a life behind bars following their certain convictions on a host of charges, real and imagined, James and the other prosecutors at the State Attorney's Office will conjure up.

"When are you going to introduce me to your family?" James asks, pulling Ebony's thoughts away from the television and back to him.

"I need to check on the food." Ebony stands and stretches in front of the sofa. She crosses into the kitchen, keeping her back toward James still sitting on the couch.

"You can't ignore the question forever, Ebony," he says turning to look at her.

Ebony pauses before turning from the stove. She tries to still her shoulders but fails. They creep close to her ears. Her resolve breaks. Her back tenses across her shoulder blades; scrunching in the middle, deepening the crease of her spine she can't seem to stretch straight. Ebony's nails find her hands wrapped in front of her body. She scratches against the skin of her veins. The raking against her skin keeps her grounded against James as her brain is clouded by picture after picture of picnics with red-checkered blankets.

The rays of the sun that heated her flushed face. The distinct outside smell of fresh cut grass clinging to every inhale. Water gun fights in the small back yard. Playing hide and go seek in the patch of grass between the garage and the front door that always proved to be fun but futile, because there was nowhere to hide; just wide-open space.

All Ebony sees is wide-open space. The space where she resides outside of her family. Her family she loves and adores but cannot introduce to James. *How do I explain to him that in my family I am non-existent. Beyond the proverbial black sheep or the yet to return prodigal daughter. I am who I am. And my family is who they are.*

"James." Ebony caresses his name on her tongue, savoring the taste of the word.

She releases her hands and soothes their nervous itch by wiping the backs on her denim-clad thighs. Lowering the flame on the front right eye of the gas stove buys her time to explain why her life does not cross paths with her parents. Why she and her family don't intersect, instead only observing them from the outside looking in. Ebony turns slowly with her hands at her chest clandestinely unbuttoning the top of her emerald green blouse. With the tops of her breasts visible she's ready to explain her familial dysfunction, hoping her measured words, timed to the rise and fall of her breasts, will distract James from listening, keeping him close instead of pushing him away.

"James," she says again. Slowly. Cooly, testing the single syllable of his name.

"We've discussed this before," Ebony continues. "My family is not your average family."

"No one's family is the average family."

She notices the hesitation in his voice. Maybe he regrets bringing up their single sore subject. The last time he asked to meet her family she left him alone on the Riverwalk with a brief kiss on the lips, before scurrying away in the direction of The Landing with a sudden work emergency. He called every day for a week. At first, confused and concerned, then apologetic. Those few apology calls finally turned into angry calls. When week three rolled around and she detected nonplussed apathy, she answered. Ebony willed herself to keep James and her family far apart, especially in conversation. That was three months ago. The first time he mentioned her family, he respected her space when she simply said she could not discuss them. He mistook her fear for emotional pain; a feeling she neither corrected nor explained. Now one year since that first mention, his persistence compels him to push past her boundaries, to reap more of the year-long investment he's already made.

In soft and measured words she says, "James, I love my family. I do. My mother, brother, sisters, Daddy. I love them all. But unfortunately, they don't feel the same way about me."

"Ebony. You've met my mother, my no-account, can't-keep-a-job, got-too-many-baby-mama's-to-count brother, my father who's suffering from early onset Alzheimer's and even my dog, who can't help humping your leg every time he sees you. And from you, I get just you?"

"Is just me not good enough for you?"

"Ebony, that's not what I'm saying and you know it."

"So what are you saying James?"

"What I'm saying is we've been together a year and I know nothing about you except what you say, and what I happen to be allowed to see."

"What more is there for you to know. I have a mother, father, a brother and two sisters. Also known as Marilyn, Dr. Ivan, Isaiah, Monica and Monique."

Staring at him Ebony takes in his broad frame. The cut of muscular thighs evident in his light gray and black pin-striped suit pants. His short, stocky arms are tamed in a crisp, white shirt with french cuffs. A vest matching his suit pants holds in the slight paunch at his midsection where cut abdominal muscles once laid flat. A skinny black tie is loosened around his thick neck. The veins there pulse with tension. Looking at his ordinary brown-skinned face, shaven down to the shadow of a beard, mustache and goatee, Ebony admits that he looks good. Almond-colored eyes dance a challenge in his pupils. Defiance blazes in her own.

"That's more than you've ever said before about this elusive family of yours."

"They're not elusive."

The shrill timbre of her voice bounces off the walls in the one story house leaving the faintest of echoes. Ebony folds her hands within themselves allowing her nails to rake against the thin flaking skin.

"Ebony, calm down."

She takes a deep breath before going on. "I am calm. I'm just over this conversation. How many times can I tell you my family is not in my life. I'm not in their lives. That history is over and done with."

"I'm just supposed to take you at your word?" James yells. "You have no past worth mentioning. Not even a hellish upbringing worth a tear or two. How am I supposed to know this present you live in, this future you're building toward, you say you want me in, won't just magically become part of an unmemorable past; a history in your head that holds no record?"

"Yes, James. You're supposed to take me at my word. It's called trust. That's what you do in relationships."

"I'll give you the benefit of the doubt on trust. But explain this to me and I'll drop it. If your mother's name is Marilyn and your sisters are Monica and Monique, and your brother's name is Isaiah and your father Ivan, how did you become Ebony?"

"Call it foreshadowing," Her voice trails off, "maybe my family always knew I'd be the outsider."

"Even before you were born?"

"That's more than one last question."

"So you're not going to answer?"

"That's three questions."

"Fuck it then. Let's just fucking eat."

"Don't curse at me."

"You want to fight about that too?"

"No. Let's eat. But I'm serious. Don't curse at me."

Ebony turns around to face the stove not waiting for a response, verbal or emotive. She buries her face in the steam of the stew pot as she listens to James storm across the tiled kitchen floor and onto the cherry hardwood of the hallway, before his feet soundlessly transition to the plush carpet of the great room throw rug. Her shoulders relax, the scrunch in her spine smooths out, her neck stretches and her hands release themselves to the sides of her thighs. Ebony turns the knob to lower the flame under the pot. Inside the stewed chicken and red potatoes begin to simmer. The smell of green peppers, celery, onions, tomatoes, thyme and rosemary waft through the house. Ebony listens to James busy himself rummaging through the stack of *New Yorker* magazines on the cracked glass coffee table. She turns around to see him just feet away in the open concept living room, dining room, and kitchen. He fiddles with the remote raising the volume on *Dawn in the Evening*. Ebony stays standing in the kitchen, silently looking as the faces of the arrested gang members scroll across the screen. Freedom comes to her again. She assumes they wanted to be free from whatever familial prison that led them to seek their family on the street.   A familiar feeling she has yet to express to James.

Ebony watches James watching TV, wishing she could tell him what he wanted to know. Her arms folded and hands scratching she wishes to feel the freedom she craves. The freedom that's eluded her leaving her arrested, like the men, doomed to a life of bondage; she mentally, them physically and spatially.

The night's dustup over her family will not be their last. They will pretend to be normal having dinner and a glass of wine, maybe two. She will ride him to snoring contentment, then lay awake beside him haunted by the freedom-seeking faces from the TV screen, reminded of the freedom she sought herself as a child in a family she made her own.

8.

Johnnie hears her family come in the house before she see's them. The alarm box in her bedroom beeps twice announcing their arrival. She does not move to greet them. She lies sprawled across the bed's new cream duvet, still in her dirty scrubs. Johnnie collapsed when she got home late in the afternoon, not bothering to pull the bedspread back and lay on the sheets, exhausted by the amount of work that rolled through the trauma center.

For Johnnie, the day was nonstop emergency after emergency since 11 o'clock in the morning when she was called in on her day off. Five bodies rolled in at once with varying degrees of injury. One she pronounced dead on arrival. Four others survived the trauma of bullets. Johnnie spent hours in the operating room on one fishing expedition after another. She extracted a bullet out of a back just inches from a spine, and pulled another that pierced a lung. The brass collected at her station in the O.R. were trophies no one would ever esteem as a testament to her medical heroism.

When she was finally relieved of her emergency medical duty she dragged herself home, shuffling her feet from the O.R. to her red Toyota Camry parked in the hospital's parking lot. Then again from her garage to the inside of her house. The drive home was a blur. Once inside, Johnnie closed every door, window, blind, and curtain in the four-bedroom two-and-a-half bathroom home. She shut herself in and passed out.

Napping is where Nathan finds her after he, Tyler and Danielle come into the house. Johnnie lays on top of the heavy cover with her arms splayed. One hand hangs off the edge of the bed as if reaching for the water bottle just inches from her fingertips.

Nathan doesn't want to wake her, but he and the kids haven't seen her since morning when he took them to school. He approaches her slowly. Kneeling at the bed he lightly kisses her lips then lays his head on her chest, listening to her heart beat.

Johnnie smells him first. Nathan's new scent awakens her senses. The same different smell she first detected on him the day before. She can't place the scent, but she knows it's nothing from the Old Spice line. Johnnie breathes in deeply, trying not to let the mystery smell annoy her. She adjusts her body to accommodate the weight of Nathan's body on her own. She settles further into the bed's pillow top mattress and lets her free hand caress Nathan's shoulder.

Nathan lifts his head. Johnnie sits up on a forearm, never letting him go.

"Hey you," she says.

"Why's it so dark in here?" Nathan asks.

"I got called in. Shooting at a funeral. Five victims. When I came home I crashed." Johnnie yawns.

"Did you eat?"

"Just drank some water." Johnnie points to the white water bottle sitting on the floor near the corner of the bed.

"Well, what do you want?" Nathan asks. "The kids are hungry and were hoping you had a little something special for them, but I think I can hook us all up tonight."

"Whatever you make is fine, Babe," Johnnie says yawning again. "I'll be down in a minute. Let me change out of these scrubs and freshen up."

Nathan leaves Johnnie alone in their bedroom. As soon as Nathan is out the door and down the steps, she closes the bedroom door behind him. She turns on the lights in the room taking in the sparse oak furniture. A bed, dresser and mirror, and chest of drawers occupy the large elongated space. More furniture could fit, a sitting room easily, but she likes it this way. Open. Johnnie walks to the chest, opening drawers and selecting bra, panties, leggings and a T-shirt. Clothes she wears around the house.

She strips off her scrubs and takes all of the clothes, clean and dirty, through to the five piece en suite. Johnnie deposits the dirty scrubs in the laundry basket standing by the shower before stepping in. She turns on the hot water; then sits on the marble bench built into one of the shower walls. She had it installed for moments like this.

Johnnie sits beneath the water until her skin begins to wrinkle. Washing away the day with her soapy loofah running over her tired body. Meticulous about grooming she washes every inch; ass to breasts, across her taut stomach, up and down her legs, between her thighs, across her arms, and to her back. She follows the wet roadmap with the sweet smelling lavender soap on her body twice before switching to a towel to scrub her face. Sit, wash, rinse, and sit. The water runs lukewarm under Johnnie's seated frame as a faint knock raps on her bedroom door.

"Mama, Daddy says come eat," Danielle calls, walking into the steaming bathroom from the bedroom.

"I'm coming, baby," Johnnie says, barely making out her daughter's shape through the heavy steam of the shower. "Just let me get dressed."

"Okay." Danielle turns and walks away.

Johnnie waits until she hears the door close behind her five-year-old. She reaches for the chrome shower handle and turns off the steady stream of water. Stepping out of the glass encased shower, Johnnie grabs her towel and dries her body.

She gives the bedspread a shake to smooth out the wrinkles; hiding the evidence of where she laid. She picks up her water bottle and tips its top to her mouth. She takes a long satisfying drink as she heads back into the bathroom smacking her lips. Johnnie opens the black cap and pours the clear liquid down the drain. It guzzles the liquid. Johnnie smells the contents. She pours a cap full of bleach, another clear liquid, behind the bottle contents to cleanse the smell before turning on the faucet. The hot water fogs up the mirrors. Johnnie reaches for her toothbrush and toothpaste. She brushes her teeth furiously. When the metallic taste of blood hits her palette, she spits the minty foam into the sink. It, too, is guzzled by the drain.

Stepping back, Johnnie squints at her complexion in the large mirror, still foggy from the steam. She slaps her face with both hands to put some color in her cheeks. She blinks her large brown eyes rapidly in an effort to bring them to life. Satisfied with the red undertones in her cheeks and the perceived look of sleep in her eyes, Johnnie dresses. Black yoga pants are pulled over her petite frame. An oversized T-shirt covers her ample bosom. The only thing ample about her. Satisfied with her at-home mommy appearance, she grabs her water bottle before turning off the light in her bathroom. Through the darkness she exits the en suite, and then the bedroom, in search of her family and something else to drink.

9.

Soleil drinks the water in long gulps. The sound of her swallows and the beat of her heart, pound in her ears. It's steady boom-boom-boom lets her know she's still alive. Her breath is labored and short. Her head throbs against her skull. Every muscle in her body is alive with pain. Her legs, thighs, ribs, abs, arms, back, and face all ache. She hurts all over, but welcomes the abuse. Right. Left. Right. Left. The punishing blows are unceasing. Right. Left. Right. Left. Each pound makes her stronger. Every punch is a moment of clarity she can fight back. Every slap a searing hot poker branding her body in a different place.

Six and a half grueling miles of not jogging, but not quite sprinting are almost over. Soleil is nearly home, her short novice-stride works overtime because her arms aren't pumping quickly enough. She runs her own way, owning this part of her life that is unequivocally hers. Every step a punishment of her own making. Every time her fists punch the air is her own brand of abuse. Every time the March wind slaps her exposed limbs is a slap she controls.

Soleil runs the last lengths of Southpoint Parkway, pacing herself against the speed of a black car rounding the bend into her apartment complex. Soleil follows the car's lead, waving her entrance pass before the gate sensor as she goes to keep it from closing on her. The tall, pastel colored buildings are an open invitation for anyone who does not live there to move-in immediately. The gates, closed and locked at all times, give the assurance of safety. Outsiders, would-be robbers, or serial killers can not get in without a code or a pass. Without a neighbor jeopardizing their safety for someone they call friend.

Soleil jogs through the parking lot passing the now parked black car she timed herself to, just before reaching the front of her building. Abruptly, she slows her space to a snail's trudge seeing him before he has the chance to see her. His bald head, shined to perfection, shimmers beneath the late morning sun. He leans against his car. A sleek, black Audi RS 5. Soleil can tell by the way his suit jacket is pulled at the corners of his shoulders that his arms are folded in front of him. She slows her walk further.

He will wait. He has already been waiting.

He turns around as if reading her thoughts; knowing she is near, but not where he expects her to be at the moment he expects.

A bright smile greets her meek one. She jogs the last few feet toward him.

"Good morning, Gorgeous," Barker says with all 32 on display.

"Good morning," Soleil responds wary of his mood.

"You went running this morning," he says, taking in her black lycra bike shorts, loose lime green tank top, and baby blue sports bra. "And in so little." He tsks.

"I figured the cool air would keep my adrenaline pumping. Besides, it's supposed to warm up."

"So I take it that's why you missed my three phone calls." His smile disappears.

"I guess."

He walks toward her. She steels her body in anticipation of his touch, trying not to flinch. His scent reaches her first. She inhales. He smells good, like the unfulfilled promise of good sex. He looks even better, wearing a dark gray suit with widely-spaced, black pinstripes, a crisp white shirt, and an off-putting lavender tie with an intricate knot at his neck. It's just shy of conservative; a not so subtle announcement of, "Look at me. Here I am."

Barker grabs Soleil's wrists and rubs them gently with his thumb. She inhales his scent, exhales her fears, and waits.

"Don't you want to know why I called, Gorgeous?" He whispers into her ear.

His murmur leaves drops of spit dotted against the lobe of her ear. The sensation and scent of the latent fluids from his breath assault her nostrils with the staleness of no longer sweet cigarettes and overly strong peppermints. It is in direct contrast to the smell of his body. The opposing scents duel as they enter and exit her nose. The sweet smell emanating from his clothing seeks to engage her desire, but his breath, filling her ear and neck reneges on the unpromised sensuality leaving her stunned. Soleil remains still, smelling all of him, unable to gauge his mood.

His wrist rubs become squeezes.

"Well." He prods. "Don't you want to know why I called?"

"Yes, Baby," she murmurs.

"I called to see if you would accompany me to a luncheon this afternoon," he whispers while tightening his grip around her wrist.

"Where are we going?" Soleil asks, keenly aware of the building pressure on her body.

"We *were* going to a luncheon with the mayor. But you didn't answer your phone."

She bows her head.

"You know how it makes me feel when you don't answer your phone, Soleil."

He says her name, dripping saliva into the edge of her ear. The feel of his spit makes her tilt her head to her shoulder to dry it out. He wrenches her wrist tighter than before as she head butts him away from her shoulder so she can clean her ear. The reflex is an involuntary slight. He squeezes harder. Soleil opens her mouth to yell, but no sound comes out. Out of the corner of her eye she sees the elderly woman who lives in the apartment across the breezeway from her. Ms. Jay. She is walking her dog. Soleil smiles at her as she passes by. Her flamingo pink sweat pants and matching jacket swish as she walks and pumps her arms. Soleil accompanies her smile with a nod in her direction. The teacup terrier at the end of her leash yips at Barker. He steps closer so his body is flush against Soleil, blocking her view of Ms. Jay. The woman's small, pale face and bouncy gray hair disappear. To the untrained eye they look like lovers enjoying stolen moments in the middle of a parking lot.

"Are you in pain, Gorgeous?" he asks as he nods at Ms. Jay and her tiny barking dog.

Soleil says nothing.

"I asked you a question, Soleil. You, like to defy, me don't you?"

She says nothing.

"You must like it more than I do." He takes one hand from her wrist and wraps it around her back until they are locked in a hug.

He takes the other hand that was cuffed at her wrist and drags it across her stomach. His hand is the only thing between them. Stuck against him again, Soleil lets her body become his rag doll as she stares out over the cars of the parking lot. Her gaze rests on the black car that beat her in the complex. She squints to see if anyone is still inside as he lifts her hydration belt holding the bottles of water from her run. The hem of her tank top follows as he pulls her closer with the one hand wrapped around her back. His other hand moves down into her bike shorts. Soleil squints her eyes at the car, to keep her body from flinching as he discovers she's not wearing any underwear. His low guttural groan is appreciative. Soleil squints, but she can't see inside the tint. She can't see if anyone is watching her molestation, through the slight slits in her eyes.

He cups her sex and moves his fingers in a come here motion Soleil's sweat and other bodily fluids slick across his hand.

"You do like to defy me, don't you, Gorgeous," he growls. "I can tell it turns you on."

She does not answer. Eyes closed, refusing to look at him, she keeps her head turned away from his face. He sees her bushy ponytail and she sees nothing at all.

"You know how it makes me feel when you don't answer the goddamn phone, Gorgeous," he says, continuing the motion of his hand in her shorts. His thumb flips across her clitoris. "It makes me think somebody else is fucking this sweet pussy. My sweet pussy. Is that what you want me to think?"

Soleil doesn't answer.

"I hate having my imagination run away with me like that. Me at home thinking another man has his dick rammed up my pussy. His balls slapping against my ass." He shoves his fist into her vagina.

Soleil's eyes fly open. Her head turns to see the sadistic smile stretch from crows-feet corner to crows-feet corner as the intrusion pushes her to the tips of her toes. She turns her head wildly to see if Ms. Jay or anyone, is looking, but all she see's is her hair slapping back and forth between her face and his. The cork-screw ringlets serve as a distraction to keep from looking at him, but her hair also blocks her view of seeing the driver step outside of the black car she paced herself against. It blocks her view of the car she focused on while stuck against Barker, before he bombarded her body with his fist.

"No one outside to help you, Gorgeous."

He does not see the woman with wild hair whose arms are shoved in her pockets, behind them as he walks toward the steps leading to Soleil's apartment. She shuffles her feet to keep up not seeing the woman, either.

"Here I was at home" — Barker pauses as they make their way up the first flight of stairs — "Here I was at home thinking someone had my pussy spread-eagle on a platter. I thought someone was patting your pretty head as your beautiful lips wrapped themselves around their dick and sucked him off, until he came down your gorgeous golden throat."

He releases her at the landing. Instead of going up the final flight of stairs fisted, the hand that was inside of her wraps around her neck. Trapped in his half headlock, the fist that smells like her, motions toward her mouth. Soleil opens.

"Suck you off, Gorgeous. Suck me clean."

She obeys until they reach her door. He uses his free hand to fish her key out of his pocket and turn the lock. He kicks the door open with his foot. They step in. They don't see the woman with the wild hair standing at the foot of the first step looking up at them. They don't see her eyes contract as the door to Soleil's apartment closes behind him.

The woman at the foot of the stairs can no longer see them. She doesn't know that inside Soleil's apartment his arm is still wrapped around her neck, and Soleil's lips are still wrapped around his fist. She doesn't know that when Barker releases Soleil she stays standing in front of him waiting as Barker waited before.

He doesn't make her wait long. Soleil is on her knees before reflexes force her to blink twice. The thud of her fall to the ground reaches the woman standing at the bottom step outside of the apartment building. The woman doesn't know a kick to the middle of Soleil's back is what catapulted her to the ground. She heard the fall, but not the cry because there wasn't one. Soleil is silent. Barker grabs her ankles and yanks her across the thin cream carpet. It burns across her knees and the exposed meat of her thighs as she is pulled backward. He kneels behind her, placing her ass in his lap. His belt and zipper are undone. Leaning across her back until his lips are at her ear, he laps his tongue in the canal sending his breath into her nose, eliminating her last feelings of fondness wrapped up in the heady smell of his body. She smells hate as he follows the lap of his tongue with a blow of rank breath. Hovering over her, he peels her shorts over her ass and lifts her shirt and hydration belt higher on her back. Ass to dick, he leans further over her exposed back and whispers, "This pretty ass of yours is going to fucking suck me dry."

The woman at the bottom of the stairs hears none of it. She is back in her car. Her imagination unfolding the scene on her own, formulating the words between them she believes were exchanged. The woman pulls out of the parking lot hearing only her tires and the sound of her own thoughts that she misses the first few rings of her phone blaring through her car speakers.

"Hello," she answers breathlessly.

"Where are you?"

"I'm just leaving from getting my hair done. I'll be home soon."

"I'm waiting on you. We're going to be late to the luncheon."

"No we won't. All I have to do is my makeup, and take a shower."

"We're going to be late."

"I'm on my way James. It won't take me that long to do my makeup and shower."

"Whatever you say, Ebony. I'm sitting in the car outside waiting on you."

"I'll be there soon."

Ebony disconnects the call as she hops on the highway headed back to her own home. The radio in her car is off, the interior of her carriage silent save for her own thoughts racing through her head. She rushes home from the apartment she's visited for the third time this week, the twenty-first week since they've been dating, wondering if she was seen. It is the first time she's gotten out of her car and gotten so close since she saw him find her at Cracker Barrel in September. It is the first time she's heard the audible sounds of his abuse against someone else's body. Ebony rushes home with the sound of the thud playing bass on her brain, looping uninterrupted for miles, until her phone beeps with information.

Ebony taps the screen making it come to life and reads the message:

Dawn Anthony hosts luncheon for Judge Barker Gordon, Doctor Jonelle Edwards and others honored by the mayor. Watch live on 9NewsNow.com.

I'll be there live.

Ebony drops the phone back in her cup holder and accelerates on the highway. She hurries home to meet James; promising not to take too long doing her hair and makeup, and taking a shower.

10.

Dawn jumps out of the shower hearing the heavy knock on her door at ten minutes to 11. The knuckles on the other side rap three times in hard, quick succession.

"Coming," she yells from deep inside the condo.

Dawn snatches her robe from the cream ottoman inside her bathroom and throws it around her wet body. The silk of the fabric clings to her skin. The residue water from her shower bleeds through, creating wet spots on the small of her back and under her breasts. She turns to face her full- length mirror in the far right corner of the bathroom. Not paying attention to her reflection she pulls her large, satin covered sponge rollers from tufts of her hair one by one. They fall to the floor in a haphazard pile around her feet. Dawn shakes her head, glances in the mirror, and adjusts the long layered bangs of her bob before exiting the bathroom, passing through her bedroom, and into the main space of the condo toward the door.

She pauses before opening, breathing deeply to slow her racing heart beat.

"You're early," she says smiling widely at Victor standing in her doorway.

"And you're not dressed." He leans in for a hug.

Victor wraps his arms around Dawn's upper body squeezing tightly and pulling her close. Dawn stiffens her back, aware she is nearly naked against him. Victor, feeling the tension, releases her and thrusts the bouquet of calla lilies he's holding in her face.

"These are for you."

"Thank you. Come in. I'll be dressed in a few minutes."

Victor takes a quick step over the threshold into the one bedroom condo and stops. Dawn walks around the furniture dodging the low sofa and arm chairs, and the line of four beanbag chairs separating the living room from the kitchen. She lays the flowers on the peninsula countertop before turning to face Victor.

He's the first man to set foot inside her condo in four years, an intentional act, choosing to keep her trysts, when needed, relegated to waterfront hotels. She gazes at him while his eyes wander around the walls staring at the hand-crafted African masks, wood works, and original canvas artworks. Copper sculptures and other knickknacks line the floating shelves along the wall of the condo that leads from Dawn's bedroom to the kitchen. The opposite wall of floor-to-ceiling bay windows overlooks the St. Johns River and the scant downtown skyline. In the center of it all is Victor Russell. A tall, thin man whose clothes are perfectly tailored to fit his frame. He's dressed in a simple black, slim fit suit. A mint green tie adds color to the monochrome attire. Monogramed silver cufflinks glimmer in the sunlight pouring from the window.

"Nice place," Victor mumbles taking in the view.

"Thanks. Make yourself comfortable."

"I think I've died and gone to architectural heaven. But what's with the bean bag chairs."

Dawn laughs. "The furniture is just for show. My attempt at adulting. I've had the beanbags since college. They're way more comfortable."

"Gotcha."

"Make yourself comfortable. I'll be right out." Dawn sidesteps toward her bedroom.

"I'll be here." Victor smiles.

"I won't keep you waiting long. I promise."

"Not like Thursday?"

"You're not letting that go, are you?"

"Not if I can make TV's Dawn Anthony feel guilty and be nice to me."

"Let me get dressed," Dawn says backing into her bedroom; her real smile plastered across her face.

Thursday night after *Dawn in the Evening* wrapped, Dawn sped out of the 9 News Now parking lot in downtown Jacksonville toward the city's Southside. She arrived at the St. Johns Town Center, the city's premier shopping and dining locale, in 15 minutes. On the outskirts of the high-end outdoor mall is where she parked, behind J. Alexander's restaurant, where Victor was already waiting for her. She breezed through the doors and made her way to the booth where the hostess said he was seated.

"Sorry I'm late," she said once she reached the table.

Victor stood up to greet Dawn. She offered her hand. He leaned in for a hug. The awkward half-embrace broke the ice between them, giving her comfort as she slid into the booth with a toss of her hair and an easy smile.

"I was watching your show," Victor said, striking up a conversation.

"And what did you think?"

"It was good. Seems like you know what you're doing?"

"Thank you for thinking I'm competent to do my job."

"I hope I didn't offend you. It was good," he falters. "*You* were good."

"Thank you. Maybe we shouldn't talk about my work."

"Why not? It's the reason we met."

"Touché."

Six weeks ago Dawn held a panel on her show about the city's plan to improve the Brooklyn neighborhood. Victor, the lead architect on the 220 Riverside complex, was a guest. After the show they exchanged cards. The next day he left her a voicemail where he hinted at meeting on less than professional terms. After six weeks of texts, emails, casual phone conversations, and one off meetings around the city, they were finally sitting down together for dinner without any time constraints to adhere to.

"What are you drinking?" Victor asked.

"Wine please," Dawn said, letting her lips creep up into a small smile. "You can't come to J. Alexander's and not have wine."

"True," Victor nodded toward the focal point of the dimly lit restaurant. The glass-encased wine cellar in the center of the restaurant separated shelves of wine bottles by red and white.

"Thanks for meeting me tonight," Victor said after placing their order for wine and appetizers.

"No problem." Dawn looked up from the menu. "I'm happy to be here. Definitely better than anything else I was supposed to do this evening."

"Yeah? Like what?"

"I was supposed to be apart of this panel for this women's group I'm not even in, and never agreed to join or moderate. This is a much better time than that would have ever been."

"You don't mean the SENT panel tonight, do you?" Victor asked, looking at Dawn over his menu.

"That's the one. How do you know SENT?"

"Margo Westscott."

"Me too. That woman is relentless."

"Well, I'm sure you know why she was hounding you to come tonight, don't you?"

"I never cared to know. So no."

"Well, look at you. You're beautiful. In a highly-visible career, and single."

"That almost sounded like a compliment. *Almost.*"

"It was," Victor affirmed. "What greater testimonial for SENT could there be, then Margo Westcott helping the great Dawn Anthony find a forever love."

"You sound like Johnnie."

"Who's Johnnie?"

"*She's* a friend. Short for Jonelle. She and Margo tag-teamed me at another event a few years ago. Margo invited me, and when I got there, Johnnie gave a testimonial about how Margo built her business off her back."

"I'm listening."

"Margo introduced Johnnie to her husband 17 years ago. Johnnie, is a surgeon at Shands. Nathan was an engineer for the city. They've been together ever since. Married for 16 years. Two children. Though Nathan is more of house-husband now than an engineer."

"Sounds like a solid couple to build and brand a match-making business."

"So they've been telling me." Dawn sighs. "I just don't need, or want, a whole organization of people in my life telling me yay or nay on how to land a boyfriend, turned fiancé, turned husband."

Victor didn't speak. He believed he was allowing Dawn the space to be herself and air her true feelings. A glimmer of her dropped guard stopped him from saying anything that might make her raise it again. Dawn, aware of expressing that she indeed wanted to be married and was looking for a husband, didn't know how to take back the words she just let tumble out in her truth.

"What's your story with Margo?" She asked.

"She tried to recruit me to go to the panel after meeting me at the construction site at 220 Riverside. She was looking at getting an apartment there, and maybe leasing an office space on the ground floor."

"And she thought you were an ideal candidate to listen to the panel because?" Dawn pressed.

"Because as she said, 'I don't see a ring on your finger so it can't hurt,'" Victor mimicked. "She never let me get to the part that I already had a date with you."

"Why would a man like you, need a panel like that?"

"Dating is not just difficult for women."

"Who said it was difficult?"

"I wasn't talking about you Ms. Anthony. Calm down. But from the dates I've been on, present company not included, it's hard out here for women and men."

"So did you *ever* seek Ms. Westscott's services?"

"I looked up the site after I thought you stood me up tonight."

"Ha, ha, ha. I wasn't *that* late. But seriously, did you ever look at any dating website, SENT or otherwise?"

"Are you grilling me, Ms. Anthony?"

"Sorry," Dawn said sheepishly. "It's hard to turn it off sometimes."

"You're like a dog with a bone when it comes to a story."

"Now you've insulted me. You have to finish the story."

"Let's just say I checked out the SENT site after she told me about it, more out of boredom than anything else, and I clicked one too many links while browsing and received a phone call the next day that was an interview with questions, deeper than things I've shared with my doctor."

"I told you. That woman is relentless."

"That she is. That she is."

"Well, I'm glad you decided not to go to the panel tonight." Dawn scans the menu.

"And why is that, Ms. Anthony?" Victor leans in toward Dawn.

"Well, Mr. Russell." Dawn sighed, "Instead of single, ethnic and not taken, I'm hoping I am single, ethnic, and taken," Dawn answered revealing her uncomfortable truth as she put the menu down.

"You are hoping right. Ms. Anthony, as of tonight you are single, ethnic, and taken." Victor offered his hand across the table.

Dawn placed her hand in his, sealing their new relationship. Over the course of the meal they explored more of each other's backgrounds. They were both only children, but their upbringings were markedly different. Dawn was born and raised in Virginia by parents who allowed her the freedom to do and say almost anything as a child, as long as she was respectful. She was brought up with southern sensibilities and big city ideals living in the DMV. On the other hand, Victor was the product of a southern grandmother who believed children were better seen and not heard. Though he did credit her with giving him his interest in architecture. From as early as he could remember, at the end of their day, before he went to bed, he would crawl into his grandmother's lap with his bucket of Legos in tow. Dumping them all out into the fabric of her skirt so they could build something with every brick from the bucket, was his night-time routine.

Dawn and Victor talked until they were the only ones left in the restaurant aside from the tired wait staff, who impatiently waited for them to leave. Victor walked Dawn to her car learning along the way that she didn't have an aversion to water when the sky opened up and poured rain. Instead, she slowed down and twirled in the fat drops from heaven. Her open, peanut-butter trench coat created a wide ark around her as she laughed before rejoining Victor. Before saying good bye she invited him to the luncheon for the mayor she was emceeing. He agreed, kissed her on her forehead, and closed her car door, as she adjusted her purse with the unopened umbrella still inside.

"I'm ready," Dawn says emerging from her bedroom dressed in a form fitting, sleeveless, white sheath dress. A forest green, faux, snake skin belt cinches her waist.

"You look amazing," Victor says standing from the low-seated navy sofa.

He brushes his hands across his black suit pants and strides to Dawn, standing in front of the beanbag chairs.

"Thank you."

"You're most welcome."

Victor touches Dawn's chin with his index finger. He slowly lifts her face, looks into her eyes, then leans in closer to gently kiss her lips. Her body melts and her lips follow Victor's lead, engaging in a more relaxed embrace than before. Their kiss is slow and tempting. Promising. Victor eases his tongue between Dawn's lips tasting her briefly before she pulls away.

"I think we should go." Dawn attempts to walk toward the door.

"What's the rush?" He asks holding her back.

"I'm going to be late and I have to host."

"Exactly. The show can't start without it's emcee."

Victor leans into Dawn's lips again. His kiss is quick, strong and urgent. He explores her mouth with his tongue, suckles her bottom lip, biting it gently between his front teeth before letting go. Dawn pants slightly when he abruptly releases her.

"Now we can go." Victor declares.

"Are you sure, Mr. Russell?"

"Trust me, Ms. Anthony. We can't stay."

Dawn follows Victor out of her apartment. As she closes the door, she notices the bouquet of flowers still sitting on the kitchen counter where she placed them when Victor first arrived.

11.

James and Ebony arrive in the grand ballroom of the Jacksonville Marriott 30 minutes after the program for the awards luncheon began. He is the first thing Ebony sees when they walk in. Standing in the middle of the ballroom floor, hands clasped behind his back, he listens to the mayor give a speech about his few honorable characteristics.

"Judge Barker Gordon, we present you with the trailblazer award today, for having the courage to prosecute cases, instead of settling them, even when the law favored defendants, and for striking a balance of fairness and justice for both victims and suspects from your post on the bench. Congratulations."

Ebony stares as James erupts in applause, "woofing" at Barker from across the room. He is the last one to finish clapping.

"I think we should find our table now," Ebony says flatly.

James leads her by the hand around the maze of tables until they reach the one filled with his colleagues. Ebony takes her seat and tunes out the program that carries on for the next two hours. She focuses her attention on him. Barker is seated in the center of the room at the table with the other honorees. Staring through her periphery she watches him struggle, like the rest of the luncheon goers, to break down the overcooked chicken breast, gummy rice, and soggy vegetables. The five-piece band breaks down and is replaced by a DJ without her missing even one of his blinks. Smooth jazz remixes of classic R&B and pop hits keep the dance floor empty and her sideways glances at him unobstructed. James doesn't notice that she's no longer there with him. He holds court of his own with several assistant prosecutors from the State Attorney's Office. Their wives and girlfriends chat amongst themselves, indulging in the latest local political gossip. They don't extend their conversation to Ebony, nor does she care to join in. She keeps her gaze and attention on him until she feels the eyes of someone else looking in the same direction.

Another woman takes a seat at one of the two empty chairs remaining at the table. Her approach is silent; her greeting is nonexistent. Ebony watches as the woman puts her small, pearl clutch in the seat beside her to save for someone else. The woman's hauntingly beautiful face is immediately recognizable. Her curly, medium-brown hair is pulled into a messy topknot at the crown of her head. A few loose tendrils hang along either side of her face close to her ears, and against the nape of her neck. The thoughtless hairstyle adds to the elegance of her strapless, lavender dress. Her makeup application is the finishing touch to her look with iridescent eyeshadow smoked to perfection, and a deep plum blush drawing out the mystery of her charcoal-lined eyes. Her blank face holds a quiet sadness in the moment she dares to look up from her fingers in her lap.

Ebony lowers her head in her own seat across from the woman. Their eyes catch. She raises her gaze hoping the woman follows.

"I'm Ebony," she says once they are eye level.

"Hello," she answers meekly.

Ebony stands from her side of the table and makes her way around to the woman, when she notices her back stiffen. A hand is there. His large, gnarled hand grips her shoulder. Ebony's eyes incline to meet his gaze; her body forgoing taking the seat meant for him.

His dark pupils glow with a glare that catches them both off guard. His ghastly smile is wide and masks the thrill of torture and fear lighting in his eyes. Ebony adjusts her course away from the table, away from his seat, and away from the woman who just arrived. Before she is out of earshot, she hears him say, "Well, hello, Gorgeous." Ebony's not sure which one of them his standard greeting is meant for, but she knows Barker will not let her leave the luncheon without cornering her for an inappropriate conversation.

Ebony quickens her pace out of the ballroom to the hotel bathroom. Visions of knotted and calloused hands cloud her mind. She enters the stuffy powder room with her arms crossed; nails raking long scratches into the tops of her hands. The small suite is empty. Keeping it that way, Ebony closes and locks the main door to the restroom behind her. A candle burns a floral scent, but only one smell floods her senses. A stored stench of Swisher Sweet and Southern Comfort; his smell from their last close encounter two years ago.

Two years ago, in the heat of August, Ebony laid on her sofa in panties and a wife beater. With her air conditioner broken, she did her best to keep cool in the stifling house with every light off, and every ceiling fan spinning on high. Ebony was on the couch under the fan when her doorbell rang. She knew who it was before she answered. There was no need to yell "Who is it?" Expending her breath, especially in the heat, would only add to the agony of a Florida summer without AC. Ebony opened her front door in her wife beater, no bra, and panties and returned immediately to the living room sofa to continue cooling herself under the fan. Barker followed behind.

Neither of them exchanged any words. No greetings, no pleasantries, no kisses, no hugs. He followed her through the cave-like darkness until he joined her on the white suede couch. The salmon and canary colored pillows were quickly tossed to the floor to make space for his body. She plopped her feet in his lap without a glance or second thought. It was the least amount of effort required to show some modicum of affection.

"I'm surprised you're home," Barker said after several moments of silence.

"I had Chuck cover my session at the gym tonight," Ebony answered with her eyes closed. "The repair man was supposed to come by and take a look at the AC but they canceled on me."

"You never told me that."

"You never asked."

Ebony regretted her words as soon as they settled on the air. His grip on her ankles tightened.

"What's wrong?" she asked, softening her heat induced frustration.

"I just don't understand why you would make plans to have a man come to your house and not tell me," he said, squeezing her ankles as his thumb and forefingers made rings around their circumference.

"What man?" she asked still not looking at him.

"Now you want to play like you're dumb? Gorgeous, you are far, far from stupid."

Ebony sat up on her elbows to look at him. His eyes were tight, squinted and beaded. The corners of his face lined in unmasked anger. His one word was a trigger letting her know how far she had pushed him.

"Baby," she said, opening her eyes to him as she sat all the way up on the couch and reached for his arm. "I just needed someone to come look at the AC in the house. I didn't think it was a problem since it needs to be fixed."

"Don't Baby me, Gorgeous. You know better than to treat me like *I'm* stupid. Like I don't know what you're doing."

"What are you talking about?"

He dropped her ankles and stood up in front of the couch. Stretching his arms wide, he arched his back. His body cracked from the movement. Ebony kept her feet stretched out on the couch, as she watched him take off his black suit jacket. He laid it on the arm of the couch. She waited for his next move.

"You know, Gorgeous, I really hate when you try to make it seem like I'm the dumb one and you're smarter than me. If you were waiting on the AC repair man, I highly doubt you'd be waiting in your underwear."

"Baby, I took off my clothes after the man canceled on me."

"Gorgeous, there's only one way to tell in matters like these," he said, yanking her ankles and forcing her to fall. Ebony bounced on the carpet from the impact. The throw pillows on the floor did nothing to cushion her fall. Her head barely missed the edge of the cracked glass coffee table.

"What are you doing?" she screamed.

He wasn't listening, no longer interested in anything she said. His jealousy and irrational logic, gave him the conviction he needed for his violent behavior.

Barker dragged Ebony from the living room, around the couch, down the hall, and into her bedroom. The backs of her legs and the sides of her thighs burned as they forcefully slid across the carpeted living room throw rug, squeaked across the hardwood, and rubbed along the plush carpet of her bedroom.

Once inside, he picked her up and threw her on the bed. Again she bounced. Her body tumble-landed in a crush of decorative pillows. Ebony had no time to recover. No time to roll out of his reach. He leapt on to the bed with his pants unzipped, his penis hard and hanging. She was pinned with one hand on top of her chest as he used his other hand to pull her panties down just below her knees. She was exposed.

"This never lies." He snarled, shoving his middle and index fingers inside of her.

He stirred them around, then brought them to his nose.

"The sweet stench of pussy sweat. Now for the real test."

He rammed his dick inside her and pumped away. One hand kept her chest pinned to the bed. The other hand, with his fingers dripping of her, smothered her lips. She was trapped beneath his weight; her own underwear kept her legs bound in a vice. Only her arms were free. Ebony pumped her hips in time to his beating motion, willing wetness to form at her center. He met her challenge and raised the fucking stakes, beating at her walls. Pushing her further into the pillows, he rammed every inch of himself inside her. His head thrown back in ecstasy, eyes squeezed shut in sadistic gratification, he clinched and gritted his teeth as his balls slapped at her perineum, giving it it's own beating in the process.

Smashed into the bed, Ebony kept her hips moving in time with him and let her hands roam beneath the pillows. She made angel wings as she pushed her arms and hands deeper beneath the pillows until she rubbed what she was looking for. The cool steel fit right into her hand. She gripped it beneath the pillow and brought it to her chest, just above where his hand pinned her down. He pumped. She stopped. She laid still beneath him and cocked her Lady.

His eyes fluttered open as Ebony put the barrel to his forehead.

"Get out, Gorgeous," she said with one finger on the trigger.

Barker laughed heartily as he pulled out of her.

"Gorgeous, you should know better than to pull a gun on a judge," he said, stepping back from the bed with his dick still hard and hanging, pulsating, and dripping of her.

"And you should know better than to rape a woman."

"That's how you want to play this, Gorgeous?" He asked as he zipped over his erection.

"That's exactly how we're going to play this. Get your shit, get out, and don't come back; and I won't blow your head off. This would count as self-defense right, Your Honor?"

"You're smarter than you look. I guess you have learned something from me," he said, sauntering toward the living room.

Ebony pulled up her underwear with one hand, never lowering the gun, never taking her finger off the trigger, she followed behind him; arms extended and aimed. Barker slowly gathered his jacket. He carried it with one finger over his shoulder as he made his way back to the front door.

She followed behind with her Lady still trained to the back of his head. He unlocked the door, turned the knob, and swung it open wide.

"Good bye Gorgeous," Barker said with a cheshire grin.

He chuckled to himself as he walked down the lone step toward his car. Ebony slammed the door behind him, but his last words still made it inside.

"I'll see you again soon."

"What took you so long?" James asks as Ebony returns to their table from the hotel bathroom.

"I didn't feel well." She sits beside him.

"Are you okay now?"

She nods not wanting to talk.

"Well then, how about a dance?"

"How can I say no."

She takes his hand, concealing the fresh, deep scratch marks she raked into her skin. James escorts her from the table. In his arms, she allows herself a lingering look at the entire table. Barker and the woman are gone. Disappointment and relief simmer in her stomach as she glides on to the empty dance floor with James. She wraps her arms around his neck as he pulls her closer. Eye to eye they dance to a song Ebony recognizes, but can't name. Her mind drifts back to the mysteriously beautiful woman. The stranger who wasn't, who was no longer sitting across from her when she returned to the table.

"Mind if I cut in?"

The voice belongs to him. Barker and the woman stand in front of them.

"Judge Gordon. Congratulations. How are you?" James breaks his embrace with Ebony.

He slaps Barker on his back further greeting him.

"I'm well," Barker says. The woman stands beside him silent and obedient. Her head is down, refusing to look at anyone or anything except her feet.

"So how about that dance?" Barker asks.

"It's up to my lady. Judge Gordon, this is Ebony. Ebony Jones. My girlfriend."

"Nice to meet you Ebony." He says extending his hand. "So how about giving an old man a shot on the dance floor."

"Only if your date doesn't mind," Ebony answers, looking him dead in his eyes.

"She doesn't mind," he answers for her. "James, this is Soleil."

Barker releases Soleil with a shove. She stumbles. James catches her.

"I told you I'd see you again, Gorgeous," Barker coos taking Ebony's hand.

"My name is Ebony."

"Gorgeous, don't be so mean. It's been such a long time and we've got so much catching up to do."

"Barker, I already told you my name is Ebony. Keep your abusive pet name for Soleil."

"Don't be like that, Gorgeous."

"What do you want, Barker."

"I've missed you, Gorgeous. No one has put up quite a fight like you did."

"In case you've forgotten, I don't fight fair."

"You mean your little gun stunt?"

"Seems like Soleil enjoys being away from you." Ebony nods toward where she dances with James.

Barker's eyes tighten as he watches the two slow dance, James's arm around her back; Soleil's arms around his neck. She laughs when James says something only she can hear.

"Don't get mad, Gorgeous," Ebony taunts. "This arrangement was your doing."

Barker ekes out a smile through clenched eyes and gritting teeth.

"I'll deal with her later."

"No you won't." Ebony breaks free of his hold. "James, Baby, why don't you and Judge Gordon catch up and let Soleil and I get to know each other better."

Ebony takes her hand, not waiting for James to agree. She walks toward the doors of the ballroom not allowing anyone else the chance to say no. Soleil drags behind her in silent protest. Ebony stops at the door and looks at Soleil who stares over her shoulder at a seething Barker. Her eyes plead with Ebony to stop, but Soleil doesn't speak. She doesn't voice her concern or speak up in protest. Ebony takes her silence as consent and pulls the beautiful stranger through the doors, wanting to tell her everything will be okay, but knowing it will only get worse before it ever gets better.

12.

"Red Bull and Vodka, please," Johnnie says to the bartender.

The pasty-faced barkeep rinses an already wet glass and places it on the counter. Johnnie watches as he takes a can of Red Bull from the glass refrigerator and a bottle of Ciroc from a mid-level shelf, and pours the dueling liquids into the glass. Her fingers drum the counter as she waits for the bartender to finish his flourishes with a lime wedge and bright red stirrer that matches the clip-on bow tie of his uniform.

"Will that be all for you, ma'am?"

"Aah." She smacks her lips.

"Ma'am? Would you like another one?"

"No, but I'll have one," Dawn says approaching Johnnie beside the bar.

"Hey Lady." Johnnie smiles.

"Hey yourself. Just wanted to tell you congratulations again."

"I think you said enough with that speech you gave."

"I did make you sound kind of awesome, huh?"

"Kind of awesome? You had me looking around like 'who is she talking about?'"

"Here you are, ma'am." The bartender interrupts pushing Dawn's drink close to her.

"Thanks," Dawn says. They both drop $10 bills into the large wine glass the bartender designated for tips.

The two sip their drinks as Dawn follows Johnnie back to her table where Nathan waits. Even though Johnnie is off work, she is surrounded by colleagues and their spouses, save for Dawn, who pulls up a seat beside her. Every year the hospital buys a table for the mayor's luncheon. This year the hospital bought two tables to celebrate Johnnie's honor as a "trailblazer" in the city. The designation was made up for 14 random citizens to disguise the political grandstanding, gladhanding and securing of donations.

The annual March luncheon takes place no matter who is in office or how far off the city election. The reclusive mayor is in rare form. He joked through the program and made his way around to all the tables. If there were babies in the room, he would have kissed them.

Johnnie, on the other hand, is not as jovial. Tired of the pose and exhausted from her week, she is ready to go home and get out of her uncomfortable dress.

Whoever believed corsets and boning were a good idea never actually wore one.

Johnnie eases in her seat next to Nathan and tunes out the conversations around her to talk to Dawn.

"Don't think I didn't see you stroll in here with that young, hot, tenderoni on your arm," Johnnie says. "You can front like you want to congratulate me all you want, but I saw him. Is that the guy you went out with the other night?"

"First of all who says "tenderoni" anymore? What decade is this again?" Dawn chides. "And second of all, yes, that is my date from Thursday. You were supposed to see him."

"So I guess you don't need me, Margo, and SENT, after all?"

"That's what I keep trying to tell you. And her, for that matter. I got this."

"Okay, Miss Thang. Well, now that you have a man, I want details. Where'd you meet, how old is he, and does he do it to you good?" Johnnie asks muffling a liquor heightened cackle.

"Why you gotta be so nasty? Damn, Johnnie, we're at a classy event."

"So you're going to hold out on me until when?"

"Until the next time we get drinks. You decide since you stay so busy."

"Alright, Miss Lady, I'll hold you to it. But at least tell me his name."

"Victor." Dawn stands up. "I gotta go and make my rounds."

"Okay, see you later."

"Let me know before you leave. I'll walk out with you."

"Cool."

Dawn moves away from Johnnie and walks across the room to another table. Johnnie faces her colleagues. Dr. Taylor Thomas, the Dean of Medicine at the hospital and Johnnie's mentor, is regaling the other doctors about the hospital's rapid expansion. Bored with the small talk, Johnnie pretends to listen, plastering an enthused look on her face as she curls herself in the nook of Nathan's arm. The sweaty glass of energy and alcohol doesn't move from her lips. Her succession of sips provides peace to her agitated energy, and prevents her from chiming in with her real thoughts about the hospital's expansion.

Johnnie sips, inhaling Nathan's new scent: lemongrass and jasmine. The floral fragrances are foreign to Old Spice, Nathan's chosen brand of cologne for the last 17 years. She inhales deeply and sighs through her mouth. Looking into Nathan's chestnut eyes, she can't reciprocate the smile he beams down at her.

"You smell good," Johnnie whispers, nuzzling her nose against the stubble of his cheek.

"Old Spice, Love" Nathan grins, giving Johnnie's shoulder a squeeze.

Lie number one. "I'm ready whenever you are. Love." Johnnie places her empty glass on the table.

"No protest here."

Nathan stands and smooths the wrinkles out of his worn blue suit. The button at his belly lays flat against him despite the jacket's ill fit. Nathan rolls his shoulders forward to adjust his lanky arms, then pulls Johnnie's seat and helps her up. She picks up her small, black clutch from the table and turns to face her colleagues.

"Until next time," she says over their conversation to announce her departure.

"Until next time."

Dr. Thomas stands and shakes Johnnie's and Nathan's hands, then wipes his own on the front of his tuxedo jacket.

"Call me if you need me," Johnnie says to Dr. Thomas while looking at Nathan.

"I always do, Johnnie. I always do. And congratulations. Good work."

A chorus of half-hearted "congratulations" follow Johnnie and Nathan away from the table.

"What was that about?" Nathan asks once they're out of ear shot.

"I have no idea." Johnnie answers. "Habit I guess."

"Racist habit."

"I doubt it. He's a doctor. He probably doesn't like being touched," Johnnie defends.

"Don't make excuses for him. You're a doctor and you let me touch you," Nathan says sliding his hand from the small of Johnnie's back to her nearly non-existent behind.

"That's different." She giggles.

The innuendo is just enough to turn Johnnie's thoughts from suspicion to relief.

"Hold on one second," Johnnie says, stopping Nathan at the door.

"What is it, Love?"

"I told Dawn I would tell her when I was leaving."

"Oh. By all means, wait for your friend."

Johnnie scans the ballroom until she see's Dawn at her own table with Victor. She stares in Dawn's direction, waiting to catch her friend's attention. When Dawn looks up, Johnnie waves her to the door. After a whisper into Victor's ear, Dawn leaves her table and strides to where Johnnie and Nathan wait to leave.

"Hey, Nathan," Dawn says, reaching them at the door.

"Oh, now you see me?"

"I'm sorry. It's just. You know. Me and this girl never get to catch up anymore." Dawn throws her arm around Johnnie's waist in a hug. "She's always so busy."

"Don't I know it." Nathan mutters.

"Now that we've established how busy I am, can we go?" Johnnie looks between her husband and friend.

"After you, ladies."

Nathan walks behind Johnnie and Dawn in relatively content silence, as they chat. Outside, Nathan hands their car ticket to the valet and waits behind Johnnie and Dawn, where two others wait in the valet line.

"Miss St. James," Nathan says tentatively to the tall woman standing beside Dawn.

She turns to the voice that called her name, smiling slightly when she recognizes Nathan's face.

"Mr. Edwards. Good to see you again. And please call me, Soleil. We're not in school. "

"Okay. Good to see you, too. You remember meeting my wife at the beginning of the school year," Nathan motions toward Johnnie.

"We talk on the phone all the time. Dr. Edwards how are you? And, Dawn Anthony, nice to see you again too?"

"How do you two know each other?" Johnnie inquires.

"I read to her class yesterday. I forgot to tell you. I saw Danielle. She is super cute. And getting so big."

"Well, it's a small world after all," Nathan says behind the women's reacquaintance.

"And who is this?" Dawn asks, staring at the woman standing beside Soleil.

"Dawn, Dr. Edwards, Mr. Edwards, This is Ebony." Soleil introduces them.

"Hi," Both Johnnie and Dawn say warmly.

"Hi," Ebony replies. "I'm a huge fan," she says to Dawn.

"Thank you. Thank you for watching."

"Nice to see you again, Soleil," Johnnie says, picking up the original conversation. "Danielle is doing really well."

"She's a great student."

"Thank you."

"So what are you doing here?" Nathan asks.

"I'm here . . . on . . . a . . . date." Soleil lowers her head.

"I did see you with Judge Gordon," Dawn chimes in. "I thought that was you, but I wasn't sure."

"It was them alright," Ebony says aloud.

"How long have the two of you been dating?" Dawn asks.

"Six months," Soleil answers just above a whisper.

"Good. How's it going?" Dawn grills.

"Damn, Dawn. Don't interview the girl. And I know you're not asking questions about a relationship and you won't even come off the details of yours."

"Touché, Dr. Edwards. Touché," Dawn says.

"Well, it's good seeing you again, Soleil." Nathan jumps back into the conversation.

"Likewise. Dr. Edwards, you'll still be joining us for our field trip Wednesday, won't you?"

"Yes. Danielle, won't let me forget."

"I bet she won't. That's all she's been talking about since she turned in the permission slip you signed."

"Oh, I know."

"Have a good one, Soleil, Ebony, Dawn," Nathan says stepping through the women as the valet pulls their 4Runner to the curb.

"You too, Mr. Edwards. Dr. Edwards," Soleil replies as Nathan helps Johnnie into the car.

"See you soon. You guys, have a good day," Johnnie says to Soleil and Ebony. "Dawn I'll call you to set up a time for drinks."

"Sounds like a plan," Dawn says. "You know, you guys, should come." Dawn extends the invitation to Soleil and Ebony.

"Yeah, sure," Johnnie responds.

"If you're not leaving we can exchange numbers inside."

"We're not leaving yet. Just catching up away from the guys," Ebony says.

"I heard that. I'm going to run to the bathroom and I'll see you guys inside."

"Are you ready?" Nathan asks impatiently from the driver's seat.

"Sorry, ladies. Hubby is ready to go. See you soon."

"See you . . ." Soleil, Ebony, and Dawn all say together.

Dawn walks away from the group and back inside the hotel as Nathan pulls the SUV away from the entrance. He and Johnnie ride in silence, their windows rolled up, the car air conditioner humming along, adding to the white noise of the radio commercial. Closed in the car, the scent of lemongrass and jasmine finds Johnnie again. Her agitated suspicion returns. She sucks her tongue in her vodka-dry mouth, letting her taste buds find the remnants of the liquor's soothing balm as Nathan sings along to Shirley Murdock's voice, coming through the radio.

13.

"You should really hold your head up more," Ebony says, watching Nathan and Johnnie disappear from the hotel curb.

Soleil doesn't respond to Ebony's admonishment. She waits, where she's been waiting, for what, she's not sure.

"So you're a teacher." Ebony says, still not looking at Soleil.

"Yes."

The valet pulls a sleek black Acura RLX to the curb. Ebony steps forward. Soleil waits where she stands looking between Ebony and the car, and back again. Ebony watches Soleil compute the information in front of her. She sees the look of recognition alight in her face before she shakes her head, dismissing what she believes to be a doppelgänger or coincidence. Soleil waits, shifting in her stance, unsure of Ebony's plan, and why she must be apart of it.

The valet gets out of the car and glares at Ebony for longer than what is necessary. His eyes roam over her stacked, petite frame in a royal blue bandeau dress. The plunging neckline offers him only a peek at her slight breasts, but it is what is behind her that makes the dress worth his while. The valet gawks with open mouth at the diminutive amazon. His gaze travels from the mass of perfectly positioned wand curls framing her face, over the ridged cuts of her arms, across her tight hips, down the jutting muscles of her quads and calves, to the onyx nail polish painted on her toes. Ebony clears her throat, forcing the valet to look her in her eyes. Shame shows in his downcast eyes as he finally hands over her keys; but not enough shame to keep him from looking once more at the supple and geometrically perfect creation on Ebony's back.

She shakes her head from side to side as she steps into the car.

"Get in." She commands across the hood.

Soleil approaches the car tentatively. Opening the door to the luxury sedan, she gathers her dress around her ankles before sliding in. Ebony pulls off as soon as the door slams, but she only drives a few yards, parking her car in a space to the right of the hotel's entry way.

They sit in silence. Watching. Waiting. Soleil wanting to learn the purpose of their clandestine adventure, but Ebony avoids her gaze. Both of their masks of pretense during their meeting with Dawn and Johnnie are removed. Manicured bushes covering the ground floor of the hotel keep Ebony's attention. Her determination wanes, and the adrenaline fades from the rush she felt on the dance floor, or in Soleil's apartment complex parking lot. She stares at the rooms and the windows casting large enough shadows to keep the car cool, despite the blazing sun above them.

"How long has he been hitting you?" Ebony finally asks, breaking the uncomfortable silence.

Soleil doesn't confirm or deny Ebony's observation. Her history with Barker was obvious from the way they danced together. Hushed words and pretend smiles. The familiarity between them was different from the awkwardness between she and James.

"You don't have to answer. I know how he is. He used to hit me too," she admits, still looking straight ahead.

Ebony's voice is distant though she's sitting right beside Soleil. It's tone cold, deflated; the kind of cadence used to recall memories you've tried to forget all your life.

"You two have been dating for six months?"

"Yes."

"We dated two years ago. But only for three months. It wasn't so bad at first, but then . . ."

Her voice trails off. She doesn't have to finish. Soleil nods, knowing what comes after then.

"How did you guys meet?"

Soleil considers the curious question, "Cracker Barrel at Regency." She answers. "You?"

"He goes there every Sunday." Ebony says under her breath.

"What?"

"Nothing." She shakes her head. "We met at a private gym on Baymeadows near 295. I used to work there."

"Used too?"

"I was a personal trainer there. I specialize in boxing."

She pauses before continuing.

"Barker used to have an appointment with a trainer named Chuck right after I had an appointment with a client of my own. He would always come early and hang out around the ring while I was in a session with my client. In the beginning, he would just sit on the floor and pretend to stretch or do push ups or sit ups. As he became more comfortable, he would walk up to the ring and hang on the ropes and just leer at me."

"What did you do about it?"

"This went on for weeks. In the beginning I ignored him and just focused on my client. But after awhile, he made himself noticeable.

He would groan anytime my back was turned to him and lick his lips when I would wipe sweat off of me."

Soleil sits and listens, looking at Ebony's profile as she triggers memory after memory of her first days with Barker, knowing firsthand the creep in him. Ebony's admission proves she knows him.

"One day I told my client to take a break," Ebony continues. "I waited until she was out of eye sight and earshot before I approached him."

"What did you say?"

"I told him to get away from my ropes and to step back from my ring."

"And he said?"

"Don't mind me, Gorgeous, I'm just admiring your work."

The sharp inhale in the car is audible. Soleil processes the involuntary breath with the words that were nearly identical to the phrase he used when he approached her in the rocking chair. A predator with the same strategy. The compliment always comes first.

"I told him to admire from out of my sight, perhaps outside the gym since I was conducting a private session. He, of course, respectfully declined."

"Where was the other trainer? Chuck?"

"He hadn't arrived yet. Most trainers lock the gym doors once their session starts, but that's a fire hazard and an unnecessary risk."

Soleil remains silent, waiting for Ebony to continue her own story at her own pace.

"In the end, I guess Barker was an unnecessary risk as well." She sighs. "Instead of backing off he became more annoying and more persistent every time I saw him, until I'd had enough."

"What does that mean?"

"It means, one day after his game of cat and mouse had been going on for weeks, I cancelled my client's appointment and waited for him to show up on his own. He was predictable; always arrived 30 minutes before his session, smiling and chomping on a peppermint. When he walked in the gym and saw me alone beside the ring he smiled wider. It was almost sexy if it wasn't for his eyes."

"He is a beautiful man." Soleil sighs. She gave truth to words whose veracity made them both feel shame.

"Especially that day. White on white on Black." Ebony smiles, at the memory. "He strolled over to the ring, dropped his gym bag on the floor beside him, and just stared at me. I refused to look at him, just put my gloves on and climbed between the ropes."

"And of course he followed," Soleil says knowing his aggressive, dogged pursuit.

"He followed. I was ready to teach a lesson I hoped he was ready to learn."

Soleil raises an eyebrow to the side of Ebony's face. The muscles visible through her dress suggest strength, but she still stands a foot below the top of Barker's head. Ebony doesn't negate her facts. She stares straight ahead at the hotel's brick facade rising above the freshly manicured bushes.

"The only thing I learned," Ebony says turning to face Soleil, "is he's not afraid to hit a woman."

Soleil stares at Ebony's face, now that she's being allowed the chance to truly see it. There are no visible scars, no well-covered bruises, no painted over, broken blood vessels and veins similar to the ones hidden beneath Soleil's own drag. By comparison, Ebony's face is perfect underneath the light contouring of concealer, heavy black eyeliner, and thick mascara. If Soleil is Ebony's mirror the cracks of her reflection do not reflect back.

"So you fought?"

Ebony does not answer right away. She keeps her guest waiting; the question hanging in the air, knowing the conversation hinges on her answer, knowing it will lead the way into his history and the depths of his bottomless depravity.

"I guess you can say that," Ebony says reluctantly. "He swung at me with everything he had. I bobbed and weaved around his punches as much as I could. He landed a few, I landed a few. In the end we laid sprawled on the mat; sweaty, out of breath, and silly with whatever fucked up hormones were floating in the air between us. It marked the beginning of what could have been an almost normal relationship."

"Almost doesn't count," Soleil says, trying to keep Ebony's honesty from drifting into fantasy.

"I know."

Their eyes meet but reveal nothing. The shared experiences between the two of them are lost in the coldness they've both developed to cope; Soleil in the present and Ebony in an attempt to block the past.

"How did you leave?" Soleil asks wanting to know more about how Ebony's three month saga with Barker ended, then what happened before he became himself.

"He hit me," she says, pushing a few curls away from her forehead.

The move is revealing. Ebony's earlier perfection is ruined. There on her forehead; uncovered, unconcealed, and unpainted is a curved scar above her left eyebrow. Soleil's own forehead holds its identical twin. They are scars from Barker's backhand. The curve made by the scratched gash left in flesh once his heavy, spiked titanium ring ran across their faces.

"He hit me, fucked me raw, and left smiling, whistling and smacking on a fistful of peppermints like I was his favorite stress reliever."

"The next day he showed up with flowers," Soleil says, not needing Ebony to tell her what she already knew. "An assortment of long stem roses in red, white, and pink. The colors of blood, pus, and exposed skin meat."

"I never thought of it like that, but yes." Ebony repositions her curls.

Soleil reaches up to her face, with Ebony's permission, she moves the hair away from the scar. She wants proof that she is not the only one marked. Gentle fingers brush across smooth forehead skin leaving Ebony's face as exposed as her own.

"What did you do after he hit you?"

"I followed behind him as he left out the door as jovial as could be, and threatened to call the police."

"He laughed, didn't he?"

"He laughed. He made his case while I bled from my forehead in my own doorway. He asked me, 'Who would believe a judge, a public servant, and an honorably discharged Navy man actually hit a woman he's never met and for no reason? What 9-1-1 dispatcher would even send police to investigate once they heard the name of the alleged assailant?' He made his case, laughing and smacking peppermints all the way to his car."

"And you broke up after that one time? No other fight? No other protest? No amazingly attentive I'm sorry sex?" Soleil asks — angry, curious and incredulous.

"Not immediately. There was one other fight three weeks later and that's when we broke up. But in between I was able to manage his fits of jealousy and rage. As for the I'm sorry sex, he was only attentive that once, but the orgasms he gave me didn't erase the sting of his ring. My wound was still fresh and I fucking hate roses."

"That still doesn't explain how you left."

Ebony, still in the driver's seat, lets her eyes roam over Soleil's face with more questions than answers. The pleading look in her eyes show she is willing to take and not give. Soleil huff's angrily; not in a giving mood either. She sucks her teeth waiting for Ebony to answer and keep the conversation going, since this tete a tete is of her own design.

"All that matters right now, is that you leave." Ebony finally advises, ignoring the question.

"And how do you suggest I do that?"

"Do something that will make him never come back."

"Is that what you did?"

Soleil's question hangs in the stuffy car air between them. Ebony turns away from her and reclines her seat all the way back. She doesn't answer, escaping into her own thoughts instead. Spent of the energy needed to push for answers to rhetorical questions, Soleil lets her own mind wander to the beautifully-ugly man inside. His eyes find her and squint. They're mashed together like a dog's mouth ready to growl. Soleil shudders from a chill running down the length of her back. His new forms of pain and punishment that await her inside her apartment find their way to her mind. Her torturous imagination forces her to squeeze her muscles, knowing the fisting was only par for the course.

"I need to get back inside," Soleil resigns after getting no more answers from her would-be sister in survival.

"I know."

Ebony takes Soleil's trembling hand and delays her exit. Caressing her fingers in an attempt to comfort, Soleil accepts the gesture and waits to leave. She waits to leave the safe space for the brutal unknown.

"I meant to tell you earlier," Soleil begins, "you look familiar."

"I know," Ebony admits in an inaudible breath that reaches her passenger's ears as air.

Soleil looks over the body of the woman laying beside her. The woman that got away. The body that fought back. Their hands are clasped. Ebony's olive brown coloring entwined with her burnished cream. Their fingernails rest against one another displaying the color of wickedness as black as the plans Soleil had yet to learn encased Ebony's heart.

14.

Dawn stands in the entrance to the bathroom when she sees Soleil and Ebony walk down the hallway toward the ballroom. She watches them walk, waiting for them to get closer before speaking. Ebony, short and statuesque, holds up Soleil, tall, thin, and waif. They approach with their heads down, exchanging whispers. They do not see her waiting.

"Hey, ladies," she says aloud stepping out of the shadow of the bathroom doorway.

"Hey. We didn't see you there," Ebony says dropping her arm from around Soleil's waist.

"I can tell." Dawn smiles. "You two must have caught up a lot. You were deep in conversation."

"You could say that."

"Do, you guys, still want to get drinks, with Johnnie and I? I'm sure it'll be sometime this year."

"Let's set it up." Soleil laughs lightly, knowing Dr. Edwards is not the most reliable person, or parent, to make and keep to set plans.

"Would you mind taking a picture with us too?" Ebony asks as they walk back inside the ballroom. "My phone is at the table."

"Not a problem."

Dawn follows Ebony and Soleil as they walk between the tables, maneuvering around the extended chairs of guests who have already left. They reach the table at the edge of the ballroom floor. Dawn recognizes a few prosecutors from the State Attorney's Office. Nods, half-smiles, and slight waves are had all around. She sees Ebony bump past one attorney, deliberately brushing her ample ass against the front of his pants. He says something to her, she playfully pushes his shoulder. An invisible speck of lint is lifted from his suit jacket. Dawn's stomach knots at the suggestive scene tugging at her heart, telling her to scan the room for Victor. She ignores her internal advice. An anchor on duty, she waits to comply with the request of a viewer. But she is not alone in her wait. Soleil stands inches away from her, head bowed, arms folded tightly across her stomach.

"Soleil, Dawn, this is my boyfriend James," Ebony says approaching them.

"James Parnell. Nice to see you again," Dawn says dropping her anchor smile for a genuine one. "Thanks for all the quick responses during the Michael Dunn trial."

"You know her?" Ebony asks incredulous. "How come you didn't introduce us."

"Because I know how big of a fan you are," James soothes. "Dawn, if I don't get a hold of this girl before eight o'clock then I might as well not even try until nine. Fan doesn't even begin to describe her. If I weren't her man, I'd think she was into you."

"Well, I'm glad you enjoy the show. How about this picture?"

Dawn grabs Soleil's hand and tugs her closer, as Ebony and James take their place to Dawn's left. Ebony holds her phone out in front of the group to capture the moment.

"Alright, you guys," Ebony says. "On the count of three. One, two . . ."

"I know you guys aren't going to take a picture without me." Barker booms approaching the group. "Ebony, James, Gorgeous, and the lovely Dawn Anthony."

"Congratulations," Dawn says, letting go of Soleil's hand, who seems to squeeze tighter at that moment.

"Why, thank you." Barker bows at the waist.

Soleil turns her head away from him as his grin touches the grody corners of his eyes.

"When am I going to see you in my courtroom again?" Barker asks Dawn.

"The next time you have a high-profile trial."

"Are we ready?" Ebony asks impatiently.

"Sorry," Dawn says smiling. "Judge Gordon, why don't you join us for the photo." She makes room between her and Soleil for Barker to fit in.

"Don't mind if I do," he says, stepping into the open space. "I'll stand right beside my Gorgeous, whom I see you've already met."

Barker squeezes against Soleil even though there is nothing behind him that warrants such a tight fit. He holds tightly to her left hand. Soleil reaches for Dawn with her right.

"If we're all ready now," Ebony snaps glaring at Barker.

"We're ready, Baby," James kisses the side of Ebony's face to ease her tension.

"Alright, on the count of three. One, two, three."

The camera makes a single snapping noise capturing the moment.

"Thank you." Ebony says graciously.

"No problem," Dawn replies. "Send it to me. Take my number down so we can get together."

Ebony taps the screen of her phone inputting Dawn's information as she dictates it. Neither of them see Barker snake closer to Soleil. He wraps his hand around hers, which is clasped tightly in front of her stomach. Chatting amongst themselves, Dawn and Ebony don't see Barker gripping his hands into Soleil's shoulder, pushing her down into an empty seat at the table. They only look up to find her sitting, and Barker behind her talking to James; his hand still pressing into her shoulder. Ebony eventually sees the tensioned stretch of his gnarled knuckles holding Soleil down. Dawn doesn't know to look.

"Call me if you ever need anything," Dawn says to Soleil. "You've got both of my numbers on the card I gave you at the school Friday."

Soleil nods as Dawn walks away. Her gaze comes back to Ebony who stares past her face to where Barker's hand presses into her shoulder. She starts to speak to the woman she's gotten in trouble, but no words come out. Mannequin still, she witnesses the beginning of Barker's tirade. Ebony watches Soleil; Barker and James, focus on something other than her. James is engaged in the conversation. Soleil meditates through her pain. No one else sees Barker's arm move from Soleil's shoulder to curve into a subtle noose around her neck. Even Soleil doesn't see it; reacting in slow motion — unable to stop the hurt before it starts — unable to do anything that will make him never want to come back.

"James, Baby, I'm ready," Ebony says, stepping between him and Barker.

"Your girlfriend is gorgeous," Barker says with a churlish lick of his lips.

"I know," James says, pulling Ebony backward to lay against him.

"Let's go."

"Judge Gordon, the Lady's waiting. I'll see you Monday."

"See you Monday." Barker hugs James and claps him on his back.

See you Monday, Ebony thinks to herself as she and James stride away from the table to the ballroom doors. Ebony doesn't look back to see Barker take the seat behind Soleil, still with his arm around her neck. She doesn't look back to see Barker pull Soleil closer to him with that same arm. The subtle noose is now a chokehold. Her gasps for air invisible to the waning crowd. The beginning of Barker's torture is unseen because she looks like his lover, laid with her back against his stomach. The "trailblazing" Judge, loving and attentive, holds his girlfriend tight, stroking her cheek with the back of his ringed hand, whispering reviling words in her ear.

The entire scene is lost on the lingering crowd, including Dawn. She stands in the center of the ballroom rattled by her journalistic intuition and unanswered questions, but she refuses to turn around to see Soleil laying in physical, emotional, and mental pain as Barker's ring digs into her skin, nearly piercing her flesh. Dawn stands in the middle of the ballroom, pushing her inquisitive thoughts to the back of her mind, refusing to turn around to see the teacher named after the sun, eclipsed by the dark side of the moon. She shakes her head and walks further away, stomping anxiety beneath the click of her heels. Dawn counts every step as she crosses the faux wood of the ballroom floor to her table. She doesn't notice Victor's approach.

"There you are." He smiles at her.

"Hey," Dawn says, plastering on her anchor smile to arm herself against questions she can't answer.

"The band is gone and the DJ has broken down, I do believe your MC duties are over."

"Has the mayor left already?"

"Yes, Ms. Anthony. He ducked out while you were in the bathroom. What took you so long in there?"

"I ran into a fan. She insisted on a picture. Saw a few other people I sort of know."

"All in a days work, huh, Ms. Anthony?"

"I guess."

"What do you say we do now?" Victor asks with a gleam in his eye.

"Oh, I don't know." Dawn shrugs.

"I've got a few ideas." Victor lowers his face to meet Dawn's forehead.

"Oh really, Mr. Russell?"

"Yes, Ms. Anthony, I do."

"And what do those ideas entail, might I ask?"

"Let's just say we finish where we left off, before we left your home for here." Victor grazes his lips across Dawn's smooth forehead.

The static connection is enough to dissipate Dawn's disquietude. She forgets the unease and anxiety simmering in the pit of her stomach. The feeling she refuses to follow to watch the background of her next story unfold behind her in real time.

Part 2

"The Lord will work everything to it's proper end. Even the wicked for a day of destruction."

— Proverbs 16:4

15.

Wednesday, March 19, 2014

Early morning darkness clings to the clear sky. The hazy, blue black of the heavens cloud the cars on I-95. The only lights cutting through the lanes of traffic come from street lamps, brake lights and headlights on the other side of the highway. Ebony maneuvers her car through the quick, moving traffic for the third day in a row, fishtailing her way through the lanes of cars, and missing the daily slowdowns that are still an hour off. The time on the interior clock reads 6:35. She nods her head at the numbers knowing she is right on time. The numbers glow green inside her car. The colon separating the hour from the minutes flashes to the beat of every second in time with the thumping of her heart. It pounds out the rhythm of the thoughts in her head. The thoughts she hasn't been able to shake for the last four days. The thoughts that led her to scratch her hands until they were red and ready to bleed. The thoughts of two people who have clouded her mind, entered uninvited into her daydreams, and smiled grotesque grins and marred masks in her nightmares.

They are the thoughts that made her lie to James, and pick a fight with him after the luncheon Saturday so he would not stay at her place the entire weekend. They are the thoughts of Soleil's torture by Barker. Saturday night she listened outside of Soleil's door. What she heard propelled her out of bed Monday, made her dress in the color of shadows, and drive in the cool dew of the morning with one destination in mind.

Monday, Ebony guided the curves of her car North on the highway. Armed with her conviction and Barker's condemnation, she drove to the courthouse and parked near the side entrance where the employees enter. She waited until she saw his car come down a side street and park in a lot behind a chain link fence. Her mind willed herself to get out of the car but she never moved her body. Watching from the car, she saw him walk from his parking spot and cross the street into the courthouse. He never knew to look in her direction. He didn't know she was waiting for him. Just like he didn't know she heard him Saturday and Sunday night.

"Bitch, you're going to tell me what she said."

His words to Soleil came back to her Monday as she watched him walk into the courthouse through her rearview mirror. Tall and regal in navy blue, the slight sheen from his suit dazzled light across his chiseled features. Ebony watched Barker stride with purpose from his car to the courthouse with a slight bounce in his walk. It was a happy walk from his parking space to the domain where he reigns. He never looked in any direction except the one he intended to enter; never even spoke aloud to anyone who threw him a quick "Hey, Judge."

Ebony watched his arrogance in defeat. She drove away from her unpaid meter and circled the city until she ended up in Arlington, on the perimeter of the teacher's parking lot at an elementary school, waiting to see Soleil's face. With her car hidden between two pick-up trucks, Ebony watched from her driver's seat as the blue coupe pulled into the lot. Soleil hurried out of her car, only turning in Ebony's unknown direction for a brief moment. She couldn't see what the teacher was hiding behind fluffy curls, covering the cheeks of her face, and large sunglasses that hid everything from the scar on her forehead to the bridge of her nose.

Ebony memorized the image. Stamped in her brain, the photographic memory forced her out of bed Tuesday morning to try again. She drove the same stretch of highway, at the same time, with the same drivers she lane-changed with the day before. The new car in the morning rush that was part of their daily routine. Her heart pounded in time with the silent flashing of the clock colon as she drove to her destination. She did not look up into her rearview mirror to see the car that got behind her as she exited the highway into the belly of the city center. She did not notice the driver in the car behind her through her mirrors or windows, until she was parked in her same spot from Monday, waiting for Barker. James's face contorted in confusion when he knocked on her window, peering at her through the tinted glass, demanding she acknowledge him. Ebony rolled down the window to finally confront her boyfriend she'd been ducking for days.

"What are you doing here?" James asked annoyed.

"I came to see you."

"You never come to the courthouse to see me."

"There's a first time for everything. I came to make up with you."

"I have some cases I need to prepare for this morning. Why don't you make it up to me tonight."

"I'll meet you at your place after my last session."

James leaned into the car window to seal their deal. He kissed the lying lips of his girlfriend satisfied with their arrangement. Engaged in the moment, he didn't know her eyes were open behind his head. He didn't know she watched from his shoulder, waiting for Barker to emerge after he parked his car behind the chain-link fence. Caught in the rhythm of her tongue, James didn't know Ebony watched as Barker rushed into the courthouse with a crush of other employees. His stride was insistent and deliberate, instead of insouciant and buoyant. Ebony watched him nearly run from the street corner to the side courthouse door. He wasn't late, but he appeared unprepared as he walk-jogged the few feet to his destination; his briefcase blowing behind him even though there was no wind.

Ebony kissed James and watched Barker as he glided quickly across the street. Both men oblivious to her following eyes that trailed the line of Barker's jaw as he chomped peppermints to mush. She watched him, still connected to James, until he broke their lip embrace and crossed the courthouse grounds to the State Attorney's Office, on a side street more than a football field away. She tasted him in her mouth but the visceral memory didn't stick. Sitting in her unpaid parking space, a picture of Soleil's curls and shades impressed itself before her eyes. Her nose was assaulted by dueling scents of hard liquor, local cigarettes, and pure peppermints. Ebony drove away Tuesday making yet another tomorrow promise to herself.

It's this promise that got her out of James' bed while he snored happily beside her. At five in the morning, Ebony tiptoed along the old hardwood of his Mandarin home. She cajoled his Husky to keep quiet with treats, as she crept out to her car and headed to her own home five minutes away. Her mind on overload, she showered away her anxiety and forced herself back into her car. Still convinced of her convictions and his condemnation, she armed herself for the drive for the third day in a row, with one hand on the wheel and the other on her Lady.

Ebony feels the cool, rounded weight in her hand. Her palm runs back and forth over the metal, slowing her breath with each pass, calming the beat of her heart timed to the blinking of the car clock. She focuses on the shifting lanes of the highway, pushing her personified lucid memories to the depths of her being. Outside her car, mothers and fathers, secretaries and executives, half-full school buses, and filled to the last seat mini vans drive with her from the Southside toward the lackluster urban sprawl of downtown. She doesn't notice the texting drivers, the ones talking loudly on their phones, or chomping through their brightly-colored, paperbag breakfast of fried and saturated fat. The women applying mascara, blush, and eyeliner as they hurry to beat their faces to perfection before the work day sweats off their effort, are oblivious to Ebony as she drives. She is blind to the commuters sipping from coffee cups, all bearing the Starbucks label, and a barista's order scrawl. The drivers and passengers who mainline fast food and caffeine in an effort to self-medicate their morning, are ignored. If there was a way for them to get their fix without ever having to detour off the highway, the interstate would be lined with tolls like drive-throughs, offering a temporary high instead of a hassle-free ride.

Ebony whips past these drivers, unconcerned with their distractions, embodied by her own thoughts that have lingered for the last four days. The singular sound from inside Soleil's door, the image of her face in curls and shades, the taste of James's lips and tongue as her eyes caught Barker in their unimpassioned crosshairs, carry her around curves and bends, through construction zones for highway widening, and into the far right lane to make her exit into downtown. She crosses the illuminated blue of the Main Street Bridge and comes to a stop at the light. The distinct smell of freshly brewed coffee hangs in the air from the Maxwell House warehouse near the eastern edge of downtown. Immediately before her is the Chamber of Commerce with it's bold sign and many flags, welcoming business visitors to her left. An empty parking lot tells the true tale of Jacksonville's downtown real estate market on her right.

The light turns green and Ebony turns left onto Bay Street. She stays in the far right lane passing by businesses rarely noticed, except by the homeless and the optimistic few who live in the the area, believing the urban core will be re-birthed into a true city center. The time on her clock reads 6:55. In 12 minutes she will be late. She is caught behind a city bus inhaling black exhaust. The fumes force her into a coughing fit and she nearly misses her turn on Clay Street. The jewel in Jacksonville's crown, the mecca of the city, the new Duval County Courthouse looms large in front of her. The grounds are sprawling and immaculate. The stone and glass structure is a marvel for any metropolitan area, even if it is a reminder for all those who pass to always visit by choice, instead of by force when choices of future and fate are no longer yours to make.

Ebony makes her own choice and turns left on Adams Street. A right at the next light and a block and a half up, gets her into the same metered space in front of the Sikes & Stowe auto body shop that she hasn't paid for the last two days. The time on her car clock now reads 7:02. With five minutes to spare, Ebony turns off her car and listens to the engine and transmission settle. She listens to the hum of traffic as it passes by, letting the whir of wheels and the purr of engines distract her from the replaying thoughts and faces who have sent her here. Their faces are what force her to get out of her car after two days of playing chicken with her mission. Her left hand takes the door handle. It is the first time she's removed it from her Lady since she placed it inside the front pouch of her black hoodie. On the sidewalk into the dewy dark haze of the pre-dawn morning, Ebony watches the sun flirt with the horizon before rising. She leans her body against the curve of her car door and waits for whom she has come for.

He doesn't keep her waiting long. The cat-eye lights of his German engineered car cut the corners of the streets as he pulls into the parking lot behind the chain-link fence. It is 7:07. Always the same time. Always punctual. Always predictable.

She waits for him to join the trickle of courthouse employees he crosses the street with everyday. They come in clusters, arriving in pairs or trios, and walk in groups into the courthouse. Some are in suits, some in ill-fitting pants with pleats, some in ankle length, shapeless skirts; all with lanyards around their necks connected to IDs and security keys to let them inside. It is their shortcut to avoid the offenders, defenders, family members, and the curious few who are forced to file through the court's front doors.

Ebony watches him from her lean against the car. She watches as he gets caught at the temperamental light. Tuesday he made it; Monday he didn't, even though his timing is never off. He chomps the mints in his mouth in muted irritation, refusing to jaywalk despite the empty street in front of him.

"Good morning Gorgeous," Ebony yells from her post against her car.

He turns his head sharply at her voice. The range of motion in his neck is restricted by the top button of his shirt and the eldredge knot Ebony knows secures his tie. His love of the skill required to make the knot is unparalleled and unmatched, even when compared to the love of his favorite loafers.

Barker spots her alone against her car; both hands shoved into the front pocket of her hoodie. Her unkempt, four-day-old curls frame her face with unsexy bed head. He jogs across the street catching the last few seconds of the yellow light. His squared, black briefcase bounces off of his knee with each stride. Barker blends in with the lingering darkness of the night. His black on black suit conceals his body and folds into the ebony of his skin. His smile is what cuts through the monotony of his ensemble and surroundings. His teeth shine white against the backdrop of the still dark morning. From a distance he is beautiful, unmarked, and emanating joy. It is only when he gets closer that she see's the distant joy is a front for hubris. His scars come into focus and his smell assaults her senses — Swishea Sweet, Maxwell House coffee, and peppermints.

"I knew you missed me, Gorgeous," he says, stalking the last few steps toward Ebony.

"Call me by my name."

"Don't be like that Gorgeous. You came to see me."

"I did."

"And to what do I owe the pleasure?"

"Trust me, the pleasure will be all mine," Ebony says, rubbing her hands across her hidden Lady.

"I'm all ears, Gorgeous. It must be important for you to get here before court."

"I'm not your Gorgeous," she says, taking a deep breath. "And neither is Soleil. You need to leave her alone. Let her go and find somebody whose not afraid to treat you like the man you are."

"You mean like you, Gorgeous?"

"No, not like me. And this is the last time I'm telling you. Call me by my name."

"Gorgeous, if you don't want me, why do you care what I do with Soleil?"

"So you do know other words besides gorgeous?"

"You're really trying my patience. Don't push your luck."

"And if I do. What are you going to do in the middle of the street as the sun comes up?" Ebony points to the pink in the sky.

"You know me better than that, Gorgeous."

He steps toward where she lays against her car. The rounded toe of her running shoes kiss the pointed tips of his Oxfords. He sets his briefcase on the curb beside them, leans over her, and rests his forearms on the curve of her car door. They are close enough to kiss. The personal space gap between them is closed. His body relaxes in proximity to her. Ebony grips her hands tighter to her Lady and takes a breath.

"You two bitches have a lot of nerve," he whispers angrily in her ear.

Spittle from his mouth drips inside. The moisture makes Ebony lay her head on her shoulder to dry it out against the cloth of her hoodie.

"That's right, squirm, Gorgeous. You know how I love to see that body move."

"Back off of me, Barker." Ebony pushes with one hand against the hard strength of his chest.

He grabs her left wrist and laughs.

"Ah, ah, ah, no touching. This concrete is nowhere near as soft as the padded floor of your ring or your bed; even if you did bounce off that pretty, soft ass behind you."

"Let me go you, bastard."

"Now who's calling names," he says, pressing the front of his body against hers. His erection is prominent against her thigh as he arrests her wrists above her head.

"Let me go, Barker. Do you really want to make a scene in front of your coworkers."

"There's no one out here but us, Gorgeous. No one to save you *or* Soleil for that matter."

"She might need saving, but I, for damn sure don't," Ebony spits. Dribbles of her saliva land at the corners of his eyes. She smiles seeing it glisten in the lines of crunched crows feet.

"I got rid of your abusive ass once, I can for damn sure do it again *and* take Soleil with me at the same time."

"Gorgeous, you will never take Soleil anywhere with you. She knows better now."

"What did you do to her?" Ebony forces more spit out of her mouth. This time it lands in a glob on the silk, candy black ascot tucked into the breast pocket of his suit.

"Why does it matter, Gorgeous? Unless you want to join us for a night."

"I don't want shit to do with you. The dick ain't that good."

Ebony spits again as she tries to shake her wrists and arms loose from over her head.

"Stop struggling, Gorgeous."

He releases her wrists and takes hold of her shoulders. Ebony takes advantage of her minimal freedom and places her hands back into her front pocket. They meet as he squeezes his grip into the blades of her shoulders. She lives one of her memories — his hands crush her as they crushed Soleil Saturday.

"Let. Me. Go."

He doesn't respond. The edge of his patience dissipates with the single syllable of her last word. He pulls her shoulders toward his body, squeezing his rough hands deeper into the blades. The pain becomes an afterthought as heat radiates across her back. The sound of glass cracks behind her.

Ebony levitates in the space between him and the car. Lifted by her shoulders, her feet hover just above the ground as he slams her against the door. Three times back and forth, her head bobbles on her spine. Three times, strands of hair rip from her scalp into the cracked glass of her broken tinted window. Every time he pulls her forward, he wraps his arms around her in a bear hug, squeezing her arms at her sides. Her hands, trapped in a vice grip, fumble in her front pocket over her Lady.

Ebony looks right and left. No one is in sight. No one waits at the light to cross to the courthouse. No one is behind them at the auto body shop; not even a courthouse security guard walks the grounds in their direction. They are together alone. Two predators facing off and one quickly becoming the other's prey.

"I told you there is no one here to save you, Gorgeous."

His lips press against her ear with his body prostrate against her own. One leg between her straddle stance, the chiseled muscles of his thighs pin Ebony to her car. She feels his heart beat through his suit; his dick pulses through his pants.

"There is no one but us, Gorg . . ."

His last word is cutoff by a ringing in her ears and the smoky smell of fiery powder. He staggers two steps backward, releasing her arms. His hands clutch his stomach and chest. He raises them from his body and stares at his fingertips. Eyes spread wide with fear, the crows feet corners spread into an automatic facelift. He flips his hands. Ebony sees the flesh of his fingertips. They are wet with redness. He coughs twice. Red spills from his mouth. He stumbles further backward. With the last of his own force, he throws himself forward and coughs as he falls to a knee.

"I can't breathe."

Ebony is frozen. A witness to their own torrid affair. She stares at Goliath delaying his downfall, not understanding the only explanation available. She sees herself as she pulls open the door handle, tucks her battered body into the driver's seat and slams her door shut. The shattered glass raining on her head and lap makes her jump. The noise mixes with the clang of car tools coming from the body shop.

On autopilot, Ebony starts her engine and pulls into the one-way traffic. Stuck behind a bus again she inhales black exhaust. Sucking down the fumes, she delays the coughing fit itching at the back of her throat. She inhales the smog until the light turns green. The bus goes straight. She turns left. Checking her rearview, a broken man on bended knee clutches his heart that could never be won.

Ebony races down the street passing boarded up brick buildings with realty signs on the front. The fire station's aluminum doors are still down. She runs her car through the stagnant green light on Jefferson and peels another left. The fire station siren begins to blare. She prays to the timed traffic gods that they be with her as she runs through the green light on Monroe. The next light turns red, but she makes a right on red and keeps running. The streets pass by in a blur. The landmarks, the Salvation Army and a fleet of AT&T trucks all blend together as she catches green, after green, after green all the way to the I-95 on ramp.

She follows the signs for 95 South, trying to make her dented and dinged car blend into the morning rush. To draw less attention to the missing window on the driver's side, Ebony rolls the other windows down until they disappear. The warming morning air washes over her. It blows against her face with a steady breath. The pace of her race slows. She moves with the flow of traffic in the middle lane, avoiding the speeding cars drawing attention from the motorcycle cop hidden in plain sight less than a mile ahead. The slow pokes mosey beside her in the right lane, shaving minutes from their lives with every frustrating moment that passes by.

I am a normal woman, making my morning commute, and there is nothing wrong.

She repeats the mantra over and over in her head as she passes the exit for San Marco Boulevard. She passes the motorcycle cop next, turning her head away from him.

I am a normal woman, making my morning commute, and there is nothing wrong.

The St. Johns River the city gets its nickname from comes into view. Water sparkles in the early rays of the sun. The light pings back and forth from sky to water as the rays dance on the shimmering, blood red surface. Ebony shakes her head furiously until the mirage disappears and the river is clear. She changes her focus from the water to the skyline. The bridges to everywhere stand across the pathways of the city. The red Mathews Bridge to Arlington, the green Hart Bridge to the Southside; the Fuller Warren in her rearview to I-10 and the

Westside. The monuments to progress stand tall as drivers trust their construction with their lives.

Ebony keeps going. She passes Baptist's downtown campus, Nemours, and Wolfson Children's Hospital. The Blue Cross Blue Shield of Florida and Aetna buildings are visible from the highway and nearly every window of each medical center. A cruel, ironic joke of urban planning telling patients, parents, and the public in general what they need in case of an emergency, and where they can get it if they find themselves lacking, Obamacare be damned.

The sporty sedan curves past the last of downtown's relics: EverBank Field. Home of the Jaguars. The team most in the city love to hate to love. This year, even fair-weather fan curiosity is peaked by the construction of cabanas, pools, the world's largest video boards, and which quarterback will be picked in the draft.

With EverBank in her rearview and the sardine can of cars finally thinned out, Ebony picks up her pace as she makes her way closer and closer to Southside territory. She moves into the left lane after the Emerson exit to avoid the coming slowdown at JTB. Flying by cars taking their time in front of her, weaving in and out of lanes the same way she did when she was first headed to her destination, she flees. A flashing overhead sign says Philips Highway is only five miles and five minutes away.

I am a normal woman, making my morning commute, and there is nothing wrong.

Ebony chants the phrase to herself until she is off the highway and making a right onto Philips. She drives past the Regal movie theater. The empty lot is devoid of the weekend box office crowd. She drives past businesses whose names she's never learned, a stone company with an outdoor fountain, a gas station, and another auto body shop until she's forced to stop at the light. Green. More businesses, a bridal shop, small diners, a used car lot, and an old white clapboard church come into view and disappear behind her. She turns left on Sunbeam Road.

Ebony's body bumps as the car jumps over railroad tracks. The jostling movement aggravates the pain in her shoulders and across the swath of her back. She winces, repeats her mantra, and lets her right foot continue to lead against the accelerator until she's made the last mile journey into her neighborhood.

I am a normal woman, making her morning commute, and there is nothing wrong.

Ebony whips a sharp right into her driveway, hitting the garage door as she turns. It opens. Inch by inch she pulls the car in until she's completely parked. By the time the garage door reaches it's full height, it's coming down again.

Out of the car and on her own in the garage, she coughs. Ebony expels the bus fumes she swallowed. She coughs away the slight carbon monoxide built up inside the garage before she turns off the car. Shaky legs lead her out of the car, through the garage, and inside her home.

Two strides through the laundry room and crossing the hallway into her bedroom, relief finds Ebony when she turns directly into her bathroom. The door slams. Her body leans against it in darkness. A hand finds the light switch illuminating the room from the skylights in the ceiling and the bright makeup lights stretched across the vanity. She faces the mirror and sees herself for the first time since she forced herself out of the house after leaving James's place this morning. Her hair sparkles from the flecks of glass sprinkled throughout the ends of her curls. Small dots are clumped in sections toward the bottom of her face. She leans over the vanity to see the red freckles up close in the mirror.

He got me.

The clumps of chicken pox-like red dots are drops of blood from his two stumbling coughs. Ebony presses the button at the bottom of the mirror. Water streams from a hole in the wall into the glass bowl sink. She picks up the white beauty bar and rubs it over and over in her hands until the lather begins to build and spills over into the sink bowl. Ebony drops the bar of soap, closes her eyes, and slaps her hands to her face. Lather floods her skin; nails rake across her cheeks and forehead until her face is raw to touch.

Ebony lowers her face to the stream of water and lets it pour over her skin. She turns her head back and forth until the soap is rinsed from her eyes, face, and around the edges of her hair. Satisfied, she feels for the button on the mirror to stop the water. The bottom of her hoodie meets the front of her face. It knocks against the weight of her forgotten Lady.

Ebony stumbles backward and sits on the edge of the extra-long, porcelain Jacuzzi. She produces her Lady from her pocket. Inside it is the evidence of a crime she did not commit. Empty casings fall into her hand, telling the truth as the smell of smoke enters her nostrils, and clouds of red cover her eyes in a milky river haze.

16.

"Mama, aren't you glad you're coming on my field trip with me?" Danielle asks from the backseat.

"Yes, baby." Johnnie pulls her Camry into the school parking lot.

"What animals do you want to see, Mama?

"All of them. Come on, get out of your seat." Johnnie turns around to unhook Danielle from her booster.

"But what's your favorite, Mama?"

Danielle asks the question with her head cocked to the side. A pink barrette rests against her cheek. Bright chestnut-brown eyes bore into Johnnie's honey-colored face waiting for a real answer.

"The turtles, Dani. Now come on, let's go."

"Can I get my own backpack out of the trunk?"

"Yes, baby."

Johnnie waits until Danielle is at her side before popping the trunk. Danielle reaches in first to grab her pink Minnie Mouse backpack. She bounces on her toes while Johnnie hefts her own large black book bag onto her back. The first aid kit and their brown bag lunches jostle inside until Johnnie gets the straps settled against her shoulders. She reaches into the depths of the trunk again this time hoisting out her leather tote purse. Johnnie lobs the bag on her shoulder, slams the trunk and grabs Danielle's hand as they march their way toward the school.

Danielle pulls and tugs on Johnnie's hand, impatient and anxious to get into the class with her mother. She chants as she pulls.

"One, two buckle my shoe. Three, four close the door. Five, six pick up sticks."

Danielle stops. Johnnie doesn't notice until she realizes she's tugging on her daughter's hand and not the other way around.

"Dani, why'd you stop? What's wrong?"

The zoo field trip is all Danielle's been talking about since Monday when she went back to school and realized her big trip was just days away. She'd even made Johnnie mark the days off on the calendar hanging in their kitchen. Her sudden silence and stillness jars Johnnie's instincts.

"Sing with me, Mama."

"Oh."

"Did I scare you, Mama?" Danielle asks doubled over in a fit of laughter. The melodic sound of her joy blends in with the default ringtone of Johnnie's phone.

"Hold on, Dani. Mama's phone is ringing."

Johnnie holds tightly to Danielle with one hand and uses the other to rummage through her purse until she finds the phone ringing and buzzing inside.

"Hello," she answers annoyed.

"Johnnie, I need you," the voice on the other end snaps.

"Who is this?"

"Taylor," Dr. Taylor Thomas snaps again.

Johnnie pulls the phone from her ear. "Let's keep going," she whispers to Danielle, who's looking at her once again with her head cocked to the side, eyes inquisitive and all knowing.

"Taylor, I can't," Johnnie protests.

She takes Danielle's hand again and walks with her daughter, who's still chanting the nursery rhyme.

"Johnnie, I wouldn't call if I didn't need you. This isn't an ordinary patient. He deserves the best. That's you. You need to be here in the next 10 minutes."

"It's a gift and a curse."

"What was that?"

"Nothing. Look, Taylor, I won't make it. I can't make it. I promised Danielle. I'm not even on call. Not even for the Pope."

"Good thing you live in Jacksonville and not the Vatican. Johnnie, this is not a request. I will see you here in 10 minutes. Make it work. Tell Danielle I'm sorry."

The line clicks. Johnnie drops her cell phone into her tote, then reaches for her white water bottle in the mesh side pocket of her book bag. She pulls the bottle top open with her teeth and gulps the liquid as it burns down her throat.

"Come on, Mama, let's go," Danielle tugs.

"Hold on, Dani." Johnnie drops to one knee to be eye level with Danielle.

"What's wrong, Mama?"

"I'm sorry, baby, but Mama can't go to the zoo today."

"But why not?" Danielle cries. "You promised. You even signed the permission slip."

"Mama has to take care of an emergency at work."

"You always have an emer, an emerg, an emergency."

"I'm so sorry, Baby."

Johnnie pulls Danielle close. She hyperventilates her sobs into Johnnie's chest.

"Come on now, Dani. Stop crying. You know I have to go to work. I have to help people when they need me."

"But you said you were coming to the zoo today no matter what."

"I know, baby. But Mama can't."

"But what if I have an emergency? Will you come help me?" Danielle's tears stream down her face.

"Of course, baby, you always come first."

"Are you sure?"

Johnnie sniffs back tears of her own as Danielle questions her place in the hierarchy of her mother's life. She reaches for the white water bottle and takes another long, burning gulp of the liquid inside. The contents settle on top of her empty stomach. She takes another swig before replacing the bottle in the book bag. Armed with the liquid courage, she dabs at the corners of her tear-stained eyes, trying to hold back the waterworks, and be strong in front of her daughter.

"I'll tell you what," Johnnie says, lifting Danielle's chin so they're eye to eye.

"What?" Danielle sniffles.

"If Mama finishes her work early, I'll meet you at the zoo. If I don't finish before the trip is over, then this weekend when I'm off we'll go stay in a hotel and have a sleepover, just us girls."

Danielle silently considers Johnnie's proposition. Her head is tilted sideways to mull over the new promise to make up for the zoo.

"What do you say, Dani?"

"Okay, I guess. I just wish you could come to the zoo with us like Daddy did last time with Miss Jessie."

"Who is . . .?" Johnnie lets the tail end of her question fizzle on her tongue. "Come on, Dani, give me your hand. I don't want you to miss your trip."

Johnnie and Danielle walk the few feet from the parking lot to the open outdoor hallways of the school in silence. Once inside the main building, Danielle pulls Johnnie the rest of the way through the corridors; back outside through the maze of trailers until they reach the front door of her portable classroom. They walk inside hand in hand and approach Soleil, sitting behind the desk.

"Miss St. James." Johnnie says formally to get Soleil's attention.

"Dr. Edwards, it's good to see you again."

"I wish I could say the same," Johnnie replies.

"I'm sorry, what was that?"

"Nothing. It's just that I'm not going to be able to go with you all on the field trip to the zoo today. I've been called in."

"I'm so sorry to hear that. Danielle was really looking forward to you coming with us today."

"I know."

"Well, I hope everything is alright," Soleil says.

"Likewise."

Johnnie looks beyond the hair covering Soleil's eyes to the yet to heal broken blood vessels beneath her made up skin. The airbrushed foundation, concealer, eyeliner, shadow, and blush are a convincing facade to the untrained eye, but Johnnie sees through the pancake mix to her bruised face.

"Miss. St. James, may I join Miss Lisa's group?" Danielle asks.

Soleil hesitates, looking to Johnnie for approval.

"Miss St. James," Danielle whines. "Can I join Miss Lisa, please?"

"Only if your mom and Miss Lisa don't mind," Soleil defers.

"If Miss Lisa doesn't mind, I don't mind, Dani?"

"Thank you, Mama. I'm going to ask her." Danielle scampers off.

"Who's Miss Lisa?"

"My assistant."

"Oh, well Dani should be fine in her group." Johnnie ignores Soleil's hesitation. "Dani, you're not going to even tell Mama bye?" Johnnie yells across the room.

"Sorry, Mama." Danielle runs back.

Johnnie drops to one knee. "Be good, Dani. I'll try to make it if I can. And if I don't, then it'll be just us girls this weekend. Okay."

"Okay, Mama." Danielle throws her arms around Johnnie's neck.

Johnnie squeezes Danielle in a tight hug. She looks up at Soleil beaming down on them. Johnnie mouths the word 'thank you' before letting Danielle go.

"Let me put your lunch in your backpack and then you can go join your group. Okay."

"Okay."

"Turn around, Dani."

Johnnie sets her purse beside her, removes one arm from the book bag strap, unzips the largest pouch, and pulls out two brown paper bags. She stuffs both inside Danielle's backpack and zips it up.

"You're good to go, Dani. I love you." Johnnie says as Danielle runs back to her group.

"Thank you," Johnnie says to Soleil. "I'm so sorry I have to bail on you like this, but duty calls."

"It's okay, Dr. Edwards. I understand. We'll manage."

"Thanks again. Oh, I put the extra lunch I packed for myself this morning inside Danielle's backpack just in case one of the children or their parents forget. I hope it helps."

"Thank you, Dr. Edwards. I'm sure it'll be a big help. Have a good day."

"I'll try. I'm sure I'll need a real drink after leaving the hospital today."

"We are supposed to get together for drinks with Dawn and Ebony. Tonight could be as good a night as any once Dawn's show is over."

"That doesn't sound like a bad idea." Johnnie smiles. "I'll call Dawn later today and have her set it up. She likes planning stuff."

"Sounds good to me. Have a good day."

You too.

Johnnie doesn't let the words escape her lips before turning out of the classroom door and into the quiet, outdoor hallway. Her mood disturbed, Johnnie shakes her head, wondering what could have caused Soleil's black eye. The scratches from the apple of her cheeks to her jaw line; the bruises around her chin and neck cloud Johnnie's thoughts as she leaves the school thinking of two people: Soleil and Miss Jessie.

The triple ring of the school bell clangs through Johnnie's brain, interrupting her thoughts. Even in the parking lot the blaring sound alerting all students, parents, teachers, and neighbors that the children have just five minutes until their day starts, is loud and obnoxious. The sound of the bell clatters in Johnnie's ears long after it goes silent. The ringing stays with her as she grabs her cell phone from her purse, then shoves it and her book bag into the passenger seat of her car.

Johnnie dials Nathan's number and waits the obligatory four rings until his voicemail picks up. *Why isn't he answering the phone.* An automated voice instructs her on how to leave a message she's left a thousand times. When the phone tone sounds, she speaks into the receiver, alerting Nathan to the emergency, telling him to pick up Danielle after her field trip.

With the parenting formalities taken care of, Johnnie tosses the phone into the passenger seat with her purse and backpack. She grabs her white water bottle peeking out from the mesh pocket of the book bag and brings it to her lips. The last of the clear contents in the bottle sting their way to her belly as she backs out of her parking space. Johnnie exits the lot as the final bell to start the day sounds. Her phone rings through the speakers of her car's bluetooth interface. The name on the navigation screen reads Dr. Taylor Thomas. Johnnie hits ignore and drives off.

I'll be there in 20 minutes, she thinks, smacking her lips "ah," savoring the last drops of her salvation lingering on the front and back buds of her tongue.

17.

Soleil creeps out of her classroom and heads to the teachers' lounge in the main building. She enters the nearly empty break room and heads straight for the Keurig, K-Cup in hand. Her mug beneath the machine waits for the fresh, hot caffeine. The silver face of the coffee maker makes her squint at what she can see of her own reflection. She takes her fingers to her face and dabs at the concealer and color corrector on her cheeks, smoothing it in beneath her bronzer and highlighter.

"I didn't know you had it in you, Miss Girl," Troy startles Soleil as he saunters over to where she stands.

"Troy, you're going to make me burn myself." Soleil turns around from the machine and wipes her makeup stained fingertips on her jeans.

"No, you're going to make you burn yourself, leaning so close into the coffee. The Keurig ain't a mirror."

"I know."

"Well, let me see your face. Let me see what you did."

Troy steps more closely toward Soleil. He gives her a once over, taking her chin and turning her face from side to side in his hands. He inspects her airbrush makeup application. The one he insisted she start using when he saw the bruises on her face Monday, that she tried to hide behind big hair, big sunglasses, and pinkish purple blush. He even chipped in half of the money for Soleil to buy the expensive system, saying it was a necessity if she "planned to keep coming to work looking like she'd lost a fight with 100 flights of stairs."

"I see you got the hang of the airbrush good, girl. If your face wasn't so jacked up underneath, I'd say you could start a YouTube beauty page."

"Gee, thanks, What do you want?"

"Oh, don't play like you don't know. You know what I'm talking about."

"No, Troy, I don't, and I have no time to play charades with you to figure it out."

"First of all, it's not charades. You can't talk during charades. We'd be playing *Taboo*. And secondly, I know you know what I'm talking about because you're in here all smiling and happy, making coffee and checking out your face instead of hiding in some corner. I knew one day you'd reach your breaking point and put that sorry faggot, wish-he-could-box, bastard, wannabe in his place."

"Troy. What are you talking about? I have to get back to class," Soleil says, lifting her mug from the Keurig.

"I guess you haven't seen the news this morning?"

"No, I haven't. Just say what you have to say so I can go."

"No need to snap at me, honey. I just thought that maybe you did a drive-by at the courthouse before coming to work this morning."

"For your information, Barker and I made up this morning. But, what happened at the courthouse?"

"I guess you rode that bastard straight to hell, because according to the news somebody got shot where all the employees go in."

"I have to go."

Soleil bumps past Troy clutching her coffee cup tightly in her hand. On auto pilot, her feet carry her out of the main building and back down the path of open-air hallways to her trailer, for a classroom. Fingers white-knuckle the coffee mug in her hand. Troy's words echo out of order in her head. Shooting. Courthouse. Employees. Troy's nasally tenor is on repeat at the expense of everything else. Her senses are drowned in a pool of his voice. Other noises arrive silent against the drum. The outside ambient sound a vacuum of white noise. Soleil's feet follow the muscle memory of her brain and carry her back to her classroom.

Her hands are on autopilot as well. The coffee mug is shifted to her left hand. She reaches for the classroom door handle with her right. The door swings wide. She moves forward to step through the gap, but something blocks her. Something is in her way and searing her arms, stomach, and legs with a hot poker.

"I'm so sorry. Are you alright?" A voice asks in what sounds like a whisper to Soleil's ears, still ringing with white noise. The voice seems to come from in front of her, but she can't tell. She can barely make out what it is saying as she feels fingers and hands dabbing and tugging at her clothes.

"Miss St. James." The voice says her name over and over again.

"I'm alright," Soleil mumbles, standing up.

She tries again with her feet, hands, mug, and door. The mug is in her left. She barely notices that it feels lighter than when she first came from the teachers' lounge. Now for the door. She swings it wide with her right hand and steps through. Nothing is in her way. The plain school-issued metal desk with the faux lacquered wood on top, is her destination. She sits in the high backed, wooden chair and places her coffee mug on the coaster near the laptop. Breath returns. Slowly, sound returns. The children in their groups laugh with their chaperones. Bits of their conversations find their way to her desk. Talk of zebras, and giraffes, the new tigers, and who would win in a jungle fight; the king of the jungle or Asia's most wanted, striped, four-legged predator. The young voices wash out the white noise and give Soleil her senses back.

"There you are, Miss St. James," one of the chaperones says coming in the door.

"Yes."

"I got you some paper towel from the bathroom to clean yourself up." The older woman shoves the rough napkins in her face.

"Oh."

"I feel so bad. You spilled your coffee all over you. I hope it wasn't too hot. And you're going to need another shirt. Your polo is ruined."

"Yes," Soleil says again, unable to offer anything more than monosyllabic answers.

She takes the paper towels from the woman and looks down at herself. Liquid stains the thighs of her dark wash jeans. The brown color of the black coffee is splashed in splotches along the mid-section of her yellow school polo. Soleil's mind catches up to her senses, remembering the searing pain she felt the first time she tried to come into the classroom. It reminds her of the pain beginning to subside in her body. The pain of Barker's punishing blows that created the bruises healing on her face and ribs.

The thought of his name sends Soleil lurching into the bottom drawer of her desk. She takes her cell phone out of her purse, and scrolls to their last set of text messages, typing rapidly with her thumbs,

R u alright?

Soleil watches the clock face of her phone, waiting for a message to slide across the slate gray background. The minute changes. 8:41. No message. The time stares a minute more. 8:42. No message. No snarky remark of "Why wouldn't I be, Gorgeous?"

She tosses the phone back into her purse, but leaves the drawer open just in case it dings. Soleil flips open the laptop, logs online, and types in the address for 9 News Now. The brain of the computer takes it's time catching up to her commands. The home page of the website loads slowly, but the breaking news screams in bold capital letters from the bright red banner head: **Duval county courthouse on lockdown after shooting.**

Soleil clicks the link and waits until the article comes up. The first image to appear is a picture of the side of the courthouse with the Jacksonville Sheriff's Office signature red and white police tape, blocking off the crime scene. Taped inside the police confines is an empty street with glass on the ground. It tells her nothing. Soleil scrolls below the picture to read the article.

JACKSONVILLE, Fla. -- 9 News Now is following Breaking News in downtown Jacksonville.

Homicide detectives with the Jacksonville Sheriff's Office are investigating a shooting outside the Duval County Courthouse.

Investigators say the shooting happened in front of the Sikes & Stowe auto body shop near the corner of Monroe and Broad Streets just after 7 a.m. Wednesday.

At this time the identity of the victim has not been released, but investigators do say the victim was transported to the hospital in critical condition with life-threatening injuries.

Right now investigators say they are canvassing the area and talking to witnesses to get a description of the suspect.

As a precaution, the courthouse is on lockdown and all court proceedings have been suspended for the day.

9 News Now's Tarren Tyler is at the scene gathering more details on this Breaking story. She'll have the latest in a live report starting at 11 a.m. on a special extended edition of 9 News Now at Noon with Julia Gillé and Dawn Anthony.

The article says little more than the picture of the crime scene. Shooting. No victim. No suspect. No witness. Soleil looks at the clock in the corner of her computer screen. 8:46. The phone in her desk drawer is black in uncommunicative silence. It's face still upward. No ding. No vibration. No message. She kicks the drawer closed, sealing away the torment from the phone that refuses to ring. Closing her laptop, fear and hope flood her, telling her the worst happened.

Soleil tries to dismiss the intrinsic feeling, but her body holds on to it. Hands shake at her sides, calves quiver in jeans. Unsteady on her own two feet, she leans forward and grips the smooth edge of her desk with both hands. All eyes in the classroom are on her. The students and the chaperones, their beady and small, round, brown pupils stare. They look through her. She clears her throat to speak, but when she opens her mouth, nothing comes out. White noise roars back around her, even though everyone in the classroom is nearly silent. The quiet murmur of anxious, five-year-old voices is distant against the deafening cloud of fog and unsettled thoughts in her own head.

Soleil reluctantly raises one hand from her desk and motions to Miss Lisa. Lisa bounds to the front of the room on tiptoe and stands beside Soleil.

"You alright?"

"I'm fine." Soleil lies. "Just starting to feel the pain from when I spilled the coffee. Would you mind getting the children lined up in their groups and ready to get on the bus. I just need to step outside for a moment."

"No problem, Soleil. Go take care of yourself. I got this."

Soleil takes the few steps toward the door of the classroom, swings it wide and steps outside. The air is cool, humid and muggy, still filled with the dew of the morning and the chance of rain yet to fall. Laying against the cheap siding of the trailer, Soleil gulps air in gasping breaths. The white noise ringing in her ears doesn't clear. Like ears that won't pop after takeoff, she lays against the trailer listening to the echoed sounds of her own mind. It subsumes her as she watches Lisa organize the class.

Soleil watches her call roll from the square window in the door. Lisa rises up on her tiptoes as if to see far into the back of the room to call the names of the children whose faces and desks are beyond her limited height and scope. She bounces back down on her heels when she gets to the names of the children in the front of the room. Up and down, Lisa rises and falls with the placement of the names. Her butt bounces firm in her green capri cargo pants when she lands on a name in the front of the classroom. The motion deepens the crease of her school polo shirt into her lower back, creating the perfect carpeted shelf for an imaginary tray of cocktails. Lisa's look from behind is a marked difference from the way she looks in the front. From behind she is a grown woman without question; ripe, fecund and nubile, but straight on her shirt falls over her scant chest with barely a twin bump in the road. It hangs nearly limp like a wet T-shirt on a hanger from her olive-toned skin.

Soleil stares and times her breath to her assistant's bounces. Up and down. Inhale and exhale. The courthouse crime scene and Troy's words. Soleil watches Lisa's ass rise and fall with dedicated purpose as the white noise in her ears softens and her thoughts compartmentalize into a manageable place in her brain where the memories of physical pain are stored. Soleil stares at Lisa and wills herself back to composure when she sees what she's been trying to figure out for the last four days. *Why does she seem more familiar to me now than before?*

The answer to her own question is clear in the rise of Lisa's body and her buoyant fall. Soleil realizes Lisa is the doppelgänger for her relationship twin. A spitting image of who and what she's wished she could sometimes be for the last four days. The woman whose words have haunted her thoughts in the night-time hours when she lays trapped in her bed beneath his body. *Do something that will make him never want to come back.*

Soleil wonders if the olive-skinned woman, with more ass than anything else, who advised her to "do something," knows of the glass-riddled courthouse crime scene. She wonders if she has seen the same thing, if she knows more information than the blurb on Dawn's station website. Does she know if the victim in today's random act of violence was taken to set her free?

I wonder if she knows?

18.

They lay across the baby blue sateen sheets a mass of arms and legs. Their bodies huddle against one another; her back to his front. They are snug and geometrically congruent; an amorphous clump of limbs entwined in the aftermath of what could look like love.

Dawn stirs first in the bright spring light streaming through her bedroom's windows. She shields her eyes with one hand, and sits up on the elbow of her opposite arm. Gently she scoots her butt away from Victor's naked form, still haphazardly wrapped between the loose and fitted sheets. In the rare moment of uninterrupted quiet, Dawn smiles down at her new lover; the man who has met her every night in her bed for the last four days.

Four days ago, Dawn and Victor returned to her condo after the Mayor's luncheon. The 20-minute car ride from the Southside hotel to the Southbank was filled with unmitigated silence and frequent caresses that both eased and added to the tension of the moment.

Once inside Dawn's doors, Victor allowed her the space to make a decision for the both of them. A decision she weighed hesitantly, backing away from him and busying herself in the kitchen. She rummaged through the lone wall of cabinets, opening and closing the cupboard doors until she selected what appeared to be the perfect vase. Victor watched as Dawn made a full scale production of lifting the vase from the shelf, delicately carrying it to the sink, and then turning on the water ever so slightly, so that it streamed into the vase.

Once the water reached the desired level, Dawn set the vase to the side and grabbed the plastic wrapped bouquet of flowers still laying on the counter. The cellophane was peeled and removed piece by piece. Packets of flower food fell to the counter before her. Setting the flowers down again, she meticulously tore through each pouch of food and poured it into the vase of water. Every detail was perfected with a flourish only one accustomed to a camera could muster.

The flower food settled into pebble-sized clumps at the bottom of the vase. Bouquet stems landed on the food once the flowers were splayed into place. Dawn studied the budding bouquet, her head angled in deep concentration, but she did not touch them for further arrangement. Seemingly satisfied she walked around the peninsula, vased bouquet of flowers in hand, to where Victor stood, still as a mannequin with a surveillance camera for an eye. She gave him her back as she placed the flowers on the edge of the peninsula where they previously laid.

His heat was behind her. When she turned around she was eye level with his chest, Victor reached one finger toward her chin, tilted it up toward his face, and leaned in with his mouth. He kissed her first on her forehead, then on the tip of her nose, before finally descending to her lips. The kiss was at first all lip, gently taking in the slight taste of Dawn's chocolate gloss. They were innocent as they played upon the pillowy softness of their mouth pads. She relaxed enough for him to nibble a corner with the nubs of his teeth. Dawn encouraged the motion with a bite of her own, giving fleeting access to her tongue. They stood facing each other, connected at the mouth, Dawn's back pressed into the marble slab of the peninsula, reaffirming their decision they both had waited hours to make, when Dawn side-stepped away.

She surreptitiously removed herself from their tongue lock and backed behind the marble to fidget in the kitchen. Victor, again a mannequin with a roaming eye, understood the indecision of Dawn's decision. He watched her rummage through the cupboards again. The cabinets where she placed every item now seemed foreign to her, as she opened and closed doors in search of something. A glass. She ended her search with a glass clutched in both hands. Delicate hands squeezed the glass like a coffee mug as Dawn walked to the refrigerator, opened the french doors, and removed the clear, plastic filtered water container.

She filled the liquid to the brim and took a long gulp before replacing the pitcher in the cool air of the fridge. Their eyes met across the kitchen, staring at each other with a slow burn in their pupils. Neither of them moved as Dawn made the fastidious choice every woman must make when she's determining how much of her woman she wants a new man to see.

Dawn drained the glass of water in two more long gulps before she approached Victor. The caps of her stiletto heels made no noise as she transitioned from the scant wood of the kitchen to the plush carpet of the living area. Fluid motion pushed his suit jacket from his shoulders until it fell with ease down the length of his arms to the floor. Her hands traveled to his tie to loosen the simple windsor knot, leaving the long, loose ends hanging from his collar. The buttons were next. First the top button to completely expose his neck, then another, and another. Dawn worked her hands down the length of Victor's shirt until he arrested her fingers, placing her arms at her sides.

"That's enough, Ms. Anthony," he said softly.

"No. Don't say that." Dawn stepped back.

"Don't say what?"

"Don't call me Ms. Anthony."

Victor nodded, waiting for further explanation.

"I've got to be more than just Dawn Anthony. *Victor.*"

Victor nodded in understanding. Discretion was advised, and she was not a trophy to be won.

"Dawn. Come here," Victor said, opening his arms.

She hesitantly stepped toward him hoping not to be judged by her womanhood.

Close enough to touch, Victor obliged himself and removed Dawn's belt from her waist. He placed it on the countertop behind her, then tugged at her hand, forcing her to step closer. Her mouth was receptive as he engaged her in a kiss, encircling one arm around her waist, and using the other to slide the zipper down the back of her dress.

Their tongues danced as Victor exposed more of Dawn's body. With the zipper undone, he let go of her waist and pushed her dress off her shoulders. The fabric fell to the floor with a swoosh. Victor broke the rhythmic intensity of their kiss to admire his work. Dawn was disrobed in a demi-cup, black, lace bra and matching thong.

"We are a bit unmatched."

"What are you going to do about that?"

She stepped out of the dress pool and walked the short hallway to her bedroom. Victor followed behind dutifully, watching the muscles of her exposed ass and legs ripple and straighten with each stiletto gilded step. He stared at her ass — firm, juicy, and ready to be cupped with two dimpled indentations across her lower back, he swore were made just for his thumbs.

Inside the bedroom, Dawn waited in front of the bed until she could feel Victor behind her. Bending over at the waist, her ass rose to the top of her hips as she removed six decorative throw pillows, and pulled the camel-colored duvet back to expose the sheets of the king-sized bed.

"So you like to tease."

"You'll find I like a lot of things."

"I don't just want to find out what you like," Victor said, approaching her at the bed. "I want to find out what you love and what drives you absolutely insane."

Dawn sat back on the bed and let her actions speak for her. She unhooked Victor's belt buckle, pulling the long leather strap from the loops at his waist until it fell to the floor. Reaching in again, she unbuttoned his pants and eased the zipper over his erection. He removed the rest of his clothing, quickly twisting his hips until his pants were on the floor, and lifting the shirt over his head without opening any more buttons.

Nearly naked, Dawn took in Victor's lean and chiseled muscles from pectorals to abdomen to the smooth cuts that formed a V at the the tops of his trimmed pubic hairs peaking from his underwear. Dawn bit her bottom lip as Victor ended the mystery and removed his socks, shoes, and underwear.

"It seems we are a bit unmatched," Victor said, dropping to his knees.

He positioned himself between her legs and placed feather light kisses on each one of her thighs. His kisses ran up each leg before he let his nose travel across the lace covered apex of her pleasure. Back and forth, he teased her epicenter until her legs clamped tightly to his ears, and her hands pulled the back of his head deeper into her essence.

Victor ignored Dawn's unspoken request and pushed himself up from the floor. She motioned with her hand toward the top drawer of the nightstand beside the bed. He followed her direction and opened the drawer. Inside he saw what she wanted him to retrieve — a gold packaged condom sitting next to a tube of hot pink lipstick, he knew was not lipstick.

Victor closed the drawer with a smile as he met Dawn's unabashed look. He tore open the condom wrapper, tossed it on the floor, and rolled the slippery rubber along his length. Safety, formalities out of the way, he returned to Dawn and hovered over her.

"Lay down."

Dawn did as she was told. Victor held his body in a plank above hers and let his lips and tongue take over. He traced a pattern of kisses from the top of her head, over her nose, across her lips, and to each side of her neck where he suckled the sensitive skin just below her ear until her back began to arch. Instead of letting the sensation linger, he moved back to his path and journeyed to the mounds of Dawn's full cup. One hand behind her back freed their bounty. Hardened nipples stood erect in the open air now that their lace shield had been removed. He kneaded and massaged the mounds of Dawn's breasts before transferring his touch to her already erect nipples. He tugged and toyed with them until pleasure bumps rose on her skin. Dawn cooed softly. Still holding on to the restraint and resolve of her TV persona, Victor was determined to make her let it go.

With every inch of her taut with unrelieved stress and anticipation, he dove back into her body with his mouth, suckling her breast as gently as a newborn. Victor kept the pressure at a consistent pleasure, alternating between the two and dribbling spit between the twin peaks until it ran down her stomach and pooled in her belly button.

Coos were her yes to continue. Moans were a sensation away, as Victor journeyed away from her uneven mountains and traversed the flat plains down her stomach, stopping to lap up his excess drool in the pit of her belly.

He lifted his mouth from Dawn's body long enough to slide her underwear down her legs and over her shoes. The lace cover landed soundlessly on the floor. Both of them completely naked, save for Dawn's glistening silver shoes, smiled at each other. She watched from her perch on her elbows as Victor returned, traveling further down her body until his tongue licked her inner and outer lips. He lapped her Venus mons until it became saturated with fluid. Her mouth opened as wide as her eyes as Victor expertly worked his mop-up magic on her body until she could no longer hold herself up. Falling back, she raised her lower body to smother his face. Victor took the cue and slid into her sweet abyss.

Inch by inch, he plunged and she shuddered with the deepening. He pulled to the tip and repeated the process until they both adjusted to the natural rhythms that inspired them to dance. Victor pushed and Dawn pushed back. Their hands found one another's as their bodies glided along the length of the other. Face to face, front to front, they peppered each other with kisses on chins and earlobes, suckles on cheeks and just above collar bones; licks on skin to increase the sensation of their pumping passion.

Victor pulled and stirred Dawn's insides until her coos became soundless and her mouth opened in O form. The moan he had been working for was coming. He kept his eyes open wide as he forced her to release the Dawn Anthony she didn't want to only be, and embrace the other woman she let few rarely see.

Dawn squeezed her inner body, pulsing and pumping Victor's length and girth as the moaning scream emerged from her gut and resounded off the walls in the twilight of the evening. Her honeyed release coated Victor and expelled his lingam from her inner sanctum.

She greedily moved her body closer toward him to fill the gap. He obliged and rushed into her opening, awakening the sensations she just assuaged. Winding hips met thumping dick until her lips French kissed Victor at the base of his beginning. Over and over she kissed him deep, pumping and pulsing, and riding his length until his gentleman was unmasked. Victor gripped his hands into Dawn's waist and slammed her into him, over and over, until he held her there and succumbed to the easing pressure built up inside his body. They collapsed on the bed, warriors at the end of a lust fight, entangled in each other sated, satisfied, and ready for the next round.

Dawn smiles at the memory of their beginning as she pushes herself off the bed to stretch. Reaching her hands into the air, she inhales deeply and stretches past the length of her armpits and fingertips, until she is forced to exhale the deepest sigh that sends life and relief to her muscles, still slack with sleep. A deep inhale and she bends at the waist, wrapping her arms around the backs of her legs and binding her hands into the crooks of her elbows. She leaves her body bowed until she is forced to exhale another deep sigh and release the tension in the muscles of her thighs.

Dawn rolls her body up slowly until her head's arrival on top of her neck is almost a surprise. She tilts it side to side, ears nearly kissing her shoulders. The tendons in her neck stretch, creak, and crack. Feeling loose, Dawn twists her torso and hips until they too stretch, creak, and crack releasing the stress and tension built up in their nooks. Finally, she wraps her arms around her body, hugging herself tightly, as she turns around to slide back in the bed next to Victor.

"Ms. Anthony, I think you need a masseuse," Victor says, his voice heavy with sleep, as Dawn faces him.

"Rude. That's what I have you for."

"How often do you go through that little morning routine of yours?"

"Typically every day, though it's gotten away from me the last few days."

"I wonder why?"

"I have no idea."

"None?" Victor asks, standing up from the bed.

"None."

"I can think of a few differences in your morning that may have thrown your routine off."

"You're either psychic or I have amnesia, Mr . . . What is your name again?"

"Dawn, I do believe your mind is going. But I can make it all better."

Victor runs his hands along the sides of Dawn's torso as he slowly descends to his knees.

"Whatever would I . . . Ooh."

Victor interrupts Dawn's playful game as she feels the sensation of his finger slide to the center of her thighs and back down again. He watches her face as he works his index finger back and forth over her opening, across her lips, and up the front of her waxed mound. His strokes are slow and deliberate. Pleasure unfurls from the center of her body, rolls upward over her belly, through the length of her neck, and into her face. She is flush with red undertones dominating her dark skin.

Victor adds a second finger to his motion and continues the wave across Dawn's most sensitive area, until his fingers are slick with her anticipation and she becomes unsteady on two feet. Both of her hands find his shoulders. She steadies herself, then moves her own body across his fingers, slipping and sliding against his long, strong digits, making sure they hit every sensitive bundle of nerves to add to her wetness. His non-working hand and arm slips under her ass and moves her body closer toward him. With one hand behind her and Dawn slow riding the other, Victor bows his head to her body and adds to the sensation. He alternates his tongue and his fingers against her gyrations until she stops moving and let's him do all the work. Victor licks and finger fucks her until his whole hand and mouth are soaked.

She vibrates against him as he laps up every drop of pre-sex cum from the apex of her thighs. Her grip tightens on his shoulders, still holding on to her composure. Two fingers and a tongue slide inside and induce a gasp.

"Oh shit!"

Victor holds Dawn tight against his face as he lifts her from the floor. Her center never leaves his face as he gently places her on the bed.

"Do you remember now?" Victor asks, standing away from Dawn's squirming with her eyes closed and legs open.

Dawn opens one eye and looks at Victor's wet lips spread across his face in a satisfied grin.

"Yes, I remember," she concedes, wriggling her body closer to his upright stare.

Victor shakes his head and moves toward her on the bed. Opening the nightstand drawer, he takes a condom from a box he replaced.

"Give me," Dawn says, holding out her hand.

He places the concealed condom in her palm and stares down on her as she opens the package and removes the rubber. Dawn tosses the foil to the floor, scoots her booty to the edge of the bed, gently pulls the tip of the condom and rolls the sticky protective layer against his skin. He grins, bends down, and kisses Dawn fully on the mouth. Crawling up the bed, he forces her to lay down, positioning himself to enter her with an easy glide.

Dawn spreads her legs wider, giving Victor as much access as necessary to reach her bottom. In and out of her aura he glides as she winds her hips to his steady rhythm. Legs open. Legs close. Victor changes the rhythm. Legs open on the long slow strokes; close on the deep, punishing penetrations. Her arms wrap around his neck; his encompass her waist. They slip, slide, and slam into one another; cursing the whole time between licks of the ear.

Dawn feels her pressure building as Victor pounds into her. She tightens her inner muscles, climbing her body along the length of his, and releases guttural grunts and moans that land on his ears in layers, octaves, and butter-rich harmonies that encourage him to keep going. To go faster. To be relentless in his pursuit of their pleasure. She gasps in air, hiccuping gulps of breath, as her climax oozes from the pistil of her flower around Victor's bulging girth, away from their connection, and down her leg. Dawn squeezes until the last drops of her elixir are wrenched from her body with a high-pitched tennis scream that blends with the ringing of her phone.

The unnatural electronic sound blares like a bullhorn across the room as its steady vibration taps out an annoying beat on the wood of the nightstand. Victor arrests Dawn's body with both hands and drums into her until his own climax pours from his gut into the tip of the condom with one final skin-slapping slam against Dawn's ass, and into the depth of her center. His collapse on top of her is greeted by the final echoes of the ringtone into silence.

They lay there, he on top of her, bodies entwined from fingernails to the tips of their toes, both panting and holding on to the edges of their phantasms as the phone begins again. The annoying tone and reverberating vibrations force Dawn back to reality as she squirms beneath Victor toward the nightstand. Not yet ready to be evicted from her home, Victor leans his body toward the side dresser and grabs the phone. He holds it in front of Dawn as she slides her finger across the front of the glass face to answer.

She bursts into the receiver, "Hello," as Victor holds it at her ear.

"Dawn, sorry to call so early. It's Boyce. I need you to come in."

"Who is this?"

"It's Boyce."

"What do you want?"

"I just told you, I need you to come in."

Dawn grabs the phone from Victor with one hand and gently pushes him off of her with the other so she can sit up. Expelled, Victor stumbles as he stands, and takes a seat beside Dawn annoyed.

"Why do you need me to come in?" Dawn snaps. "It's only . . . 9:30. Isn't your morning team still there?"

"Dawn, we've got Breaking News. Marcus and Kirsten are on the desk now for a cut-in. I need you to come in and head up our noon with Julia. We're starting at 11."

"So what will Marcus and Kirsten be doing if Julia and I are doing the noon? And why is it starting at 11. Where is Linden? And does Julia know all this?"

"Yes, Julia knows. Linden is still coming in at two," Boyce says of the main male anchor in the evening. "I need my best for this coverage. Marcus and Kirsten research, and act as third anchors."

"So what's the Breaking News?" Dawn asks softening her tone at Boyce admitting she was the best. In her mind, the compliment did not extend to Julia.

"Shooting at the courthouse. Why don't you know already?"

"Because I don't check my email as soon as I open my eyes. My morning belongs to me."

"How soon can you get here?" Boyce asks, forgoing the fight Dawn's voice was goading him into.

"Before show time," Dawn answers icily, hanging up the phone.

"Duty calls?" Victor asks uneasily seeing the the change in Dawn's demeanor from sated and satisfied to all business bitch, in the matter of moments.

"Unfortunately."

"How soon do you have to go?"

"I'm sure they want me there as soon as possible."

Dawn stands up from the bed and twists her body from side to side. The creaks and cracks resound with the stretch, despite her best relaxation techniques.

"You really do need a masseuse."

"That's what I have you for." she faces him with a kind smile.

Victor, who was beginning to learn the difference in her smiles, knew this one was genuine, even if it wasn't the real one.

"So are you just going to use me, Ms. Anthony?"

"Only if you let me, Mr. Russell."

"So, Ms. Anthony. When would you like to book your next session?"

Dawn rolls her eyes to the sky before she stalks off toward the entrance of her en suite.

"How about now," she says, leaning against one post of the open door frame, "In the shower."

"As you wish." Victor watches Dawn turn away from the door and saunter into the bathroom. "As you wish."

19.

We continue to follow Breaking News this morning on a special extended edition of 9 News Now. If you're just joining us, we're following the investigation of a shooting near the Duval County Courthouse.

Julia Gillé and Dawn Anthony continue to tell the sparest details of a story Ebony already knows. Before them, it was Marcus Jordan and Kirsten Little. The entire 9 News Now team has been telling her things they know nothing about since she turned the television on, after she emerged from the bathroom. She thought the background noise would help in her effort to return to normal and drown the raging thoughts in her head, but the anchors give her no peace.

Video showing the aftermath of what she did not do are on a constant loop. Glass on the ground. Police officers inspecting and dusting the glass on the ground. Employees, attorneys, suspects, and families file out of the courthouse from all exits. Security guards patrol the grounds in an effort to look like they're on their job and did not let what some would perceive to be a tragedy, occur on their watch. Police officers roll out their candy cane striped crime scene tape. More police arrive on scene; some in SUV's, some in unmarked vans, some in their everyday squad cars with blue and red lights flashing. The whir of the silent lights is present in every video clip. The anchors and reporters talk to fill time, saying everything and nothing, all at once, as they try not to convict the suspect in a crime she did not commit.

Your time now is 11:55. In five minutes we are expecting an update from the Jacksonville Sheriff with the latest on the shooting that happened early this morning across the street from the courthouse. Dawn and Julia, back to you in the studio.

Thank you, Jorah. And thank you, to you at home, for staying with us through this Breaking News. We're going to take a quick break and be back at the top of the hour for the news conference with the Jacksonville Sheriff. Remember, for Breaking News on the go head to 9 News Now dot com or keep up with us on our app, Facebook or Twitter, using hashtag JAX courthouse shooting.

We'll be right back.

Dawn Anthony's quick wrap of the courthouse coverage leads directly into a commercial blaring loudly from the television speaker. It's for a local law firm. Each family member working in the practice gets their screen time to explain why their firm is the best to represent anyone in any situation; from run of the mill ambulance chasing accidents and the fallacious medical concoctions that are soft tissue injuries, to the most wanted, suspected mass murderer in town. They explain that their family does it all. The commercial ends with a serious family portrait, and a voice-over says their name and slogan as it appears written in a script font on the screen, *Blake & Blake. We fight for Families.*

This is the first time Ebony has ever paid attention to the commercial. Confined to the couch, she reads the number on the screen contemplating whether she wants to call. She contemplates whether or not she wants to put her future into the hands of a family who has to advertise to increase clientele. Instead, Ebony gets up from the couch for another reason. Her house phone is ringing again. It is the fifth time in a row James has called the phone, forcing Ebony to let it just ring without acknowledgment. She knows he is determined to get through to her, even if she can't get through to herself. Ebony begrudgingly gets up from the couch where she's been watching the coverage of the crime she did not commit, still unable to separate herself from the images on the news and what she saw with her own two eyes. The reports of the unknowing reporters and anchors conflict with what she knows to be true.

The ringing of the phone stops just as Ebony stands from the couch. It is only temporary. The memory of the noise blends with the ringing in her ears, still shell-shocked by the early pops of her Lady.

Ebony makes her way out of the living room across the cherry hardwood and onto the tile of the kitchen. By the time she makes it to where the phone hangs in its corner cradle, the ringing begins again for the sixth time in a row.

"Yes, James," she answers.

"Jesus, Ebony, I've been trying to reach you all morning. How did you know it was me?"

"You're the only one who has this number."

"So why didn't you answer?"

"I was busy. Usually you just call my cell."

"I did. It's off. It went straight to voicemail."

"Well, you've got me now."

"Come to the door, I'm outside."

Ebony hangs up the phone without confirmation she'll do what he's requested. She makes her way across the textures of the floor, down the hall and to the door. Turning the lock and swinging the door wide, James steps across the threshold without seeing her. Deliberately standing behind the door, Ebony further delays the inevitable.

Once James is completely inside, she closes the door behind him and turns the lock. She looks at his face to see what he knows. His ordinary brown face is composed, at first, until he takes her in from head to toe. Still in her black hoodie and yoga pants from the morning, her sneakers are off and thin black ankle socks cover her feet. Ebony's hands are shoved into her pocket holding the weight of her Lady. The only skin exposed is the sliver of space from her calf to her sock line, her forehead, nose, and chin. The hoodie encloses the rest of her head and shrouds much of her unruly hair.

"Baby, what happened to you?" James asks concerned. "Why did you leave this morning?"

"I had to run an errand. I didn't want to wake you."

"What time did you leave? I would have at least walked you out."

"I left at five, but then I had an accident with my car."

"Are you alright?"

"My back and neck are sore, but I'm okay," Ebony says, turning away from James.

The heels of his Oxford Wingtips follow behind her as they walk down the hallway and into the living room.

Breaking News right now on 9 News Now at Noon. We continue to follow the latest developments of the courthouse shooting from this morning.

Thank you for joining us. I'm Julia Gillé.

And I'm Dawn Anthony.

Right now we're waiting on the Jacksonville Sheriff to give us the latest updates from the courthouse.

9 News Now's Jorah Anderson is standing by at the podium where the Sheriff will speak in just moments. Jorah what can you tell us.

"You've been watching?"

"Of course." Ebony answers. "How are you?"

Ebony settles back into the right corner of the couch, hugging the salmon-colored throw pillow to her chest.

"I'm alright," he says, taking off his blue pinstriped suit jacket as he sits in the opposite corner. Ebony helps him kick off his shoes with her own feet to make him feel comfortable, despite her appearance and the information they will watch the Sheriff deliver together about a crime she did not commit.

"I hadn't gotten to work yet when everything happened," James continues. "The state attorney called me as I was pulling into the parking garage and told me about the shooting, and that court was cancelled for the day. I called you, but you didn't answer."

"Sorry," Ebony mumbles into her hoodie. "But at least you're okay. Pass me the remote, please."

James places the remote control in her hand. She turns the volume up as the Sheriff clears his throat to speak.

This morning at 7:20 a.m., a 45 year-old Black male was shot twice outside of the Sikes & Stowe Auto Body shop at the corner of Monroe and Broad Streets in downtown Jacksonville.

Homicide detectives with the Jacksonville Sheriff's Office and rescue units with Jacksonville Fire and Rescue, responded to the scene, immediately.

Upon arrival the victim was conscious, but coughing up blood. He was transported to UF Health with life-threatening injuries and is, at this time, in critical condition. We are not releasing the identity of the victim until next of kin is notified.

Homicide detectives canvassed the immediate area around the courthouse in the aftermath of the shooting in search of witnesses and to obtain a description of the suspect.

Witnesses we spoke to did not see the shooting happen, but remember hearing gunshots. They say the man was seen hugging a woman shortly before the gunshots rang out. Witnesses describe that woman as short, with long, curly hair, and dressed in all black. The woman is also believed to be African-American. Witnesses say the victim and the woman were standing in front of a new model black car, but the exact make and model are unknown.

It is still early in the investigation and, at this time, it is unclear if the woman seen with the victim is in fact the suspect. If you know anything about this woman you are asked to contact police immediately.

I will now take a few questions.

James turns down the television once the gaggle of reporters start peppering the Sheriff with questions he refuses to answer, has already answered, or the reporters already have the answers to.

"That was helpful," James says.

"No, it wasn't." Ebony disagrees, looking directly at him for the first time since he sat down beside her. "For all you know, I could be the mystery woman slash non-suspect, suspect they're looking for."

"Baby, don't be ridiculous. Not all Black women look the same." James laughs. "And they don't even know for sure the woman is Black."

He turns toward Ebony seated beside him. His lawyer poker face is replaced by one of ease, satisfied with the information delivered in the news brief from the Sheriff. His face is so settled and serene, Ebony can see the makings of a smile creeping at the corners of his lips. His composure is the exact opposite of her own, knowing she is a wanted woman for a crime she did not commit.

"Short, dressed in black, with long, curly hair," Ebony says, removing her hoodie from her head. "If the woman *is* Black, *I* fit the description."

James looks at Ebony seriously before responding. With her hoodie removed, he can see the mess of her mass of curls. The ends of her hair sparkling with specks of glass that don't belong. If he looks closely, he can see the haggard look in her eyes, and the skin of her face scrubbed raw with soap and the city's hard tap water. If he looks closely.

"Baby, what are you saying?" James asks cautiously. "How could you even think you fit a description of that woman when you were in a car accident nowhere near the courthouse, this morning."

"I never said where I was this morning. And I never said I was in a car accident. I said I had an accident with my car."

"What's the damn difference, Ebony?"

"There's a big difference, James."

"Ebony, don't start this cagey bullshit now. Say what you have to say. Where were you this morning? And what the hell happened with your car?" James fires the last two questions at her with agitation and intensity rising, as if she were a hostile witness and he was trying to get a confession in open court.

"Don't curse at me."

"Talk, Ebony."

"What would you like me to say, James?"

"Answer my questions. Why did you leave my house in the dead of morning? Where did you go?"

"The courthouse."

"Why the hell were you at the courthouse? You said you had to run an errand. And you never come to see me at work?"

"I came to see you yesterday."

"Not really. I saw you on the highway and followed you. I don't work at the courthouse."

"Same difference, James. I still saw you at work yesterday."

"Whatever. It's the first time you've seen me at work in the year we've been dating. To make up, you said. But some make up that was if you had to leave my house at five this morning."

Ebony doesn't respond as James puts his version of events before her as evidence that her story doesn't make sense. She doesn't contradict his sparse timeline. She waits for him to continue learning, picking up clues so she doesn't have to admit the truth about a crime she did not commit.

"Why were you at the courthouse, Ebony?"

"I wasn't there to see you."

"Then who were you there to see?"

"Barker."

"Barker?" James says the name as if it is foreign to him, until a look of recognition registers on his face. "You mean Judge Gordon. My mentor Judge Gordon. You just met him Saturday. Why did you need to see him? What the fuck is going on?"

"Last time telling you, James — don't curse at me."

"Ebony, it's my last time telling *you*. Talk."

"Saturday wasn't the first time I met Barker. We used to date, two years ago. He was abusive. I left him. He was beating Soleil. The woman he brought with him to the mayor's luncheon. I could tell. And she didn't deny it when I asked her. I went to the courthouse with my Lady to tell him to stop and he choked me, strangled me, and slammed me against my car, and my Lady went off."

The words tumble out of Ebony's mouth hurried and unrehearsed. Her entire morning's effort to be normal wasted in a moment.

"Ebony, back up. You're telling me the man who has shaped and guided my legal career at the State's Attorney's Office is a man you used to fuck, who you just happened to see for the first time in two years on Saturday. On top of that, you *claim* he was abusive." James summarized making air quotes around the word.

"That's exactly what I'm saying. But I'm not claiming he was abusive, I'm telling you he beat me and he was beating Soleil."

"So what the fuck does all that have to do with you and some lady going to confront him at the courthouse and her cursing him out? How the hell does that connect you to the courthouse shooting?"

Ebony pushes the pillow from in front of her and takes her sheathed, scratched hands out of her front hoodie pocket. Holding her Lady in one hand and the empty shell casings she removed from her revolver in the other, she places them on top of the pillow separating their sides; suspect and victim from witness and spectator.

"I didn't say some lady went with me," Ebony says, letting the presence of the Lady Smith .38 Special Revolver settle between them. "I said my Lady went off after he slammed me against the car."

"Ebony, where the hell did you get the gun?" James asks. "I didn't even know you were a gun owner. And I'm really supposed to believe Judge Gordon, a man I've known for damn near a decade, and have never known to be violent, slammed you against the car and the gun just went the fuck off. That doesn't make any sense."

"James, whether it makes sense or not, it's what happened. I've had the gun since Barker slapped me the first time and left this fucking mark on my forehead," Ebony says pushing her hair out of her face.

"You told me that was a birthmark."

"Because it's easier than saying on a third date that a man put his hands on me."

"This shit makes no fucking sense." James stands from the couch jostling the Lady. "You better pray he doesn't die." He paces.

"So what if he does?"

"Are you fucking serious?" James roars. "If he dies you might as well prepare for death too. That's the sentence you're looking at for the premeditated murder of a court officer. That's a first degree murder charge, Baby. I'd *have* to ask for the death penalty."

"Well, it's nice to know where we stand after all this time."

"Ebony, don't you dare do that to me." James roars again as he slams his body down on the couch. The heavy movement jostles the Lady some more.

"You're sitting here telling me you purposefully took a gun to the courthouse, to confront a man you used to fuck, who you haven't seen in two years, about a woman you don't know from Adam, and that you killed him and fled the scene! Do I have that right?"

Ebony says nothing. Her silence is neither submission nor confession. It is silence for silence's sake because she knows words are inappropriate.

"What am I supposed to say to that?" James continues. "How am I supposed to react to that? I'm supposed to take it like you're telling me the sky is blue or the day is fucking Wednesday. Sorry, Baby. If that's what you were expecting, I'm not the one."

James ends his tirade where the conversation began, he and Ebony sit on opposite ends of her sofa. The Lady sits between them. The business end faces Ebony with the handle closest to James. It is the nascent making of a would be crime scene where James is the primary suspect in an accident he didn't mean to happen, and in a murder he did not commit.

"Like I said: It's nice to know where we stand after all this time."

"Ebony, what the fuck do you want me to do, leave my job and represent your ass? I can't represent you. I don't even trust you. And I for damn sure don't know you."

"You've known me for the last year," Ebony offers weakly.

"Ebony, I don't know shit about you. Not about your family. You just told me about your parents and your siblings last week. And now you're telling me about you and Barker. This convenient boyfriend from two years ago who beat your ass, and you decided to kill on a whim."

"He's not dead . . ." Ebony says, leaving her sentence unfinished. "And secondly, why do you need to know so much about my past? I keep telling you my parents, my family, they are not in my life, and my last boyfriends don't matter because I'm with you."

"What the fuck ever, Ebony."

"Fuck it, James. What do you want to know? About Barker? What do you want to know?"

"Anything. I need to know how the fuck you two got together. I need to know about this alleged abuse. And I need to know how the fuck you got it in your head to drive to the fucking courthouse, with a gun, and shoot him. Ebony, I need to know it all, because it looks to me like your ass is still chasing after him. If that's true, what the fuck do you need me for? Why am I here? Why are we together? I need to know something because, right now, I don't see where I fit in to all of this."

"You don't see where you fit in. Is that what you just said to me. You don't see where *you* fit in? Well, James, here's where you fit in. Me going to the courthouse to see Barker . . . today wasn't the first time. Yesterday, when I saw you first, wasn't the first time, either. My trips to the courthouse to see him are the reason we met."

"What the fuck?"

"You heard me. You want to know so much so bad. Here's something for your ass. Barker. Your mentor, Barker. He's the reason we met."

20.

Breaking News: State Attorney Barker Gordon Appointed to 4th Judicial Circuit Court by Governor Rick Scott.

Ebony received the app alert on her phone early one morning a year ago. The six a.m. message from the 9 News Now app cut right through her sleep with the tone of its delivery. In the blackout curtain darkness of her room, she reached for her phone on the nightstand and brought the screen to life to read the message. She immediately regretted her decision. Staring at the screen with cold still in her eyes, his name stared back at her with dignity and importance, an urgency and worthiness of her time she knew he didn't deserve. Ebony read the short alert over and over again, re-illuminating the screen of her phone to scan the words that hadn't changed since they'd first been delivered.

Unable to discern any more meaning from the headline, Ebony touched the message to go to the 9 News Now website. One touch took her to the live stream of the morning news. Marcus Jordan and Kirsten Little were anchoring. Jorah Anderson was in the field reporting from the State Attorney's Office. The office where Barker worked. Jorah was camped outside the office waiting for Barker to arrive; waiting to get a comment from the state attorney about his promotion. The reporter narrated the empty scene, describing the sleepy downtown area as Ebony got out of bed.

She listened to Jorah detail the last cases Barker successfully prosecuted. The reporter hailed Barker as a measure of balanced fairness seeking the toughest punishments against career criminals, and prosecuting children as children instead of sending them through the criminal justice system as adults. Ebony listened to Jorah drone on about the momentous occasion in the life of the state attorney she was sure, he only knew from pictures and his side of the television screen. Jorah and the anchors called Barker a hero; a crusader for justice. She remembered his hands dragging her by the foot from her living room to her bed.

Ebony listened to the news about Barker as she pulled on her clothes. Leggings and sports bra beneath ripped jeans and a shrunken white tee. Her ears listened to the live stream while the attention of her mind traveled back to the last time Barker stood before her; his dick hanging with excitement as she aimed her Lady in a menaced promise. Sneakers on, the news still playing from her phone, his last laugh cackled in her ear on his final walk from her door with his head held high. He whistled, and crunched peppermints in his mouth that was forever stained with the smoke of Swisher Sweets and the residue of hard liquor.

Ebony was driving North on I-95 when the next hour of news began on her phone. It beeped signaling a low battery. Her muscle memory grabbed the carjack to charge the phone. Marcus, Kirsten and Jorah talked about the breaking news for Jacksonville's justice system. Ebony listened as she drove, winding her car down the highway, over the bridge, and into the bowels of downtown to the State Attorney's Office. She planned to wait with the city's reporters to see the man of the hour, before his ascension to judgeship.

She pulled up to the stone-faced office connected to the new courthouse just in time to grab the last metered parking space in front of the building. Ebony parked behind a large news truck; her car nearly hidden by the massive size of the mega van with it's mounted satellite dish raised high to heaven. In her car, behind the truck, she listened to the news as it was performed in front of her. Her car clock and phone agreed that it was almost 8 o'clock. Ebony and the reporters agreed that Barker would arrive momentarily. They hoped he would be in a generously giving mood and bless them all with an interview about the biggest news they could ask for on a slow news morning.

Ebony loitered around her car, hanging behind the news trucks, waiting with everyone else. She circled restlessly around her squares of the pavement; walking from her car and across the street to the tree-lined edge of the courthouse grounds. Back and forth Ebony paced, her arms folded in front of her; her nails raking scratches deep into the already scabbed backs of her hands. Her phone in her back pocket, no longer played the news. She was the background in each reporter's scene, filling the space behind them with her journey from courthouse grounds to car, until she saw what all the reporters had been waiting to see.

Barker's black car pulled down the side street in front of the State Attorney's Office where they waited. He didn't stop. Barker drove past them all to the corner of Monroe and Julia Streets. The reporters and their photographers followed him to the corner, gathering outside his rolled up windows, their camera's peering through the tint, hoping to get a glimpse of the justice system messiah inside. Ebony watched the reporters rush Barker's car to further their story. She watched as Barker drove ahead and made a quick right into the looming parking garage. The news crews ran back to their respective trucks and got in position in front of the office. They all assumed Barker would enter through the front door where they waited. In the background, Ebony watched the show in front of her unsure of what she would do if he noticed her before she saw him.

"What's with all the reporters?"

The question came from behind. The voice distinctly male, and apparently irritated, asked no one in particular.

"They're here to see the state attorney."

Ebony answered without turning around. She leaned along the hood of her car watching the reporters watch the parking garage, hoping to get a glimpse of Barker as he emerged.

"All this because he was appointed judge?"

"I guess so."

"What brings you out here this morning? I know you're not with the TV stations dressed like that."

The insult made Ebony snap her head to look at the man who sparked a conversation with a stranger. She looked him over before responding to his question. He wore a black checked suit and gray vest that brought out the lining of the suit pants and coat. Red tie, handkerchief, and cufflinks added flare to his mix and match ensemble. Insulted and intrigued, Ebony obliged the handsome man.

"I have a parking ticket I need to pay for. I'm waiting for the courthouse to open." Ebony lied.

"Good luck with that. By the way, I'm James," he said, extending his hand.

"Ebony."

Their hands embraced and lingered at the fingertips as they gazed at each other.

"Nice to meet you," James said, breaking their gaze, but not letting go of her hand.

"Likewise," Ebony stared down at their connection.

They would have stayed standing like that, staring at each other when the other wasn't looking, connected at the fingertips, if the reporters and photographers had not all run across the street from their live trucks, at once. They clamored to get video of Barker as he approached the front door of the State Attorney's Office. James and Ebony broke their hand embrace as if they, too, were caught on camera. They stared at the mock mayhem playing out across the street in front of them. Three young reporters, each with their microphone in hand, pushed to the top of the steps hollering questions at Barker to get him to open up about his appointment. James and Ebony watched as he faced them all, smiling from ear to ear; his grin glowing in their camera view finders. Barker held court on the steps of his office, answering one question from each reporter before disappearing into the building.

"That was nice of him," James said as the reporters cleared the scene.

"Seemed pretentious to me."

"It wasn't like he was going to give them a full interview on the steps."

"Then why bother answering any questions at all?"

"To remain media friendly. They can be annoying, but we need them sometimes as much as they need us. He has to keep the symbiotic relationship going, keeping all sides appeased."

"If you say so."

"Though they would have done better if they caught him on a Sunday morning after church, before breakfast."

"Okay, I'll bite." Ebony smiled. "Why is that?"

"He's always in a good mood after service at Bethel, and he's always at Cracker Barrel after service because he's got a thing for fried catfish, grits, and pecan pancakes."

Ebony didn't respond as James told her information about Barker she never learned on her own in their three-month relationship.

"We sometimes go there together on Sundays if we have a big case to prepare for that week," James continued. "We talk out strategy, evidence, testimony, witnesses, everything over food."

"You work here?"

"Don't seem so surprised. Don't I look the part?" James asked, holding out his arms and turning in a circle. "Assistant State Attorney James Parnell."

"Ebony Jones, personal fitness instructor." Ebony twirled in a circle of her own.

"I could use your services." James said patting the paunch of his belly.

"Here's a pro tip, lay off the fried catfish and pecan pancakes on Sunday's with your boy."

"That's cold." James chuckled. "But you might have a point. Maybe you could give me some more pointers over lunch?" James asked, losing his chuckle for an anticipating smile.

"Give me your card."

James fumbled over his outer jacket pockets for his business card. Ebony watched with laughter dancing in her eyes as he patted

129

himself down better than the TSA. No luck with the outer pockets. James's face alighted with memory that the business card was in the inside pocket of his black checked suit coat. He produced the matte card stock with a flourish. Ebony didn't take it.

"I need a pen."

Again, James searched himself for what she asked for until he dug out a ball point pen from the brown leather duffle bag he'd placed on the ground when he first walked up to Ebony, leaning against her car. She laughed as he fumbled with the zippered compartments. He carried on going through side pouch after side pouch, until he found the pen and stood up with the bag tossed across his back and shoulders.

"This is funny to you, huh? Seeing a man get all nervous trying to ask a girl out on a date?"

"It is. No matter how old we get, we're still uncoordinated, uncomfortable pubescent teenagers on the inside when it comes to first encounters with the opposite sex."

Ebony took the business card and pen out of James's hands and wrote on the back of it before handing both items back to him.

"Both of these are your phone numbers?"

"I guess you'll have to call and find out," Ebony said, walking to her car door.

"Count on it," James said, crossing the street. "Wait, I thought you had to pay a parking ticket. The courthouse is open now."

"I'll pay it online." Ebony lied. "Have a good day."

"You too."

Ebony waited in her car until James crossed the street, walked up the few steps of the State Attorney's Office, and disappeared inside the blue gray-doors of the building. The reporters and photographers were long gone, satisfied to get the answer to three questions. Three questions they rolled into one long story on the evening news, about the city's new judge; the new face of justice.

Ebony watched the news that night and saw herself in the background of the story, but instead of paying attention to the man she initially showed up to see, she watched herself with the man she'd met. The lower left corner of her television screen showed bits and pieces of her and James. She watched, remembering James's passing conversation about Barker. Cracker Barrel. Catfish, grits, and pecan pancakes. Sunday morning after church.

It was James who told Ebony about Barker's habits the day they met. It was James who told Ebony where to find Barker every Sunday, late in the morning. It took her three weeks of visiting every Cracker Barrel in the city to find Barker. He went to the one in Regency. James's casual conversation about Barker's Sunday tradition lead to Ebony's own tradition, once she broke James of the habit of going with him.

Every Sunday since she'd found him, she'd wait for him in the parking lot of the restaurant of the less than busy shopping area. Sometimes she'd see him arrive alone to have breakfast by himself. Sometimes he'd be with a group of attorneys from the office, loaded down with bags, brief cases, and even a box of files, as James said they sometimes did when big cases were going to trial. It wasn't until 6 months into her and James's relationship, 6 months into her solo Sunday outings, that she found Barker at Cracker Barrel with a woman.

She arrived after he did and was forced to circle the parking lot for a space with a good vantage point to see him. When she finally parked, she saw he was still outside, standing along the row of rocking chairs, rapt in conversation with a woman. Trying to watch both of them from her rearview mirror was futile. Barker's back blocked most of her view of the mystery woman. It was the first time she'd seen him with a woman. The first time the thought of him being with someone other than her ever entered her mind.

She got out of the car that Sunday morning to see them both. To see if he approached the woman with the same arrogance and impudence, self-righteousness and ego he had when he approached her at the gym. Ebony watched as Barker and the woman exchanged easy smiles, flirtatious glances, and unheard words that were unnecessary when their body language expressed all she needed to know. She watched him at Cracker Barrel that Sunday as she had every Sunday before and would every Sunday after. However, it has only been since his encounter with the woman that Ebony followed him after breakfast to see where he went. His jaunts around the city led her to the woman's Southside apartment complex, where she saw her abuse from the parking lot, and heard outside her third floor door his threats and laughter as he exacted his sadistic brand of pleasure on her unwilling body.

It was James who led Ebony back to Barker. It was James who found Ebony when she only wanted to find Barker, and it was James who now condemned her for doing what he set in motion.

It was James.

21.

"Johnnie, what the hell happened in there?" Dr. Taylor Thomas asks bursting through the doctors' locker room.

The door slamming behind him startles Johnnie for the second time in as many seconds. She lost her patient. The high-priority patient she was called in to ensure his survival died while her fingers were still deep inside his chest, trying to cauterize what should have been an immediately fatal wound. Johnnie still isn't sure why the patient flat-lined so suddenly, but the monotone sound is still with her in her sulking haze.

She sits still on the bench in the locker room dressed in her dirty scrubs she wiped her bloody, gloved hands on, and a sports bra that offered no support, only backup to the heavy duty embroidered lace bra she had on beneath it. Johnnie's white water bottle, refilled immediately after the surgery from a stashed flask in her locker, sits beside her on the bench. She reaches for it, pulls the black cap open with her teeth, and takes a long drag. Taylor, red-faced, arms crossed and foot tapping, waits for an explanation.

Johnnie holds on to the sides of the bench with both hands as she straddles it. She wants to stand up, but the simple movement of turning her body sideways makes her heady.

"Johnnie, what happened?" Taylor asks with less apparent anger.

Johnnie doesn't notice the agitation and discomposure present beneath the silk layer of his goading question.

"I'm not really sure," Johnnie begins, her tongue thick and voice unsteady. She slows the pace of her speech before continuing. "I did the best I could," she enunciates, "but he was too far gone before he got to us. I tried, but I'm not God. I don't work miracles."

"Johnnie, that's up for debate. I've seen you do a helluva lot more for lesser people who didn't deserve it."

"What is that supposed to mean?" Johnnie slurs.

"It means just what it sounds like. That wasn't you in that O.R. today. That's a surgeon fresh off of residency. One I did not hire nor did I request to work on *this* patient."

"Taylor, I don't know what happened. The team and I were making progress and then we weren't. These things happen."

Johnnie tries standing up from her straddled position on the bench, knowing a seated defense is no defense at all. She is uncoordinated and nearly falls to the floor. She swings her left leg over to meet her right, but the teetering forces her to grab hold of the open door of her metal locker for balance.

"These things don't just happen. They especially don't just happen to you."

"So what are you saying, Taylor?"

"I'm saying I was watching the entire surgery from the observation deck, and what I saw was a surgeon whose team was working, but you, the leader, the surgeon in the room, was always one step behind. Your hands were shaking."

Johnnie opens her mouth to speak, but Taylor holds up one hand stopping her.

"This is the second patient you've lost in less than a week. You only lost four patients all last year. Something is wrong and you need to tell me what it is."

"Nothing is wrong." Johnnie grabs her white water bottle from the bench. She misses and the bottle fumbles out of her grasp to the floor. The open top leaks clear liquid across the cheap teal tile. Johnnie falls to both knees to recover the bottle, taking a long swig on her way up.

"Nothing is wrong," Johnnie reiterates, smacking her lips after her drink. "Nothing."

"You've got to be kidding me," Taylor exclaims. "You're drunk."

Johnnie and Taylor are nearly nose to nose in the otherwise empty locker room. Her heart beats loudly in her chest as she resists the urge to raise the bottle to her mouth again.

"I'm not drunk," she says slowly, not helping the lag in her tongue.

"You reek of alcohol; gin, vodka and whatever else is concocted in that bottle you're clutching harder than life itself."

"I'm not drunk."

"This is going to be a PR nightmare."

"What do you mean?"

"I mean, I've got a dead judge and a drunk surgeon." Taylor walks away disgusted.

"I'm not drunk," she says sitting back down on the bench, bottle still clutched between both of her hands. "And your judge didn't die because of me. Your judge died because he was shot twice by some murderer with a gun. I didn't kill him. They did."

Taylor turns to look at his defeated mentee sitting in bloody pants and no shirt.

"Maybe you're right, Johnnie." Taylor shakes his head. "Maybe you're not drunk. Maybe you didn't kill the judge. Like you said, he was too far gone before he got to us. You and your team did everything you could."

"Thank you, Taylor." Johnnie lowers her eyes away.

"But Johnnie. . . "

"Yes."

"You are suspended indefinitely. I won't announce it. You can spin it anyway you like. Taking a leave of absence for your family. Going on a religious sabbatical. I don't care. But you will not set foot in this hospital again until you get some help."

Dr. Taylor Thomas exits the locker room more solemnly than he entered. The door quietly swings closed behind him. Johnnie sits motionless on the bench, staring at the open bottle clutched in her hands. She sits listening to her inhales and exhales. Statue still she thinks of nothing. Her hands move of their own volition. They are focused on the bottle between them holding up the weight of her thoughts running through her heavy head. Motionless, she sits until the hard wooden bench begins to irritate her barely there behind.

Johnnie swings both legs over the back of the bench and stands facing her locker. She braces herself, holding the door with her right hand. The bottle is balanced in her left palm. Steady enough, Johnnie brings the bottle to her lips and knocks back the half-full contents in one shot, only wincing once all of the liquid has burned its course down her throat.

She shoves the bottle into the outer mesh pocket of her backpack, pulls her bloodied scrubs down her legs, and kicks them toward the trash can on the wall opposite the door. They end up in the red hazardous waste bin. In just her panties and two bras, Johnnie takes her time walking back to her locker. She pulls her backpack out and sets it on the bench where she had once been seated. From the zippered pack she removes her pants, shirt, and sweatshirt. Her cell phone falls out of a pocket to the tile floor. The glass screen doesn't crack with the impact. It lands face up. The time flashes 2:00 p.m.

If I hurry I can pick up Danielle from school and not break another promise.

Johnnie's thought motivates her to dress quickly, but does nothing to jog her memory that she's already asked Nathan to get Danielle from school.

22.

School dismissed early for Soleil's class once she and the students arrived back from the zoo. With four parents already on the trip to chaperone, and the others waiting in the parking lot when the school bus pulled in at 2:50, Soleil, the students, chaperones, and her teacher's assistant Miss Lisa, all descended the steps of the school bus to their cars to go home. But Soleil didn't go home. She couldn't. She drives the opposite direction of home to Eighth Street, which is eerily empty as she makes her way toward the hospital's gleaming white campus. The clustered buildings are constructed in a shape reminiscent of a medieval castle. The only difference is these towers are squared, not pointed.

Driving slowly along the last stretch of street to the hospital, Soleil delays whatever inevitable news awaits her inside, wishing her ride from Arlington across the Mathews Bridge into the city's no man's land had taken longer than twenty minutes.

The hospital campus is situated in a peculiar space. It is a stone's throw away from the city's Northside; just on the other side of I-95. On one side is the hospital, on the other is the Northside standing proud and defiant in all of it's evident, abject poverty. The hospital is not the Northside. It is neither part of Jacksonville's still developing downtown nor the historic district of Springfield. This area is now, and will always be, Shands, no matter what the blue and orange signs outside the hospital read.

Soleil passes the front of the hospital's campus and follows the signs for the ambulatory care center. It is a nice euphemism to lessen the blow of why most people end up on the hospital grounds. She turns down the narrow roadway named after a doctor no one remembers, and then again into the wide, gravel parking lot just across the street from the emergency room.

The rocks and pebbles crunch and grind beneath her tires as she slowly trolls the lanes for a parking space. Soleil rounds the bends of the lot looking without luck, until she is back where she started. Pulling out of the gravel lot she drives across the street, hoping to have better luck in the parking lot for the actual emergency room.

The ground level parking winds through an immaculately kept lot with strategically planted trees and shrubbery arranged in the well-cut grass. It is beautiful. The pride of the place is evident even in tragedy; even if Soleil may come to know someone else's personal tragedy as her blessing.

She lucks up on a space down the hill from the emergency room doors, near the sign for valet parking. Even in an emergency, the rich, well-off and those feigning importance can receive special treatment for just three dollars. Soleil shakes her head at the sign as she gets out of her car. The sound only alarm chirps notifying her the doors are locked on her little blue Honda, before she makes the short trek up the hill to the emergency room.

A siren pierces the silence with its wail as she walks. The abrupt and blaring noise makes Soleil jump and look around to see where it is coming from. The red light special of the fire truck or ambulance stays hidden, meanwhile a white hearse pulls out of wrought iron gates at the back of the emergency wing. Soleil follows the hearse with her eyes as it leaves the hospital's grounds, wondering whose cargo it's carrying inside. She wonders if it is him, even though she hasn't confirmed he was even the one shot this morning, or has even died from what the news article said were "life-threatening injuries."

Soleil continues her short walk blending with others who are also making the trek. Some walk under their own power, others are wheeled by family members. They all wear forlorn looks of sadness as they pass by a gated area filled with two dozen waste bins. A red "do not enter" sign is posted outside the black painted, chain-link fence. Just beyond that is a line of vending machines, each offering its own variety of snack food. A few hospital employees congregate around the machines on the wooden benches placed in front of them so they can snack and rest, but still be at work when they're probably supposed to be on break.

The emergency room doors appear before Soleil announced by a long rectangular red sign with the word "emergency" screaming in capitalized block letters. The sign is a marked difference from the multi-colored sign for pediatric emergency. It is written in lowercase block letters on an italic slant; perhaps to mask the pain of the reality that children, in all of their innocence, can also be killed and become victims of someone else's tragedy.

Soleil turns from the pediatric emergency sign and walks toward a reality meant for adults. The doors to the emergency room swing outward inviting her in, but she hesitates reading a small, faded, red sign posted just to the left of the doors. It announces she and her belongings may be searched, and warns her against bringing any weapons inside the hospital. The sign stands as a jarring warning of the hostility possibly waiting inside, despite the mostly serene environment.

The first set of swinging doors leads Soleil through two sets of sliding glass doors before she is confronted by an old gray metal detector. It's rudimentary in its setup, perhaps a discarded relic of airport security circa 1990, before liquids were banned and stripping and hair checks were mandatory for clearance to travel. A female officer guards the front of the metal detector instructing people to slide their purses and other belongings toward her on the rickety wooden table between the wall and the security device. Soleil walks through and surprisingly the thing beeps, but the officer doesn't give her a second glance. She doesn't urge Soleil to remove all metals, real or fake, and try again. Instead, the officer haphazardly searches through her oversized tote bag with a night stick, looking, but not.

Satisfied with whatever she doesn't see, the officer hands Soleil her bag back and grants her passage into the massive hospital waiting room with a gesture of her baton. Patient check-in kiosks stand on the half wall parallel to the metal detector. A line of three people is formed in front of a woman on the phone sitting behind a half panel of plexiglas. The sign above her reads patient information center. To Soleil's right sits a lone, disinterested male nurse behind a wooden desk in plain gray blue scrubs. She walks up to him. He doesn't acknowledge her, even though the sign above his head touts the quality of the hospital employees as being caring, committed, and priceless.

"Excuse me." Soleil interrupts his concentration from the game he's playing on his phone.

"May I help you?" He asks without looking up from the screen.

"I want to know if you have a patient here. In the emergency room. In the hospital," she says, trying to make a clear thought out of disjointed words.

"That's patient information over there," the nurse gestures with his head.

"I know, but she's on the phone and I don't know if I'm even supposed to be here."

He lifts one eye. "Who are you here for?"

"Barker Gordon. He would have come in around seven this morning. Maybe with a gunshot wound. Maybe in critical condition or life-threatening injuries."

"He's here. Who are you?"

"I'm Soleil."

"Okay, Soleil. Who are you?" The nurse demands, still playing his game.

"I'm his . . ." Soleil pauses. She's never had to define what she is to Barker because he always did it for her. He always gave whatever satisfactory explanation he could come up with to whomever was asking to quash curiosity without being too serious. Now it's her turn to do the same. She tries again.

"I'm his, —" Soleil looks down on the unshaven nurse who's suddenly interested enough to look at her eyes as she struggles for a definition of who and what she is to a man who might be dead.

"I'm his girlfriend." Soleil manages quietly.

"Well, you can wait with his mom." The nurse rudely points toward a brown-skinned, gray- haired woman sitting with her back to them.

The nurse buries his face back in his game dismissing her. Soleil turns away from the desk and walks around the back of the hospital waiting room, passing the woman behind the plexiglas with a line of five people now. She claims the last seat along the back wall. The faux leather is soft beneath her; the multi-colored, striped, cushioned back melts around her low slouch.

Soleil hides her stare of the brown-skinned woman who looks out the massive front hospital windows. The gold plated MK on the toes of her shoes gives her away as Barker's mother, even if the nurse hadn't told her who she was. She, too, apparently has an affinity for designer shoes the same as her son's love of Cole Haan loafers.

Like her son, the luxury brand shoes compliment the luxury attire. The woman is dressed in an elegant pants suit; brown slacks and red blazer. A silk scarf of reds, blues, and golds wraps around her neck and bustles from the front of her jacket, hiding whatever blouse she's wearing beneath it. She is regal; an understated relic of beauty whose soft features, even at the corners of her eyes, glow without makeup. There is no sign of the thick scars at the corners of her eyes that crowd the edges of her son's face. Her only accessories are her small, gold hoop earrings and one gold ring on her right hand. She is a saturnine woman, stoically waiting for whatever news is to come from the double doors that swing open and shut between the male nurse and the woman still denying standing, waiting families the patient information they have come for.

Soleil closes her eyes and allows darkness to find her as her other senses kick in to overdrive. Bits and pieces of conversations waft in and out of her ears, mixed with the sounds from the three flat screen televisions hanging on the wall above her head. She breathes in the conversations of cancer, and exhales banter between talk show hosts hoarding two of the televisions tuned to local news stations, and sports highlights from the third TV blasting ESPN. With each breath, she notices the smell in the air. It's not mint. Eucalyptus, maybe. What it is not is the distinct hospital smell of bleach and other disinfectants used in excess to cover the stench of human feces and death. Even in it's choice of scent the hospital exceeds expectations, considering it's locale and the nature of its clientele.

Soleil counts her breaths passing time in inhales and exhales. It's the way she passed her time earlier that morning laying next to Barker in bed. He greeted her the night before with an exotic arrangement of flowers and an array of oils for her bath. He brought the apology bouquet and gift basket after Soleil told him the same truth about her jaunt with Ebony for three days straight. After three days of blows to the abdomen, back, and face, Barker finally believed the facts that remained consistent. He rewarded Soleil with an ephemeral kindness she and her body appreciated for the moment it lasted. He spoke softly as she bathed, and turned his head at the sight of the black and blue bruises he imprinted on her body. They slept next to each other without touching and he pretended to be a shadow of the charismatic man she met outside Cracker Barrel. The man she loved, even though he didn't exist. Barker left her apartment with a smile and an "I'll call you, Gorgeous," the four-word phrase, a reminder and warning to wait by the phone.

"Mrs. Gordon, I'm Dr. Taylor Thomas," Soleil hears an unknown voice say to the woman across from her.

"It's Ms. Gordon, Dr. Thomas," Barker's mother says in a steely voice. "I've been a divorcee a long time now."

Soleil opens her eyes to see Barker's mother standing before the doctor in the three-piece black suit. She stands as well, creeping toward the outskirts of their perimeter; close enough to listen, but far enough away that they don't notice her covert invasion.

"Excuse me, *Ms.* Gordon, my apologies," Dr. Thomas says turning red in the face.

He adjusts his plastic-framed, black glasses and runs his hands through his short crop of salt and pepper hair before continuing. "There's really no easy way to say this," Dr. Thomas begins apologetically, "but we lost your son."

Soleil staggers more closely toward Dr. Thomas and Ms. Gordon as her bowels somersault inside of her. She shuffles her feet closer to the regal woman and the doctor delivering news that can only come from his mouth. The drag of each foot brings her closer to the conversation she's been waiting and wanting to overhear since Troy's earlier speculation. It doesn't matter that her first meeting with Barker's mother is without him.

"He lost too much blood before he arrived and he just didn't survive the wounds. One bullet was lodged in such a way we just couldn't get to it. I'm sorry."

Ms. Gordon says nothing.

"I'm sorry to interrupt, but are you talking about Judge Barker Gordon?" Soleil asks to reconfirm what she's already overheard.

Both Ms. Gordon and Dr. Thomas turn to her. Their eyes are daggers toward the woman with coffee-stained clothes, wild hair, and the stench of wild animals emanating from her skin.

"Who are you?"

The pointed voice belongs to Dr. Thomas. His perfected condolence coo is gone. The authoritarian of the hospital returns to question the intruder.

"I'm Soleil. Soleil St. James."

"And you are?"

"I'm his . . ." Soleil hesitates. "I'm his girlfriend," she ekes out.

"I'm so sorry for your loss," Dr. Thomas softens his voice.

He reaches his arm toward her, grazing the side of her bruised body with his fingertips. Soleil shrinks away from the foreign hand, taking a step behind herself. Ms. Gordon's hand finds her back and offers support. No words spoken between, before, or after Dr. Thomas announced her son was dead, but she offers her hand.

"Are you okay, Miss St. James?" Dr. Thomas asks quickly scanning her body.

He sees nothing from her head to her feet until he comes back to her face. His keen medical eye sees through the carefully applied paint that's long since faded with sweat. What's left is splotchy, purple coverage that no longer blends with her bruises.

"Are you okay, Miss St. James?" Dr. Thomas asks a second time. "Did you fall?"

His follow-up question leads to an easy out. It prods her for a sensible answer to a question that has no beginning. A question Ebony never asked because she knew. A question Troy never asked because Soleil told him with the confidence of a friend. Dr. Thomas is a stranger. A stranger will want to know the who, the what, the why, the where, and the when, when all she can offer is a body of bruises and last night.

"Miss St. James," Dr. Thomas snaps Soleil's name to bring her out of her stupor.

Ms. Gordon remains silent and supportive, her hand still on Soleil's back. She moves it up and down. The motion slightly aggravates the line of size 11 bruises planted there, but Soleil doesn't tell her to stop. They are allies.

"Miss St. James." Dr. Thomas snaps again. "Did you fall or have some sort of accident. You have several bruises in your face, especially around your eyes and along your cheekbones."

"I didn't fall."

"Then do you mind my asking what happened?"

"No, I don't mind you asking." Soleil answers,

Dr. Thomas's exhales a loud stream of breath. Soleil shrugs without resolve to be more agreeable or accommodating. Ms. Gordon's hand never wavers. It never stops its up and down motion along the length of bruises. It never stops working to impart comfort where only agitation, frustration, fear, and pain have lived for the last six months.

"Miss St. James, would you mind being checked out by one of our doctor's just to make sure you're alright? And Ms. Gordon you can come with me to the morgue to identify the body before it is released to the police and medical examiner."

Dr. Thomas is once again the hospital authoritarian issuing directives instead of waiting for wayward women to bend to his whims.

"Okay," Ms. Gordon and Soleil say hesitantly, though Soleil notices the older woman's voice is veritably stronger than her own.

"By the way," Dr. Thomas adds, "you may both need to give a statement to the police to help with the investigation of Judge Gordon's murder."

Dr. Thomas allows the natural pause in the conversation to linger as he reads their expressions.

Satisfied with nothing he adds, "Once again, I'm so sorry for your loss."

He turns on his heels and walks across the tile made to look like marble. Soleil follows behind him. Ms. Gordon is behind her. With every step, her reassuring hand is at Soleil's back. Dr. Thomas passes the male nurse who scans the computer screen with his eyes pretending to work. They turn in the space between the nurse and the now moving line formed in front of the woman in charge of patient information. They walk single file behind Dr. Thomas. He leads the trio across the double-doored threshold into the belly of the hospital, but Soleil and Ms. Gordon lag behind him.

Soleil hesitates in the entry way, hovering between her past and her future, staring at the wall of televisions behind her, focused on the two from the local news stations showing the crime scene footage from the courthouse she didn't see herself. The footage Troy told her about with excitement. The footage that was captured in one single picture that didn't impart the one thousand words it promised. Soleil hovers in the doorway between the waiting room and the bowels of the emergency room, watching the competing stations vie for attention with the same story. One station stays on the video, the other cuts back to the anchor. Dawn appears on television, the red banner beneath her head tells Soleil the news she already knows.

Victim in Courthouse Shooting Dies, Sheriff to Release ID

Soleil remains standing, hovering between her two worlds until Dawn disappears from the television screen and the talk show takes over in the regularly scheduled programming. She turns away from the wall of headlines and highlights to follow Dr. Thomas to the other side of the waiting room. Every step of the way, the woman who just lost her son, whom Soleil has yet to properly and formally meet, leaves her reassuring hand at her back, leading her into her new unknown life.

23.

"Who the victim is, is still unknown," Boyce says to the small crowd gathered in the station conference room. "I think that missing detail alone is enough to sustain us through the five and six."

No one gathered in the room with him speaks. Instead, three faces stare across the long oak conference table at six other faces. Boyce's long, oblong shadow is cast across the room from the late-afternoon sun beaming through the windows at the back of the room. He is the ringmaster of this news circus which, for the last hour, has resembled more of a cat fight instead of a healthy debate about coverage.

"All I'm saying is, we don't have enough to go wall to wall for 90 minutes after we just did two hours with no information." Dawn sighs.

"Dawn, it doesn't matter what you say. You're not anchoring," Julia snaps from her perch across the table.

"You're right, I'm not." Dawn stands. Kelly and Jennifer stand up beside her. "I can go and prepare for my own damn show, and you guys can figure this shit out yourselves."

"Dawn, sit down," Boyce snaps.

Dawn slams her body back into her seat, taking her time to adjust her legs and arms in the unconfined space. Kelly and Jennifer gingerly return to their rolling chairs, unsure of whether they should stay for the next round of verbal sparring or dismiss themselves ahead of time.

"We have an hour and a half until the five and we need to come up with a plan that will sustain us throughout the show. Even if we don't go to wall to wall," Boyce concedes. "But we still need big team coverage off the top and an update on the quarter."

"So far, it seems like all we have is the nuts and bolts of what happened, reactions, and security." Linden chimes in.

Linden Beale has only been at WABN a few years, but with the classic look of tall, tan and handsome, he has stolen viewers hearts with his dyed jet black hair, and deep brown eyes. He is the stud to Julia's cougar, even if he is lazy by most accounts, he can tell and sell a good story when it is necessary. He and Julia click with a chemistry most anchor teams, including the long gone days of Matt and Meredith, would envy.

"Three angles are not enough to keep us going at five, five thirty and six, even with commercial breaks, weather, traffic, and all the other bullshit pacers to get us through," Dawn says.

"Are excuses the only thing you have to offer?" Julia asks.

"No, but the solutions I offered an hour ago you shot down with excuses of your own. So one of us is going to have to put ego aside."

"Now is not the time." Boyce snaps at both Dawn and Julia as he pushes himself off the wall.

He pops his brown suspenders against his tan and white striped shirt then shoves his hands into his khaki pants pockets. The pressure from his hands forces his stomach further over the waist band of his trousers. His nervous tendencies on full display are exaggerated and exacerbated by the three shots of espresso he had in a one-hour span.

"Dawn, if you think you can line up three live interviews that will stay with us throughout, I'm fine with having them as sidebars. But you know the police won't talk when they know as much as we do right now. They barely talk when they do know something."

"Let me send three messages and I'll get you an answer."

"So it's Dawn to the rescue," Julia mumbles to Linden.

"Isn't it always." Dawn cuts her eyes at the evening anchors.

"Ladies! Not. Now." Boyce slams his fists on the cherry oak of the conference table.

Julia furrows her brow but whatever witty comeback she has in retort remains folded on the inside of her lips. She shakes her head at Dawn, whose attention is buried in the messages on her phone. Julia sighs and leans back in her stiff rolling chair and closes her eyes. She brings her fingertips to her temples and massages the growing headache from the meeting that refuses to end. A charm bracelet on her wrist makes tinkling sounds every time it clinks against the cuff button of her rust colored blazer.

For the entire time since Julia and Dawn have been off the air and the breaking news team gathered in the conference room, the only voices offering ideas on further coverage have been Dawn, Julia, Boyce, and an occasional peep or two from Linden. Morning anchors Marcus and Kirsten sit at the end of the conference table nearest to Boyce with their heads propped on their hands fighting sleep. Reporters Tarren Tyler and Owen Major sit at the opposite end of the conference table across from Dawn, Kelly, and Julia, feigning attention. Their pens and note pads are in front of them, but after an hour of argument, the two only have three lines of scribbles between them that will have to pass for two 1:15 angles in the evening newscasts.

"Dawn, any word on those interviews?" Boyce breaks the tense silence in the room.

Dawn's phone vibrates and dings on the table in perfect response to Boyce's question. She scans the brief text, then sets the phone back down on the table.

Looking up at everyone and no one, she says, "I have a private investigator and a criminology professor from UNF both confirmed to do a panel discussion with us at five-thirty." Dawn milks the moment, letting her save sink in to the tired and agitated crowd.

"Okay," Boyce says, impatient with Dawn's histrionics.

"The panel will give the reporters a break and time to try and forward their 5 p.m. angles to the six without worrying about something separate for five-thirty."

"Anything else?"

"I'm waiting on a call back from the State Attorney's Office and the Sheriff. An ASA seems more likely. The guy I worked with during the Dunn trial, I met him again this weekend at the mayor's luncheon. He might come through for me. If not for the 90 for my show, at least, and we can turn around sound or a statement or whatever we get for the 11."

"Of course, you'd get something just for your show, now wouldn't you," Julia says standing from the table.

"I might as well help myself while I'm helping you."

"Julia, we're almost done. Sit down," Boyce demands

It's now Julia's turn to fold her body into the conference room chair. She takes her time smoothing the textured fabric of her white A-line dress about her, before she sits completely. The final touch, crossing and re-crossing her legs as Dawn had done earlier, when she was ready to storm out of the room with Kelly and Jennifer in tow.

Boyce waits for Julia's grandstanding to end before proceeding.

"Thank you, Dawn," he says graciously.

Julia and Linden snicker. Boyce snaps his head at them, but does not dish out an acerbic warning or reminder of decorum.

"Here's what we're going to do." Boyce clears his throat. "Tarren, you and Owen will give me nuts and bolts in your scene setters before your pieces run. Tarren, you take reaction. Owen, you take security. Julia and Linden will include the important details of the shooting in setups and tosses before coming to you. You two, will focus on what's happening now."

Boyce paces around the room as he monologues his vision of the newscast; talking with his hands and making sure to look everyone in their eyes to drive home his points.

Dawn watches Boyce with amusement, until he comes to stand right behind Julia and Linden to stare directly at her, Kelly, and Jennifer

"We'll use Jorah Anderson's look live he put together for us from this morning in the five-thirty before introducing our panel, and we'll let that breathe for the whole half hour before going to the six. Kelly, I want you and Jennifer to take the lead on setting up the panel in the five-thirty rundown, for the anchors before starting on your show."

"Of course," Kelly says. "I produce two hours that aren't mine and another half hour that isn't mine before I even get to start on our show."

"What was that Ms. Boulden?" Julia dares.

Not backing down from the challenge, Kelly sits up straight and stares the elder anchor down before beginning, "I said, I produce two hours that aren't mine and another half hour that isn't mine before I even get to start on our show."

"The most important show is always the show that's next on air, so I'm sure the three of you won't mind helping out today with the shows that really matter," Julia says, ignoring Kelly and staring straight at Dawn.

"Keep telling yourself that," Jennifer mumbles.

Dawn and Kelly snicker aloud at the half heard diss.

"That's enough!" Boyce slaps his hands down on the table. "Dawn and Julia, Tarren, Owen, everyone, we are done! You have your assignments and you have about an hour to get them done. I want our coverage flawless."

"I can't wait to see those discreps," Jennifer mutters.

Kelly giggles.

"So help me God, I will change everyone's schedule for good!" Boyce screams. "Producer shuffles, anchor shuffles, show shuffles. Julia and Linden in the morning, and *Weekday Roundup with Julia Gillé* will replace *Dawn in the Evening.*"

"Wasn't that the show I was brought here to replace? Dawn asks, glowering at Julia and Boyce. "Good luck trying to bring that back."

With one last sideways glance at an open-mouthed Julia and a fuming Boyce, Dawn floats out of the conference room door with a satisfied smile. Kelly and Jennifer usher behind her.

24.

Down the street in a hulking building of protection and pain, remorse and regret, officers usher Ebony into a cold, gray paneled walled room. They leave her in a wobbly chair. One leg is shorter than the other. The metal table in front of her creaks anytime she rests the weight of her elbows on it's surface. She sits in the room alone, for hours, or maybe it's just minutes.

It's the room where Sergeant Jay Wilson stuck her after stripping her of whatever evidence she was wearing. Her black hoodie with the two holes in the front pocket, and the blood stains from where she was caught in the crossfire of Barker's blood-filled cough are gone. James made her give them up as she turned herself into the police. Now she sits in the cold room, nails scratching against her hands in her lap, goose bumps rising on her naked arms and shoulder flesh as she waits for Sgt. Wilson to return and tell her what to do next.

Ebony waits inside the belly of the Jacksonville Sheriff's Office downtown headquarters. It's where she and James came together after the news went off, after he processed her overload of information as a reality he could not run from; a reality that in Ebony's mind *he* set in motion. Telling him her truth made him as much a part of her morning rendezvous as her Lady.

The Lady Smith, the no longer smoking gun, is also in the hands of the police. The empty remains of what she did are with the police as well. Every piece of evidence Ebony wore or carried is now sealed in separate evidence bags and tagged with a number. Everything except her hair. They wanted what they thought was her wig, until they realized the mass of strands did not detach, but grew out of her scalp in a corkscrew curl pattern, she tamed with conditioner and a hot wand.

James stood between Ebony and Sgt. Wilson as she handed over her belongings to the police one by one. He played mediator when the Sergeant nodded at her head, asking for the glass-filled "wig" to match the strands still stuck in the cracked window of her car. James nodded his no, whispered why the hair was an impossibility, and offered an awkward smile at the officer's inherent prejudice of seeing a black woman with hair nearly as long as Ebony is tall.

The teachable moment ended with Sgt. Wilson offering an apology toward Ebony before he returned to his formalities; checking off boxes on a list of evidence he needed in custody to properly process the crime she did not commit. Now only two formalities remained after hair-gate. Sgt. Wilson needed the one item she did not bring with her. Her car. It's still in her garage with it's dented door and smashed driver's side windows. The other item they need is her photograph. Not a mugshot, but photographs of her back and head. Her own body of proof showing she was in a struggle. The blue-black marks lining parts of her skin still waiting to turn their deepest color on her back, and around her neck. This is the only evidence left to get.

The light wood door of the interrogation room opens wide and Sgt. Wilson walks in. He is dressed in plain clothes. A shabby seersucker suit and tie instead of the black, standard issue uniform of a lowly patrol officer. He shuts the door behind him, but Ebony still manages to get a glimpse of James's poker face before he disappears from her view again. The sight of him waiting as her attorney of record makes her double over from the lightness in her belly, and forget what she knows about Barker. James makes her forget, if only for a moment, the reason she sits in a cold room, in a wobbly chair at an uneven table.

Sgt. Wilson sits in the cushioned, gray pleather chair across from Ebony. It does not rock unevenly under his weight. All four legs of his chair are level on the ground. He slides a yellow legal pad and red pen across the table to her and sits back in the chair with his arms resting on the industrial strength plastic, black arm rails. The entire police headquarters could burn down, but those arm rails would remain. They would be deformed and misshapen globs of tar, standing testament to interrogations that took place before further tragedy or triumph.

"Ms. Jones thank you so much for turning yourself in this afternoon," Sgt. Wilson says in a tired gravelly voice. "I'll make sure the state attorney knows you came in on your own. Maybe that will help in how she chooses to proceed in this case."

The pack a day of cigarettes he smokes is evident in every syllable. The stench of his vice emanates from his clothing, skin, and breath. His smell detracts from the mock kindness of his words. It time-travels her back to the morning when she stared at a man in all black with an intricate tie knot, and the smell of peppermints failed to cover his natural body odor mixed with his liquor, tobacco, and caffeine habit.

". . . So all you need to do is write down what happened this morning and we'll go from there." Sgt. Wilson stands from the rickety table. It creaks from the pressure of his weight.

"Excuse me?" Ebony questions his instructions.

"Ms. Jones," he says, milking her name.

"Yes."

"I need you to write down what happened this morning before we go any further."

"I'm not sure I should do that," Ebony says, her voice rising and hands scratching.

She and James never talked about a confession on their way to the police station. They didn't talk about anything at all besides what he told her she had to hand over for evidence. Then he told her to keep her mouth shut as they walked into the ominous building on Bay Street where her life turned to unknown and uncharted criminal territory for someone who had yet to commit a crime.

"I need to speak with James."

"Ms. Jones, I'm sorry that will not be possible until I have your statement," Sgt. Wilson says losing the syrupy, gravelly drawl in his voice.

"I can't give you my statement until I speak with James. He's my attorney."

"Are you even listening. . ."

"No."

"Ms. Jones, ASA Parnell can't be your attorney. He's an ASA."

"Sgt. Wilson, I don't mean to be disrespectful, but why don't you ask him before you make an assumption about what ASA Parnell will do and be for me."

The plain clothes detective flings open the light, wooden door of the interrogation room and steps out in a huff. Ebony can hear hushed mumbles between James and the sergeant, but she can't make out their words. Her involuntary shivers from sitting in the cold interrogation room keep her from focusing on the sounds outside the door. In just a tank top and yoga pants, Ebony tries tricking her mind into telling her body she's not cold.

"She's not confessing," James yells flinging the interrogation room door wide open.

Five bodies fight to be first through the door, but Ebony only recognizes three. James manages to push himself through first, using his short height and stocky build to his advantage. The state attorney follows behind him. The click of her heels disappears from the linoleum outside the door to the thin blue carpet inside the interrogation room. Sgt. Wilson and two uniformed officers bring up the flank. They crowd Ebony in a semicircle opposite her uneven chair. The door slams closed. Their proximity in the claustrophobic room intensifies; their stares rain down on her in the wobbly chair where she rubs her hands against her exposed arms and shoulders to keep warm.

James breaches the semicircle to stand next to Ebony. She places her fingertips on the black plastic arm rail of the chair; he covers them with his entire hand. It is their first intimate touch today. The state attorney clears her throat. She notices.

With James by her side, Ebony takes the boost in her confidence to confront every one else in the room with her eyes. The state attorney's dirty blond and gray hair is cut in a severe bob. Her split ends take up most of the cut, but the original style is still evident from the round roller-brushed bangs. The framing of her hair leads right into a thick, pearl choker squeezed around her chubby throat. Matching pearl studs glint from her ears. Her only other accessory is a big-faced, rose gold watch squeezed around the fat flesh of her wrist. It appears beneath her long sleeved, navy blue frock. Sensible, two-inch, black, square-toed heels complete her ensemble.

Ebony stares into her minimally painted face. Splotchy foundation, concealer in areas where nothing is concealed, brown mascara, and eyebrow pencil around her eyes give her the appearance of a spotted duck. Though not much taller than James, she appears towering and imposing in person, even more so than when Ebony's seen her on TV.

"Ms. Jones, I presume," the state attorney says, her voice soft and full of southern inflection.

"Yes," Ebony says, sitting up straight in the uneven chair.

"Do you understand why you're here today?"

"Yes."

"Do you understand what you've done?"

"I'm turning myself in, but I haven't done anything," Ebony answers.

"Ms. Jones, that's a matter for the courts. If you choose to go to court. Otherwise, we could end this matter very quickly with a statement from you on that pad there and a plea deal worked out between James and I, in the next few weeks. No muss, no fuss."

The state attorney finishes her pitch with a smile in just one corner of her mouth.

"She's not giving a statement," James yells. "I told Jay that, and I've told you that. No statement. No deal. We'll take our chances in court."

"We?" The state attorney questions with raised eyebrows.

Ebony notices the expression amidst their spat. The line of the prosecutor's brow pencil raises more on her face than the actual hairs of her eyebrows.

"Yes. We." James says definitively. "Consider this my notice of an extended leave of absence to last through the duration of the case, trial, and possible appeals process. When it's over, I'll return to my office to finish my responsibility as an assistant state attorney."

Ebony shivers her pride in James's direction. She keeps her head down, smiling to herself, arms working against her shoulders in a self hug to stimulate warmth, when she really wants to hug him. In her chair shivering and wobbling, James's hand remains on hers, covering the manicured nails of her fingertips.

"Suit yourself, James. The charge is murder in the second degree. We just got word Judge Gordon died."

"At least there's a point to all of this now." Ebony blurts.

"Hush, Ebony," James admonishes.

"No, James, let your girlfriend keep talking. More outbursts, and this conversation will be all the confession I need."

"Ebony, don't speak." James turns to the State Attorney, "Second degree murder. That's better than what I thought you'd go for."

"And what is that James?"

Ebony follows every throw of the tete a tete between James and the state attorney with her head. Staring at his mouth, she watches him enunciate every syllable as he says, "Murder in the first."

"Now that you mention it, maybe we can convene a grand jury for first degree. . ."

"You and I both know, no grand jury will indict a battered woman with fresh bruises."

"What is he talking about?" The state attorney snaps at Sgt. Wilson.

Ebony takes the moment to finally smile at James, but it doesn't land on her intended target.

"He's talking about the mass of bruises on my sore back from when I was slammed against my car so hard my body shattered the glass and my ass left a dent."

"Say some more, Ms. Jones," the state attorney drawls.

"What would you like me to say?" Ebony goads with Schadenfreude intentions of her own.

"Shut up, Ebony," James glowers.

"No, James, let her continue."

Ebony stares silently at the prosecutor. She goes mute, letting her attention wane, diverting her eyes from person to person, every few seconds, so they can see the object of her interest jump from each of them to her shivering self and back again.

"Sgt. Wilson, I want a full report of what happened on my desk by first appearances tomorrow."

The state attorney breaks the half-circle, charging for the door.

"But ma'am, we only have witness statements and none of them saw anything, that's why I tried to get a confession."

"That's why you were being nice to me, Sgt. Wilson?" Ebony feigns hurt feelings. "I thought you felt sorry for me because I was cold. You wanted me to confess? To what? I haven't done anything wrong except be beaten and damn near strangled within an inch of my life by a man you all protected when I called 9-1-1 on him the first time it happened, two years ago."

"Goddamn it Ebony, shut the fuck up!" James yells.

His breath covers her as does his hand. His hand he doesn't realize hasn't moved from her fingertips since he first touched her.

"Trouble in paradise I presume." the state attorney mocks as she walks out of the interrogation room onto the linoleum tile of the hallway. "It's all going to come out in discovery anyway. Book her."

The wooden door slams behind her. The two patrol officers approach Ebony, one with his handcuffs drawn. She stands, finally breaking the slight contact between she and James. The one with the cuffs wrenches her arms behind her back. Ebony winces in pain but makes no noise. The silver bracelets are shackled loosely onto her wrists behind her body. Sgt. Wilson holds the door open as the patrol officers march Ebony out of the room.

She follows in the footsteps of the state attorney to her unknown future, satisfied knowing she's told her story. She's satisfied that she's given two sentences to a woman who will now have to rethink her prosecution strategy. The words that are meant to be used against her in a court of law will prove she is not a criminal, and that there is no crime committed in ridding the world of a woman-beating bastard, the bastard's mother doesn't even like.

25.

The computerized voice of the automated woman on Nathan's voice mail instructs Johnnie to leave a message. She sucks her teeth and declines for the fifth time, hitting the end button on her steering wheel. Snaking her car through the winding roads of her Arlington neighborhood, Johnnie approaches her home on the cul-de-sac. With the roof of the house in view, she taps the button for the garage on the rearview mirror. The door is completely open when she gets to the foot of the driveway, but she doesn't pull in.

There parked in the driveway directly behind Nathan's 4Runner, which is pulled neatly into the garage, is a yellow Mini Cooper Johnnie has never seen before. The vanity plate on the bumper of the daffodil-colored car reads I H8 ME 2.

I guess this isn't Miss Jessie's first home wrecking rodeo.

Johnnie rolls her eyes at her wayward thought, pushing the name Danielle dropped on her hours earlier from her mind.

He would never.

The reassurance of her mind doesn't make it to her heart. Johnnie pulls her fire-engine red Camry into the garage next to Nathan's SUV. Her tires purposefully screech inside the small contained space.

Jostling bags across her body, Johnnie steps out of the car and slams the door. The yellow semi-luxury car remains in its place behind the 4Runner just outside the open garage door. It's owner hasn't run out of her house for a quick conspicuous escape. The car, with its taunting license plate, remains in the driveway as if it belongs, instead of Johnnie and her Camry.

She shuffles her way to the door that leads inside the house, trying to balance her bags and cloudy thoughts. She fails falling into the door frame. Johnnie slaps one hand against the wall and the other against the garage door opener. In the doorway she grips the frame until the whirring of the door ends with a low thud, and the overhead light clicks off automatically.

In the silent space of the garage, Johnnie can make out noises coming from inside her house. A high-pitched, shrill laugh and giggle is the loudest. It belongs to Danielle. It's the sound she makes when she's tickled relentlessly. Her shrieks of joy drown out any other voices, and Johnnie knows there are at least two more.

She releases her grip from the door frame and tests the balance on her own two feet. Steady, Johnnie wipes her clammy palms across her jeans, then turns the handle to go inside the house. The alarm pad on the other side of the door frame beeps twice as soon as she pushes the door open. It announces her presence, but it, too, is drowned out by laughter; Danielle's and the immature giggles of adults.

Johnnie steps through the door into the kitchen, kicking it closed behind her. The alarm system beeps one time. Danielle and two grown voices continue their chorus of laughter. Adding to the discordant chaos is "Let It Go" blasting from the television where *Frozen* is playing in HD.

No heads turn in Johnnie's direction. No startled and caught faces look her way. She is home and invisible inside her own life. Johnnie comes completely into the kitchen and sets her bags on the quartz island. Nathan kills Danielle with tickles all over her squirming little body. A woman, who looks recently familiar, sits on the floor next to them laughing uncontrollably.

Nathan and Danielle roll around on the carpet for minutes more. Danielle laughing and singing "let me go, let me go" to the tune of "Let It Go" coming to an end in the movie. Johnnie smiles, ignoring the woman and focusing intensely on her daughter and her husband. Danielle is on her stomach clawing at the carpet, desperate to get away from Nathan's gyrating fingers, when she looks up.

"Mama," Danielle shrieks in giggling glee.

"Hey, Baby," Johnnie slurs.

She swallows to unstick her tongue from the roof of her mouth. The house is silent save for Danielle's babbling. *Frozen* is muted and Nathan and the strange woman clumsily scramble to their feet, uttering unintelligible words in explanation to unasked questions.

"You finished with your emer-gen-cy, Mama?" Danielle asks walking to Johnnie.

"Yes, Baby."

Johnnie turns away from the island and meets Danielle at the refrigerator. She pulls the heavy stainless steel door open for her daughter, who fits her body in the space beneath Johnnie's arm and stands in the light of the fridge. Danielle grabs her pink Doc McStuffins cup from the bottom shelf on the door, turns it up to her lips, and tilts her head all the way back.

"Ah" Danielle smacks her lips together after her shot of juice.

Johnnie shakes her head recognizing the imitation of her daughter's behavior even through her hazy, heady thoughts.

"Dani, take your juice upstairs and let Mama talk to Daddy and. . ."

"Miss Jessie," Danielle says excitedly.

"Thank you, Baby." Johnnie says looking up from Danielle to where the woman stands statue still in the living room.

She is noticeably distant from Nathan.

"Let Mama talk to Daddy and Miss Jessie, and when we're done, I'll come get you and you can help me make dinner."

"Okay, Mama," Danielle says running out of the kitchen, through the front hallway, and up the stairs to the second floor.

Johnnie waits with an assassin's silence until she can no longer hear Danielle's feet pattering above her.

"I take it that's your yellow car in my driveway."

"It is," Miss Jessie says, her voice cracking.

"Bold."

"Maybe I should go."

"Or maybe you should stay, so I can get to know you as well as *my* daughter and husband do. They seem to be very fond of you."

"Johnnie, it's not what you think," Nathan interrupts.

"And what is it that I'm thinking, *husband?*"

"Johnnie. Don't. Lisa is only here because Danielle insisted."

"So she's Lisa now?"

"Dr. Edwards, I'm Lisa Jessie," the woman introduces herself. "Danielle was in my group today on the field trip at the zoo. I'm the teacher's assistant for Miss St. James."

Johnnie looks at the woman from head to toe. The green capri pants that were hidden by children's grabbing hands when Johnnie dropped Danielle off, hug at all of Lisa's young, ripe, womanly curves. The easily dismissed white school polo that hangs from her shoulders is peppered with red, brown, and yellow smudges in the shape of fingerprints. Miss Jessie is Miss Lisa. Johnnie nods in stunned recognition.

"Nice to see you again," Johnnie says mustering a smile. "How was the field trip?"

"It was great. Danielle was a joy to have in the group."

"Was she now?"

"Johnnie, leave Lisa alone. She was just doing Danielle a favor," Nathan interjects.

"And what favor would that be, *husband?*"

"I was running late getting Danielle from the field trip. The school called me because Danielle was crying. Lisa was with her and offered to bring her home."

"That sounds all well and good, Nathan, except school doesn't get out until three-thirty. It's only three forty-five now."

"If I may," Lisa interrupts. "We got back from the field trip just before three. Most of the other parents who didn't chaperone with us were already there and took the kids home early. Danielle was the only one left, so I thought it would be good to bring her home to Nathan."

"So you two are just on a buddy-buddy first name basis now, huh?" Johnnie stumbles out of the kitchen toward Lisa and Nathan in the living room.

"Johnnie, let's not do this now," Nathan admonishes through clenched teeth.

"It seems like you two have been doing a lot."

"I'm going to go."

Lisa sidesteps Johnnie as they cross paths in the hallway separating the kitchen and living room. She stops at the door to the front hall closet, opens it, and grabs her purse from the top shelf.

"You seem to know our house very well." Johnnie observes leaning against the wall close to Lisa. "Almost as if you've been here before. Or several times."

"Johnnie." Nathan snaps.

Lisa says nothing. She slings her purse on her shoulder and walks to the front door on her tiptoes, ass bouncing in her wake. Johnnie follows behind; Nathan behind them both. Opening the heavy glass door, Lisa leaves without another look at the feuding couple. Johnnie steps forward to follow, but Nathan grabs her shoulders holding her back.

"She smells like lemongrass and jasmine," Johnnie says watching Lisa back her car out of the driveway. "I guess she wears Old Spice too."

With the hateful, yellow Mini Cooper and its driver gone, Johnnie steps back into Nathan, bumping him off so she can close the door. The lock turns before she completely turns around to confront her husband.

"I see why you like her."

Nathan says nothing. He stares at his wife with his chestnut eyes narrowed.

"She's got a big ass. I guess we'd make the perfect threesome for you. Her ass. My titties. It'd be paradise for you."

"It would be if you were sober," Nathan says evenly.

"I'm not drunk!"

"So why are you screaming?".

"Because. I'm tired . . . of everyone . . . thinking . . . I'm drunk . . . all . . . the . . . damn . . . time."

"Who else accused you of being drunk today?"

"It doesn't matter, Nathan. I'm suspended indefinitely anyway," Johnnie says dropping her punishment news. "And stop changing the subject. This is about you and Miss Lisa. Or Miss Jessie. Or Lisa. Whatever the fuck her name is. Which is it hun?"

Johnnie leans against the front door, allowing the cool glass to steady her so she can concentrate.

"Why are you suspended, Johnnie?"

"I killed a man today. And stop changing the subject. How long have you been sleeping with the teacher. I'm sorry, teacher's assistant."

"I can't talk to you."

Johnnie dozes against the door.

He turns past her and heads up the stairs. "Come on, Dani, let's go."

"Where the hell do you think you're going with *my child*," Johnnie yells up the stairs.

"We're leaving until you get yourself together."

"You can leave and follow that lemongrass smelling bitch if you like. But Danielle is staying here with me."

Johnnie pops her body off the front door and lunges toward the stairs. She tries to bound up the flight of 15 steps, taking them two at a time. On the last step she lunges too far and falls on her chest. Nathan stares down at her with Danielle in his arms.

"You need to sober up."

"I'm. Not. Drunk." Johnnie screams.

"Mama, don't scream," Danielle says through a startled sniffle.

"Look at you, Johnnie. You can't stand up straight without holding on to something, and you can't speak without slurring your words. You wreak of alcohol so badly that it's coming from your pores. You're drunk. You've been drunk day in and day out for the last two years."

"I'm. Not. Drunk." Johnnie repeats. This time in an unconvincing whisper into the carpet where she lays on the floor.

"You're certainly not sober."

Nathan steps over his wife. Johnnie grabs his leg as he begins to walk down the stairs. He wobbles and regains his balance jostling Danielle the entire time.

"Daddy, stop," Danielle shrieks. Fat tears fall from her face.

"Johnnie, let me go. If you make me fall with this baby, so help me God."

Johnnie holds tighter to Nathan's leg, using her grip to balance herself as she struggles to her feet on the steep staircase.

"I already told you I killed one man today. What makes you think you won't be next."

"Johnnie, you lost a patient. It happens. But if you were drunk during the operation you better hope no one finds out, because you will put this entire family in jeopardy."

"Oh, now we're a family if I get sued. That's what I thought. I make all the money, pay all the bills, and have all the responsibility, and we're a family. But if I take one little sip of something to soothe myself at the end of the day, then I'm a drunk who's on my own. Do I have that right, Naaaaaaayyyyyy-thannnnnnnnnn."

"Mama, Daddy, stop."

Nathan sets Danielle down on the step beneath him. He whispers something into her ear. She nods her head in return and makes her way down the stairs, sniffling and sobbing.

"Don't forget I allow you to live this Mr. Mom life," Johnnie says in raised belligerence. "I gave you that. You need to show me some damn respect."

"Show you some respect? Why should I respect you when you don't even respect yourself."

"I always respect myself. It's you who doesn't respect me, coming in here smelling like a wild tropical meadow, lying and saying it's Old Spice. On a first name basis with the teacher's assistant like I can't tell y'all been fucking. I am not stupid Naaaaaaayyyyyy-thannnnnnnnnn. I may be a lot of things. Even a drunk. But I'm not stupid."

"Well at least you can finally admit you're drunk."

"That's not what I said."

"As for this life you think you *allow* me to lead. I can go back to work at any time. I can go back to being an engineer whenever, wherever. I don't because of Tyler and Danielle. Somebody has to put them first, and it's for damn sure not you."

"Don't make me out to be a bad mom when you know good and damn well I'm not."

"Then, Johnnie, don't make it out like I'm living off of you when you know *I'm not.*" Nathan jogs down the stairs.

"Where the hell do you think you're going?" Johnnie screams as she follows Nathan.

"I'm taking *my* daughter and then I'm going to get *my* son, and then we're all going to get the hell away from your drunk ass."

"Don't have my kids around that bitch, you hear me." Johnnie grabs Nathan's shoulder as they descend down the final steps.

"Johnnie, get off of me." Nathan shrugs as he rounds the bend from the staircase into the hallway.

She follows closely on his heels into the living room. Nathan picks up Danielle, dressed in her jacket and backpack, and makes his way toward the garage door.

"Put my damn daughter down, Nathan." Johnnie yells. She beats his back with her fists.

"Johnnie, stop before you hit Danielle," Nathan says, shielding her head on his shoulder.

The alarm beeps as Nathan flings the door to the garage open.

"Put my daughter down!"

"Johnnie, you need help."

Nathan opens the 4Runner and places Danielle in her booster seat. Danielle's head bops from side to side. The cords of white earbuds appear beneath her braids. Nathan closes the backdoor and gets in on the driver's side. The garage door opens from where Nathan triggered it inside the SUV. Johnnie watches from the door. The hazy stupor she's been fighting takes over.

"Good-bye, Johnnie."

Johnnie opens her mouth to say something, but nothing comes out. The garage closes behind the removed vehicle. The heavy door lands with a thud. The noise forces Johnnie to bring her fingers to her temples and massage the space where a headache has formed. She inhales and exhales the residual fumes to slow her throbbing head and thinks to herself *I need a drink.*

26.

Dr. Thomas hands Soleil a drink of water. It is his last act of kindness toward her before he leaves her alone in a room with a bevy of nurses dressed in nothing more than a flimsy paper dress.

She lays on her back against the uncomfortable cushion of the exam table. The paper of the dress, and the paper covering the cushioned top of the table for sterilization crinkle and crack against each other. Soleil writhes in her own wad of worries with her eyes trained to the ceiling. Her mouth is closed. She breathes through her nose. Calming herself, she stops her twisting, her jactation, and lays still, eyes up, counting the speckled drywall tiles of the ceiling. She counts the tiles as the female doctor silently enters the room. A nod and a name is all she offers as she stands in front of Soleil's bent legs.

The doctor works; Soleil counts the tiles. The doctor pats the stirrups to tell Soleil to scoot down and spread her knees. She complies counting tiles. Gesture and action is how they communicate through the exam. The doctor pokes and prods at Soleil's bruised body with cold hands. She pushes the paper gown open, revealing her breasts and the line of purple-blue marks trailing from each of her nipples, down her obliques, and across her back. The doctor produces a small digital camera from one of her lab coat pockets, and photographs Soleil's body. She snaps shot, after shot, framing out the face. The doctor shoots with a director's eye starting wide, coming in midway, and then adjusting focus for the closeup. The eye of the camera shutters with a flashless flicker across Soleil's marked parts; the parts of her only she can identify, nameless, faceless, and meaningless to anyone else, including the police officers standing outside her exam room door. The camera shutter shudders across her body, capturing her shame in anonymity.

The doctor tucks the camera back into her lab coat pocket after taking nearly two dozen photos. The obvious part of the exam is over. Now she takes a seat on a stool perched between Soleil's legs. Tapping Soleil's knees to force her to open wider, the doctor digs inside with metal tool after metal tool, probing her insides and clipping and cutting tissue for bagging and testing. She works quickly, tapping Soleil's legs signaling completion. She leaves the room as quietly as she came, taking her specimens as a parting gift. The doctor leaves Soleil laying on her back, eyes trained to the ceiling, delaying facing the armed officers waiting for her to make a statement about the untimely death of Judge Barker Gordon.

Despite her protestations before the exam, the officers decided to wait. Now that the exam is over, Soleil makes them wait. She makes them wait as she peels herself off the body-warmed exam room table. She makes them wait as she dresses in her soiled, funky clothing. She makes them wait until *she* decides she wants to walk out of the exam room and face them with folded arms beneath her breasts, raised eyebrows, hunched shoulders, and shrouded humiliation clouding her eyes.

Soleil makes them wait.

She makes the officers wait as she takes her time walking to her own car, starting it up, and pulling behind their detail. They wait for her at a green light after she stalls at the previous red. The five-minute ride to the police headquarters from the hospital takes 15 minutes, with her obnoxiously behaving all traffic laws. Soleil makes the officers wait as she meanders and maneuvers through traffic until they arrive. They wait as she sits still in her car, in their parking lot. No one moves forward in the process of defining her life in terms of a boyfriend who never was; a man and a mendacious memory of love from another that never lasted.

Unready to face the future, and unable to return to the past, Soleil opens her driver's side door and touches the asphalt of the police parking lot with a tentative step. She forces the rest of her body out of the car before slamming the door behind her. The sound punctuates her internal profanity as she faces the officers wordlessly; one bald and one with a buzz cut, wait with no words to offer her in return.

"Let's do this," Soleil finally says aloud to their stern faces.

Buzz Cut and Baldy walk ahead of her from the back parking lot of JSO to the front of the police building. Towering above the three of them are 18 stone steps clustered in groups of six. They climb the steps together, Baldy on the right, Buzz Cut on the left, and Soleil straight up the middle. The officers lead the way into their second home, anxious and impatient to receive their statement.

Soleil makes them wait. They wait until she reaches the top step, until she, too, has arrived at the blacked out front doors. Baldy opens the doors for her and allows her entree into the kingdom no one wants to conquer. The cool air greets her, wraps around her body, and pulls her inside with a shiver. Baldy and Buzz Cut begin to walk through their domain, but Soleil does not follow behind. She does not get too far inside before she stops in her tracks. Soleil waits, waits for them to turn around, for Baldy and Buzz Cut to acknowledge that she's stopped. To make sure they see what she sees.

She knows.

Standing in the middle of the police headquarters Solei watches Ebony march from some back hallway with her hands cuffed behind her. James is by her side, holding on to her arm. Two uniformed officers march in front of her. A plain clothes detective keeps his distance behind her.

She knows.

Soleil makes everyone in the room wait as the thought crosses her mind for the second time. Ebony turns toward Soleil, reading her mind as she did the first time the two met. Everyone waits, watching the woman at the doors lift one hand from it's clasped twin and wave hello. Ebony manages the same; her shackled wrists behind her back be damned.

"Miss St. James, do you know that woman?"

The question comes from Baldy.

He speaks above the hum of the waiting and watching noise in the headquarters, demanding acknowledgment, attention, and answers. Soleil does not answer. She stares straight ahead at the woman who never told her how she left their tormentor. The woman who could only advise her to do something to make Barker never want to come back. Staring at her relationship twin, Soleil puts what few pieces she has of their shared puzzle together.

"Miss St. James, Lieutenant Gregor asked you a question," Buzz Cut snaps.

Soleil makes him wait.

She makes them both wait as she focuses on Ebony. The officers in front of her and behind her, have her nearly stripped. She stands in the cool, open police headquarters in a thin, midriff- baring tank top and black leggings. Her body is exposed. Ass on full display in the skin-clinging running tights. Nipples rise and pulse through the fabric of her black tank. Ebony's only warmth comes from her wild hair. The perfectly placed wand curls of Saturday are matted, frizzy, stringy, and dry, but the sheer volume of her strands drapes her shoulders and shields her face from view when James's hulking body is not blocking her completely.

Pity and relief subsume Soleil. The unmatched emotions wash over her body, forcing goose pimples to rise on the exposed skin of her forearms and fill heat into her flushed red face. Ebony is in shackles; a wild woman caged. Soleil watches her shuffle between her guards. Fists

162

pressed into her stomach, Soleil holds back the churn of guilt-riddled responsibility threatening to manifest itself on the police precinct floor.

"Miss St. James, if you know that woman, you need to tell us now." Baldy says, attempting to discern her relationship with their apparent suspect.

Soleil remains silent, leaving his request unanswered and ignored, the way she did the one before. She watches with her head tilted left, allowing air to pass over one side of her neck before switching the stretch to the opposite end. Muscles extend where her tension builds. Never breaking eye contact with Ebony, she watches her savior waiting to be led away. The woman she has denied knowing twice in her absence of an answer. Soleil watches Ebony wait for what's next, overtaken by a truth she wasn't ready to face, and answers to questions both asked and unuttered. Crippled in her stance, her fists bang at her belly trying to rid it of the incongruent feelings causing her to feel cold and hot all at once. Soleil watches and waits as the truth is drawn in front of her, colored in the red tint slashed across her body, and shadowed in purple like the deep, rich, fictitious shade covering her naked face.

"I know her."

Soleil answers Baldy's and Buzz Cut's question without breaking eye contact with Ebony.

"How do you know her?"

The question is ignored, as are the officers, as is the noise of the police headquarters. All speaking, mumbling, and the physical presences of everyone else, except Ebony and her police detail, are erased. Soleil watches Ebony with words on her tongue ready to unfold on her lips. She watches Ebony, finally ready to make a statement against the deceased, and in favor of the woman who has gathered them all together. She watches Ebony, a survivor of circumstance, a victim of a discriminate system, and a notch on the imaginary closed case nodule of the officers who are still on the clock, waiting until Friday to cash a check.

The officers who marched Ebony from the unseen hallway are on the move with her again. She is marched away from where she stands and deeper into the bowels of the police building. Soleil stares and waits until the officers and James walk with Ebony out of her sight. When Ebony is nearly gone, she sees what the arrested woman wants her to see. Her mouth. It moves, slowly, mouthing two words. *You're free.* She says it twice and then she is gone; her mouth disappeared, and only the memory of her lip-synced words remain.

Soleil turns to face Baldy and Buzz Cut. Four eyes stare back at two. The clouded guise of men who've had a long night, a longer morning, and the longest afternoon stare back at her. Their curiosity rises with every passing, purposeful moment of silence. They look at Soleil and delete the character of victim and pencil in partial perpetrator.

"I know her," Soleil begins. "That's Ebony. We met four days ago."

"Miss St. James, please follow us. We're going to need more than your statement," Baldy says, leading Soleil away from the front doors of the police headquarters.

He doesn't look back to see if she follows. Neither does Buzz Cut. Soleil walks behind them as she walked behind Ebony four days ago. Four days ago, she met the woman who knew her enough without her ever uttering one word of her story. Four days ago, Soleil listened to the woman who took her own advice and released her from her hiding. It is for her defense Soleil follows behind Baldy and Buzz Cut into another wing of the building where she will be presumed innocent until she either convinces them, or they suspect her of having criminally responsible guilt.

She does not wait.

She is done waiting.

27.

Dawn waits for the news package that's on the air to end. She waits until she hears the audible click of her microphone being turned on in the studio. John stands in front of her camera and cues her. Seeing herself on television with a knowing gaze through layered bangs, she speaks:

Inside the investigation . . .
The new details emerging about suspect Ebony Jones, who turned herself in, for killing Judge Barker Gordon.
The reason prosecutors say they're charging her with second degree murder, even though attorneys say she planned to shoot and kill the judge in cold blood.
That's next in our "Sound Off" when "Dawn in the Evening" continues.

Dawn looks at her prompter camera with a sober half smile as John finishes his silent countdown over the generic audio bed of music that takes the show to commercial break.

"Dawn, you're clear," John says from behind a camera.

"Thanks, John. How long is this break?" Dawn asks rifling through her scripts at the desk.

"Two-thirty."

"Thanks, John. Kelly. Kelly, can you hear me?" Dawn asks aloud in the studio waiting for Kelly to respond in her earpiece.

"I got you, Dawn. Wassup?"

"How much time do we have for "Sound Off" tonight?"

"None. We've got Breaking News. I just sent you the script. Are you still logged in?"

"No. I'm not. Read it to me."

"One minute," John yells from the studio floor.

"Breaking News just into the 9 News Now studio. In the last two minutes, we've learned Assistant State Attorney James Parnell will take a leave of absence from the State Attorney's Office to represent Ebony Jones in her second-degree murder case, for the shooting death of Judge Barker Gordon."

"In a statement sent to 9 News Now, Parnell says in part quote 'Ebony Jones has turned herself in for the shooting death of Judge Barker Gordon. I am taking a leave of absence to represent her in this criminal matter, because for once I would like to be on the right side of the law and help a battered woman escape her tormentor, instead of victimizing them all over again. I urge the media to be sensitive in reporting this case and refrain from jumping to conclusions until all the facts have come out,'" Kelly reads in Dawn's ear.

"30," John yells from the floor.

"Kelly, that sounds good. Did you make a fullscreen for the statement so we have something to put on screen? It's too long to be a reader."

"Jennifer just finished the graphic. I'm checking it now."

"15. Standby, Dawn," John yells.

"How much time do we have in this last block?" Dawn asks Kelly.

"Enough to do the breaking script and say good-bye."

"Dawn in five, four, three, two, one. Cue," John mouths.

Dawn looks up at the prompter and delivers the script Kelly read to her. She reads the words evenly, careful not to stumble, but devoid of the usual emotion and certitude she tries to impart in scripts she's written, read, and approved with her own eyes.

At the end of the script, John flashes Dawn the signal for 15 seconds left in the show. With more time to fill she adlibs a shorter version of the script she read, teasing ahead to the latest developments on 9 News Now at 11 with Julia Gillé and Linden Beale. As John counts Dawn out with his hands, she thanks her guests and the viewers for tuning in for another night of *Dawn in the Evening*, ending as John's hands reach zero.

"Clear, Dawn," John yells, stepping out from behind the cameras.

"John, let's go ahead and shoot the promos for tomorrow. We'll do two on the Judge shooting; one angle on the Judge, one on the suspect, and the third promo for whatever we have saved."

"I'm ready whenever you, Kelly and Jennifer are," John says, blowing air out of his mouth as he drops the camera cable he was coiling around his arm.

"Kelly, you ready?" Dawn asks aloud.

"We're ready in the control room," Kelly says.

Dawn waits for John to count her down before she starts adlibbing the promotions for the next day's show. With the first two promos complete, she waits for Jennifer to load the right script in the prompter before reading the third promotable. It focuses on the role the P-8A Poseidon aircraft, based at Naval Station Mayport, will play in searching for the Malaysian Airliner that disappeared.

After the third try, Dawn nails the pre-written promotable.

"Let's post," she yells in the studio.

Dawn removes her microphone, leaves it on the desk, and walks out of the studio. She walks along the back wall of offices, turns the corner past the bay of darkened windows from the long set sun, and strides straight into the conference room. The moon casts shadows of trees planted across the front parking lot into the room. Dawn turns the dimmer on the wall until there is enough light to see everyone's face without blowing out their eyes. Satisfied with the setting, she takes a seat in the rolling chair she occupied hours earlier, during the rundown meeting turned pissing match that, once again, fanned the flames of her illogical feud with Julia.

"Another exclusive for *Dawn in the Evening*. Why am I not surprised," Julia says sardonically as she sashay's into the conference room.

"What exclusive are you talking about?" Dawn asks, looking up from her phone.

"She's talking about the breaking news at the end of the show," Kelly answers walking in behind Julia. "The attorney guy only sent it to us. It was a response to one of the emails you sent after the noon post. He sent it directly to the *Dawn in the Evening* email list, no other stations were copied on it."

"That doesn't mean it was exclusive." Dawn dismisses.

"It does when Cameron Addison from NNB and Cori Shannon from 2, text you asking where you got something confirmed because they don't have it."

"Why does it matter where we got it? As long as they don't have it," Linden jokes, entering the conference room.

"You don't find it peculiar that Dawn got the exclusive right before her show ended, just like she said she would, when the suspect's been identified and booked since JSO's 4:30 update?"

"Julia, stop making something out of nothing?" Boyce says closing the door to the conference room.

"I'm glad so many of you could join us for our post meeting." Dawn scans the room stopping at Julia's, Linden's, and Boyce's faces.

"Before you get started, Julia and Linden are only here because I asked them to come in so we could do a proper handoff to the 11," Boyce responds.

Once again, three faces stare across the conference table at Julia, Linden and Boyce. Dawn, Kelly, and Jennifer sit relaxed in the uncomfortable, leather, rolling chairs, at ease now that they've reached the end of their day. Julia sits in the middle on the other side of the table with Linden and Boyce at her sides. Linden's hand rests atop Julia's, slowly stroking her skin back and forth.

"Well, let's get this over with," Dawn shakes her hair out of her eyes, then uncrosses and recrosses her legs in the chair.

"Dawn, since your team got the exclusive from James Parnell where do you suggest we go from here?" Boyce asks.

Dawn looks up slowly from the illuminated screen on her phone. "Say that name one more time."

"James Parnell. The assistant state attorney who's taking a leave of absence," Boyce adds.

"Holy shit," Dawn mutters.

"What is it?" Kelly and Jennifer say in unison.

"It's them."

"It's who? Who's them?" Boyce pushes.

"Ebony and James. I met them Saturday at the mayor's luncheon. Well, I already knew him. I met her. We took a picture together. They're a couple." Dawn spits out in choppy sentences.

"Now we know why she got the exclusive before anybody else," Julia says sucking her teeth. "She was out fraternizing with the murderer and her probably, crooked lawyer boyfriend."

"Julia, that's enough," Boyce snaps.

"Whatever."

Linden rubs Julia's hand back and forth alternating between long, slow, gentle rubs and taps on top of her protruding hand veins. Her hands tell the truth. Julia can hide the age in her face with makeup, and the age in her body with exercise and clothing, but the hands always tell the truth. They show the true wear and tear of what it means to live a long life.

"Since you know the players in this, Dawn, how do we forward our coverage?" Boyce asks.

"First, we need to call a spade a spade. This is going to be another stand your ground case. James set that up in the email he sent."

"Why do you always jump to stand your ground?" Linden asks suddenly.

"Because that's what it is," Jennifer speaks up before Dawn can respond.

"And how would you know what determines a stand your ground case?" Linden questions. "Aren't you an intern?"

"No, she's my associate producer," Dawn defends. "And even if she doesn't know all the legal ingredients for a stand your ground case. That's exactly what this one appears to be turning into. Think about it.

The state attorney announces a charge of second-degree murder, even though you can tell she wanted first with all that talk about premeditation and killing in cold blood. Then the statement we received from James says we need to be sensitive and wait for the facts, but identifies Ebony Jones as a battered woman. Sounds like Marissa Alexander all over again, only this time the dude is dead."

"Dawn, I'm really surprised hearing this from you," Boyce interjects. "You know as well as I do that Marissa Alexander's trial did not allow the stand your ground immunity."

"Maybe she'll get it in her retrial. Especially if that "warning shot" bill passes the legislature."

"I don't get it," Linden says incredulous. "How can you be so against stand your ground but favor the "warning shot" bill, which is being added as an extension of stand your ground. You can't have it both ways, sweetheart."

"First of all, I'm not your sweetheart," Dawn says coldly. "Secondly, I can want whatever I want in cases I have no part in, other than reporting. What I want as a private citizen and what I say as a public figure do not coincide."

"They do if your private thoughts seep into the copy of the words you say as a public persona. Especially in your Sound Off segment, where you often give your own personal opinion."

"You really want to know my opinion? Do you really want to know how I feel about stand your ground? George Zimmerman got away with murder. Michael Dunn got away with murder. Marissa Alexander killed no one. Her bullets hit no one. Her estranged husband and his two sons are alive, yet she was convicted and sentenced to 60 years in prison. Thank God the judge found a problem with the jury instructions and ordered a retrial. Hopefully, they all come to a deal and she can stay home on house arrest."

"This isn't about Marissa Alexander, George Zimmerman, or Michael Dunn." Linden says.

"You're right. It's not. But you wanted to know why I jumped to stand your ground. I'm telling you why. Ebony Jones is being portrayed by her attorney as a battered woman. Marissa Alexander was a battered woman. Ebony Jones is said to only have been defending herself when Judge Gordon was killed. Marissa Alexander said she was defending herself when she warned her husband to get away from her. Ebony Jones fled the scene because she was in fear for her life. It's the same reason Michael Dunn told police he left the gas station after pumping 10 bullets into a SUV full of kids, because he was too damn privileged to listen to some rap music for three and a half minutes Ebony Jones turned herself in. Michael Dunn surrendered to his neighbor, who was an officer once he got back home to Satellite Beach. You asked me why I jumped to stand your ground in this case, Linden. There's your answer. The names are different, the victims are different, the circumstances are different, but the parallel factors of the cases are the same."

"Sounds like simple self-defense to me." Boyce says.

"Even if James runs a simple self-defense case for Ebony, then it's still going to come down to the jury instructions, which will include the stand your ground statute. It's what happened in the Zimmerman case. It's what happened in the Dunn case. The jury can't convict if the law says a person has no duty to retreat and can use deadly force if they feel they're threatened, if their property is threatened, or if a crime is being committed."

"Then why was Marissa convicted?" Boyce goads.

"Because racism is still alive, and Marissa is a woman. The justice system in all of it's finite discernment has yet to tackle the injustice of intersectionality."

"Professor Anthony for the win." Jennifer giggles.

"Now, do you need anymore examples of case law and stand your ground, or can I get on with *my* post show meeting, with *my* producers?"

"Dawn, you can get on with your post meeting as soon as you confirm whether James is running an affirmative defense for Ebony Jones," Boyce says with a depleted sigh.

"Affirmative defense my ass," Julia says angrily. "That's just a nice way of saying he's going to use the law to help his girlfriend get away with murder."

"Here we go again." Jennifer shakes her head.

"So what if James helps Ebony get away with murder," Dawn snaps back. "It's about time someone deserving of stand your ground used it to get off. That's retribution and justice all wrapped up in one verdict."

"Nice to know we're thinking about the victim and justice for *his* family," Boyce reignites.

"Where was the justice for the victim in Trayvon Martin's case or Jordan Davis's case last month?"

"Just because *you* don't think they received justice doesn't mean they didn't. The justice system worked as it was supposed to. George Zimmerman got off. Michael Dunn will spend the next 60 years, which is basically the rest of his life, in prison for shooting at Jordan Davis's three friends, since the jury couldn't convict him of first degree murder."

"That's exactly my point, Boyce. How the hell does the jury find Dunn guilty of attempting to kill three out of the four people in the SUV. But the one person he actually killed and admitted to killing on the witness stand, they can't come to a decision on. It makes no sense."

"I'm glad our unbiased, fair and balanced, coverage and ideology is being passed from the top down. No matter how *any* of us feels, we can't pass judgement on either side until we have a verdict and actual justice."

"Actual justice?" Dawn shrieks. "You can't be serious. There's no justice for Jordan. There's no justice for Trayvon. Hell, Trayvon couldn't even get justice on an episode of *Law & Order: SVU* when he was shot by Paula Deen."

"That's enough."

"All I'm saying is, stand your ground is a license to kill and Ebony Jones might as well get off using it."

"You need a lesson in facts," Julia speaks up for the first time since she incited the legal and ethical debate.

"Oh really now," Dawn taunts.

"Yes. You do. Stand your ground is not a license to kill. It is the law in the state of Florida passed by the legislature in 2005 and signed into law by Governor Jeb Bush."

"Thanks to the NRA," Dawn retorts.

"Enough," Boyce says, pushing back from the table in his rolling chair.

He stands up and adjusts the suspenders holding up the front of his pants against his bulging waistline.

"Dawn, what can you get on this?"

"It may take some time to setup, but I'm sure I can get us a few exclusives with James and Ebony, and maybe even Judge Gordon's girlfriend."

"Judge Gordon's girlfriend," the room responds.

"Well, if someone had let me finish my thoughts before inciting a damn near riot in the conference room, you would know she was at the luncheon Saturday with Judge Gordon. I took a picture with all of them. James, Ebony, Judge Gordon, and his girlfriend Soleil."

"Everyone's a fan of Dawn." Julia rolls her eyes, standing up from the conference table.

"If you spent more time in the community, maybe you'd have fans too."

"I have scripts to read."

"Me too," Linden replies.

Linden and Julia both knew when it came to popularity in their viewing area Dawn was unmatched, even though Julia had been a staple on the anchor desk for decades.

"Dawn, good work tonight," Boyce says, allowing his lassitude from arguing creep into his voice. "Setup what you can as soon as you can with those interviews. I'll touch base with you in the morning about what we can do for tomorrow. Linden, Julia, and the rest of the nightside team should be good to go more in depth with the statement."

"Okay," Dawn answers.

"Let's just make sure that statement is sent out to the entire newsroom," Boyce adds.

"Asshole," Jennifer says after Boyce clears the conference room.

"Pretty much," Kelly adds.

"He can't be too much of an asshole anymore. He needs me." Dawn stands up from the conference table. "See you in the a.m."

"When do you want to go over the segments for tomorrow?" Kelly asks.

"Before show time."

"That early, huh."

28.

It is early afternoon. James and Ebony sit at opposite ends of her white suede couch, a peach throw pillow between them. It separates their difference in thought and position. Client and defendant. Accused murderer and attorney. They are no longer a couple, they are individuals. She is Ebony Jones, suspect; innocent until proven guilty in the eyes of the law, yet guilty until proven innocent in the eyes of the city. He is James Parnell, former rising star at the State Attorney's Office who's taken an abrupt leave of absence to defend the suspect in the city's second high-profile murder trial of the year.

She is the suspect who appeared in court this morning for her first appearance. The only suspect who entered the courtroom at 8:30 in the morning in an orange-red jumpsuit amongst a sea of criminals outfitted in deep forest green. She was marched into the courtroom in a chain gang, shackled at her ankles and wrists. Cameras clicked covertly from the reporters who snapped pictures in their pews reserved for spectators. The distinct sound of cell phones produced a chorus of flashing shutter whirs as the reporters gave the city it's first glimpse of Ebony Jones. This was as close to a perp walk as anyone would get, Ebony shuffling her feet into the courtroom, face a somber mask, juxtaposed against her smiling mug shot that was taken and distributed after she turned herself in.

The smiling mug shot she purposely posed for so that at the end of her life, it would look just like any other picture. A mug shot where the people who saw it would decide guilt or innocence based on the look of the assumed suspect. Ebony smiled for the cameras at the police headquarters, unashamed of the curve of her lips, just as she was unashamed of the curve of her hips and ass in her orange-red jumpsuit. She sat next to another suspect on the bench of jailbirds and waited with her eyes closed for the judge to call her name. The inmate beside her took her quiet solace as his opening to smack his lips in appreciation. He made sucking sounds with his mouth Ebony knew came from his gut. The sounds were so low only she could hear them. Only she could be disturbed. Tortured. Punished.

Then it was her turn. Standing before the judge she made eye contact the way James told her to, she spoke when spoken to, and listened respectfully as James and one of his former colleagues, argued over whether she should be remanded until trial or given house arrest James argued for house arrest since this was her first offense, she had visible scars, and the damage to her car indicated a struggle occurred before Barker was shot. He prevailed. Prevailed in advocating for his client, his first step in getting his girlfriend acquitted. However outward appearances and advocation in court is completely different from personal persecution and prosecution from the man who promised to protect her. At home, Ebony's home, she is confined to her own personal prison until a verdict is reached at trial.

They sit on the couch arrested in their own thoughts. The surface of the cracked-glass coffee table belies what's beneath their visage. On Ebony's side is an assortment of products lined up in the order of their failure. Lotion, cocoa butter, shea butter, coconut oil, tea tree oil. They've all failed in alleviating the itching that started as soon as the GPS monitor was secured around her ankle. The blinking itching anklet that reminds her with every passing second that she can't go anywhere past her front or back porch. Even the scant square space at the back of the house, passing itself off as a yard, is off limits under the terms of the court conditions.

On James's side of the table are stacks of documents and old court cases tucked tightly in brown expandable folders. One folder thrown haphazardly on top of his stack is the thinnest of them all. It is the first and last one he opened when they came home. The contents of the file made him mute.

He has been quiet since Ebony made her confession yesterday, but never has he been without words. Now they sit at opposite ends of her sofa, a pillow between them, and an ocean of thoughts separating their sides. He refuses to look in her direction as once her defender and persecutor, champion and nemesis. In an all black three-piece suit James is Ebony's dark knight, and she is the two-faced heroine who will be glorified, thanks to his sacrificial gift to the city desperate for a villain, when the real villain is now a martyr.

"Speak," Ebony says forcefully as she tries to fit her fingers in the narrow space between the ankle monitor and her skin to rub the itch she hasn't been able to reach.

"What do you want me to say?"

James asks the question with his eyes closed. His face pointed toward the silent television and noiseless entertainment system mounted on the living room wall.

"Say anything." Ebony dares.

"Like what, Ebony?"

"Like why are you so quiet?"

"Around you it's better to be quiet. The less you say, the less I'm told, the less I ask, and the less I know will be better for the both of us."

"What's that supposed to mean? You already know me, James. You've known me for a year."

"You keep saying that, Ebony. You said it yesterday. You're saying it today. Just because you say something over and over again doesn't make it true. The truth is I don't know shit about you," James spits out, finally turning to look at her.

"Don't curse at me." Ebony sits up as she ends her quest to relieve the itch.

"Don't start with that bullshit. You want to talk? Talk about this," he says flinging the thin file from atop the pile on the coffee table at her.

"What the hell is your damn problem?"

The papers inside the folder scatter across Ebony and the pillow. The folder falls to the floor. James drills holes into her face as Ebony gathers the papers to find out what's behind his sudden anger. She snatches the first sheet that fell into her lap, letting her eyes quickly scan the page. What's made him angry is evident. It is a name. A name she hasn't uttered in at least 20 years.

Ayana.

Ebony takes the page with Ayana's name and places it gingerly in her lap. She gathers the other papers strewn about and shuffles them straight. Those papers go on top of the sheet in her lap. Ayana's page is last. With the papers arranged in a neat stack, Ebony kneels to the floor, picks up the folder, places them back inside, and hands the folder to James. Ayana's paper is hidden, but James has not forgotten what he's seen. His almond eyes seethe anger in his ordinary face, burning fire into her body.

It is now Ebony's turn to be mute. Her nails find the tops of her hands in her lap. She presses her flesh into the back of the couch cushions, her face points toward the soundlessness of the television and entertainment system. She's a mirror of James's own stature, forcing herself to be comfortable in her anxiety, working to calm herself at the precipice of his fury.

"Now you don't have anything to say?" James asks.

"What do you want me to say?"

"You can start by telling me why you lied."

"What did I lie about now, James?"

"What did you lie about? You've got to be fucking kidding me." James stands up from the couch.

The folder filled with Ayana's papers falls off his body to the floor.

"Don't curse at me," Ebony says without conviction.

She focuses on the sensation of her nails scratching deep into her hands, while she stares at the red-tinted insides of her eyelids.

"Ebony, you wanted to talk. This is what we're talking about. Your mother. Ayana. Ayana Edwina Jones."

"I know her name."

"Obviously you don't. Last week your mother's name was Marilyn."

"Marilyn, might as well have been my mother."

"And why do you say that?" James asks, hovering over Ebony.

"Because she should have been?"

"Tell the whole story, Ebony."

"For what," Ebony snaps, releasing her hands and sitting up straight on the couch. "It seems like you already know. Go read your fucking file and you can find out why I lied."

"I shouldn't have to read a fucking file when my girlfriend is sitting right in front of me with all the fucking answers."

"Oh, so I'm still your girlfriend?"

"I don't know. Are you?" James glowers. "And don't change the subject. Our relationship or whatever the fuck this is, is not important. We're talking about Ayana."

"Ayana was a drug-addicted bitch who didn't give a shit about me. Is that what you want to hear, James? Is that what you want to talk about. My mother who blamed me for her problems because I was born, and not the doctors and the fucking pill pushers who got her hooked in the first fucking place."

Ebony stands from the couch. Her abrupt movement makes James stumble from where he stands over her. It interrupts his interrogation and ends her explanation.

"Now we're getting somewhere. Keep going."

Ebony ignores his encouragement, walks across the wood of the hallway onto the tile of the kitchen, and makes her way to the refrigerator. She sticks her head inside the cool stainless steel doors. Scanning the shelves she sees nothing she wants.

"Who are Marilyn and Dr. Ivan, Monica, Monique and Isaiah, Ebony?"

James's question falls on deaf ears. Inside the refrigerator, Ebony ignores what he asks. She's already said too much, revealed too much, told too much of the truth. Once the truth is told it can be used against you. Pulled apart and twisted into someone else's interpretation of what they thought you said. Then it is no longer the truth, but something in the middle of the way it was lived and the way the person you told it to received it, processed it, and re-imagined it.

"Ebony, you can't go anywhere," James says.

Ebony paces past him toward the front of the house. She ignores her first reaction to say something back, and instead walks, sans satisfaction, into her bedroom. It is as she left it. Tranquil. The sheer silver curtains keep the room relatively dim, no matter how bright the sun shines through the three windows lined behind her bed. A silver blanket is folded across one corner of the white duvet. The accent piece matches the gray and silver throw pillows lining the queen-sized bed. The space is as she wants it, designed to fit the vision of her mind.

The black nine-drawer dresser sits against the wall shared with the bathroom. A silver sunburst mirror is above it. Another mirror, one meant to stand vertically so she can see her entire self, is mounted horizontally on the wall in front of the bed.

Whenever Ebony enters the room, she is forced to confront herself. The mirrors force her to admit the truth whether she chooses to speak it aloud or not. Right now, she confronts a woman more worn than the day before. Hair more a mess. Appearance ashen and unrested. Eyes dim and sunken. If she is truly honest with herself, Ebony will admit she is the spitting image of the woman she can never forget. She is Ayana with a different set of troubles.

"So you're just going to hide?" James asks from the bedroom doorway.

"I can never hide in here."

"What happened, Ebony?"

His question is loaded and open. Open enough for Ebony to paint in broad brushstrokes or meticulously fill in the blanks of her life with sharpened color pencils. Vivid details versus a synopsis. The unabridged novel; the unredacted details versus the Cliff's Notes.

Ebony looks at James and remembers his candor when he described his mom, dad, and brother months ago. He considered it a warning before her formal introduction. She looks at James wrestling with whether she gives him the same candor. Whether she owes him the parity of openness? Does she tell him Ayana had her when she was 22? Does she tell him she was too big to fit through her little body and so she ripped her wide and Ayana couldn't take the pain? Does she tell him the doctors pumped Ayana with drug after drug, each one more powerful than the last, until she was finally so numb she liked the feeling of not feeling, of not seeing her baby girl clearly, of not hearing her colicky screams and her loud cries. Does she tell him Ayana sought everything that would make her feel, see, and hear nothing that would ever remind her of her shame and loneliness?

Ebony looks at James and wrestles whether to tell him that she had no father or grandparents to know? Ayana's parents were both dead by the time she graduated college the year before she gave birth. Does she tell him that both of her parents were only children, so there was no more family to be had? There were no cousins to play with, or loving aunts and uncles on either side to step in and make up for Ayana's own shortcomings. Does she tell James that Ayana covered the pain left by the disappearance of her sperm donor with pills meant for the pain she no longer felt in her body? They soothed her when Ebony should have, and because Ayana sought comfort else where, to Ebony Ayana stopped being mommy and became Ayana. Does she tell James that she calls Ayana by her name to spite her, but that same spite still left her void with a hole she had to look outside to fill?

Ebony looks at James and wrestles whether to tell him that outside her window every night she watched Marilyn Washington kiss her daughters Monica and Monique before they went to bed. Through the living room windows she could see her do the same to Isaiah, and if she was quiet enough, or Ayana high enough, Ebony could sneak into her room and watch Marilyn kiss Dr. Ivan before Ebony covered her eyes to hide them from seeing what they weren't supposed to.

Marilyn and Dr. Ivan were open. No curtains, no blinds, there home was Ebony's home. She watched them from her windows at night after she'd already worn out her invited indoor welcome in the afternoon. Marilyn and Dr. Ivan liked Ebony from a distance because they pitied her in person. Monica, Monique and Isaiah tolerated her because their parents told them they had to in whispered conversations they thought Ebony didn't overhear. She loved them all because she had no one else to love. Ayana had already proven herself unworthy, saying she didn't love Ebony at all.

Does she tell James how much of a latchkey kid she really was? Does she tell him how her latch was broken? How her surrogate family was taken from her? Does she tell him about the day she returned early to her own home because Marilyn and Dr. Ivan were taking Monica, Monique, and Isaiah on vacation for spring break during their seventh grade year? Ebony watched them load up their van with suitcases and climb into their seats. Dr. Ivan was driving, Marilyn was beside him, Monica and Monique shared the captain's chairs behind them, and Isaiah sprawled out on the bench behind his sisters. She watched Monica and Monique close the sliding doors to their van and Dr. Ivan drive away. They left, forcing her to live with Ayana inside the house left by Ayana's parents, that she never made a home.

Inside that house on that same Friday the Washington's left, Ebony channel surfed while Ayana slept. She flipped back and forth for two hours until she saw something that caught her eye. Something that looked familiar. A van, flipped on its head and crumpled on all sides. Ebony listened to a young Julia Gillé narrate the tragedy she already understood. They were gone. Marilyn, Dr. Ivan, Monica, Monique, and Isaiah all lost in a chain-reaction crash they did not cause. Once on the road, the girls and Isaiah had taken off their seat belts inside the van. They were ejected. Marilyn and Dr. Ivan killed on impact when their braking van slammed into a spinning semi-truck.

Ayana emerged from her room as Ebony cried on the couch facing the TV. In a rare moment of lucidity, Ayana said with a sigh, "I'm the only the family you got, girl." The words were true, and she apparently said them to herself. They resigned themselves to their new truth, making the most of their last six years together.

Ebony looks at James remembering the van, remembering the Washington's, hearing Ayana's voice. Does she tell James the story of Ayana and Ebony? Where does it begin? Does she start with her birth or their resigned decision after the family she chose was taken away.

James stands in the doorway waiting. Waiting for Ebony to tell him the truth as she knows it. To learn as much about her as she knows about him as both his girlfriend and client. The woman he will prosecute in private and defend in public.

Ebony raises the eyes Ayana gave her, and tilts her head to invite him in. James tentatively crosses the threshold, taking his time as he makes his way to her. He sits beside her on the edge of the bed. It's the closest he's been since her confession. Now he's ready to hear another.

"Ayana had me when she was 22, and apparently I was too much to handle," she says with sanguine laughter to begin the story that even she barely understands.

29.

"Ebony, put your seat belt on," Ayana said to her daughter in the backseat.

"I can't reach it, Mommy. I need help," Ebony pleaded from the beat-up seat of the old Cutlass.

"Put your seat belt on, Ebony. Mommy has to go," Ayana snapped from the driver's seat. "You're a big girl now. You can do it."

In the back seat, Ebony didn't respond. She pulled the seat belt across her little body and held the hook next to the clasp. Ayana started the car without checking her daughter's belt. Dressed in a tattered, full silk slip, Ayana lowered all the windows in the car, lit a cigarette and pulled off. She didn't turn around to see Ebony shivering in a thin, ripped, cartoon nightgown of her own. She didn't look in the mirror to see her daughter holding the seatbelt hook with one hand, and her body with the other, working to keep warm in the chill of the November night.

At six years old, Ebony knew to ride in silence. She knew not to say anything about not being able to reach the seat belt again. Saying she was cold was not even an option. Shivering in the backseat, one hand holding the seat belt, the other wrapped around herself, Ebony tucked her legs beneath her body to keep them warm from the cool breeze blowing through Ayana's open windows.

She rode behind her mother out of reach of her loose hand that flicked glowing embers of cigarette ash around the car with every uncontrolled swerve, and loose turn. It was silent in the back of the car as Ayana raged in the front. She yelled at drivers moving slowly in the single-file right lane of the road reserved for semi-trucks and road trippers. Her screams flew at cars doing just barely above the speed limit, and strings of curses were delivered to drivers urging them to speed up, hurry up, and get out of the way.

Ebony shivered in the backseat, holding her seat belt as she rocked about the car with Ayana's lane changes and swerves into the highway lines from the grated shoulder of the road. She coughed from the cold and smoke of Ayana's second cigarette. The glowing tip illuminated her face. Her tight cheeks inhaled and held the cancer. One glassy eye looked somewhere between the steering wheel and the road. Ayana's lips flapped when she wasn't smoking. They muttered about the drivers, the darkness of the road, and not being able to see her exit until it was too late.

Ebony fell across the backseat with Ayana's near turn across the lanes of the highway to the far left exit. She laid there, her hand still holding the seat belt wrapped beneath her body. Where they were going was an unknown. Inhaling the stench of stale cigarettes, Ebony pressed her face to the thin cushion of the cloth seat, balled up her body, and curled her legs under her nightgown, trying and failing to tuck her feet beneath the ripped fabric.

She stayed that way until the car came to a complete stop. This was not her first late night run with Ayana. At six years old she knew it wouldn't be her last. Ebony crawled her body back into position behind her mother, still holding the seat belt, unable to fasten the clasp. She sat and waited until the man Ayana was looking for approached their car. His long, scraggly mustache and beard covered his mouth. A cap, sitting low on his forehead, covered his face. Ebony hid her eyes when he looked through her open window, only listening to the conversation between he and her mother.

"You're back again, Yana?"

"Just give me what I need, Joe."

"Yana, I just gave you a bottle last week."

"And I'm here for you to give me a bottle this week."

"You're taking too many, Yana."

"What do you care how many I take. As long as I pay you, that's all that matters."

"Yana, you haven't paid me in two weeks. I'm starting to feel taken advantage of."

"Yeah, Joe, well when I get some money it all goes to that girl. She eats everything. She grows out of everything. I don't have enough left over for me, or what I need."

"Yana, you don't need this."

"You grew a conscience overnight or something? I didn't come here for your lecture. Give me what I need or point in the direction of somebody who can."

"Why don't you give me what I need," Joe said, leaning in to Ayana's window.

Peeking through her fingers, Ebony saw the man breach his head into Ayana's face. His lips nearly met her cheek, but his facial hair interfered.

"Get the fuck off of me, Joe. I told you from jump I ain't doing no favors. I ain't turning no fucking tricks. Give me what I need or get the fuck outta my face."

181

Ebony watched her mother ream the man sniffling at her skin. She saw Ayana demand what she wanted, and refuse to accept anything less. It was a lesson in knowing your worth Ayana had taught before. *Never settle for anything less than what you want, and when someone can't give you what you deserve . . . take the shit anyway.*

"Yana, I can't give you shit until you run me some money."

"Fine, how much you need?"

"What you owe for the last two weeks, and what you're paying for the next two weeks. I can't have your crazy ass coming around here on a weekly basis when I'm supposed to be low key and shit."

"Whatever. Give me my shit. I'm a write you a check. I had to refinance my house playing with yo' ass."

Ebony removed her hands from her face to see the man Ayana called Joe back away from the car. Still in her ball, mute and unmoving, she watched Ayana hand the flimsy paper through the window. The man handed her mother two brown bottles.

Ayana rattled the bottles beside her ear checking the weight of her saving grace. She popped the top of one, and quickly shook out two pills from the unstuffed lid. She downed them without water, and swallowed over and over with her dry throat, determined to get them down.

"This check better be good, Yana."

"Even if it ain't, I'm still not fucking or sucking you off. So you can go and get the hell on with that bullshit."

"Get the fuck outta here, Yana, with your crazy ass," the man said, waving them away.

Ayana made a U-turn and reversed course back to the highway. Ebony was once again belly down in the backseat to keep up with the motion of her mother's driving.

She fell asleep on the ride home, comforted by the stench of stale cigarettes, and cool air coming through the windows. She was still with Ayana and safe in the car; not popped, bruised, beaten with a belt, or burned with a cigarette for a flip mouth and recalcitrant attitude. Ebony slept in the backseat comforted by the fact that the scary man was not with them, that her mommy was still winning. Ayana's mantra on repeat:

Never settle for anything less than what you want, and when someone can't give you what you deserve . . . take the shit anyway.

In the morning, Ebony awakened in the car half parked between her driveway and the neighbor's yard. The neighbors were already up and preparing to take their kids to school. Ebony's classmates, though she had never been able to call them friends.

Climbing out of the open car window, Ebony walked to the front door of the house. She didn't look back at the eyes watching behind her, she ignored the mumbles and snickering from the girls who refused to speak to her during lunch. She pushed the door open and marched directly to Ayana's room. There on the bed, Ayana laid with the bottles of pills beside her. One was still full another was half empty. Ebony tiptoed arounds Ayana's body to grab her purse from the floor.

Ebony rifled through the worn leather of the nearly empty bag until, she found Ayana's wallet. She opened the ripped, faux, cowhide and took the few singles left inside. Folding the money in her hand, Ebony left Ayana's room for her own, where she pulled out her school clothes and took them to the bathroom.

Ebony washed and dressed quickly. Ready for school, she took the money she lifted from Ayana's wallet and shoved it into the too-tight pocket of her too-small clothes. The jeans came up just above her ankles, and the button at her waist no longer closed. Ebony covered the top of the jeans with an oversized T-shirt, and wore flip flops with her pants to bring less attention to her exposed ankles. She walked outside leaving the front door unlocked.

The neighbors were still outside.

"Good morning, Mrs. Washington," Ebony said cheerily, walking down the driveway.

"Good morning, Ebony," Marilyn Washington said back. "Do you need a ride to school today."

"My mommy wants to know if you can take me?"

"Ebony, go ahead and get in the backseat with Monique and Monica. Isaiah, sit in the chair and let the girls sit together."

"What happened to your hair?" Monique asked Ebony from the back of the van.

"My mommy didn't have time to do it. I got a ball, can you put it in a pony tail for me?" Ebony asked both the sisters.

"Give it here, Ebony," Marilyn said from the door of the van.

Ebony took her money out of her pocket and untied the hair ball from around the wad of folded bills.

"Thank you," Ebony said, handing over the hair ball as she stuffed the money back in her pocket.

"Ebony, why do you have so much money?" Marilyn asked taking a rough hand to Ebony's head in an attempt to smooth her mass of hair into a ponytail.

"Mommy, gave it to me for breakfast and lunch at school?"

"You didn't have breakfast this morning?"

"No. Mommy is tired. She's not feeling well, and I think I slept too long."

"All done Ebony," Marilyn said, turning Ebony around to look at her face. "What's wrong with your mommy?"

"She just doesn't feel good sometimes. But it's okay. We went and got her medicine last night."

"Oh, okay." Marilyn nodded with a smile.

"Get into your seat belt beside Monica and Monique. You guys are going to be late."

"Can you help me with my seat belt please?"

"Of course, baby. Sit back. Let me get it."

Marilyn fastened Ebony into the seat belt beside her own daughters. She checked to make sure everyone was secure, then closed the van door and walked around to the driver's side. Ebony stared out the window with one hand on the glass and the other on the ball of cash in the too-tight pocket of her too-small jeans. She watched the badly parked Cutlass she slept in, and the cracked doorway of the house where Ayana was still asleep disappear from view.

Never settle for anything less than what you want, and when someone can't give you what you deserve... take the shit anyway.

Ayana's mantra echoed in her head as Marilyn pulled away from the curb. One hand on the window, one hand on the money, Ebony looked at Marilyn and mouthed "Mommy."

30.

Saturday, March 28, 2014

Johnnie didn't want to come, but here she sits, slouched inside the driver's seat of her car, peeking out of the bottom of her window at the city draped in blue. The sky is a brilliant marina hue, while the hundreds of police officers who show up to the historic downtown church paint the crooked, cobble-stone street that houses Bethel Baptist, a sharp, pressed navy. She sits in her car, as she has for the last hour, watching the arrival of true mourners, and the city elite who have come to pay their respects to the man who lost his life on her operating table. So far, the latter outweighs the former. The mayor, city council members, the state attorney, several prosecutors and staff from her office, along with the sheriff and the portion of the police force who weren't working the funeral, all made their way inside the church. Everyone but Johnnie. With a long swig from her white water bottle, she marks the passage of another cowardly hour smacking her lips "Ah," praying to the clear liquid inside for the courage and strength to do what she has done for all of her lost patients.

Johnnie, all you have to do is go tell the man you're sorry for putting him in his forever box. If you go say you're sorry, then you can go home.

Johnnie's thoughts attempt to persuade her to lift the handle of her door and exit the car. They fail. Instead she reclines as far back as she can and watches the thin parade of people walk up the stone steps and into the church that beckons mourners with the choir's slow dirge version of "Soon and Very Soon." The harmony of voices replaces the earlier instrumental that was piped out into the street for all to hear. Instead of the lush, floating and flowery sounds of harps and flutes, Johnnie is bombarded with the sounds of imminent death; an entire chorus of voices proclaiming how close we all are to the end.

No more dying there
We are going to see the King

The choir starts the third verse. The slow, three-part harmony turns the normally five minute ditty into a reflection on the very essence of life itself. Johnnie lets her thoughts roam inside the safety of her mind, tucked away inside her car, as she waits for what she still does not know.

The first and only limo pulls past Johnnie's parking space in front of the church. The blacked out Lincoln stops a few feet in front of her

Camry. The driver hops out immediately after the tires screech to a halt. He opens the back door for two women who emerge in white: Soleil and an older, shorter, darker skinned woman whose gold and white scarf, and silver gray hair radiate under the white rays of the shining sun in the clear blue sky.

Why is she here?

Johnnie's mind rolls over the reasons for Soleil's attendance at the funeral. She involuntarily reaches for her white water bottle nestled in the car's cup holder. The open cap of the bottle top teases her lips as Soleil and the older woman walk away from the town car.

It's now or never, Johnnie.

She replaces the bottle in the cup holder and finally pulls the handle on the car door. The warm afternoon air rushes in foreshadowing the steamy summer yet to come. Removed from the dim interior of her window-tinted car, Johnnie stumbles over her own feet as she tries to stand up straight. One hand shields her eyes from the sun, the other grips the car door handle.

"Good. After-noon," Johnnie says slowly to Soleil and the older woman as they head up the stone steps of the church.

They stop as Johnnie slowly makes her way around the front of the car to where they paused their procession into the church.

"Dr. Edwards," Soleil says tentatively. "I'm surprised to see you here."

"Like-wise," Johnnie slurs. "He. Was. My. Pay-tient. Wasn't he your boyfriend?" Johnnie asks, putting together Soleil's connection to the funeral for Judge Gordon.

"Yes," Soleil answers quietly looking at the older woman standing next to her.

"I re-mem-ber," Johnnie says loudly. "You were talking about him when Dawn grilled you outside the mayor's luncheon when you were standing with that lady. What was her name again?"

"Ebony." Soleil hesitates.

"Is she coming?"

"Doubt it."

"Well, damn. She should be here to support you. I mean, you just lost your boyfriend. You two were a good-looking couple. The finest ones in the room."

"Thanks," Soleil says still looking at the older woman. "Dr. Edwards, this is Barker's mother. Ms. Nona Gordon," Soleil says, taking the older woman's hand and squeezing it tightly.

"I'm. So. Sorrrr-rrry. For. Your. Loss." Johnnie slurs as the alcohol continues it's wavy rush to her head. "I'm. Sorry. I. Couldn't. Save. Him."

"It's not your fault."

"I'm. Sorry. I. Killed. Him." Johnnie mutters her drunken apology.

"Was he your emergency you ran off to when we went on the field trip?" Soleil asks.

"Soleil, we need to go inside," Ms. Gordon says, giving her hand a squeeze. "We're already 20 minutes late for the start of the service."

"The city will wait for Barker today," Soleil says dryly. "There's still one more song before the procession."

"Look the news is here," Ms. Gordon says staring at the large white van wrapped in 9 News Now insignia.

The three women watch as the van parks illegally across the street from where they are standing. The driver cuts the engine and the passenger door opens immediately.

"That's just Dawn," Johnnie says, watching her friend jump down from the truck.

Dawn's black peplum top flops up and down with her landing, revealing a sliver of flat skin where her black pencil skirt is cinched at her waist.

"It's Dawn Anthony," Soleil reassures Ms. Gordon.

"I just told you that. I know what *my* friend looks like," Johnnie chides.

"Hey Dawnie." Johnnie waves with a slurred yell as Dawn joins the triumvirate gathered in front of the church.

"Hey-y, Johnnie," Dawn says startled by her friends disheveled appearance beside the two well-dressed women. "Soleil, how are you doing? I'm so sorry for your loss."

"I'm here." Soleil answers, leaning on Ms. Gordon for support.

"It's time," Ms. Gordon says forcefully. "They're playing the last song."

The older woman marches up the steps of the old church as the choir launches into their third song of the prologue before the processional, "Move On Up a Little Higher." Soleil follows. Their white linen jackets blow in the sudden breeze behind them, showing off the older woman's opaque white stockings and two-inch heels, along with the bottom of Soleil's bandeau dress, bare legs, and feet stuffed into five-inch silver pumps. The women reach the top step, link arms, and walk inside the old white-washed church doors as the choir belts out, *Gonna move on up a little higher.*

"I guess it's just us," Dawn says to Johnnie.

"It sure is, Dawnie." Johnnie relaxes against her car.

"Are you going in?"

"Now, Dawnie, you know I have to go in there. I kill 'em, I say good bye to 'em," Johnnie says, pushing her body off of her car with her hands.

The lurch forward sends her stumbling into the white banister running down the center of the stone steps. Johnnie clutches the post and lays the top half of her body prostrate against the railing.

"Johnnie, what the hell is wrong with you this morning?" Dawn stoops beside her friend.

Johnnie doesn't look up to meet Dawn's eyes. She is afraid of seeing the same judgement she saw in Nathan's eyes a week and a half ago.

"I'll. Be. Fine," Johnnie says hurriedly to the post. "I'll be right behind you. I just lost my footing. Funerals make me jittery."

"Johnnie. Are you drunk?" Dawn sniffs the air around Johnnie.

"Why does everyone always ask me that? I'm. Not. Fucking. Drunk!"

The back pews of mourning police officers turn to look at Dawn and Johnnie through the open doors of the church. The women are crouched around the rickety painted banister of the historical church's steps with eyes burning into their backs.

"Johnnie, you smell like a bar. How much have you had?"

"I don't know, Dawnie. A few. It makes me feel better. Gets me in the game to say good bye."

"Whatever, Johnnie. You know I hate it when you get like this. You can't control your liquor."

"I can too. Damn it, Dawnie, why you gotta bring up old shit?"

"Ain't nobody bringing up nothing. I'm going inside. You need to get your shit together."

Johnnie watches Dawn turn away from her, her face contorted in disgust.

Johnnie, just stand up, go up the steps, go up to the box, say goodbye, and then you can go.

She lays on the banister letting her own encouragement build up. She waits listening to the music from the inside the church; the chord changes, the key changes, the amplified sound coming from the organ pedals. Johnnie waits, laying on the banister. Dawn, Soleil, and Ms.

Gordon all long gone down the processional aisle to the front of the church to say their final good-byes.

Get up.

Johnnie slowly pulls herself off the banister. With one hand on the railing and the other on her hip, she takes each step one at a time, like a toddler, waiting until both feet are on the same step before testing her unbalanced gait on another. Up the stairs Johnnie walks until she reaches the top. Her point of no return. Closer to the casket then to her car, she doesn't look behind her to what awaits inside the cup holder of her Camry. Instead, she moves down the center aisle, the last of the procession of friends and family, though she is neither. Down the aisle she sways, almost in time with the choir as they belt out their last line of *It'll be always howdy, howdy and never goodbye.*

Johnnie reaches the beautiful forever box with one tear forming in her eye, arms wrapped around her swaying body. As the organist and pianist strike their last notes on their instruments, she bends down in front of the familiar corpse and blows in Barker's unhearing ear, *I'm sorry.*

31.

"There will be sorrow more, no more," the pastor bellows from the foot of the grave.

His words wash over Soleil as the cool dirt spills through the spaces of her fingertips and knuckles. She catches it with her other hand as the military trumpeter begins playing "Taps" at the end of the pastor's second sermon of the day. Soleil listens to the solemn military hymn playing the hourglass game with the dirt she's supposed to throw on Barker's coffin. She counts the seconds until the dirt is transferred from one hand to the other, blocking the forming memory of the memorial service to the man who always proved to be less than honorable. Soleil spills the dirt from hand to hand, waiting until it is her turn to throw it on the face of Barker's coffin. It will be her final "fuck you" salute to the man many did not know, though they heralded him as kind and fair.

The mayor eulogized Barker as a hero among mortals. In the home-going speech he saluted Barker for his Navy service and time served as a former state attorney and judge, instead of as the arrogant, abusive, bastard he was. The mayor eulogized Barker in flowing language meant for those who had been sick and shut in and were finally relieved of their pain, not a man who enjoyed inflicting afflictions. Soleil, forced to listen to the esteeming of the man very few really knew, grievingly smiled when condolences were offered to her on the front pew at the head of the open casket. Her eyes respectfully conveyed emotional sadness she did not feel, while her mind wished to see the naked bullet wound that did what she had yet to figure out she *could* do.

Soleil sat on the pew during the funeral service staring at Barker's closed eyes. The crows feet corners battered in makeup appeared even and soft against the rest of his smooth, ebony skin. Closed, sewn shut, and dead, his eyes were no longer menacing. They no longer glowed dark and lurid, inciting fear behind simple pet names and mundane requests. His crossed hands, which clutched a Bible centered on his chest, no longer looked threatening. The long, wide fingers that marked her body with their prints, were tamed. Their only weapon, Barker's spiked titanium ring, which had already left her damaged, was now a parasitic accessory on a dead predator's hand.

Now she stares at his closed coffin lowered halfway into the six-foot hole that still isn't deep enough to contain the terror she's supposed to bury with him. That is her answer to the pastor's prayer. His ended reign of terror is what the dirt will symbolize when she throws it on the coffin. The pastor prayed and asked that everyone give meaning, hopes, or wishes to the fists of soil they hold to send Barker off with the best of both worlds. Soleil's fistful is the terror she hopes greets him in hell when St. Peter rejects him for making her live the last six months of her life with him, Satan's incarnate.

"It's time," Troy whispers in her ear.

He showed up for the burial service at Jacksonville National Cemetery at her request. He refused to come to the funeral, saying he would spit on Barker's face and be arrested. To avoid sending him to jail for assaulting a corpse, they compromised. Troy would sit by Soleil's side only at the grave site, where she is determined to have the very last word.

Dressed in an all-white tux, Troy helps her from her seat. He takes her dirty hand as she transfers the dirt, still playing the hourglass game. Hand in dirt filled hand, Troy and Soleil follow the waning procession of people to the foot of the grave. In front of them is Barker's mother. Ms. Nona Gordon. She is the second to last person to say good bye. Soleil will be the last.

Ms. Gordon stands at her dead son's feet and waits for Troy and Soleil to walk up. The pastor and other mourners are already making their way through the neat rows of evenly cut, spaced, and placed headstones, to their cars, trucks, and SUVs.

When Soleil and Troy reach Ms. Gordon she doesn't say a word. She hasn't said much since they met in the hospital. Instead, she takes Soleil's hand holding the dirt. Ms. Gordon's hand is also filled with the cool soil. The three of them, the only ones in white, stand together dirty hand in dirty hand, inside of their own thoughts that don't mirror the sympathies some felt they had to have for the aggrieved family.

"On three, let it all go," Ms. Gordon says.

She counts in her low, velvet voice and on three, all three release their hands filled with dirt on to Barker's partially lowered coffin. The soil makes a murmured thud as it lands on top of the ornate maple and gold, emblazoned casket.

Soleil stands between Troy and Ms. Gordon, waiting for someone to give the next set of instructions. None come. Ms. Gordon faces her. She stares into Soleil's eyes with a luminescent intensity, making the younger woman's anger cower. Ms. Gordon doesn't break the gaze as she brings both of her hands to her neck, where her gold and white silk scarf is ruffled against her chin. Removing the gold brooch holding the scarf together, she drops it into the pocket of her linen coat, then tugs on the fabric around her neck until it slowly reveals her marred skin.

On her chest, just below her collar bone, is a thick keloid scar that runs from shoulder to shoulder. The sadistic cut smile is old. The scar tissue is discolored and smooth as obsidian, but the even appearance of an old scar doesn't erase the memories that will always replay as fresh as the day it was made.

The women stare at each other, their gazes hold neither shame nor empathy. Soleil stares at the older woman and sees in her a history Ebony saved her from. She resists the urge to whisper "thank you" in the windless afternoon. Keeping her specious gratitude to herself, she stands at the foot of Barker's grave with the only woman who knew him better.

"I've worn a scarf around my neck every day for nearly three decades," Ms. Gordon interrupts Soleil's thoughts. "I always thought he would be more like me instead of his father."

"I'm not sure I follow," Soleil says.

"There's not much to follow. I don't remember much about what I did the day Barker's father cut me, but I still remember the way it felt when his pocket knife pierced the flesh of my chest and swiped across, leaving me with two smiles. It burned."

Soleil doesn't respond. She stares at the mark Barker's father made, unequivocally aware that her own mark, made by Barker, stares down at his mother. The women stand in their truth; Ms. Gordon knowing she raised a son who no matter how much she nurtured him, still couldn't shake the cruel destiny of his DNA. Soleil stands knowing there is nothing of her past, or her now buried present, that presses her to establish a connection with Ms. Gordon. There is nothing for them to forge together, or dissect to the bare bones of clarity. There is nothing left between them but dirty hands and the dead man in the box just below their feet.

"I thought we were letting it all go?" Soleil asks, better understanding Ms. Gordon's words.

"We are," Ms. Gordon answers quietly. "This is the final piece. I have covered up in shame for nearly three decades for something I did not do. Today, I uncloak myself and let it all go," she says, tossing her scarf into the grave.

The light fabric flutters to the top of the coffin on an unfelt breeze. Ms. Gordon, Troy and Soleil watch the fabric land in it's final resting place, cloaking the grime and grit of the dirt with an undeserved beauty. The scarf's landing is silent. A perfect period.

"It's your turn," Ms. Gordon says, briefly looking at Soleil before turning her back on both her and her son.

She walks down the winding path through the bucolic garden graveyard the other mourners followed minutes earlier. The limo the women rode in together will carry Ms. Gordon back alone. Soleil will ride home with Troy.

"You deserved to die, you sick son-of-a-bitch," Soleil mutters.

"Soleil," Troy snaps.

"You deserved to die, you sick son-of-a-bitch," she says again with more force.

"Soleil. That's enough."

She ignores his admonishment and edges her feet closer to the opening of the grave. Dirt falls on top of Ms. Gordon's scarf from the disturbed of the earth.

"You deserved to die, you sick. Son. Of. A. Bitch!" Soleil yells at the top of her lungs.

The words exit her mouth and land empty on ears they weren't meant for. The ears of a friend who desperately tugs her hand to pull her back from whatever edge she is willingly stepping over.

"Soleil. He's not worth it." Troy says softly. "He never was."

"He ruined me," Soleil snorts.

She spits the thick, viscous saliva into the open hole. It splatters on top of the scarf.

"You ruined me," she yells.

"You're not ruined, Baby," Troy tugs.

Soleil stumbles backward. More of the disturbed earth loosens itself and falls dirt crumb by dirt crumb into the open hole. She watches the trickle of soil as Troy pulls her back. His resolve is steadfast as Soleil watches and wishes the slow erosion she's created with her feet was enough to cover Barker completely. She wishes it was enough to cover her scars completely, to cover her heart completely, but the maple and gold box is still visible; smooth, rich and as lush as her own made over, scarred skin.

"Let's go, Baby," Troy pulls Soleil into his short frame.

Their embrace is awkward. Soleil towers above Troy in her heels, but with his arms wrapped just above her waist she is safe to finally spill all of her trained and uncried tears. They pour down her face, onto his white tuxedo jacket, pooling in the space between her eyes and cheeks before running down the sides of her jawline.

"There's more I want to say." Soleil cries into Troy's shoulder.

"There's no need. Do what she said and let it all go."

"I don't have 30 years worth of scarves to throw away," Sole[il] says, standing up straight and wiping her face.

"No, but you do have six months of purple makeup you ca[n] toss."

Soleil laughs. She laughs thoroughly from her gut as Troy guide[s] her away from Barker and onto the winding path to his car that wi[ll] take them out of the cemetery.

"Thank God this relationship is finally over."

"You act like you were in the relationship," Soleil says, cuttin[g] Troy a sideways glance.

"Sometimes it felt like I was."

"I doubt it."

"When someone you love is hurting, you hurt to. At least I do," Troy says seriously. "Just because I didn't physically feel your pai[n] doesn't mean I didn't feel it emotionally. Everyday I looked at you an[d] pushed you to leave that motherfucker was every day I pushed for yo[u] to see that one, you're so damn gorgeous, and two, he was never eve[n] even worth it."

"Well, I know now."

"Do you?"

Soleil lets Troy's question go unanswered, as he intended, as the[y] walk the last few feet to his car in silence.

Tucked inside his Kia coupe, Soleil stares out the window as Tro[y] makes his way out of the cemetery. Her gaze lingers on the fountain[s] spewing water into the still ponds, amidst the low cut bushes, se[t] against the backdrop of an uncut stand. It could be Eden. A heroe[s] paradise thanks to the rows of American flags, flying half-staff, at th[e] entrance of the cemetery. The stars and stripes droop at the mid lengt[h] of the pole without a swift breeze to make them blow freely. It is as i[f] Old Glory herself is decrying her own actions, her own mendaciou[s] salute, one of many flying across the city, to a hero who wasn't.

Part 3

"In a lawsuit the first to speak seems right, until someone comes forward and cross-examines."

Proverbs 18:17

32.

Thursday, August 21, 2014

      Dawn turns off the lamp on her nightstand as the sun comes fully through her white sheer, curtain covered, bedroom window. She stretches her arms above her head before diving back into the work surrounding her. A laptop sits atop the tan duvet covering her legs, a tablet is to her right near the nightstand and her phone is on her left, near Victor's sleeping body. Stacks of highlighted papers form a semi-circle enclosing her and the high-end technology.

      Dawn types furiously on her laptop, making notes from the papers scattered around her as she prepares for the first of her exclusive set of interviews. In the afternoon she will meet with Ebony Jones and James Parnell for the first time since seeing them at the mayor's luncheon. It will be the first time she's seen them in person since the shooting of Judge Gordon. The one-on-one interview has Dawn up early in the morning typing out questions, potential answers, and definitive follow-ups, despite her late night with Victor.

      "What are you doing up so early?" Victor asks in a groggy voice with his eyes still closed.

      "Working."

      "You're always working." Victor rolls toward Dawn's seated frame in the bed.

      "Watch out." She snatches her phone from beneath Victor's dead weight and places it on the nightstand.

      "My bad." Victor sighs a laugh. "What are you working on?"

      "I have to get ready for this interview," Dawn answers, scribbling notes with a pen and highlighter on one of the pages in front her.

      "Why don't I help you with that?" Victor asks, running his nose and tongue along the length of her exposed leg.

      "And how would you do that?"

      "The same way I helped you relax last night."

      Victor pushes the bottom of Dawn's silk, cream nightgown up over her thighs. He licks her leg at the point where the hem of her nightgown and her flesh meet on her thighs. His tongue runs from the fatty tissue just on the periphery of her ass to the inner corners where her thighs meet.

"Let me move my stuff." Dawn moans breathlessly, still sitting upright, but fingers no longer gliding across the computer keys.

"Leave it." Victor breathes into Dawn's legs.

She doesn't protest as Victor buries his head between her legs. He slowly encourages them to open and part as he runs his nose across the widest patch of her lace panties that cover what's no longer a secret. Back and forth, he runs his face until he feels his nose and upper lip dampen from the wetness soaking through her underwear. With his teeth and hands, he peels Dawn's black lace panties from her body, leaving her exposed to his predilection. Beneath the covers, Victor licks her forward, backward and in circles, bumping the back of his head against the bottom of the computer in her lap.

Struggling to neatly clear the bed, Dawn sets the computer and tablet on the floor, then slides the majority of her body down to give Victor better access to all of her. She pulls her already raised nightgown the rest of the way over her head and off her body. It drops to the floor on top of the laptop and tablet. Completely naked, Dawn draws her widened knees into her chest leaving herself perched perfectly for Victor's tongue to caress and glaze over her now protruding epicenter of pleasure.

She stares at the top of his head as he angles his mouth over her essence. Soft and airy moans escape her lips; eyes flutter to stay open. They do not see the widening semi-circle of papers blurred in her sex-driven vision. Dawn throws the pillow supporting her head and neck over her and Victor's gyrating frames. It lands with a crackled plop on papers at the edge of the bed, before falling down the bed bench to the floor, at the entrance to her en suite.

Dawn pulls Victor's body up to hers until her eyes are level with his waist. She takes her hands and runs them down the chiseled sides of his obliques, to his hips, sliding his navy blue boxer briefs off his body as she goes. Exposed and erect before her, Dawn brings her hands back to his base and works them up and down his length; massaging and stroking, she gives him heat from their skin to skin friction.

The stroking motion makes beads of dew form at Victor's tip. She uses the milky drops of lust to moisten her hands and further encourage his growth before she brings him to her lips. Dawn kisses his head before slowly opening her lips, allowing him in, inch by inch. She suckles Victor in her mouth until it is full of saliva. With her mouth, and the head of Victor's dick sopping wet, she takes more of him in until she's nearly kissing the base of his erection. Pulling her head back, Dawn guards her teeth with her jaws and gives Victor pressure and slow suction. Forth and back, Dawn works Victor until he pulses between her cheeks.

He brings his hands to either side of her head, pulling and pushing her deeper as she sucks him slow. Victor pushes the hair that usually frames Dawn's face behind her ears, so he can watch her face inhale him. He watches as he disappears inside of her. Eyes closed, lashes resting on her cheeks, face relaxed and damn near peaceful, her mouth is a perfect circle as she allows him to ride inside. He leans his head back on his neck and savors her sucking; the smooth thin skin ridges at the roof of her mouth enclose the top of his shaft. The taste bud-lined top of her tongue licks and tickles the underside of him as she suckles him into submission.

Victor tightens his hands on the sides of Dawn's face and pulls her further into him, until her forehead touches his navel. Feeling Victor's excitement building, Dawn slowly exhales him until they are separated and the mixture of their juices drip over her naked body.

In a single motion, Victor flips Dawn over with one hand and slams into her opening. She greedily pushes her ass back against him, making him lose his balance. Neither of them notices the abrupt motion sends more papers over the edges of the tan duvet to the floor. Victor grabs Dawn by the waist to steady himself. He runs his hands across the length of her back, letting it ride the curves of her licorice skin as he pounds into her.

She meets him stroke for stroke, pushing back as he pushes in. The wall is his balance, the headboard becomes hers. They ride each other's rhythms with quick staccato thrusts, tapping out a steady drum beat of delayed gratification finally satisfied.

He palms both of her breasts with his free hand, kneading her supple mounds until they are pliant and malleable to his will. Fingers alternate between each nipple, rolling her sensitive raisins, careful to squeeze and tug with just enough pressure to force her head to flail back onto his shoulder, as she tries to control her mounting orgasm.

With her nipples taut, Victor removes his hand from Dawn's breast and pushes against her back, making her body flush with the headboard. He increases his pace. Keeping his strokes short and steady, the intensity enhanced against her most sensitive spot. Dawn wags her ass back against Victor's pounding dick and writhes against the overwhelming pleasure. Her hips wind clockwise and back again, forcing him to keep up with her every twist and turn, as she grinds against every stroke he strikes deep within her.

Hands beat the headboard and then the wall as Dawn rides the waves of her own orgasm. It shakes through her, out of her control, ejecting Victor from her body and sending him falling backward on to the bed of papers. Dawn grabs at her own breasts and hair as her liquid lust runs down her legs in a warm stream. Victor rears back up on his knees as she comes down from her release. He rushes to her, catching the last trickles of her orgasm as he rubs his dick against her opening before obliging himself back inside.

Enveloped in her wet warmth, Victor holds Dawn steady at the waist and strokes her furiously. The punishing rhythm forces her to squeeze the sheeted mattress with both hands. Victor's pillow that had been beside her falls to the floor, taking several sheets of highlighted and notated paper with it.

She relaxes her ass muscles around Victor and squeezes him from the inside, giving him firm pulses and a soft cushion as he pushes his way through her entrapment. The combination forces him to slow his quick strokes as his own orgasm becomes apparent. He brings Dawn into him, savoring her with every pound until, at last, he holds her steady against his throbbing stiffness. His own pleasure arises spilling into her. He holds her with one arm around her bent waist and the other on top of her breasts, until she has wrenched him dry. Pulling her backward, she collapses into him as he collapses onto the tan duvet. A sheet of paper crunches beneath him as they fall onto the bed.

"Oh. Shit," Dawn whisper yells, as the fog of phantasmagoria clears and she sees clearly the mess of her bed.

"Baby, what is it?" Victor asks through closed eyes.

"I told you to let me move my stuff," Dawn yells in her full voice as she scampers off the side of the bed. "But you said leave it. And now look at this mess. All my notes. Scattered."

"We can put it back together, Babe. Your interview is not for another few hours. Don't worry."

"That's not the fucking point."

"Excuse me." Victor leans up on one elbow.

The sheet of paper underneath his back further crunches with the shifting of his weight.

"Get up. Get up. Get up," Dawn yells, gathering papers from Victor's side of the bed.

"What is your problem?"

"Right now, you're my problem. You don't fucking listen. This is why I didn't want to see you last night. I knew this would happen."

"I'm sorry. I thought you'd appreciate seeing your man for the first time in damn near two weeks," Victor says, sliding off the front of the bed onto a stack of papers.

"Move your feet."

"My bad. Damn."

"And it's not like I was on some damn vacation." Dawn rushes around the room picking up the scattered and crumpled papers. "I was in fucking Ferguson covering Michael Brown and the damn riots."

"They weren't riots. They were protests."

"Same fucking difference. Those protests turned into riots the minute they burned down the damn QuikTrip," Dawn says, picking up her laptop and tablet. "And can we not get on this "whole media over sensationalizes" shit conversation, right now. I can't."

She snatches her cream silk robe from the headboard and throws it around her naked body. Her arms get tangled in the sleeves.

"Do you need any help." Victor chuckles.

"From you? No," Dawn answers as she finally gets the robe on. "And what's so fucking funny?"

"Nothing."

"You need to leave. I have work to do."

"No problem, but you need to calm the hell down." Victor snatches his underwear from the ground. He pads across the carpet to his side of the bed to retrieve his clothes from where he left them the night before.

"I would be calm if you'd have let me work."

"Whatever," Victor says sitting on the bed.

The weight of his body causes the stack of papers, Dawn's laptop, and tablet to topple and slide across the tan duvet.

"GET. UP."

He stands quickly with one leg inside his dark wash denim.

"Calm down. I heard you loud and clear the first time. I'm up. I'm going," he says, stepping into the other leg of his jeans.

"Then hurry up. I have shit to do."

"Baby, don't stress yourself; this interview is not that big of a deal."

"Excuse me?"

"I said, this interview is not that big of a deal. You're stressing for nothing. People get killed and people kill every day. What makes Ebony Jones or you interviewing her, so special?"

"What makes her or my interview so special? You've got to be kidding me. Why don't you Google me and find out what makes my interview with her so special."

"Google you? Baby, this is local television in Jacksonville. Not CNN, not NBC, ABC, or HLN, or whatever other bullshit network you watch 24/7. When this trial is over, no one's going to remember this chick or your interview with her."

"If that's what you need to tell yourself to make *you* feel better about dating *me*, Dawn Anthony, then do it. You knew who I was before we got together. Remember, you left me the first message. Not the other way around."

"Thank you for reminding me of memories I need to forget. Good luck with your *little* interview."

"Call it what you want, but know that between this trial, Michael Dunn's retrial next month, and my work the last two weeks in Ferguson, I won't be in Jacksonville much longer."

"If you're going network, then congratu-fucking-lations."

"I don't think I am. I've already got the offer."

"Then I guess we don't have shit else to talk about."

"I guess not."

Victor walks around the bed, past Dawn, and out of the bedroom. She stands still in her room until she hears the front door to her condo click shut behind him. Once it does, she snatches her cell phone from the nightstand to check the time. The illuminated digital display reads 10 a.m. She has less than two hours to finish her notes, get dressed, and head over to Ebony's house for the interview. Dawn sits back on the bed and sorts through her papers, careful to keep them out of the sticky wet mess she and Victor left in the center of her bed.

33.

Three men from the *Dawn in the Evening* crew buzz back and forth around Ebony's living room. They've been buzzing around her space for the better part of an hour. They have transformed the living room from her prison into their studio. Her white suede couch and cracked- glass coffee table are cast off in favor of two multi-colored striped arm chairs. The men have arranged them so they face each other with little distance between the two for leg room. If Ebony or Dawn sneezes during the interview, one will fall into the other's lap.

The men work meticulously, first setting up the chairs, then the lights, then their tripods, before finally affixing their cameras to the tops of the stick figure stands. One camera is set up in the middle of the interview set. The other two are positioned at an angle from each armchair to capture each of their faces as the questions are asked and answered.

Ebony watches the men work from her perch on a barstool at the kitchen peninsula. They work while two young women give orders. The spray-tanned, Lucille Ball wannabe gives most of the orders, while the younger brown-skinned woman takes notes. With the final camera locked into place on the tripod, the crew disappears past Ebony, down her hallway, and out the open front door. Their matching outfits, denim and white polos with the 9 News Now insignia emblazoned in the top left corner, tells the world murder suspect Ebony Jones is going after her 15 minutes of fame. If their shirts don't tell the story to all the new neighbors who drive slowly past her house before making a U-turn out of the subdivision, then the news truck and cars wrapped in the same signage make up for the subtle communication.

James approved of the interview with Dawn and Ebony, much to Dawn's delight and Ebony's dismay. He reasoned with Ebony, saying the interview will help shape the narrative of her case even, if it doesn't air until after the trial. He explained that if she's convicted it will help with her appeal, and if she's acquitted it will give blood thirsty Nancy Grace fans a human look at the woman they've come to know as "Judge Killer." Ebony disagrees.

She focuses her attention to the makeshift interview set adding to the circus she's lived for the last five months. Sitting atop a bar stool, she watches the crew watch her as they try not to get caught staring at her blinking ankle monitor, keenly aware it is their first time seeing her in person. When the crew arrived earlier, James let them in. He showed them the way around her space. He made them comfortable in the residence that's become his second home since he began prepping Ebony last week with mock questions Dawn Anthony might ask, to help her craft the perfect answers. When the doorbell rang at 10, James and Ebony wrapped up their last practice session so that he could do what she could not. What she is forbidden to do. Go outside her own front door.

Ebony, trapped in the house until she is either convicted or acquitted, keeps her blinds and curtains closed, or else her new neighbors may get a *Media Takeout* worthy snapshot of the caged "Judge Killer" in her natural habitat. She has settled into her life of house arrest, wondering if she would have been better served by spending the last five months in jail, instead of working to avoid the wondrous eyes of the inquisitive and curious who wait to catch a glimpse of a suspect in a murder, a crime she did not commit, living in the easily accessible, second home from the entrance to her subdivision. House arrest has forced her to stay "smile for the cameras" ready when she tries to enjoy her brief reprieve with fresh air, when opening the door for James. A reprieve she has missed in the last week since he's nearly moved in.

"You ready?" James asks, sitting on a wooden barstool beside her.

"As ready as I'll ever be," Ebony answers without looking at him. "Just waiting on the woman of the hour."

"Well, we both know that's you."

Ebony hears the smile in his voice, even though she doesn't turn to see the expression. It is one of many kindnesses he has offered to comfort her over the last five months. A smile here. A touch there. An optimistic lie about her chances at trial every now and again. He is sanguine for Ebony's sake, and because of it, they are becoming friends in addition to lovers; bonding over their commonalities since Ayana forced Ebony to let him in.

"I'm going to touch-up my makeup," Ebony says standing. "Dawn will be here any minute."

Her heels click clack across the hardwood floor as they follow the path Dawn Anthony's crew takes in and out to the outer world. Ebony mirrors their steps until she arrives at her crossroads. As much as she wants to take the extra step across the threshold outside, the persistent itching at her ankle reminds her to turn into her bedroom and then bathroom.

The cool, semi-darkness of the bathroom greets her. Eucalyptus, sage, and spearmint candles burn on the vanity where Ebony's sparse makeup collection lays on the counter. She flips the light switch to illuminate the room, but the glow from her incandescent bulbs makes her squint. She flips the switch again and lets her eyes readjust to the burning dimness.

In front of the bathroom mirror, Ebony looks at herself; both of her selves. The two versions of self, she now sees anytime reflective glass faces her. There is the painted puppet James suggested she transform into, and the marked "Judge Killer" with wild, glassy hair unrepentant eyes, and blood spots speckled on her face. Ebony sees Barker's ring gash on her forehead beneath her contouring. She sees the curly fro potential of her hair flat ironed to it's full length. In the glass the recalcitrant fighter dressed in all black with a hoodie full of reflective heavy metal dominates over the angelic looking girl woman outfitted in an all white sheath dress.

From the front and the waist up, Ebony is Black Barbie minus the breasts. She is safety personified; inviting calm and understanding. It is the only way she will be seen through the camera's lens, from the waist up, an un-intimidating, uninspiring, child's plaything. She will not be seen standing to avoid the cameras catching a glimpse of her shackle. Views from the side and behind are banned. Dawn's viewers will not see the muscular cuts in her arms definitively carving out her triceps and biceps. Their singular point of view will make sure they never know to fear the strength and power in her hips, legs, and ass. Seated, from the waist up, will force anyone who watches to focus on her scars hidden beneath her flawlessly made-up face.

Ebony picks up the open tube of pale pink lip stain and swabs the applicator brush across her bottom lip. She closes her eyes and presses her lips together. Red illuminates before her sealed lids. It is her constant reminder every time she sleeps, every time she blinks, of the intransigent red spots that still dot her cheeks, chin, nose, and lips, even though they've been scrubbed and washed away more times than she can count.

Ebony opens her eyes to her dueling reflections and stares at the fractured woman before her.

"Come on in, Dawn. Ebony's just touching up her makeup," James says from the hallway.

The woman of the hour has arrived to interview Jacksonville's "Judge Killer." Ebony picks up her fluffy powder brush and runs it across her entire face, spending extra time and attention on the apples of her cheeks, chin, forehead, and the bridge of her nose. She rubs in with powder the long washed spots some will see as her body's revolting admission of guilt, despite her not guilty plea.

Satisfied with her attempt at making two into one, Ebony sets the brush on the vanity and takes a deep breath. The cleansing fresh scents of the candles waft through her nose with her deep inhale, and filter out of her mouth with her sighing exhale. The calm meditative aura the scents invite is addictive. She breathes in whatever healing properties are associated with the burning herbs and uses them to steer her out of her bathroom, through her bedroom, and to the hallway, pausing at the door frame to scratch her ankle. The itch alludes her. She closes her eyes. Red appears. Again.

"I hope you found my place okay," she says to Dawn's back from the doorway.

"No problems at all," Dawn says, turning to face Ebony.

She catches up to Dawn and James standing at the peninsula. They observe the crew standing in the corners of the room. Dawn looks from them to the studio they've constructed, and nods her head in approval.

"Thank you for doing this," Dawn says, turning toward Ebony and James.

"No problem," James replies quietly.

"I must admit I'm nervous," Ebony says looking at James.

His eyes are static, eyebrows stationary, and lips dry. His face is ashen and his body is flooded by the fabric of his clothes. The paunch at his belly is no longer prominent, and his strong stocky arms no longer fill out every thread of the sleeves of his crisp, white shirt. He is a shadow of the man she met more than a year ago. The doppelgänger for the man who argued with her with fierce tenacity five months ago. She stares at what's left of him, the man who told her just that morning that she was ready to show the world her real face. Looking closely at him now, Ebony sees his kind words were a specious front to conceal his own concerns.

"Don't worry, I'm sure you'll do fine," Dawn reassures.

"Don't forget I've seen your show. You don't go easy on people."

"That may be true, but just because I ask a question doesn't mean you *have* to answer it."

"I guess."

"Dawn, we're ready for you," the Lucille Ball wannabe says from the makeshift interview set.

"Great. Ebony, James these are my producers Kelly and Jennifer," Dawn says, referencing the two women standing in the midst of the armchairs, cameras, and lights. "They'll get you guys set up with mics so we can get started."

"Are you alright?" Ebony asks James. "You look worse than I feel."

"Thanks," he says without looking at her.

"Ms. Jones, Mr. Parnell, we're ready for you," Jennifer calls.

Ebony walks to where she stands holding a microphone. Jennifer runs the cable up her back and clips the small black audio piece to the front of her white dress.

"This you can put behind you in the chair," Jennifer says, handing Ebony the square battery pack. "Good luck."

"Are you ready?" Dawn asks.

"As ready as I'll ever be."

Dawn takes a seat in her armchair. Sitting back against the cushions, she crosses then re-crosses her legs. In the end, she sits straight up, not touching the cushions, with only her ankles crossed. Dawn shakes her head to push wisps of her elongated bangs out of her face, even though they fall right back in her eyes. She is the personification of poise, juxtaposed against a red spotted and dotted Barbie Doll whose makeup, clothing, and accessories do nothing to hide the villainous vixen underneath it all. Ebony looks at the camera viewfinder, knowing she is ill-prepared for the questions she's supposed to answer.

"The first question is always the easiest," Dawn begins. "Say and spell your name, just so we have it on the record."

Dawn's request is warm and inviting, encouraged by her flawless, toothy smile she flashes every night at the start and end of her show. Ebony focuses on her face as she complies with the request. Her relaxed brow and unclenched jaw offer comfort; a serenity Ebony tries to emulate as she awaits the first question.

"So, Ebony, we're going to jump right in. Why did you kill Judge Gordon?"

"She's not answering that question," James says from the barstool beside Ebony, just out of range of the camera's view.

"But it's the question everyone wants to know the answer to."

"I don't care who wants what answers. She's not answering that question. Move. On."

"Ebony, why did you bring a gun to the courthouse the morning Judge Gordon was shot and killed?"

"She's not answering that question either," James snaps again.

Dawn stares from Ebony to James and back again. Her wrinkled nose and furrowed brow tells them she is used to asking and getting answers to whatever she wants from whomever she wants without any intrusion. So far, her first two questions, James already prepped Ebony to answer, have been shot down.

"Let's start with something easier and then work our way up to the shooting," Dawn suggests, offering a small, all-lip smile.

"Ebony, tell me about your family. Mother, father, brothers, sisters? How did they influence you, and how are they doing as you prepare to stand trial for the murder of Judge Barker Gordon?"

Ebony waits for James to interject. He doesn't. Silence consumes the moment. Dawn leans forward waiting for an answer. Ebony sits still in her chair, back straight, without an answer to give. She and James did not practice for questions about her family. About Ayana. Questions whose answers she cannot give. She breaks eye contact first, looking down to her hands in her lap. The scratches against the veins on the tops of her hands call to her subconscious.

"I need a break," Ebony says standing.

"But we've just begun," Dawn protests.

Her pout falls on deaf ears as Ebony unclips the microphone from the top of her dress and lets it fall into the armchair. She sidesteps her way out of the makeshift interview set, leaving Dawn leaning forward for an answer to a question she will not receive. The light rings bathe her in a luminescent glow as she walks away from the cameras, with the unconcerned crew boring holes in her back with their eyes. Out of the living room, down the hall, she arrives back at her crossroads, where her only option is to to go into her bedroom.

Ebony collapses onto the unmade bed and brings her knees into her chest wrapping her arms around herself. She lays there inside her own warmth, inhaling the cleansing scents from the candles burning in the bathroom, ignoring James at the door.

"Are you going to the finish the interview?" He asks, staring down her body.

"I don't know. Is she going to ask any more questions about Ayana?"

"How do I know. I'm not her. She told me she was going to ask whatever she wanted but you don't have to answer if you don't want to."

"I was prepared to answer her first two questions, but you said no." Ebony sits up in the bed, "Ayana was never on the table for this interview. She is not up for public discussion."

"Why do you hate her so much?" He asks, taking a seat beside her.

"James, we've been over Ayana. And as I've told you before there is no hate, just a mutual agreement that we're best off when we're not in each others lives."

"The agreement can't be mutual if she never agreed to it."

"How do you know she didn't agree that we both keep our distance?"

He looks away, casting his almond eyes down into his lap. The silent omission tells his truth.

"When were you going to tell me that you've been talking to her?"

He remains mute.

"How long?"

His sigh breaks the icy, turgid silence. It is heavy. Weighted with the burden of being both Ebony's attorney and boyfriend. It tells more than the kindnesses of his words ever will. Inside, his sigh are his true feelings, whereas his words are the lies he thinks she needs to be comforted.

"She wants to see you."

"If she wants to see me, all she has to do is watch the news."

"Seriously, Ebony. I think she wants to make things right between you two."

"The time for her to make things right was when my family was killed in a car accident. But no, she gloated and shitted on their deaths."

"You've got to let that go, Babe. She's a different person now."

"How would you know what kind of person she is? You've been talking to her for what, four, five months. She's being whoever she thinks you want her to be."

"I've been dating you for more than a year and I'm still learning what kind of person you are, so what difference does the length of time make?"

"Whatever."

Her eyes rest on the tops of her hands. The white scratch marks along the path of her veins have gone deep enough to peel the skin. It is her tell. Her truth of the feelings inside of herself when her words to express them are ineffable lies.

"I just wanted to know more about you."

"Then you should have just asked me."

"You don't talk to me, Ebony. Any time you've ever told me something about yourself truly worth knowing, it's been in a fucked up argument that makes me regret asking in the first place."

Ebony nods her head in agreement.

"You should go finish the interview," James says, staring at Ebony's hands as her nails rake across her skin.

"Not if she's going to ask about Ayana."

"Ebony, at some point you're going to have to confront your mother and all of your feelings about her."

"James, I confront her every time I open my eyes and look in the mirror. I have her name *and* her face, what more confrontation do I need."

"Whatever it takes to get over what happened."

"Some things in life you never get over."

"If you love someone enough you do."

"I doubt there's any love lost between us."

"I wasn't talking about you," James says, "I was talking about me."

In the year and a half they've been dating, Ebony and James have never had a conversation about how they feel for each other. They met, clicked, and became an us. Their arguments never tore them apart, and their make ups were always enough to remind them of why they keep hanging around each other, despite the lack of any pronouncements of committed love, like, or pure infatuation. James's ill-timed confession adds to the confusion of Ebony's life, instead of providing the comfort professions of love give to relationships in trying times.

"You don't have anything to say?" James questions.

"What am I supposed to say, James? You're telling me you love me four days before my trial starts. You want me to believe you love me. You want to hear me say it back. Say it after the jury delivers a guilty verdict, and see how much love we have for each other then."

"But you're not guilty."

His words are both statement and question. He needs Ebony to confirm her innocence so they can both believe in the truth she's created. The corners of his eyes turn down in his face, pleading in earnest for her to make the reasonable doubt he will feed the jury in her defense, the truth.

"Just because we both say it, doesn't mean it's true," Ebony says standing up from the bed.

"Well, then, you better go convince the city it is."

The time for living inside their own fantasies is over. Their time for inception has come to an end. Ebony walks out of the bedroom knowing James is behind her. His bare feet shuffle behind the clicks of her heels. They keep count as time winds down between them living inside the truth as they know it, and her case as the jury, the city, and the entire country will hear it presented.

"I'm ready," Ebony says once she reaches Dawn.

"You can ask your original two questions if you wish." James offers an apologetic smile.

Jennifer comes over to help Ebony with her microphone. Once again, she runs the thin black cable up the back of Ebony's dress and clips the audio piece to the fabric, just below her mouth. Jennifer's nimble fingers drag softly against Ebony's arm as she finishes her work. She is subsumed by the energy, even though Jennifer is not holding on to her anymore. Instead the youngest of the crew members holds Ebony's gaze intently, as if to impart some message without speaking aloud. There are no words exchanged between them, just the warmth emanating from the dark glow of Jennifer's eyes, speaking to her belief of the truth Ebony lived five months ago.

"Ebony, why did you kill Judge Gordon?"

Ebony takes one last look at Jennifer's trusting eyes before turning to Dawn.

"I didn't kill him."

34.

"One last question," Dawn says, leaning back into the armchair that's been her interrogation stool for the last hour.

"Okay, shoot," Ebony says with an unmitigated smile.

"It's a two-part question. First, if you're convicted, what do you plan to do before you go to prison? And secondly, if you're acquitted, how do you plan to celebrate?"

"I'm only answering the second part of your question because the first one doesn't apply."

"Why is that?"

"Because I'm not going to be convicted. I didn't kill anyone. I didn't murder anyone. I did not willingly and thoughtfully commit any crime. The jury will understand that, and there's no reason for me to believe or prepare myself for going to prison. But the second part of your question I have thought a lot about. What am I going to do once I'm acquitted? I'm going to take lots of long walks outside in the air for several days, weeks, months even."

"Not doing to well on house arrest, are you?"

"Not at all."

Ding Dong

The doorbell resounds throughout Ebony's house as the perfect audio marker to the end of her interview with Dawn.

"I'll get it," Ebony says, standing from her interview chair.

She unclips the mic and lets it fall back into the chair behind her as she stretches her arms above her head.

Ding Dong

"I'm coming," Ebony yells down the hallway.

She kicks off her shoes and leaves the make shift studio set to answer the door. Two people lean against frame. One with her back on the ornate stained glass of the heavy wooden door. The other has her face pressed to the glass, begging for a glimpse inside. They were invited at her request. She hasn't seen either of them since March, and only one of them in the aftermath of the crime she did not commit.

Ebony pulls the door open and watches both women stumble to stand up straight.

"Come on in," she calls from where she stands several paces behind the back edge of the door.

Johnnie and Soleil step across the threshold into the house. The three women face each other. Johnnie stares face to face with the woman the news identified as the suspect, the accidental murderer, and "Judge Killer," in some of the most egregious reports. She stares at Ebony Jones; the woman taking the fall for something she did.

"How are you doing?" Soleil asks, pulling Ebony close to her in a bear hug.

"Be careful before you set off my anklet," Ebony remarks with a sardonic chuckle.

"I'm sorry. I didn't mean to."

"No worries. It's not your fault I can't go anywhere."

"How is it?"

"House arrest? It is what it sounds like. It probably wouldn't be so bad if my ankle didn't itch like crazy from this damn monitor. I have a permanent rash there now."

"Oh." Soleil says with a forlorn look at Ebony's ankle.

"How are you otherwise?" Johnnie asks filling her space in the rhythm of the budding conversation.

"I'm living." Ebony rolls her eyes. "Come on in. Get out of the heat. We just finished up."

"May I trouble you for some water?" Johnnie asks.

"No trouble at all," Ebony answers.

The three walk down the hallway without another word. Soleil, clad in stonewashed jeans and a yellow tank top, follows closely behind Ebony. Johnnie behind them, in white shorts and a tee, brings her empty white water bottle back to her lips. She sucks the air from the cap as she closes the door behind her, following the victim she already knows and the suspect the morning news introduced her to, in the haze of her hangover the morning after Nathan left with Danielle. Johnnie follows Soleil and Ebony until the three arrive in the living room where James and Dawn stand in what's left of the interview set, as the crew works to rearrange the furniture the way they found it.

"What are you guys doing here?" Dawn asks surprised.

"We were invited," Johnnie says with attitude.

"What are you trying to say, Johnnie? I wasn't."

"Were you?"

"She was," James interjects.

"So really. What are you guys doing here?"

"We came for drinks," Soleil says. "You remember those drinks we were supposed to have way back when we all met. That's why we're here."

"Sorry for the delay, but something came up," Ebony says from the kitchen.

"You don't say," Soleil says, deliberately rolling her eyes.

Johnnie studies Danielle's now former teacher as she brings her empty water bottle back to her mouth to suck more emptiness out of it. Today is the first time she's seen Soleil since the funeral. The first time she's seen her without makeup. Her usually heavily made-up face is unadorned. Her complexion, that was marred by healing, broken blood vessels and veins, is clear. Johnnie notices only one scar on Soleil's face. A jagged half-moon on her forehead above her eye. It is the only apparent battle wound left on the woman Dawn, and the rest of the news channels, identified as the battered girlfriend of the late Judge Barker Gordon.

"Am I invited to stay for drinks?" Dawn pouts. "I mean, it was my idea."

"That's why we're doing it now," Ebony says, coming out of the kitchen and handing Johnnie a glass of ice water. "I figured we would finish the interview, and then we could all have drinks. It'd be almost like I have friends."

"Aww, Babe, I'm your friend," James says coming over to hug Ebony's shoulders.

"You're not invited," Ebony says flatly.

"Oh, I see how you do. You get some girls around and just kick a brother to the curb. That's okay. I don't stay where I'm not wanted. But I know you're going to want me back."

"You're right. I need you back by Monday. Who else is going to run my defense?"

"Just use me up. That's all you do is use me up," James says walking out of the living room.

"It's nice you two can joke like that with all that's going on," Johnnie says wistfully.

"There's a first time for everything." Ebony sighs. "I don't even know where all that came from."

"Dawn, what time should we tell Boyce you'll be at the station?" Kelly asks, coming over to where the women stand by the bar stools. "You know he's going to want a full accounting of this interview."

"I'll be there before show time."

"Well, alrighty then," Jennifer exclaims. "Drink one for us. We'll be at work."

"I am working. It's called community service and enrichment."

213

"I'll be sure to tell Boyce that, once he stops screaming down our throats."

"And see, that right there, that's called character building. Everyone's got to pay their dues in this business."

"If you say so."

"I do say, my young squire. I'll see you soon."

"Later," Kelly calls, walking down the hall and out the door. Jennifer follows behind with the three men from the camera crew behind her. They walk out of the house, closing the door as they go.

"What would everyone like to drink?" Ebony asks.

"Doesn't matter to me, but I can only have one glass," Dawn says.

"I'm drinking water," Johnnie says not looking at Dawn. "I have to get Danielle and Tyler later this afternoon," she explains her sobriety.

Her sobriety that began after Dawn's admonishment of her behavior at the funeral. The funeral she arrived to, drunk from the days before. The days before when she realized Nathan and Danielle and Tyler weren't coming back. They hadn't come home that day, or the day after she argued with Nathan. The Thursday morning after they left when she woke up on the couch to the news of Ebony's first appearance and Judge Barker Gordon's death. The morning she woke up to find herself unlisted among the key players in the case. The morning she woke up searching for her water bottle she'd dropped in her drunken sleep. The morning she watched the news standing in her refrigerator, one hand wrapped around her white water bottle, black cap removed, and the other hand holding on to the neck of a half-empty wine bottle, ready to refill her drink.

That morning, in her heady drunken stupor, she stared at the images on the television screen of Ebony's mug shot, Judge Gordon's official photo from the court, and the group picture Dawn, Ebony, James, Soleil and Judge Gordon took after she and Nathan left the mayor's luncheon. In her drunken stupor, that Thursday morning, Johnnie watched the news, and looked at the pictures on the screen until long after they'd changed to video and images of something else to go with another story. That Thursday morning, Johnnie stared at the images until they made clear a thought through the fog in her head. She stared until the pictures were imprinted on her mind. The mugshot, the cropped picture of Ebony Jones and her boyfriend, and the group picture where Soleil appeared to put distance between her body and the body of the man Johnnie failed to save, because she was too drunk to even save herself. Full of alcohol, Johnnie remembered the final photo of the man with the tight, piercing, gleaming eyes and draconian smile, who implored her to meet all of her ghosts who'd yet to haunt her.

That Thursday morning, standing, drinking in the refrigerator, one hand on her vice, and the other on its means of delivery, Johnnie vowed not to drink again. A vow she didn't fulfill until two weeks later, the Monday after Judge Gordon's funeral.

"I have Jack, gin, Goose, and SoCo," Ebony says, pulling bottles from the cabinets.

"Anything but SoCo," Soleil says. "Bad memories."

"Yeah, sorry. I forgot," Ebony says, putting the bottle of Southern Comfort back in the cabinet. "That bottle's about two years old. He bought it."

"He who?" Dawn asks from her perch at the kitchen peninsula.

"Barker," Ebony and Soleil say together.

"Why would he buy you alcohol?" Dawn asks.

"Because we used to date," Ebony says matter of factly.

"Why didn't we discuss *that* during the interview?"

"Because you didn't ask."

"It was the one question I didn't think to ask."

"How did your interview go?" Soleil asks.

"Okay, I guess. Dawn? Thoughts?"

"It went well, save for the fact that I forgot to ask the most important question. How did you know Judge Gordon?"

"We all forget something," Ebony says without sorrow.

"That doesn't sound too bad," Soleil breaks in. "It makes me less nervous for mine tomorrow."

"Taped or live?" Ebony asks.

"Live," Soleil and Dawn answer at once.

Johnnie half listens as Ebony, Soleil, and Dawn talk about their interviews. Instead, she focuses on Ebony's face. The smooth olive skin, dark eyes, small nose, and full lips. Her face is symmetrical and plastic surgery perfect without the surgery, minus the half moon scar on her forehead. The small scar nearly hidden in her complexion jumps out at Johnnie as she looks from suspect to victim and back again.

"Johnnie, what is it?" Ebony asks, staring at her intently.

"You two have the same scar," she says softly.

"He beat us both," Ebony says.

Johnnie nods her head in acknowledgment that the *he* Ebony speaks of is the reason they are all finally together. He is the connective tissue that binds them together as a haphazard collection of almost

215

friends, instead of almost strangers. Johnnie sits against Ebony's hard saddle bar stool, her hands clutching her white water bottle, refilled with water, because of him. Acknowledging the absence of his presence brings a cold sobriety to the room. The earlier jokes associated with his name subside for the gravitas of the circumstances that have contributed to this otherwise airy conversation. Johnnie knows this is not a visit between friends or strangers. It is a visit deemed necessary by tragic happenstance where two of the parties involved will be judged, and the actual executioner who played God and lost will, remain anonymous.

"I'm sorry." Johnnie apologizes.

"For what?" Ebony asks, zeroing in on her vapid expression. "It's not like you pulled the trigger."

"Be careful of what you say," Soleil admonishes. "I have to testify."

"James told me," Ebony says still looking at Johnnie.

"I'm just sorry you're going through all of this," Johnnie begins. "I'm sorry I didn't save him. I'm sorry . . . I . . . "

"Johnnie, you didn't kill him," Ebony interrupts.

"Neither did you." Johnnie says, getting as close to her unfinished apology as possible.

"Well, at least somebody believes me." Ebony laughs. "Can you be on my jury Monday?"

Soleil, Dawn and Johnnie laugh with Ebony, but Johnnie can't help but hear the heartache behind her own levity. She knows she is facing two victims. That what she'd heard on more liberal news reports were true. Ebony was beaten. Judge Barker Gordon had a history of beating women. And the shooting, while Johnnie isn't sure if it was accidental, she is convinced Ebony is not a murderer. That title she reserves for herself, and the God she knows will judge her if Ebony is martyred by a jury who will never know the truth.

"Ladies, if you'll excuse me, I'm going to go and get out of this dress," Ebony announces, leaving the kitchen and heading down the hallway.

Dawn watches until Ebony is out of sight.

"Johnnie, what do you mean you're sorry, you didn't mean to kill him?"

"You said the same thing at the funeral, too," Soleil adds.

"I meant just what I said. I didn't mean to kill him."

"Then why do you feel guilty for killing him, when the bullets had already done their damage before he got to you?" Soleil asks.

216

"That's what Dr. Thomas and I came up with after he died on my table."

"Then what's the truth, Johnnie? And not the one you concocted," Dawn demands.

"The true story is I could have been a lot better at my job that day. That I should have been able to save his life but I couldn't."

"Johnnie, stop talking in shoulda, coulda, woulda's. Are you the real suspect? Is James defending the wrong woman?"

"What the hell do you mean?" Johnnie asks incredulous. "What doctor do you know who's been charged with murder for trying to *save* a life? I feel guilty for not being on my "A" game during his surgery, but I'm nobody's suspect." Johnnie assuages her own culpability.

"What are ya'll talking about in here?" Ebony asks coming down the hallway,

Johnnie sucks her teeth and brings her water bottle to her lips. She pulls the black cap open and tilts her head back. The ice cubes from the glass Johnnie poured into the bottle crunch as they jostle around the plastic. The cold liquid glides easily down her throat.

"Ah," Johnnie sighs, smacking her lips at her quenched but dissatisfied thirst.

"Would you like some more water?" Ebony asks.

"No, thank you. This should hold me until I pick up Danielle and Tyler from Nathan." Johnnie stands.

"How is she doing?" Soleil asks. "She is definitely among my favorite students."

"She's doing great. Excited about starting first grade Monday."

"Her class will be right next to mine so she'll still get a chance to see Miss Lisa and I."

Johnnie smacks her lips and rolls her eyes at the mention of the name that triggers the smell of lemongrass and jasmine, unanswered questions from Nathan, self-aggrandizing vanity plates, and sounds of laughter set to the tune of "Let It Go." It's been five months, and she had yet to let anything go except one bad habit and Danielle's favorite DVD.

"Would you like me to walk you to the door?" Ebony asks.

Johnnie can tell from Ebony's pleading, earnest eyes her offer is more out of polite decorum demanded by the laws of southern hospitality than by an actual want to follow her to the door.

"Don't worry about it," Johnnie responds.

"I'll walk her out Ebony. I need to get to work anyway," Dawn chimes in.

"Well, alright. Thank you for coming by," Ebony says with a smiling sigh as Johnnie and Dawn leave down the hallway.

"No problem," Dawn says. "And thank you to you and James for doing the interview. I think it's going to be great; especially when you get off."

"It's good to know I have some support."

The words stop Johnnie in her tracks. She doesn't turn to face the woman accused of a crime she knows she did not commit. Instead she stands in the hallway separating the living room from the kitchen with her back turned away from the two victims and her friend, who has ascertained the truth on her own.

Johnnie turns around slowly, still waiting for the right words to come into her head so she can speak them out of her mouth. As she waits for intelligence to arrive she avoids looking at Dawn, focusing only on Ebony and Soleil. Their half-moon scars jump out at her from both faces. The self-evident evidence the judge, esteemed to be a man of great moral and civil character, was just a man with his own secrets, demons, and confirmed bad habits.

"You'll always have my support," Johnnie finally says. "I'll see you in court Monday."

"Then we'll all be there," Soleil says. "I'm on leave from the school until the trial is over, or until I feel ready to get back to work. And Dawn you'll be there, too, for coverage, right?"

"Of course."

"Well, then, it's a date," Johnnie says. "See you Monday."

Johnnie doesn't wait for Ebony, Soleil or Dawn to add anything more to the conversation. She turns away from them all and follows her feet down the hall; her white water bottle in hand. It's not until she's out of the house and standing in the doorway of her car that she stops for Dawn, who is just a few paces behind her.

"Why are you running?" Dawn asks, holding Johnnie's car door open so she can't close it.

"I'm not running, Dawn. I just don't have time for your third degree right now. I have to pick up Tyler and Danielle from Nathan."

"Why do you have to pick them up? Why can't they all just meet you at home?"

"Because they don't live with me anymore."

"What do you mean, they don't live with you anymore?"

"Just what it sounds like, Dawn. They don't live with me anymore. Nathan and I are separated."

"When did this happen?" Dawn asks, dropping the interrogative edge from her voice.

"The day of the shooting."

"Your separation doesn't have anything to do with your half-assed confession in there, does it?"

"What confession?"

"Johnnie, don't play dumb with me. We've been friends long enough now for you to come clean. Whatever happened the day Judge Gordon died led to your separation. You've been feeling guilty for months, and you've apparently stopped drinking. All the times I've been around you, I've never known you to turn down a cocktail."

"Aren't you the perceptive one?"

"It's my job."

"I'm not your job, Dawn. I'm your friend."

"Then be a friend and tell me what the hell is going on so I can be there to support you, instead of leaving me jumping to my own conclusions. You know my imagination is pretty wild."

"Yeah, I know," Johnnie sighs. "I'm on leave from the hospital for what happened with Judge Gordon."

Johnnie waits for Dawn to follow-up with another question, but she doesn't. They stand there in the blazing heat of the August sun standing their ground, both waiting for the other to further the conversation. Dawn waits for Johnnie to answer questions she feels she shouldn't have to ask, and Johnnie waits for Dawn to ask the questions so she can give the answers her friend is looking for.

"Nathan left you the same day you lost your job?" Dawn cowers to her need to know.

"Yeah. I came home from the hospital and he and the teacher's assistant from Dani's school were playing family with my child like I didn't even exist."

"In *your* house?"

"You heard me."

"That's fucked up."

"Tell me something I don't know," Johnnie sighs, pushing the car door open further.

Johnnie sits on the hot sun-baked leather, rocking side to side to alternate the burning on the underside of her thighs. She uses the break in the conversation to roll down her windows and let the heat trapped inside of the car escape. Beads of sweat form on her neck, chest and back in an attempt to cool her.

"Johnnie, what happened? Weren't you just telling me how to be a ho for your husband?" Dawn asks outside the window. "You guys have been together so long. If anyone knows how to make it, I thought it was you two."

"Dawn, I wish I knew, when this became my life. I've been a good wife. I've been a faithful wife. I've been a nasty wife. I sucked and fucked him four times a week for nearly two decades. Even learned how to surfboard. Sometimes forever just don't last."

"I guess not."

Johnnie sighs in the seat she's now adjusted to, relaxing in the warm leather chair, her head and neck reclined, eyes closed. Muscle memory makes her grab the white water bottle with the black cap. She pulls it open between her teeth and guzzles down the liquid inside. The water slides down her throat without protest, without burning it's taste into her buds.

"I've got to get to work, Johnnie, but you can call me if you need me. You know that, right?"

"I know, Dawn."

Johnnie waits until Dawn walks away from her car, crosses the street, and gets into her own vehicle. She doesn't turn the key in her ignition until Dawn is out of the subdivision. The air conditioning blasts her in the face with warm outside air. Johnnie turns it off, sits up in her seat, puts the car in gear, and curves it into Ebony's driveway. She makes a full turn until she drives forward, pulling out of the subdivision as another car pulls in. In her rearview mirror, she sees the car pause in front of the home she just left.

What happened?

Dawn's last question lingers in Johnnie's mind. Complex in it's simplicity, Johnnie turns the loaded two-word inquiry over and over.

What happened?

She drives to pick up Tyler and Danielle with Dawn's last question, and the determination that she will see the outcome of her unvanquished ghosts until someone's justice is served, knowing it will never be her own.

35.

Soleil sits in her own sweat and shivers in the news studio that is hot and cold all at once. Her adjusting body is split into two distinct hemispheres. From the waist down, the stubble of the hair on her legs stands straight up, but her body's attempt at keeping her warm fails against the high-powered air conditioning of the studio. Meanwhile, the high strung, bright lights beam down on her back and head from where she sits at the *Dawn in the Evening* set desk. They warm everything from the top of her head down. Sweat beads on her scalp rain down her head, and roll over her temples, ears, and the back of her neck.

Soleil waits in her sweat and shivers for Dawn to get around to interviewing her, hoping she doesn't look like a sweaty, nervous reck when the cameras start rolling and the signal begins broadcasting her. She hopes her sweats and shivers won't make her look like an unreliable witness who can't be trusted to the tell the truth. The opinion the state attorney says the jury will have of her if they see any sign of weakness on the witness stand. Body water is bad; both sweat and tears are a sign of weakness. Soleil has trained herself out of producing one, but the other pours from her dank body, in an interview that's set to be her trial run.

"One Crime. Two Killers. Ahead on *Dawn in the Evening* . . . The other side of the story. The girlfriend of the late Judge Barker Gordon speaks to me one-on-one about her life with the judge before the courthouse shooting, and why she says she feels responsible for his murder."

Dawn finishes speaking into the camera with a broad, toothy smile. John counts her down, from behind the camera with his fingers, as music plays in the studio. The music stops when his hand reaches a fist.

"Three minutes," John says aloud as he steps back behind the cameras.

"Are you ready?" Dawn asks, turning to Soleil.

"That was some promise you made."

"We have to tease the best part of the interview," Dawn answers with the same smile she gave the camera.

"I guess."

"Besides, when you told me in our pre-interview you feel bad because you believe Ebony *allegedly* shot the judge to help you get out of the relationship, I just knew we had to use that. That's our hook."

"I thought that was off the record."

"Nothing is off the record unless you explicitly say it is."

"Oh."

"Two minutes," John yells from behind the three cameras that envelop the long glass news desk.

"You may want to touch up your makeup," Dawn says, leaning in toward Soleil. "These lights can be harsh and the camera is always unforgiving."

"Ooo . . . kay," Soleil says unsure.

She bends down from the stool John gave her to sit on and picks up her black leather tote from where she stuffed it under the desk. Rummaging inside, Soleil tosses her brush and two small compacts holding her purple palette of eye shadow and blush, into a corner in the bag, and takes out the compact holding her pressed powder. She dabs the sponge in the makeup and presses it into her flesh, making small circles around the circumference of her face. Her actions are meticulous and methodical as she applies the makeup, careful to dab away the shine from her forehead, blend the highlighter and bronzer of her cheekbones to the edges of her hairline, and powder her chin before blending the contour of concealer across the sides of her nose, and up through her T-zone.

"One minute," John yells, stepping in front of the cameras. "Dawn, when we come out of break you'll be on camera two, and then turn to one for the interview."

"Thanks."

"What camera should I look at?" Soleil asks aloud, as John steps back behind the cameras.

"Don't worry about that," Dawn answers. "Just focus on me and you'll be fine. The camera will capture you as you are naturally."

"30 seconds," John calls.

Soleil takes one last look in the small mirror, and uses her fingers to smudge in a few spots on her face near her temples that she missed with the sponge. She swipes each eyebrow with her index fingers laying down the hairs of her unruly arch. Satisfied with her appearance she closes the compact.

"15 seconds," John yells.

Soleil drops the makeup back in her purse and lets it fall to the floor beside her. Meanwhile, Dawn picks up a large hand mirror from a hidden shelf beneath the desk. She pats her hair into place and presses her deep plum-colored lips together, further spreading the stain. The hue of the lipstick blends effortlessly into her lightly made-up face, and compliments her scoop neck, burgundy sheath dress. Soleil stares at Dawn. Her hands find her own waist, smoothing the wrinkles between her sapphire blue blouse and black skirt.

"10, nine, eight . . . " John counts.

"Get ready," Dawn says.

Soleil focuses on the side of Dawn's head as John silently continues the countdown with his fingers. Her hands fidget at her waist. She tries to keep them from fanning herself as heat rises from her armpits and breasts. The inside of her silk blouse girds the top half of her body in a sauna of fabric, leaving her body an unwilling inhabitant.

"Welcome back to *Dawn in the Evening*," Dawn smile talks to the camera in front of her. "Tonight we have a special guest in the studio with us. Soleil St. James. The girlfriend of the late Judge Barker Gordon."

Dawn talks to the camera and tells it Soleil is a teacher. She lists her guest's credentials in the community as if she's vetting her for trial, and not simply asking Soleil her own opinion on her life. As Dawn talks, pictures of Soleil flash on the television screen sitting below each camera. They are the pictures Dawn asked for ahead of the interview. She asked for pictures of Barker and Soleil together, but Soleil told her she didn't have any. It is the truth. The only picture of the two of them together is from the group photo at the mayor's luncheon which Dawn already had.

Soleil stares at the group photo as it comes up on the screen. It is her first time seeing Barker's face since the funeral. Since she sat on the front pew next to Ms. Gordon and watched the funeral director close the top half of his exquisite coffin. Looking at him now, she sees he is just a man. A beautifully-flawed man. In the picture, the smile on his face appears genuine. His thick lips are stretched to show off his perfect teeth. His eyes don't glow with the mean, irascible spirit inside of him. They appear happy. Maybe because he knew just hours later that he would be able to get off on torturing her. The thick scar of crows feet corners at his eyes are undetectable in the picture. In the picture, his ebony skin is unmarked by the remnants of adolescent acne or adult age. He is perfectly beautiful, but then again, a devil always is. No one has ever been tempted by anything ugly.

"Soleil, thank you for joining us this evening," Dawn says, turning to her at the desk.

"Thank you for having me," Soleil says, looking into her eyes.

"When was the last time you saw Judge Gordon?"

"The morning of the shooting," she answers.

"What happened?"

"He left my apartment to go to work. He had spent the night the day before," Soleil recalls. "He brought me flowers," she says softly. "Roses."

"For what?"

Soleil sees Dawn's anxiousness to get to what she calls the hook of the story. She already knows why Barker brought the flowers. She knows what happened the last time Soleil saw him. The veiled threat poorly masked by his charm.

"Soleil, why did Judge Gordon bring you flowers?" Dawn asks again.

"To apologize," Soleil answers, resisting the urge to fidget and fan as three drops of sweat stream down her back to the top of her skirt's cinching high waist band.

The sweat beads, bubbles, and flows from the nape of Soleil's neck underneath the collar of her blouse to the skin enclosed in the rest of her shirt. Her body's mechanism to keep itself cool works in overdrive as she sits and bares the heat under the spotlighted gaze of the news set, and Dawn's earnest stare.

"What did he have to apologize for?" Dawn asks, her smile slightly diminished.

She lowers her head and catches Soleil's eyes with her own. Soleil lifts her head to meet Dawn.

Focus your eyes.

The words of the state attorney come to Soleil as she wrestles with her answer. She blinks to regain control of her thoughts as words fight to be first about why Barker had to apologize.

"Soleil."

Dawn saying her name coaxes the gentle version of the truth.

"The flowers were his way of apologizing for beating me."

"What do you mean, beating you?"

Soleil visibly scoffs on camera. She can see in the monitor her head involuntarily fly back on her neck, and her eyebrows raise. The expression appears on her face before she can compute to her brain to control its emotional outburst, her synapses firing in overdrive with responses fueled by the right side of her brain. Dawn's question is not one she expected. Dawn wants specifics. Details. Idioms. Graphic pictures painted in words. Her question requires an answer Soleil's never given. Not even to Troy.

Watching herself in the monitor she blinks again, feeling the beads of sweat running across her temples, neck, and back again. She can feel Dawn waiting on an answer. This question she has not asked twice to encourage an answer like before. Silence subsumes them. Soleil resists turning to the camera to break her stare. She blinks.

Focus your eyes.

The voice of the state attorney returns to her subconscious. The face of the prosecutor takes over for the anchor. She is conducting the interview instead. Her icy stare and smug smirk, dubious and disbelieving as Soleil told her truth in the police station months ago.

"When we took that picture with you at the mayor's luncheon, he was squeezing my waist with his hands," Soleil says slowly and firmly, unshaken by the inviolability of her answer. "He had hard hands. That night and the two days after, he used his hands and his feet."

"What does that mean?"

"It means he left me with cracked ribs, a bruised back, and a black eye."

"Why did he hurt you?"

She said hurt instead of hit or beat. Her use of the euphemism imparts judgement in her words. Dawn is holding court of her own. The spotlights forcing Soleil to sweat through her blouse are Dawn's very own interrogation lamps used to build or destroy whatever story she deems necessary. She is worse than the state attorney, because she doesn't need Soleil to make a case. Dawn makes the case all on her own. This studio is her courtroom where she presides as both judge and jury.

Soleil blinks.

"I met Ebony."

"He hurt you just because you met murder suspect Ebony Jones?"

"She wasn't a murder suspect when we met. But yes, he hurt me because we had a conversation."

"Is that why you believe you are responsible for his murder, and not Ebony?"

Dawn's question is leading. She is using Soleil to build her case in the court of public opinion. Dawn is as James will be on cross examination, but Dawn, like James, already knows Soleil's answers.

Soleil sits up higher on her stool and looks just above Dawn's eyes. She blinks and ignores the heat from the lights above, ignoring the sweat rolling on her body.

She blinks.

"I am the only one who benefitted from his death." Soleil answers.

"Did you ask Ebony to kill the judge for you?"

"No."

"Why did she do it?"

"I don't know that she did."

"Did she say anything to you the day you met that gave you an idea that she would kill Judge Gordon."

"She told me to leave him."

"What made her tell you that?"

"She knew him. How he was. Who he was. What he did."

"What did he do?"

"Beat women."

"How did she know?"

"She dated him two years ago."

"Did she leave him?"

"Yes."

"How?"

"She didn't say."

"She just told you that you should leave the judge as well?"

"Yes."

"Why didn't you?"

Again, Dawn's question elicit's a visceral, unspoken response from Soleil. A question that forces her to look down at the bridge of her nose as she ponders an answer she doesn't have. The question Troy asked her for months. A question Soleil asked herself regularly during the course of her relationship.

Do something that will make him never want to come back.

Ebony's words from the car echo in her ear. She hadn't done anything. Soleil suffered in silence, content to continue a relationship she mostly didn't want. Dawn's question hangs in the air unanswered. Soleil's true answer, "I don't know," hangs on the tip of her tongue unspoken because she knows "I don't know" is not good enough. Soleil blinks her eyes and looks into Dawn's. The dark caverns of the anchor's face are obscured by ambiguity. They are vapid and vague as they search for an answer to a question Soleil doesn't have an answer for.

She let's her silence be her answer. She stays mute waiting for Dawn to move on. Dawn remains equally as silent. The impregnated pause of a now awkward live interview creates tension on television. Neither woman, anchor or interviewee, moves. The only motion in the studio is off screen. John in the background, behind the cameras, holds one finger in the air. Dawn nods her head ever so slightly in acknowledgment of the visual cue.

"Soleil, do you think Ebony Jones went to meet Judge Gordon on your behalf?" She asks, moving the interview forward.

"I can't say why she went to meet the judge. But if she did it for me, I can't say I'm not grateful."

"Are you happy Judge Gordon is dead?"

"I'm happy we're no longer together."

"Why does that make you smile? Judge Gordon is dead."

"I know."

"Thank you, Soleil, for joining us tonight on *Dawn in the Evening*."

"Thank you for having me."

"And thank you, to you at home, for watching," Dawn says, turning away from Soleil and back to her camera, focused toward the center of the desk. Soleil turns her head away from the side of Dawn's face, but avoids looking into the camera pointed in her direction. Her eyes follow John who steps to the side of Dawn's camera with his hands raised high in the air as his fingers count backward from 10.

"Stay with 9 News Now for continuing coverage of the murder trial of Ebony Jones," Dawn continues quickly in her camera. "Ahead at 11 with Linden and Julia, the impact verdicts of past self-defense trials could have on this case. And don't forget jury selection begins Monday morning at 9 a.m. I will be in the courtroom for all of the proceedings, and have the very latest Monday night on *Dawn in the Evening*."

"That's a wrap," John yells aloud.

"Thanks Soleil," Dawn says over her shoulder. "I'll show you out."

"Don't worry about it, I remember the way." Soleil stands from the stool.

She picks up her purse off the floor and flings it on her shoulder. Soleil steps off the set and walks to the side doors of the studio as the hot overhead lights in the room go out one by one. The sound of the last light shutting off resounds with an electric buzzing hum as she exits the studio.

Dawn Anthony's unanswered question dances in her head. The words walk with her to the rhythm of her scampering feet.

Why didn't you?
Why didn't you?
Why didn't you?

Soleil hears the question over and over, replaying with the nuanced inflection of Dawn's voice. The judgement, the curiosity, the confusion.

Why didn't you?

Dawn's question takes Soleil through the cool hallway. The cold air conditioning from the studio is blasting throughout the building, chilling the last sweat drops on her body.

Focus your eyes.

The voice of the state attorney comes back to battle for Soleil's attention. She steps out of the back door of the news station into the muggy heat of an August night in Jacksonville.

She blinks.

The outside heat immediately warms her cold body.

She blinks.

Why didn't you?

She blinks.

Focus your eyes.

She blinks.

Why didn't you?

Dawn's three-word question carries Soleil to her car, out of the electric security gates of the station, down Bay Street, over the Main Street Bridge to I-95, and all the way home to her Southside apartment. Dawn's voice stays with her for the entire ride. It greets her on the other side of her apartment door. It's in the bathroom where she strips out of the high waist, black pencil skirt and the sweat-stained, sapphire blouse.

Why didn't you?

Dawn's voice resounds in Soleil's skull as she stares at her reflection in the mirror. Naked and marked, her skin is dented with uneven lines around her waist where the tight skirt pinched the blouse against her body. The indentations run around Soleil's stomach, sides and hips brushing against the places that were once bruised blue, purple, and black. The clothing lines paint wispy brush strokes against the surface of her back that used to hold the permanent print of a Cole Haan loafer. These marks are only temporary. They are incomparable to the mark staring back at her from her face; clear skin clouded with scar tissue a shade darker than her creamy complexion. A constant reminder.

She blinks.

Why didn't you?

"Why didn't I?"

36.

Monday, August 25, 2014

Chants of "Stand Down to Stand Your Ground," greet Dawn's ear before she sets foot on the courthouse grounds. The chorus of voices comes from throngs of women who crowd the front lawn of the Duval County Courthouse. Dawn watched as they arrived by the busload throughout the morning while Marcus and Kirsten were on air. Now just 30 minutes before jury selection begins, she is face to face with them and their vocal and visual protest.

The chanting demonstrators all have on shirts with a message. One woman's shirt reads "Ebony Did What Janay Should Have." A few others display the monikers from the Michael Brown protests, "Hands Up, Don't Shoot" and "Black Lives Matter." Out of the corner of her eye Dawn catches the back of one woman whose shirt reads "Black Women Matter." Another woman wears a double sided poster over her body. One side displays the young faces of Trayvon Martin, Jordan Davis, and Michael Brown with the words "We Stand Up for our Black Men." The back of the poster shows the faces of Marissa Alexander and Ebony Jones with the words "But What About our Black Women?"

Dawn side-steps her way through the crowd, ignoring the camera crew following behind her. They pause every few steps to get close-ups of the protesters, their shirts and signs, until they make their way up the steps of the courthouse, inside the building, and through security. With their court press passes accepted, they're waved through the immaculate building to the bay of elevators, where one is already on the ground level to take them upstairs. The sliding doors close with a muffled ding, drowned out by the loud tone of Dawn's phone.

She reaches into the pocket of her white blazer and sees the text message banner across the locked home screen.

Good Luck with your trial coverage. I hope it gets you where you want to go.

Dawn clears the message from Victor as she steps off the elevator behind her crew. She follows them blindly to their designated room; phone in hand, fingers hovering above the letters of the animated keyboard, both ready and unready to type a message in response.

"Ma'am, you're going to have to silence your phone inside the courtroom. Judge's orders," an officer says as she prepares to enter the courtroom.

Dawn taps out a hasty response and then turns off the ringer. She drops it back inside her blazer pocket before stepping inside the fifth floor courtroom. Three benches behind where Ebony and James sit at the defendant's table, Dawn joins Soleil and Johnnie. They're both dressed in black. Another woman beside them is in a royal blue, red, and gold print dress.

"Good morning, ladies," Dawn says to the women seated.

"Good morning," Soleil and Johnnie reply.

Dawn says, "Soleil, I'm surprised to see you here with school back in session. I thought you just had to come the day you were testifying."

"I'm on leave of absence until after the trial," Soleil says. "My TA, Miss Lisa, is handling the class until the jury goes into deliberation."

Johnnie roll her eyes.

"I forgot, you did say that." Dawn shrugs. "Good morning. I'm Dawn," she says turning to the stranger sitting in the corner of their bench.

"Good morning," the woman says back, never turning to take Dawn's hand. "Ayana," she says staring at the back of Ebony's head.

"All rise."

The booming voice of the bailiff brings the murmuring chatter in the courtroom to a swift silence. Everyone comes to their feet as the bailiff announces Judge Marisol Shaw into the room. Judge Shaw, one of the few Hispanic judges in the Duval County court system, sweeps inside with the bangs of her short pixie cut bouncing in her eyes. She tells everyone to quickly take their seats and with a flip of her hair and a flick of her wrist, she bangs the gavel to call the court to order.

"How long do you think jury selection will take," Soleil whispers to Dawn.

"It's expected to take a week, but who knows for sure," Dawn says, staring at the back of Ebony's head.

"Did you guys say anything to her when she came in the courtroom this morning?" Dawn asks Soleil and Johnnie.

"She smiled at us for a quick second, then her face went blank. It was weird," Johnnie answers.

"That's because of me," Ayana says turning to the trio.

"What do you mean?" Dawn asks.

"Her face probably looked like that because she saw me," Ayana says in a cool voice. "I'm her mother. We're not . . . We're not . . . We're not . . . very close," she sighs.

"You two look just alike," Dawn observes Ayana with new eyes. "I don't know why I didn't see it when I sat down."

"Thanks. But don't let Ebony hear you say that."

Dawn takes in Ayana's oval face, olive skin, wide nose and supple lips. She notices the only differences between the two women is their age, nose and hair. Ayana's face is harder, filled with the lines that only come from well learned lessons and life experience. Her hair is cut short. The curls of her tiny afro are coiled tightly to her scalp nearly hiding her graying edges.

"How are you doing?" Dawn asks.

"Just praying for my baby," Ayana answers, away from the group.

"I'm sure she's grateful for that." Dawn prolongs the conversation.

"Maybe."

Dawn watches Ayana stare intently at the back of Ebony's head. She squints and refocuses her small wire-rimmed glasses on her eyes, studying every detail of her daughter. The wild hair from her mugshot is pulled into a sleek low ponytail just barely showing off small diamond studs glinting from her ears. Slivers of Ebony's skin are visible at each shoulder left uncovered by hair or the collar of her sleeveless cream blouse.

"Ayana, I'm not sure if you know who I am," Dawn starts up the conversation again.

"I know you," Ayana interrupts. "James told me. You work at Channel 9. My baby has watched that station religiously since she was 12."

"Well, I would love it if you would be my guest on the show this evening," Dawn says, offering her real smile with her interview pitch.

"Thank you for the invite. I saw the two of you on Friday." Ayana nods toward Soleil. "But I don't think I can do it. The only person I'm interested in telling all my secrets to, is my baby, right up there."

"Oh."

"It's been too long," Ayana mutters, crossing her hands in her lap.

Dawn watches Ayanna rake her nails across the tops of her hands, as she rocks from side to side in the corner of their bench.

"I saw your interview Friday," Johnnie interrupts Dawn's observations. "It was good."

"Thank you," Dawn and Soleil say together.

"A little tense though," Johnnie continues. "Dawn, you could've gone a little easier on her. I mean, you guys are friends."

"When it comes to my job, Johnnie, I don't go easy on anyone."

"See, that's why you don't have any friends. Well, at least you have a man. You still have a man, right?"

"Y'all, are a mess," Soleil says.

"No. She's the hot mess. I'm just fine," Dawn chides.

"Then answer the question, Dawn. How's Victor doing?" Johnnie challenges.

"How's Nathan?"

Johnnie doesn't say anything. She looks at her friend who stares back at her with lips pursed and body poised, ready to have a conversation that let's Johnnie know they may not remain friends.

"Oooh, oooh, oooh. Someone ask me. I want to play." Soleil bursts in with a smile to ease the tension.

"How's your love life, Soleil?" Johnnie asks.

"He's still dead."

The women laugh at the morbid joke that's eased the tension between them. Johnnie leans her head on the edge of the spectator bench in the courtroom, staring at the backs of James and Ebony's heads. Dawn follows the same gaze as Johnnie and Ayana; each woman wrapped in her own warped thoughts of present, past, and the potential of the future on reconciliation. The potential of the future in the world outside their kindred kinship, evolved away from the tragedy that's brought them together, and threatened to take away everything they once loved, or at least thought they liked.

"Johnnie, when you see him, tell Nathan I said hey," Dawn says, not looking away from Judge Shaw.

"Tell Victor we need to get together for drinks," Johnnie says.

"My turn." Soleil smiles.

"Tell Barker to go to hell." Dawn laughs cutting her eyes at Soleil.

"He's already there," Soleil cackles, covering her mouth.

"I can't believe they just dismissed her," Ayana says abruptly "She would have been a good juror."

"What happened?" Dawn asks through her own muffled fit of giggles.

Ayana doesn't answer. She doesn't turn to Dawn and give her a recap of the nascent beginnings of jury selection. She sits in her own corner, on the opposite end of the bench, staring intently between Judge Shaw and the back of Ebony's head as Ebony watches James and the state attorney in their preliminary round of questioning to find the most preferable jury.

"Let me start taking notes so I don't miss what the hell happens in court," Dawn says aloud.

Dawn pulls out her cell phone and illuminates the screen.

Her text message response comes up. There is no reply. There is no notification on the message at all, besides that it has been delivered. Dawn sucks her teeth and changes screens to her notes app Turning the phone sideways, her thumbs hover above the keys, ready to type or change screens again in case a message vibrates in her hand.

"How was court," Kelly asks Dawn, stepping into her office.

"Interesting," Dawn says, not looking up from her computer screen.

"What was interesting," Jennifer asks, coming into the office behind Kelly.

"Court," Dawn says curtly.

"What was so interesting about the first day of jury selection?" Kelly asks, sitting in one of the chairs in front of Dawn's desk. "We can't even report half of what happened."

Jennifer sits beside Kelly. Dawn looks up at her two producers and slides away from her computer. She glances at the screen of her cell phone sitting atop the stacks of papers sprawled across the desk. The empty black screen belies nothing. Not seeing what she's looking for, Dawn looks up at Kelly and Jennifer.

"The actual jury selection process was typical. It's the person who was in court that's interesting."

"Like who?" Kelly asks.

"Ayana. Ebony's mother."

"Really," Kelly says leaning forward in her chair, "What was she like."

"Quiet. Sad. Something happened between the two of them. I can tell."

"You couldn't tell from the interview last week when she just got up and left the room when you asked her about her family?" Kelly asks with a raised eyebrow.

"Leave Ebony alone. Some people just don't like talking about their family," Jennifer speaks up.

"So quick to come to her defense like you two are best friends."

"You two can do this later," Dawn interrupts the makings of their argument. It was one of many they'd had in the last few weeks leading up to the trial.

"Dawn, can you work some details on Ayana into tonight's show?" Kelly asks. "We definitely have the room."

"I'll see what I can do. And what do you mean we have the room?"

"We're three minutes light," Jennifer says. "That's the reason we came in here in the first place."

"Oh. I'll write up as much as I can on Ayana. There might be a couple shots of her sitting in the courtroom that we got for cutaways. That should eat up some time, but you two need to get back to work and go find me some news."

"It's Monday. The only news we have is Ebony Jones, and the latest from Ferguson." Kelly shrugs standing up.

"We could put the two stories together," Jennifer stands as well. "Michael Brown's funeral was today. And it's the first day of jury selection for Ebony Jones. The umbrella lead will take us right into our interview segment with the defense attorney and African-American studies professor from UNF, and I'm sure the interviews will go way over."

"Sounds like a plan." Dawn picks up her cell phone.

"You can build that out in the rundown." Kelly storms out of the office.

"Oooo-kayyy," Jennifer says following behind her.

"What's that about?" Dawn asks, looking up at Jennifer from where the cursor on her phone blinks in the text box.

"I don't know. I'm not her enemy." Jennifer says with a shrug of her shoulders. "Maybe she's jealous or something. Thinks I'm going to take her job."

"Not with a shirt like that on," Dawn calls behind her, phone still in hand.

"What's wrong with my shirt?" Jennifer asks wide-eyed stepping back into Dawn's office.

"No one needs to know your politics. Especially on divisive issues like race, gender, religion, politics . . . "

"Basically, everything we cover."

"There's nothing wrong with having a position. But wearing it on your back when you work in a newsroom is a bit much. And showing up to a protest with it on could be seen as a conflict of interest and grounds for suspension."

"You saw me?"

"You know we saw you. That's why you turned your back toward the camera when you saw us coming up the walk toward the courthouse steps."

"All my shirt says is 'Black Women Matter'."

"What the shirt says isn't the entire problem, Jennifer, and you know it. It's the fact that you wore it today, to the protest at the courthouse where you were caught on our own cameras, and then to work."

"If you say so." Jennifer stands again.

Dawn watches Jennifer walk out of her office. The back of her shirt screams to everyone who gets behind her that "Black Women Matter," including Julia Gillé who walks by Dawn's office heading to the news set. Dawn watches as Julia reads the back of Jennifer's shirt. She waits for her to turn to her. She does with an icy stare and a shake of her brunette and blonde hair. Dawn waits until Julia completely passes by her office window before she turns back to the open rundown on her computer screen. She moves her hand to type, when she realizes she has to first put down her phone. Jostling it between hands brings the dark screen to illuminated life. Her one word message stares back at her eight hours after she first sent it.

Thanks.

There is no response. No ellipsis blinking on the screen to let her know Victor is in the midst of a response. Her message only shows that it's been read. Dawn sets her phone back down atop the papers across her messy, desk and turns back to her computer screen. The framed Post-it Note catches her eye. "I'm not your enemy." Dawn mouths the written words on the small square paper to herself as she studies every loop and curl of the cursive script.

"Good evening and welcome to 9 News Now at five. I'm Julia Gillé."

Julia's voice resounds from the television hanging in the top right corner of Dawn's office. She picks up the remote control beside her computer, and hits the mute button.

"Maybe *you* are my enemy," Dawn says aloud.

37.

"The defense calls Ebony Jones to the stand."

James's voice resounds among the murmurs in the mostly silent courtroom. He looks at Ebony after he speaks waiting for her to make her move. His face tells her his voice came out louder than he expected. Her face says the same. The lingering reverberations of his tone denotes a baritone beyond the degree of loud that equates being assertive. James was loud and overcompensating. His resounding voice in the closed, claustrophobic courtroom is followed by the echo of silence as heads turn and eyes watch for Ebony to take the stand.

The jury and spectators all look to the defendants table where for two weeks Ebony sat silently in her seat, at the table with James and listened to acquaintances, strangers, medical professionals, and police officers talk about her and what they believe she did. For two weeks Ebony sat silently at her table, engaged in the trial for her own life, taking in the evidence both for and against her: grainy surveillance videos, autopsy photos of Barker and enlarged glossy photos of her own bruises. For two weeks she has watched the facial expressions of the six member jury change in response to persuasive arguments and an even more persuasive reenactment. Now it is her turn.

Ebony rises from her seat at the table making eye contact with no one. Not even James. She allows her movements to speak for her. The swishing back and forth of her white, wide legged pants is the only discernible noise in the packed to capacity courtroom. Sure steps take her from the table where she has sat as a passive defendant to the witness stand where she will finally take an active part in her own defense. The too long hems flit against her skin as she walks. They are a salve for the itch at her ankle as they sing their shuffling song. Whether it is the rhythm of the chain gang or the promising hymn of freedom is still to be determined.

In the witness box, facing the courtroom, all eyes come to her. The strength of their pupils aim at her like daggers. Even the ones that are not present. The gaze of the the camera lens is sharp and focused from its strategically posted position meant to capture all the action; all expressions, all truths, half truths, and outright lies crafted by each side in an effort to determine her innocence or guilt. Ebony ignores them all.

"State your name for the court," the clerk says in a bland voice.

"Ebony. Ayana. Jones."

She inhales at the sound of her own voice. The quickly muted gasp instigates internal notions of surprise. Her voice is softer than she intended, the timbre more timid than practiced. Her effort to remove the emotion from acknowledging her middle name in front of Ayana fails. She knows Ayana has seen her try and fail at indifference. Ebony's fingernails find the tops of each of her hands before she can stop them. They scratch away as she solemnly swears to tell the truth, the whole truth, and nothing but the truth so help her God.

She adjusts her white blouse and blazer against her pants before she takes a seat in the cracked leather chair in the witness box. Her arms, legs, ass and ankle monitor are completely covered by the swaths of loose white fabric. She is once again demure and angelic, and most of all un-intimidating without any false hints of guilt. It is the way James says she must appear on the stand. Ebony catches his eyes with her own and sees his grimacing nod toward her still scratching hands. She covertly places them under her thighs hoping to lessen the attention to her habit that's already told the court she's nervous, because they don't know she's prepared.

"Ebony, what do you do for a living?"

James asks his first question of their rehearsed verbal tango in a casual tone as he approaches Ebony in the box.

"I am a fitness instructor and personal trainer," she answers looking only at him.

James begins his line of questioning as they practiced. He told her each question would build on the previous answer to lay the foundation of who she is, and what she is all about before taking her to the day the jury, the courtroom spectators, the city, the country and even some parts of the globe have questions about. The crime she did not commit.

"Where do you work?"

"I am on leave of absence from LA Fitness in Kernan."

"Have you always worked there as a fitness instructor and personal trainer?"

"No."

"Where did you work before?"

"Fitness 4 You. A private gym on Baymeadows Road near 295. But it's changed names since I've left."

James pauses to look at Ebony before his next question. His stare is hard even though he's managing to keep his face soft. She nods knowing what he wants. Short answers, no explanations unless they're asked for. The tilt of her head translates that she knows her last answer was too long. It is her answer of understanding to the boyfriend she cannot answer like a girlfriend, while testifying for her life, and ignoring an itch at her ankle and the one creeping across the tops of her hands still stuck beneath the heavy muscles of her thighs.

"How long did you work there?"

"About eight years from the time I graduated college?"

"What college did you attend."

"The Florida State University."

"What did you study?"

"I graduated with a Bachelors of Science in Athletic Training."

"And after graduation you began working at Fitness 4 You until about two years ago?"

"Yes."

"Why did you leave Fitness 4 You."

"My professional relationship with my clients was compromised."

"How so?"

"By the ending of my relationship with the client of another trainer."

"Who was that client?"

"The late Judge Barker Gordon," Ebony says, giving Barker all the respect and deference James insisted he deserved since he told her she is *allegedly* responsible for his death.

Ebony bites her bottom lip after saying his name. It rolled off her tongue evenly. Whereas she said her own name with fear haunting the acknowledgement of herself before her future mirror; resurrecting the ghost of the man who tormented her into a crime she did not commit comes with apathy rather than her expected antipathy.

"Why did you end your relationship with the late Judge Gordon?"

"He became abusive."

"How was he abusive? Mentally, physically, emotionally?"

"All of the above."

"Can you be more specific."

"He was physically abusive. We got together after first boxing each other at the gym. The first time he beat me he slapped me across my face leaving this scar on my forehead," Ebony says bringing both hands to her face.

It is the first time she has moved them from beneath her thighs since James began his questioning. They no longer itch with anxiety. Instead they are numb and unexpressive doing as she wills them to instead of as they involuntarily please.

"He was also mentally and emotionally abusive," Ebony continues bringing her hands to her lap. "He would call me pet names with a grimace. Gorgeous was his favorite. He would caress me with one hand while squeezing me hard with the other, and send me flowers with notes where his words were more threat than the concern of an over protective boyfriend."

"How long were the two of you together?"

"Three months."

"When did he first hit you?"

"The first time he hit me we were boxing each other. But it wasn't in anger. That was how we started dating, but about a month after that he backhanded me leaving me with this scar on my forehead."

Again, Ebony brings her hands to her face just above her eye to call attention to the permanent reminder of what happened to her. James waits for her to finish gesturing and for the courtroom and cameras to finish taking in her scar before continuing.

In their final practice session, sprawled in the middle of Ebony's living room last night James told Ebony he wanted her to talk about her scar in as many answers as she could so that they could flip sympathies and make the jury believe she was the true victim. He said he wanted to make her more sympathetic by pointing out the reminder of a scar they could still see in person, instead of just the hi-definition poster sized pictures of the bruises after the accident with her car. James assured her the scar on her face in addition to the pictures of her bruises would prove to the jury that she too is a victim. Ebony cared less about the latest strategy for her defense. Sitting in one of her multi-colored striped armchairs last night, she barely listened as James rambled about tricks, tactics, and logistics like he was going to war, she was only concerned with what he believed.

It is the same concern she brought to the courtroom now that she is no longer pretending to testify. Sitting in the witness stand she knows she must convince not just the jury, but James as well. His belief in her testimony will truly transform her into a victim, a belief she knows he did not have as they strategized one last time. He paced the open square space of the living room in black boxers, while she lounged in his oversized undershirt and ever itching ankle monitor, neither of them acknowledging that he still did not trust her version of events. He replaced any care or concern for the truth with a will to win. Looking at him now as she delivers the answers he has already heard, Ebony looks for his sympathy. She looks to see if he believes whether she is a victim or perpetrator.

"So you began your relationship in violence?"

"Yes."

"Why?"

"We boxed in the gym because I was tired of him interrupting my training session with my client. I was trying to get him to leave me alone but it didn't work. Instead I was drawn to him."

"Ms. Jones how tall are you?"

"Five feet and two inches."

"How tall was Judge Gordon?"

"More than six feet."

"And you thought you could beat him? A man nearly a foot or more taller than you, in boxing, and make him leave you alone?"

"I didn't think I could beat him in boxing. But I knew I could hold my own. At the very least he would have to work to catch me and land a punch."

"Is it safe to say you enjoyed his abusive side?"

Ebony controls the grimace threatening to erupt on her face. She hates the question. She told James that two months ago when they first started preparing. To Ebony, it sounds like he's blaming her before they even get to the crime. He said he wanted to be both prosecutor and defense attorney in his questioning so that she doesn't get caught off guard on cross examination; so that she can answer any question, in her favor or not, calmly as her truth says it happened.

"No. I wouldn't say I enjoyed his abusive side. At the time I didn't know he was abusive. Obsessive maybe but not abusive."

"Do you think boxing with him showed the potential of his abuse?"

"In retrospect yes."

"But you decided to move forward with the relationship and date him anyway even though you thought he was obsessive? Then a month later he became physically abusive when he slapped you across your forehead and left you with a scar?"

"Yes."

"Was that the only time he was physically abusive toward you?"

"No. There was one other time?"

"What happened in that circumstance?"

242

"He raped me."

"How did he rape you if you were his girlfriend?"

Another question Ebony hates. Another battle with her face in front of the jury, the spectators, Ayana, and the cameras. She's forced to wage war with herself, and win, to keep her unassuming appearance of innocence. To James it didn't matter how much she protested since he first sprang the question on her last night. "How does this help me?" She asked him. His answer was that she had to play to both the men and the women on the jury because she didn't know who would be judging her if the verdict was close. He said women are more forgiving of rape victims than men are. He reasoned that if she could convince the men she had been raped by a lover than they would take up her cause, become her champion, and try to save her from a punishment she did not deserve, since they couldn't save her from the man who put her in the position of a criminal even though she never committed a crime.

"I was sitting on the couch when he grabbed my ankles and pulled me to the floor," Ebony recounts. "He dragged me by my ankles from the living room in my house to my bedroom. My thighs squeaked as they rubbed across the waxed hardwood floors of my home and were left with burns as he roughly pulled me across the carpet of my bedroom."

"Ms. Jones, while that is a horrible story to imagine it does not constitute a rape," James interrupts.

He wants the three men on the jury to hate him. He wants them to see him as Barker, the bad boyfriend, and for them to put themselves in his position, the good boyfriend. The champion. The defender. It is legal theater and Ebony is the costar; the supporting actress in her own drama.

"When we got to my bedroom he picked me up, threw me on my bed, yanked down my panties, unbuckled his pants and forced himself inside me saying 'This never lies.'"

"Did you tell him to stop?"

"No."

"Why not?"

"Because I was trying to reason with him that I hadn't done anything wrong for him to flip out on me the way he was."

"What did he think you had done?"

"He thought I was cheating on him."

"Did you?"

"No."

"So why would he think that?"

"Because I was half dressed when he came to my home."

"Why were you half dressed?"

The battle begins on Ebony's face as she reaches for the answer she's prepared. She looks to her row of support she knows is for her, Johnnie, Soleil, Dawn and even Ayana. Ebony looks at the faces on the one row in the courtroom she knows is rooting for her to settle her face and answer yet another question she told James she hated as they worked through the new line of questioning. He said every question is intentional. Looking at Soleil's stunned face she can see his working theory is having it's desired effect. Victim blaming and slut shaming. A purpose she didn't understand when he began last night; a purpose with a dubious value as she prepares to deliver the answer he's waiting for. His answer to her uncertainty was that he'd rather be the one to tear her down than someone else.

"It was the middle of summer and the air conditioner in my home was broken. I was trying to stay cool?"

"And he thought you were cheating on him?"

"He thought I had an affair with the repair man, or someone, because I hadn't told him about the repair in advance, even though the repair man never came."

"So you two had an argument and he raped you."

"We didn't have an argument. You didn't argue with Barker. You never got the chance to. You have a conversation and then you're not having a conversation because he's hitting you or raping you."

"So while he raped you, on your bed, in your house what did you do?"

"I reached for my gun."

"Where was your gun?"

"Under my pillow."

"Why did you have it there?"

"For protection."

"Protection from what?"

"Barker."

"So you knew he was going to rape you in your bedroom?"

"No, but I knew he would do something and that the gun would protect me."

"When did you buy the gun?"

"After the first time he hit me leaving this scar on my face."

"So he backhands you across your face one month after the two of you began dating? You buy a gun, and then another month passes and that's when he rapes you and you pull a gun on him?"

"Objection. Leading," the state attorney yells from where she stands behind her table.

Her ice blue eyes lock Ebony in a stare with the same cold her ill fitting navy blue skirt suit emanates. She is Medusa beneath teased tresses and pearls, but Ebony refuses to scare herself into statue stillness. She holds the gaze of her oppressor until Judge Shaw renders her verdict on the call.

"Sustained," Judge Shaw says looking at James.

"I'll rephrase your honor," James says with a glint of a smile. "Ms. Jones, what did you do after you reached for your gun?"

"Once I was able to grip it, I pulled it out and placed the barrel of the gun on his head."

"What happened after that?"

"He stopped and opened his eyes and I told him to get out."

"Did he leave?"

"No. He laughed."

"What did you do?"

"I cocked the gun and pressed the barrel harder into his forehead."

"Did he leave then?"

"Yes."

"From these stories some would say you're prone to violence. Boxing. Staying with a man after he slapped you. Pulling a gun on him. They would say you wanted the late Judge Gordon dead two years before you killed him. Would you agree with their assessment?"

"No."

"Why is that?"

"Because after he walked out of my door I left my job so I wouldn't see him anymore, and I didn't for two years until this past March."

James walks to the table after Ebony's answer. He doesn't follow up with a question about her seeing Judge Gordon after his appointment to the bench. He didn't work out and rehearse the question last night, or a week ago, or two months ago, and he doesn't begin to rehash history that has become his own. Or maybe he doesn't remember. A year is long time to forget what was never meant to be retained.

Instead, James reaches for his plastic water bottle and brings it to his lips. It is a practiced pause. A cue to let Ebony know they are going to shift from the past to the present. While he drinks his water Ebony takes the opportunity to cross her legs at the ankles, and wrap her arms behind her chair. She scratches the tops of her hands and shackled ankle until her skin satiates in the relief of cotton fabric and her own raking nails. Ebony lets both of her pants legs and nails drag across the itching parts of her body until James turns back toward her.

She uncurls her ankles and releases her hands as he smooths his own against the breasts of his black suit jacket. His all black three piece suit is another layer to their legal theater. He in all black and she in all white. After the jury was selected two weeks ago he said he would help her win the men. Her job is to keep the women.

"Ms. Jones, where were you when you saw Judge Gordon on Saturday March 15th."

"I was accompanying you to a luncheon held by the mayor at the Southside Marriott."

"What did you do when you first saw Judge Gordon at that event?"

"I ran to the bathroom because I was upset."

"Did you have any one on one encounters or did you just observe him from a distance?"

"He asked me to dance?"

"Did you oblige his request?"

"I said only if his date didn't mind."

"Who was his date?"

"Soleil St. James," Ebony says pointing to Soleil nestled between Dawn and Johnnie on her favorite spectator bench.

Her rock of women have been seated on the same bench in the same order every day for the last two weeks. Johnnie, Soleil, Dawn, Ayana. Even the latter woman's presence had become a comfort. Despite the shakiness of her voice at the acknowledgement of her name, over the last two weeks Ebony's eyes never flutter when they find the face that's beginning to look more like her own.

"Did Miss St. James mind if you danced with Judge Gordon?"

"I don't know. He didn't care if she did or not."

"What happened?"

"I danced with Judge Gordon and Soleil danced with you."

"Did you and Judge Gordon just dance or did you all talk."

"We talked but I don't think you can call the words we exchanged a conversation."

"Why not?"

"Because I didn't want to talk to him."

"What did he say to you?"

"He said we had a lot of catching up to do. He said he missed me and that no one else had ever put up a fight like I did."

"And you said?"

"I told him I didn't fight fair. Then I told him Soleil was finally enjoying herself dancing with you."

"How did he react to that?"

"He became angry."

"Did you say it to make him angry on purpose?"

"Yes."

"Why?"

"Because he deserved it."

"What did he do after he saw Miss St. James dancing with me?"

"He said he would deal with her later."

"Did you two continue dancing after he threatened Miss St. James?"

"No. I broke away from him and went outside with her so that we could talk."

"Did she want to go with you?"

"No, but I made her."

"Why don't you think she wanted to talk to you?"

"Objection, Your Honor. Hearsay," the State Attorney says standing from her table.

"How is it hearsay when Miss St. James has already testified that she did not want to speak to Ms. Jones in seclusion on the day in question?" James asks.

"Overruled," Judge Shaw says banging her gavel.

"Again, Ms. Jones, Why don't you think Miss St. James wanted to talk to you?"

"Because she knew Judge Gordon would beat her."

"When you two spoke did she tell you that he was abusing her."

"She didn't have to."

"So she never said out of her own mouth that she was being abused?" James asks turning away from Ebony.

He is turning into the villain. His questions are quick and gruff. His voice taking on an aggravated and disbelieving edge. His peppering back and forth is purposeful. He is bringing Ebony closer to the day their lives changed, to the day she became the victim in a crime she did not commit.

"She admitted to the abuse once I told her my history with Judge Gordon. We have the same scar."

"Did she want you to do something to help her get out of the relationship?"

"No."

"Did she ask your advice on how she should get out of the relationship?"

"No."

"Did you offer advice for her to get out of the relationship?"

"I told her she should leave him."

"Did you help Miss St. James devise a plan to get out of the relationship?"

"No."

The answer is a half truth. A half truth Ebony tells while looking at Soleil. Johnnie, Dawn and Ayana remain blurry through her periphery as Ebony focuses on Soleil alone. Her tightly coiled ringlets pulled to the top of her head show off the scar on her face with pride. It is uncovered as is the rest of her face. No purple blush or iridescent eyeshadow or heavy black eyeliner. Her face is fresh and more beautiful than the day they first met. The day they bonded over her misery. The day Ebony told Soleil to do something to make Barker never want to come back. The honest truth neither of them has told. Soleil didn't say it to Dawn during her interview. Ebony has never said it to James in any of their practice sessions, and she won't say it to him or the world now. Ebony stares at Soleil's hauntingly beautiful face, honing in on her light expressive eyes, to tell her their unspoken pact is in tact.

"Did Miss St. James ask you to confront the late Judge Gordon on her behalf?"

"No."

"Then why did you go to the courthouse on Wednesday, March 19th?"

"To tell Judge Gordon to leave Soleil alone."

"Why did you do that if she never asked you to?"

"Because I felt like it was the right thing to do."

"Why is that?"

"Because I understood what she was going through and knew it was getting worse because she had been with him for twice as long as I had."

"So what did you plan to do once you confronted Judge Gordon that Wednesday morning?"

"Talk to him and tell him to leave Soleil alone."

"How did that go?"

"Not well."

"Explain what happened."

"He said, 'You two bitches have a lot of nerve.' He grabbed my wrists and slammed me back against my car. He kept slamming me until my gun went off."

"Where was your gun?"

"In the pocket of my hoodie."

"Why did you bring your gun with you?"

"For protection?"

"Is it the same protection you were seeking when you first bought the gun after Judge Gordon hit you leaving that scar on your face?"

"Yes."

"Is it the same protection you were seeking when you pulled the gun on Judge Gordon as he raped you?"

"Yes."

"Did you know you would need protection when you tried to save Miss St. James?"

"I knew the threat of the gun would help keep me safe."

"Did you have any intention of using the gun that morning when you met Judge Gordon?"

"No."

"So why did you bring it with you?"

"Just to feel safe and to keep him from jumping on me."

"Did Judge Gordon know you had the gun the morning you met him?"

"No."

"Did you ever tell him you had the gun while you two were together that morning?"

"No."

"Did you threaten him with the gun when you two met that morning?"

"No."

"If he didn't know you were armed, and you never threatened him with the gun, how was it supposed to keep you safe?"

"It didn't."

"What do you mean?"

"When I told him to leave Soleil he got angry and pushed against me to intimidate me.

"Objection Your Honor," the state attorney says jumping from her wooden chair.

"On what grounds?" Judge Shaw asks after the murmuring in the room dies down.

"She can't purport to know the victim's state of mind or intent in his alleged actions. Judge Barker Gordon is not the one on trial here. Ebony Jones is on trial for the second degree murder of Judge Barker Gordon. I think we need to make clear who is the victim and who is the suspect in this case, Your Honor."

The state attorney finishes her diatribe with an exasperated sigh.

"I'll rephrase, Your Honor," James smiles refusing to argue with his former boss.

"Keep your questions straight, Mr. Parnell."

"Yes, Ma'am, Your Honor."

"Ms. Jones," James says walking back to face Ebony in the witness stand. "Why don't you think your gun kept you safe while you were asking Judge Gordon to leave Miss St. James alone?"

"Barker got angry when I told him to leave Soleil," Ebony says pulling out her default answer James made her have in case of objections. "He pushed his body against me. I think it was to intimidate me. At least that's what I felt. I tried to push him back and that's when he grabbed my wrist."

"So how did you end up shooting him?"

"I didn't. The gun went off on its own when he slammed me against my car."

"Did you know you had shot the judge when the gun went off?"

"No. The gunshots startled me."

"What did you do next?"

"He let me go and I got in my car to drive away."

"Why?"

I can't breathe.

Barker's last words to Ebony as he stumbled to his knees rush back to her brain as she prepares to answer James' question. They are his last words she has tried to forget. His last words she thought she didn't hear. The last words she ever heard Barker speak.

I can't breathe.

He coughed up the blood that landed on her face as he struggled for breath.

I can't breathe.

"Why did you drive away, Ms. Jones?"

"Because I was scared."

"Take me through what you did once you got into your car."

"When I slammed the door my window shattered. It cracked when I was slammed against the car. That scared me even more so I pulled into the morning traffic on Broad and drove home."

"Did you ever stop to see if Judge Gordon was alright?"

"No."

"Why not?"

"I didn't know he was hurt."

I can't breathe.

"Did you think he was hurt once you heard the gun go off?"

"At the time I didn't know my gun went off. Like I said the noise startled me. I thought the noise startled him too and that's why he let me go. I wasn't thinking about him."

Ebony bites her lip regretting the words immediately as she says them. They are not part of what she and James practiced, but they are the truest words she has spoken in this revisionist version of history. James' expression is irritation personified. He doesn't appreciate the actual truth. His wrinkled forehead, furrowed brow, and steely brown eyes tell her she has testified to too much. His countenance urges Ebony to stick to their script, to their version of the events, to the final draft of the testimony they finished perfecting last night. James turns away from Ebony in the witness stand and walks toward their table.

"I just wanted to get away and get to safety," Ebony blurts to his back.

His shoulders relax as she goes back to their script, but he doesn't turn around again. Ebony crosses her legs and arms again and scratches as he picks up the water bottle on the table and takes another long drink. It is another cue. His drag on the bottle tells her they are nearing the end of her testimony. With the gulps down his throat he relays that she is almost finished telling her truth. Their truth, even though Ebony still doesn't know if he believes her.

"You didn't feel safe even though you had your gun with you?"

"No."

"Did your gun keep you safe?"

"No."

"Were you hurt by Judge Gordon that morning?"

"Physically? Yes. I had deep bruises all down my back from where he slammed me against the car. He slammed me so hard my body dented my door and cracked my window which shattered."

"Did the force of your body being slammed against your car door cause your gun to go off?"

"I'm not a gun expert but I believe it did."

"Did you pull the trigger of your gun to kill Judge Gordon?"

"No."

"But your fingerprints are on the trigger."

"It's my gun."

"Did you kill Judge Gordon?"

"No."

"Did you plan to kill Judge Gordon?"

"No."

"Why did you bring a loaded gun to your meeting with Judge Gordon?"

"To keep me safe."

"Did that gun keep you safe?"

"No."

"But safety from him is why you bought the gun in the first place?"

"Yes."

"Did you feel safe knowing you had the gun when you were around him?"

"At first. Then he slammed me against the car and me having a gun no longer mattered. Against him my gun didn't matter. Against him I knew I would never be safe. No woman would."

"Your witness," James says to the state attorney walking back to his own table.

38.

"Ms. Jones," the state attorney begins from her chair at the prosecution's table. "I'd like to go back to the first time you said you saw Judge Gordon after your break up two years ago? When exactly was that again?

"The date of the mayor's luncheon. March 15th," Ebony answers confidently.

"Are you sure that's the first time you saw him since the two of you broke up?" She asks now standing at the front of her table rifling through a stack of papers.

"Yes."

"Ms. Jones, I'd like to remind you that you are still under oath and under penalty of perjury if you are lying."

"My client knows her rights," James says standing from the defense table.

"What is this about?" Judge Shaw asks the state attorney.

"Your Honor, the people are just trying to truthfully ascertain the first time Ms. Jones was reunited with Judge Gordon."

"That question has been asked and answered four times now," Judge Shaw says emphatically. "Please move on."

"Ms. Jones, did you see Judge Gordon at any time during March of 2013?"

"No."

"Again, Ms. Jones, you are under penalty of perjury if you are lying so I'm going to ask you again, did you see Judge Gordon at any time in March 2013?"

"No," Ebony answers vehemently.

The state attorney stalks to where Ebony sits upright in the witness box with a stack of papers in her hand. Her easy gait, and soundless shoes, leaves the courtroom quiet save for the sway of papers against the polyester of her ill fitting burgundy skirt suit.

"Ms. Jones, on what day did you meet Mr. Parnell?"

"Objection, relevance," James says quickly standing again.

"Your Honor, if you'll allow it I promise this will all make sense very quickly," The State Attorney pleads.

"Then you better make it quick," Judge Shaw nods with growing irritation.

"Ms. Jones, again, on what day did you meet Mr Parnell?"

"Monday March 11, 2013."

"Isn't that the same day then State Attorney Barker Gordon was appointed as a judge by Governor Rick Scott?"

"I guess," Ebony answers unsure of where the state attorney is leading her.

"It is," the state attorney affirms. "And where did you meet Mr Parnell on Monday March 11, 2013?"

"Outside of his office," Ebony answers recognizing the trap being laid for her.

"And what office is that, Ms. Jones? Please be specific."

"The State Attorney's Office," Ebony answers begrudgingly.

"And did you meet Mr. Parnell before or after his work day began?"

"Before."

"Did you happen to see then State Attorney Barker Gordon that same day you met Mr Parnell?"

"I guess."

"So the mayor's luncheon on March 15th of this year was not the first time that you saw Judge Gordon correct?"

"I guess not."

"And isn't it true you saw Judge Gordon several more times after you met Mr. Parnell?"

"No?" Ebony questions her own answer.

"Your Honor, I have in my hand the destinations Ms. Jones traveled to over the last 18 months pulled from the GPS of her car that's already been entered into evidence as defense exhibit 1. Permission to please approach the witness with these findings."

"Permission granted," Judge Shaw says with intrigue coating her voice.

The state attorney trudges quickly to where Ebony sits in the witness box. Her hulking, boxy frame looms over her, the strong scent of floral perfume mixed with sweat emanates from the prosecutor's long sleeved skirt suit and wafts into Ebony's face making her eyes water. She coughs to clear the smell from her nostrils, taking the distracting opportunity to wipe the tears from her eyes.

"Ms. Jones, please tell me your location according to your GPS on Sunday March 31, 2013?"

"I can't see the papers," Ebony stalls.

"It's this line highlighted in yellow," The State Attorney says shoving the papers into the bridge of Ebony's nose. "Can you read it now?"

"I can read it."

"What does it say, Ms. Jones?"

"It says I was at the Cracker Barrel on 438 Commerce Center Drive in Regency Square."

"And where does it say you were on Sunday, April 7, 14, 21, and 28th, Ms. Jones?

"The same."

"And what about on Sunday, September 8, 2013. Where does your GPS say you were that day?"

"The same."

"Your Honor, I fail to see the point in this line of questioning," James says seated from their table. "My client has a penchant for southern food on Sunday's. Sounds to me like she's following in the old negro tradition of Sunday dinner which last time I checked is not criminal."

"Mr. Parnell is right," Judge Shaw says stifling a yawn. "Please get to the point or I'm going to instruct the jury to disregard this entire line of questioning."

"Your Honor, here is the point right here," the State Attorney says graciously. "Ms. Jones, who else besides yourself frequents the Regency Square Cracker Barrel on Sunday mornings?"

"I don't know. The people who live in Arlington and Regency."

"Ms. Jones isn't it true that Judge Gordon used to frequent that same restaurant every Sunday?"

"I don't know. I'm not his keeper."

"Isn't it true you followed Judge Gordon to that restaurant every Sunday for the last year?"

"No," Ebony answers technically telling the truth.

"Ms. Jones would you read this highlighted line of GPS data please? Where does it say you were on the evening of March 13, 2014."

"The Coventry Park apartments."

"Your Honor, I would like to refer the court back to State's evidence, item 19, the statement of Judge Gordon's girlfriend Soleil St. James. That is the same apartment complex where she lives."

"So noted," Judge Shaw says with a bright lilt to her voice.

"Ms. Jones, what day did you meet Soleil St. James?"

"The day of the mayor's luncheon on March 15th."

"Then why were you at her apartment complex two days before?"

"She's not the only one who lives there. I do have friends you know," Ebony says with a smile creeping up on her lips.

She chances looking at James sitting at their table. His face i
drained of it's normally rich brown color. His cheeks are hollow an
gaunt and his skin is pale. The masked front he put on to present hi
case with his star witness is gone. What's left is the willowy man wh
joined Ebony for her interview with Dawn. The fiery, argumentativ
prosecutor and boyfriend is gone. The unbelieving defense attorne
who remains is learning with the jury, the court spectators, and Ebony
bench of support who the "Judge Killer" really is.

James does not make eye contact with her. He stares at th
yellow legal pad before him, either taking notes or doodling. Avoidin
her gaze he loses himself in his scribbled timeline of his relationshi
juxtaposed against the ghost timeline of Ebony's deception.

"Ms. Jones, isn't it true you saw Judge Gordon at Cracker Barre
on Sunday, September 8, 2013?"

"I don't know," Ebony answers.

"And isn't it true you saw him the day he met Soleil St. Jame
which was September 8, 2013?"

"I don't recall," Ebony answers.

"Isn't it true you followed Judge Gordon to Soleil St. James'
house between September 8, 2013 and March 15, 2014."

"I don't recall," Ebony answers.

"Isn't it true, Ms. Jones, that you were jealous that Judg
Gordon had moved on from you?"

"No."

"Isn't it true that you went after Judge Gordon on the mornin
of Wednesday, March 19, 2014, not to tell him to leave Miss St. Jame
alone, but to tell him to take you back because you were jealous?"

"Why would I go back to that woman beating bastard?" Ebon
asks aloud.

"Your honor please instruct the witness to answer th
question."

"Ms. Jones, yes or no answers please," Judge Shaw demands.

"No. I did not go to see Barker to tell him to take me back.
was already in a relationship."

"Ms. Jones, you say you bought the .38 caliber Lady Smith anc
Wesson after Judge Gordon allegedly slapped you?"

"Yes, he left this scar on my face, that's correct."

"Before the day Judge Gordon was murdered had you ever sho
the Lady Smith?"

"No."

"You never went to the gun range to learn how to handle your weapon?"

"No."

"Did you take any classes on firearm safety to prepare you to have the weapon?"

"Yes."

"In those classes you never shot the gun?"

"No. Not without assistance."

"Which is it, Ms. Jones? Have you ever shot the gun. Yes or No."

"Yes, but . . . "

"So, Ms. Jones, you were just untruthful?" the State Attorney interrupts.

"No I wasn't."

"Have you shot your gun before? Yes or no?"

"With assistance . . . "

"Yes or No," the state attorney demands loudly facing the spectators in the courtroom.

"I can't give you a yes or no answer?"

"Then what's your answer, Ms. Jones."

"I've never pulled the trigger. I only shot My Lady with assistance and even then I had my hands positioned around the concealed carry instructor's hands and he shot the gun. I've never shot it on my own."

"But your fingerprints are all over the trigger, Ms. Jones. Can you explain that?"

"As I said earlier, it's my gun. My fingerprints are going to be all over it, including the trigger."

"Ms. Jones, if you only bought the gun for protection from Judge Gordon, why did you keep it after you two broke up?"

"Because it was mine."

James puts his head on the defense table in front of him. It lands with an audible thud. Both Ebony and the state attorney turn and look in his direction. Their eyes do not entice him to lift his head. He feels the stares of everyone in the room. He knows his actions are un-choreographed ad-libs that could make the minds of the jurors dance away from his carefully crafted piece of the truth to their own conclusions. But he does not lift his head. Not right away. His eyes raise first, followed by his mouth moving in inaudible mumbles, then his head rolls to the top of his neck. The water on his face is apparent. Sweat from his forehead, or tears from his eyes, stream down his cheeks in rivulets. His countenance assumes the guilt Ebony doesn't feel. She looks away from him and back to the State Attorney.

"Did you ever have any intention of shooting your gun, Ms Jones?"

"No."

"Then why did you bring it with you on the morning of Wednesday, March 19, 2014."

"To keep me safe?"

"But the gun didn't keep you safe did it?"

"Around Barker nothing keeps you safe."

"In fact you put yourself in more danger by having the gun with you, did you not?"

"No."

"Well, Judge Gordon is dead because you say he allegedly bumped you the wrong way and the Lady Smith suddenly fired through your hoodie into his stomach. Couldn't that have been you?"

"Objection, Your Honor," James says weakly from the desk. "Cause for speculation. My client has already said she is not a gun expert."

"Your Honor, the people aren't looking for Ms. Jones's expertise, only her opinion."

"Overruled. And Mr. Parnell, do you need a recess to get yourself together?" Judge Shaw asks.

"No, Your Honor, I'm fine."

"Then act like it while you're in my courtroom. Sit up. And wipe your face," she admonishes.

The reprimand sends murmurs through the courtroom. Chatter picks up, stares at James increase with turning heads on each bench of the courtroom. He is now in the hot seat instead of Ebony. His actions and inactions are in question instead of her own.

"Ms. Jones," the state attorney says getting back to her cross examination.

"Yes."

"Couldn't you have ended up being the one shot and left for dead from your own gun when you say Judge Gordon bumped you against the car."

"First of all, it was more than a bump," Ebony corrects vehemently. "Secondly, I don't know if I could have been shot. Maybe it's a possibility."

"Thank you, Ms. Jones…"

"What I do know is that I didn't shoot him."

"Thank You, Ms. Jones."

"It's kind of hard to point, aim, and shoot someone, through clothing when you're just trying to brace yourself to be slammed through a car window."

"Your Honor," the state attorney pouts.

"That's enough, Ms. Jones," Judge Shaw bangs her gavel.

"I was fighting for my life out there," Ebony yells undeterred steering the case back in her favor.

"The jury will disregard Ms. Jones's last statements," Judge Shaw bangs her gavel again. "Another outburst like that, Ms. Jones, and I will hold you in contempt."

"Thank you, Your Honor," the state attorney says. "Ms. Jones who was shot and killed on Wednesday, March 19, 2014?"

"Barker."

"Whose gun is the murder weapon?"

"Mine."

"The people rest, Your Honor?" The state attorney says walking away from Ebony back to her table leaving the list of GPS coordinates at the witness stand. She walks with pride back to her chair, sitting with a smug smile, and a whisper of satisfaction to the assistant state attorney beside her. The ASA who took James's position as protege when he left to defend Ebony.

The exchange between the prosecutors is not lost on him. Their camaraderie fuels him as he stands from the defense table and faces Judge Shaw. His face is dry and composed. The color returned to his cheeks.

"Redirect, Your Honor?" James asks Judge Shaw.

"Make it quick," she says annoyed.

"Ebony, what injuries did the doctors in the infirmary of the Duval County Jail say you had after you turned yourself in, in the death of Judge Gordon?"

"They said I had fractured ribs and a bruised appendix."

"Were there any other injuries?"

"I had cuts in my scalp from my head flailing against the glass when Barker slammed me against it."

"Were those injuries incurred before or after the gun went off?"

"Before," Ebony answers confidently riffing off of James' new found energy.

"Were you able to reach for your gun as your body was being slammed against your car, and your head bobbled on your neck against the glass?"

"No?"

"Did you shoot Judge Gordon?"

"No."

"That is all Your Honor," James says sitting back at the defense table he never moved from.

Ebony sighs her appreciation without looking at him. Her eyes drift to the only place she's allowed herself to look, other than the judge and jury, the entire trial. She looks to her bench. Fresh tears fall freely down the dried streaks of Soleil's eyes. She knows Ebony was not following Barker, but following her. Her tears acknowledge the attempt by the then stranger to keep her safe. The tears she taught herself not to cry for the last six months fall unchallenged and unrestrained. They are tears Ebony cannot cry herself. The stream of Soleil's waterfall rains down her face in big round drops. Ayana, with moist eyes and clammy hands, rocks the bench with one arm wrapped around Dawn and Soleil. Johnnie's arm meets her hand. Dawn, in the middle of the emotion leaves her face expressionless. Ebony sees her belief has waned though not yet erased. She stares at her support system being rocked by Ayana, her face contorted in pain with emotions too numerous to properly display. She rocks, staring at her daughter, one arm around the women, the other scratching a leg in place of a hand.

Their cavalcade of emotion forces Ebony to finally look at the other faces and eyes staring at her in the room. She faces them all with the freedom of expressionlessness until she reaches the guises of the jurors. To them she gives them their due respect looking at each of them one by one. The three women and the three men. It is unclear if they believe her; if they will find her innocent or guilty, but she does not look at them to discern her judgement. She looks to see the impact her testimony has made. Some of their lips are twisted and curled others have their eyebrows raised. The expressions of others are more subtle; finger taps, bouncing knees, chewing mouths, and gritting teeth. They are uncomfortable, adequately agitated, but for whom is still unknown.

Ebony finally brings her gaze back to James as he sits facing her. The water bottle on the table beside him has long been empty. The papers and files stacked in front of his seat are again neatly organized into an even and dense square pile. All except the yellow legal pad holding his two scribbled timelines. Their legal theater is over and their lives are beginning again. He is no longer her villain and she his victim. They are back to Ebony and James; lovers playing court in their underwear, reluctant attorney and ungrateful client, skeptical defender and defiant defendant.

"The defense rests, Your Honor."

39.

"Is the defense ready to present their closing argument today," Judge Shaw asks after Ebony returns to their table.

"Yes, Your Honor," James answers.

"Is the prosecution ready?"

"Yes, Your Honor. We're ready to proceed and see that justice is done."

"You don't need to testify about justice, Madam State Attorney. That's what we're all here for," Judge Shaw admonishes. "We will take a one hour recess. Closing arguments will begin at 1 p.m. sharp."

Judge Shaw's bang of the gavel dismisses the courtroom. Johnnie, Soleil, Dawn, and Ayana rise from where they're seated on their bench. They side step their way in the narrow walk space between the pews until they reach the aisle. Johnnie walks forward to where Ebony and James sit. Soleil and Dawn follow. Ayana waits behind.

"How do you feel?" Johnnie asks in a thick voice, and heavy tongue stuck between her teeth from hours of not talking.

During Ebony's testimony the women did not exchange words. Their communication was non-verbal. Head nods, neck snaps, tears, hand-holding, and body rocking. Sometimes one at a time. Sometimes all at once. They sat silently and listened to their friend describe her state of mind and motivations.

"Do you think you've won them over?" Dawn asks behind Johnnie.

"I assume that question is for my attorney," Ebony deflects.

"It is," James interjects in an irritated and gruff voice. "Dawn Anthony we have no comment to the press at this time."

"Then off the record," Soleil says stepping into the conversation. "Do you think you guys won them over. That was one helluva testimony."

"Off the record," James whispers, "I think our fight is just beginning. I think they're intrigued just enough to be persuaded either way, especially with the GPS evidence."

"Then you better have a damn good close," Ebony says without a smile.

"You did good, Baby," Ayana says from her perch against the court bench.

Ebony nods in Ayana's direction. It is her only acknowledgment. The simple gesture sends Ayana with tentative steps forward. Indecision resounds with every flat plant of her foot. Johnnie sees Ebony's body tense up. She looks between mother and daughter. Daughter and mother. Tension bubbling with every pace Ayana takes to close the gap. The roiling boil of bitterness between them is palpable. It radiates off of Ebony's skin. Ayana's redemption will not be as easy as prayer after the benediction. Ebony is not interested in redemption, only James's pragmatic approach to making sure she's saved.

"Ms. Jones," James utters. "It's been nice to see you on our row these last two weeks. You've been a welcome sight among these three," James says nodding toward Dawn, Johnnie, and Soleil.

"It's nice to meet you, James. Even under these circumstances," Ayana replies. "I wish I could hold you," she says to Ebony.

Ayana's voice breaks as she presses the bottom half of her body against the wooden apron separating her from Ebony.

"You never wanted to hold me before," Ebony says not looking at her.

"Don't do this now," James pleads.

"I'm not doing anything."

"I wish I could hug you," Ayana reaches her hand across the apron.

"You never wanted to hug me before."

"I've got to go guys," Johnnie blurts out. "I gotta get Dani."

Johnnie scampers out of the courtroom and heads for the emergency exit stair well. She races down the five flights of stairs as tears rain down her eyes. Out of the exit, through the ground floor rotunda, and out of the main doors of the courthouse Johnnie bolts. She rushes the dozens of protesters chanting in clusters on the lush green courtyard outside. The gathered groups have ramped up their steady chorus of "Black Women Matter, Black Women Matter." Everyone else may be on a lunch break but the protesters are not. They chant for change as Johnnie flees the scene. Her feet carry her quickly away from their chorus of couplets, away from the failed reunification of mother and daughter, and away from Ebony's testimony. Testimony Johnnie will never give in the trial where she will never be the defendant despite her own guilt. Speed walking to the parking garage across the street from the courthouse Johnnie tries to trample her bubbling emotions.

I didn't know he was hurt.

Bits of Ebony's testimony swirl around her head as she jogs up the three flights of stairs to the level where she left her car. *He was hurt but not fatally wounded* Johnnie thinks to herself as what happened on her operating table five months ago comes back to her in fuzzy pieces.

The bloodied body of Judge Barker Gordon comes into clear focus in her eyes as she hits the alarm to unlock her car. She sees the two gunshot wounds in his chest as she puts the car in gear. His shallow breath before his body was hooked up to a ventilator is in time with her. The scalpels and other medical tools clanged as a nurse hurriedly laid them out on a metal table behind her. Johnnie's steering wheel morphs into bloody gauze in her hands as she rounds the square corners of the parking garage and heads out into the street.

She remembers the feel of her fingers fishing inside Judge Gordon's chest. The turn of her scalpel following the paths of the body cavity she memorized long ago. Then the drone of tone. The long steady beep that told Johnnie her fingers turned the wrong way, her scalpel curved in the wrong direction, and just as quickly as a breath can be taken to continue the business of life, it can be taken away by the bankrupt finality of death.

Johnnie remembers the last living moments of her patient as the pad of her foot presses into the accelerator and carries her a long way away from the judgement of a woman who should not be on trial. She remembers the taste in her mouth when the tone sounded, when Dr. Taylor Thomas confronted her, when she confronted Nathan, and when the television told her what she had done and who was being blamed for what she was ultimately responsible for.

She reaches for that taste. Her fingers curl around the white plastic water bottle nestled in the car's cup holder. Unholstering the bottle, Johnnie brings it to her lips, pulls the black cap open with her teeth, and knocks back the liquid inside. It goes down without the smooth burn she craves, landing in the pit of her empty gut without a sting.

"This is not what I want," Johnnie says draining the bottle. She smacks her lips with a dissatisfied "Ah," going through the motions of enjoying her drink even though the tastelessness of water doesn't give her the escapism she's desperately seeking. The escape that allowed her to hide inside her own catatonic dreamless sleep. The escape that cost her her loves in life. The escape she wishes could be hers just one more time as she maneuvers her car into the parking lot of Danielle's school.

Johnnie spies Nathan's 4Runner parked near the school's main office entrance. She trolls the lanes of the lot and finds a space along the tree lined back fence. Backing in to the tight spot, Johnnie keeps her eyes on the 4Runner waiting to see if Nathan will emerge. She sits and waits sipping her water until the bottle is empty and her cravings for stinging scream to be satisfied.

Stepping out of the car Johnnie shakes her head back and forth clearing the images that collided in her mind during Ebony's testimony, and Ayana's attempt at a reunion. Johnnie breathes against the thoughts that ran laps around her brain as she sped her car from one side of the city to the other. Her kinky, twisted curls that are usually pulled into a puff high on her head sweep her face with the motion. The feel of the soft strands against her cheeks fills Johnnie with another memory. A memory of Danielle in her arms, sleeping on her shoulder. Her little girl's virgin hair rubbing on her neck just below her ear as she tossed and turned her head trying to get comfortable. Johnnie brings her hands to her cheeks and lets her knuckles brush against her curls. It is the closest to calm she's felt since she stopped escaping inside her white water bottle.

Arming herself with a new calm, Johnnie walks through the parking lot to the school's main office door. The secretary at the front desk buzzes her in.

"I'm here to pick up Danielle Edwards," Johnnie says to the older woman sitting behind the desk.

"Would you like to go to her classroom or wait in the office?" The woman asks in a lilting voice meant for children.

"If I can wait outside her class that'd be great." Johnnie says.

"Let me just notify her teacher, but it shouldn't be a problem your husband is already here."

"Oh."

She knew Nathan was on the school grounds when she saw his SUV parked out front, but the secretary mentioning him as her husband entices nerves to rumble in her belly. She and Nathan hadn't been husband and wife since he walked out with Danielle. Since he told her to get herself together, to sober up. If it weren't for text messages from Tyler she wouldn't have been able to see her children everyday.

Everyday Tyler, looking more and more like Nathan when he and Johnnie first met, sent her pictures of him and Danielle. Sometimes he sent them in the morning, sometimes he sent them in the evening. Sometimes the two of them just smiled. Sometimes the two of them made funny faces. Every now and then over the last five months he would send a quick video of the two of them holding a conversation that only a teenager and a little girl just out of toddlerhood could pull off. Johnnie didn't know who the impetus was behind the pictures and she told herself she didn't care, but with Nathan in proximity for more than a head nod Johnnie's stomach bubbles with fear and freedom. She wants to both escape and make renewed debut. She craves the taste of the old, distilled, smooth and dry but knows she has to opt for what is crisp, clear, clean and bland.

"Dr. Edwards, you can go on back. Danielle's in building 3 classroom 2103," the secretary says.

"Thank you," Johnnie says with a warm smile to the older woman's smooth milk chocolate face.

Johnnie is buzzed through the door that leads out of the main office and into the maze of indoor and outdoor hallways that make up the elementary school campus of mostly portable classrooms. She navigates the so called corridors until she gets to the block that houses Danielle's new classroom. Just as Soleil said it is right next door to her old room. Nathan stands outside the door with his back to her.

He doesn't see her steady approach, until she stops outside of Danielle's old classroom and stares at Lisa Jessie standing on her tip toes and bouncing on her heels. She stares at her rival's olive skin, short stature, and low ponytail. Lisa wears khaki pants and a fitted white blouse that still doesn't fit. Staring down at her own attire, Johnnie takes note of her worn and faded black jeans, and gray tank top that rides up at the waist because of her breasts. The blazer she wore in court she now wishes she'd kept on, instead of throwing it in the backseat of her car. She alternates her gaze from herself to Lisa and shakes her head seeing the woman she just left; Ebony in all white Johnnie stares at Lisa and sees guilt when their eyes meet. She deliberately sends her pupils to the sky and continues her walk just a few steps forward until she is arm distance from Nathan's back and he is forced to turn around to discover who is behind him.

"You look good," he says.

"Thank you," Johnnie responds as casually as she can muster "How long have you been here?"

"About five minutes. Just waiting on the bell to ring. They're basically done in there."

"Oh. Okay."

Johnnie opens her mouth to say more and closes it again. She stands beside Nathan in an uncomfortable silence no longer knowing how to keep their conversation going as specious as it may have been.

"It's amazing how distance can erode the memories of time," Nathan says after the silence settles loudly between them. "16 years

266

together, five months apart, and now we can't even talk for a few minutes while we stand in each others' space."

"I'm not the one who insisted on the distance," Johnnie cuts with her words.

"You needed it."

"Perhaps I did."

The echoes of Johnnie's soft-spoken confession lingers between them as the school bell interrupts the makings of their reconnection.

"What do you have planned for them this weekend?" Nathan asks raising his voice to be heard above the crush of excited children exiting their classrooms.

"Nothing yet, I've just been following the trial."

"Tyler told me you've been going to court. I don't know why you're doing this to yourself," Nathan says letting warmth enter his voice.

"Because I have to."

"Well it's out of everybody's hands now except the jury."

"Yep. They should be on verdict watch by the end of the day."

"Mama, Mama, Mama," Danielle shrieks running outside the classroom.

"There's my big girl," Johnnie says as she bends down.

Danielle runs into Johnnie's open arms. Her pink Minnie Mouse book bag and long braids flap against the back of her peter pan collar shirt. Johnnie scoops Danielle up and throws her high on her shoulder. Immediately Danielle snuggles into the neck space between Johnnie's ear and shoulder. Their heads touch and their hair blends strand against strand, kinky curls against matted braids and barrettes. The memory Johnnie recalled in the parking lot is real again. Her calm becomes real and her need to escape melts away from her body she didn't realize she was holding tense. Johnnie sucks in Danielle's smell. The clean and crisp scent of unscented white soap, the mild notes of pink baby lotion and A&D ointment.

"Mama, will hold you as long you want her to. Mama will always hug you," Johnnie whispers through Danielle's braids into her ear.

"Mama you're squeezing me," Danielle squeaks in a giggle.

"Sorry." Johnnie giggles herself as she sets Danielle back on her feet. "Somebody's got to get their hair washed this weekend," Johnnie tugs one of Danielle's lopsided braids.

"Can Daddy help you do it?" Danielle asks looking up at both her parents. "His hands feel good when he washes my hair."

"Only if your Mama doesn't mind," Nathan steps closer to Johnnie.

She pauses before responding. This is the closest she's been to Nathan in months. The last time he was this close she smelled lemongrass and jasmine. She inhales through her nostrils twice blowing her nose wide open, detecting nothing. The scent is gone.

"I suppose so," Johnnie says looking down at Danielle. "I'm probably going to wash it tonight. You can just come back with us."

"Yay," Danielle shrieks. "Mama and Daddy together. Mama and Daddy together."

Johnnie stares into Nathan's chestnut eyes and breathes. The eyes she sees every time she looks at Danielle. She breathes. She inhales twice more letting her nose play detective again. It comes up with nothing, again.

"You smell different," Johnnie says still staring into Nathan eyes.

"I needed to."

"Did you . . . "

"Not here, Johnnie. Not now."

"We're going to have to talk about this," Johnnie turns her head. "Come, Dani. You can ride with Mama," she says taking hold of Danielle's hand as they walk down the path of portables to the main office.

Johnnie stops once more in front of Soleil's door where Lisa Jessie has finished conducting class on her own. She stares at Lisa and sees two women at once, feeling guilty for both of them. The one woman who will soon be judged for something she did not do, and the other woman for giving her false hope that she could fill a role never meant for her.

"Can I say bye to Miss Jessie, Mama?" Danielle asks peeking between Johnnie's legs into the open classroom doorway.

"Not now, Dani. We have to go," Johnnie says softly.

"Johnnie, we have a lot to talk about," Nathan says following his wife's gaze to Lisa.

"I suppose we do," Johnnie says walking with Danielle again. "I suppose we do."

40.

Monday, September 15, 2014

It is now 4:30 on your Monday afternoon. We continue to follow the second degree murder trial of Ebony Jones where the jury has been deliberating over the last three days for more than 34 hours.

Soleil adjusts her earbuds as she begins her run to talk radio. The talk on the radio is about Ebony. They have been talking about Ebony every day for the last two weeks on her every run. Analysis of the jury, analysis of the testimony, and now analysis about the overall trial with the world on verdict watch. Every day the pundits square off with the host who operates as moderator.

Just because you're battered doesn't mean you have the right to take someone's life. Just because you've been battered in the past doesn't mean you have the right to defend yourself by picking a fight today. Furthermore she should have never been battered in the first place.

The conservative commentator concludes his argument. Soleil pounds the pavement hearing the voice's smug smile through her headphones.

Are you really going to blame the victim.

I'm not blaming anyone. She got into a relationship by fighting? Who does that? Who fights their way to love?

I'm not going to even address that. How she and the judge started is irrelevant. It has no bearing on this trial.

If their history didn't have any bearing then why did she testify about it. She talked more about their two years dating on the stand then she did about the day she killed the man.

Allegedly killed him. And he backed her into a corner.

Soleil runs and nods as the host makes one valid point on Ebony's behalf.

Are we going to forget the fact that she tailed him. She stalked him. She sought him out.

It would be different if she approached him with her gun drawn. She didn't. She has a concealed carry license. She can conceal and carry wherever she chooses.

Soleil exits the radio app on the favorable argument. While she's been starting her run with their voices, and their arguments, they never make it with her to the end of her route. She leaves the men behind to debate what she already knows, counting the hours she's counted for herself ever since Ebony stepped down from the stand and the jury was swept behind closed doors to decide the next course for her life. The pundits, moderators and anchors will rehash every question the jury's had and Judge Shaw's flippant answers. Soleil will rehash the same her constant thoughts on the six who will decide the fate of the woman who did what she was unable to do herself.

Soleil runs distracted. As distracted as she was earlier during her first day back in class. Her mind drifted to the three men and three women who stared at her expressionless when she testified for the State. The three men and three women who showed no hints of concern or compassion when she told them about her injuries, about the diseases she contracted from him, how she masked her pain in pale purples and deep plums. When she got home, alone, her mind drifted to the three men and three women who listened to Ebony with varying questions of disbelief visible as she explained what drove her to the courthouse. Now, Soleil rounds the final curve of Southpoint Parkway into the parking lot of her apartment complex in silence. The radio men are silenced, not allowed to discuss the jurors whose indecisiveness or confounding reading of the law has forced them to meet in secret everyday to decide who is lying; the battered women or the dead judge.

Soleil sprints the last yards of her run, slamming her feet into the asphalt of the parking lot, jettisoning between the cars on her toes until she reaches the foot of the stairs. She takes the wooden planks two by two continuing her sprint until she reaches her third floor door. Only then does she slow down. Only then does she walk; pacing back and forth across the breezeway between the apartments to slow her beating heart. She walks in time to her slowing breath. Her short inhales and exhales turn into long, slow, deep breaths. Soleil fishes her key from the inside pocket of her bike shorts and shakily puts it in the door. She holds it there until the tremors in her hand subside.

Turning the key, cool air from inside the apartment greets her. The air conditioning and her two ceiling fans all run on high. They blast the rivers of sweat running freely down her body now that she is inside and out of the heat of the September sun. Soleil slams the apartment door and turns into her bathroom stripping as she goes. She drops the loose, red, men's tank top on the cheap, cracked tile of the bathroom floor as she walks through the adjacent door into her bedroom.

She stops just over the threshold. Her room is in disarray. It is not as she left it. Her mattress hangs off the edge of the broken bed.

frame which kisses the carpet. On the bed is a mass of tangled wires and debris. She can make out pieces of the smooth, wooden fan blades among the wreckage. She looks up at the ceiling and sees a hole where the fan used to hang. Creeping closer to the pile, wood and glass crunch beneath the checkered soles of her running shoes. In the middle of her bed are small petal shaped globes that encased four of the light bulbs. They are smashed in jagged pieces. The fan blades are cracked; some in half, some in thirds or fourths. Their wood is splintered. Something is missing. The large center globe of the ceiling fan is not in the pile. Soleil runs her eyes up the mounds of debris to the pillows of the bed. There the remnants of the center globe are scattered in pieces on just one of the pillows. She looks further up the the pillow to the headboard and sees what happened. The hole in her DIY headboard is bigger. Rounder. It's no longer broken into the shape of her head. The wood where her head banged through is now more gashed, more fragmented, more splintered.

The scene sends Soleil side stepping through debris out of the bedroom and into the kitchen trekking bits of wood and glass across the carpet onto the vinyl flooring. She squats in front of the cabinets beneath the sink and opens the plain brown doors. Bottles of Windex, Lysol, and bleach on the front line of the storage space are moved out of the way until she touches the plastic of the tool box sitting under the drain pipes. It's the toolbox she bought to construct her headboard. The one she hasn't used since. She slides the box forward, pops the tabs open, and grabs what she needs.

Her knees creak as they straighten. The impact of her run begins to take hold of her body. She ignores the warning for ice and heat and walks back into the bedroom with her hammer in hand. The metal of the unwrapped handle is cool against her palm. Soleil swings the weight of the hammer back and forth. It brushes past her exposed legs as she surveys the damage. Her eyes jump across the room as the hammer swings at her side. They hop from the sagging mattress on the broken bed frame to the dented headboard. They flit from nightstand to nightstand to the dresser and mirror in front of the bed until they arrive at the woven white rocking chair just beside it. The hammer in constant motion swings at her side as her gaze scans the room again until she's staring through the dark cavern in the middle of the wooden carrying crates.

The jagged wood of the hole is inches from her pupils, in eyes whose lids are stretched wide against her face. A spiked ring hand is around her neck. Her breath is short, gasping through a congested nose overcome by the smell of Southern Comfort and Swisher Sweets. His wetness roll down her skin and her shaking legs throb with pain.

Then it is gone. Smashed by the hammer that no longer swings in her hand.

She released it. Set it free. It crashed into the headboard above the fan debris. Soleil walks crunching steps to the pillow where the hammer landed and picks up the cool metal weight. Back and forth it swings beside her legs, engaging her rhythm, until the forward and backward strokes are as long as they are strong, and then she swings the hammer into the other side of the headboard by the pillow where she lays her head to sleep. Soleil plows the hammer through the remnants of the jagged hole that sometimes contained her head. The carrying crates collapse under the power of her even swing. The wood crumbles in pieces onto the sagging mattress, over the edges of the nightstand, and down to the floor leaving the wall behind it swathed in bland beige.

The hammer swings, forwards and backwards, backwards and forwards. It's motion carries Soleil from her side of the bed to the front of her dresser. She sees herself in the glass. The mostly clear skin of her face and body. No unnatural marks around her neck, down her sports bra covered breasts, around her ribs, or across the sides of her abdomen. Her body is clear. Almost. Soleil's eyes settle on her face. The jagged scar.

The hammer swings.

High above her head the hammer arcs until it completes its circle with a decisive land on the seat of the rocking chair. The painted wood stutters. The hammer swings. Another high arc. Another hard landing. The wood cracks. The hammer swings. Another high arc and an easy landing, straight through the center of the chair. The seat is destroyed. The hammer swings again. It smashes through the arms then the rocking legs until the seat back collapses on its own with nothing else to hold on to. The hammer swings, and swings, landing again and again on top of the white pile of wood. The paint chips and flakes to the floor and the woven pattern of the chair is undetectable amongst the jagged, splintered pieces that were once hand crafted.

The hammer swings. Back at her side, beside her leg, it swings leisurely as Soleil walks out of the bedroom and back into the kitchen. She squats down in front of the open cabinet, replaces the hammer in the rectangular tool box, and grabs a black garbage bag from the corner.

She shakes the bag loose from its folds and walks back into the bedroom setting it in the middle of the floor. Soleil rolls the sides of the plastic over to keep it wide open. First into the bag is the pile of white wood. The pieces land in the bag in clumps. Dust, made of wood chips and paint, rise from the beaten chair's final resting place.

The pile on the bed is next. Soleil tosses pieces of the broken blades into the bag one by one until all that surrounds her is glass and wire. She steps away from the bag to her nightstand. The one on her side of the bed. She opens the drawer and pulls out the note. The cursive script slightly faded since it was first printed on embossed and glossy 3x5 card stock.

Hope you help yourself.

She tosses the note into the open bag, rolls up the sides, and double knots the open mouth. Hoisting it on her shoulder she carries it out of the bedroom, through the bathroom, and to the front door.

She opens it in time to see her neighbor taking her dog for a walk.

"Good Evening, Ms. Jay," Soleil says.

"Are you okay, dear?" She asks. "I heard a lot of noise coming from your apartment. I wasn't sure what was going on."

The older woman's eyes reveal that she knows what used to go on in the apartment across from her. Her eyes tell that she's been watching the news and reading the paper. She knows the headlines. Now, her earnest, imploring eyes traverse Soleil's face in a quest to know more. Her eyes tell she wasn't just coming out to take her dog for a walk, but had instead been standing in the breezeway waiting for Soleil to emerge so that she could look at her more closely.

Soleil squares her body to Ms. Jay so she can take all of her in. The older woman's unmitigated stare is free, unabashed, and unashamed. Her eyes rove from her little dog who sits lazily at her feet to Soleil's running shoes, up her legs, past the waistband of her bike shorts, across her bare and unbruised stomach, up the lengths of her arms, and over her neck until she settles on Soleil's face. Her mostly unmarked face. This is where Ms. Jay's gaze rests. On Soleil's face, just above her eye, seeing what she already knows to be true.

"I'm fine," Soleil says allowing Ms. Jay to stare longer than necessary. "I'm just taking out the trash."

41.

Breaking news right now in the murder trial of Ebony Jones.
Nine News Now has learned in the last 10 minutes that the jury ha
reached a verdict.
Good Evening and welcome to Nine News Now at five.
I'm Dawn Anthony.

Dawn pauses and waits while Linden introduces himself to the viewers through the camera. She listens as he introduces the team coverage from reporters Tarren Tyler and Owen Major until her name appears in the prompter again.

We begin with Tarren Tyler who is waiting to be let back in the courtroom where the jury will deliver the verdict.
Tarren.

An audible click in the studio signals to Dawn and Linden their microphones are off. Dawn thumbs through her scripts barely glancing at the words knowing the other stories in the show will die due to the imminence of the verdict. She reaches the end of her scripts and gets to what she is really looking for. A manila envelope she pulled out of her mailbox when she arrived at work. There is no indication of who the envelope is from, only a typed label on the front that reads confidential in bold block letters.

Dawn intended to open the envelope once she got in her office but Boyce was there waiting for her when she breached the doorway. He stood up as she walked in but said nothing. Dawn followed his lead and didn't inquire about what he wanted. She offered her cursory good morning and waited to find out how her day would play. Boyce told her she would anchor all of the evening shows in addition to her own and walked out of her office.

Dawn didn't ask about Julia and Boyce didn't offer. When Linden came into the newsroom a couple hours later he refused to look at her. When they sat in the rundown meeting to discuss the coverage for the evening newscasts he ignored her still. Now on set they present to the viewers a happy anchor team color complimenting each other through their suits. Linden in light gray, with a white shirt and topaz tie, and Dawn in a teal dress and slate blazer. They look as if they enjoy working with each other even though Dawn and Linden both know they are far from friends.

"Looks like you've got some big news there," Linden whispers looking at Dawn's envelope.

"I don't know. I haven't opened it yet."

"Standby Linden," John yells from the floor.

"Thank you, Tarren," Linden says to the camera. "Picking up our team coverage is 9 News Now's Owen Major. Owen you're outside the courthouse with the protesters. Have they said what they will do if the verdict does not turn out in their favor?"

The click in the studio sounds again. Dawn and Linden are alone to listen to Owen's speculative report and wait for their next cue. She takes the time to finally peek inside the envelope. Sliding her index finger beneath the spit closed seal, the flap breaks, and Dawn reaches inside and partially pulls out a thick stack of stapled papers. The words "employment agreement" are printed in all caps on the first page.

Dawn scans the offer she now knows Boyce put in her mailbox. The words "five year agreement" and "main anchor" jump out at her from the first page. Dawn drops the contract back in the envelope and lays the package on the glass anchor desk.

"Are you going to take it?" Linden asks.

"So you know." Dawn says more to herself than her co-anchor.

"Julia called and told me this morning," Linden says swiveling his chair to look at Dawn. "She told me she was being put in review for the next six months and that you were taking her chair during that time."

"That doesn't mean anything. She can always have it back."

"Not by the looks of that envelope she can't."

"Linden and Dawn, the jury is back in the courtroom our live feed is hot," Kelly says in both their ears.

"Who do you want to toss?" Dawn asks aloud.

"We're going to come out to a two shot," Kelly answers. "Linden will wrap Owen's report on the protesters and then Dawn you toss to the live camera in the courtroom. We'll take the sound full until the jury delivers the verdict."

"Standby two shot," John yells to the anchors.

Dawn waits for her next cue. The manila envelope with the anchor offer stares at her from the desk. She lets it fall to the top of her scripts. It is her alternate focal point, besides the side of Linden's face while he talks. She waits, with a half smile, ready to report the unknown while the unknown stares back at her.

And now we want to take you live inside the courtroom where the jury ha reconvened ready to deliver the verdict in the murder trial of Ebony Jones.

The microphones click off in the studio as the audio for th courtroom replaces the voices of the anchors. Judge Shaw explains th procedures of what is to happen after the verdict is read be it guilty o not guilty.

"So are you taking her chair?" Linden asks looking at Dawn.

"It's an offer I have to consider," Dawn says looking at th courtroom feed.

"You have other offers?"

"Yeah, hold on," Dawn says, pulling her vibrating cell phon out of her blazer pocket.

I'm watching.

The words greet Dawn on the locked screen of her cell phon A text from Victor. The first response since her reply of "thanks more than two weeks ago. Dawn taps out another hasty thanks on th glass keypad and then puts the phone on the desk.

"So where are you going?" Linden asks.

"I don't know yet," Dawn answers as the phone illuminate again.

Dawn taps the text. The cursor in the message box blinks at he daring her to type another message.

I may be staying in Jacksonville after all.

Dawn sends the unsolicited information to Victor then darken the screen to watch the television just below her prompter.

She watches the face of Judge Marisol Shaw as she waits for th jury foreman to announce the verdict. On her screen the jury is no seen. Their identities still as secret to the viewers as the day they wer selected. But Dawn remembers them. She remembers their faces fron sitting in the courtroom. Their varied ages. Dawn brings the images o the three men and three women into her mind's eye as she watches th television. Her phone buzzes on the desk.

I hope you get what you want.

She reads the text from her anchor chair but does not respond. She looks back up at the television, and then the manila envelope staring at her from the desk. Dawn ignores the faces Linden makes to the side of her head. Watching the television the shot cuts from a close up of Judge Shaw to a wide shot of the courtroom with Judge Shaw sitting in the center. The backs of Ebony's and James's heads are visible as well as the back of the state attorney.

The audio from the courtroom camera shot crackles.

Judge Shaw's voice comes through the studio instructing the jury forewoman to give the verdict to the clerk for certification. Dawn focuses on the television, ignoring the buzzing on the desk. She doesn't look down to see Victor's unanswered text beckoning her for a response. She studies the scene in the courtroom. Only Ayana is on the bench that she, Johnnie, and Soleil, inhabited through the duration of the trial. Ayana is in focus in the camera's view, she's dressed in all white, matching her daughter. Her head bounces with the movement of the verdict as it is passed from the unseen forewoman, to the clerk, and back again.

Judge Shaw's voice comes through the studio.

"Ladies and gentleman of the jury, have you reached a verdict?"

"We have, Your Honor."

Author's Note and Acknowledgments

If you're still reading, I know you're mad. Please don't be mad. I know. You don't know the verdict and you want to know if Ebony, is guilty or innocent right? Right. So here's why you don't know . . . I don't know what the verdict is. No, that's not some artistic author cop out. It's the truth. As the author and creator of these characters I could not bring myself to convict Ebony. At the same time, I didn't think it a realistic ending if Ebony was acquitted. Instead, I've left the verdict unknown, not because I'm itching to write a sequel. I'm not, but because I think it's worth discussing. Whether you think Ebony is guilty or innocent I think there's a conversation waiting to be had about the role of Black women, domestic violence, and the visibility of women in all parts of the Black Lives Matter movement; as both protesters and as worthy victims in need of defense. And, you never know, there may be a sequel in the works. :)

And now, for a quick round of thank you's. Thank you God for giving me the patience and perseverance to finish this book twice and then do two major revisions and countless rounds of edits just to get it to where it is now. Destiny and purpose is a journey and I know all things work together for my good. Thank you, Lord. To my family: Jermaine, Mylen, Erik, Jace, and Romello for being patient with me during all my bouts of writing. To my mom for always encouraging me and to Janet Johnson and my bestie Ashley Grant for the help with the legal scenes. Thank you John Tintera and Katherine Carroll Trowbridge for forcing me to do those two major revisions. To my editor, Mrs. Arvita Roberts-Glenn, who didn't think I was crazy when I cornered you in the library during the book fest, your eye for grammatical and stylistic mistakes is a machine I'm thankful to have had gone over this novel. To my brother for the dope design of my imprint, and to the designer of the dopest book cover, Gisette Gomez, you took a quick synopsis and Nina Simone's song and made magic beyond what I thought I wanted; Thank you.

— Nikesha Elise Williams

About the Author

Nikesha Elise Williams is from Chicago, Illinois. She attended The Florida State University where she graduated with a B.S. in Communication: Mass Media Studies and Honors English Creative Writing. Nikesha works as a news producer and is a two time Emmy nominee. She won the Florida Associated Press Broadcasters award for Best Breaking News in 2014. Nikesha lives in Jacksonville, Florida, but you can always find her online at www.newwrites.com, Facebook.com/NikeshaElise or @Nikesha_Elise on Twitter and Instagram. *Four Women* is her first novel.

50154738R00169

Made in the USA
Columbia, SC
02 February 2019